PRAISE FOR STEPHEN GREENLEAF AND

THE DITTO LIST

"From the first sentence readers will know they're in very good hands.
The Washington Post

"The writing crackles with new insights, the characters are defined in real dimensions and the dialogue rings with smart—sometimes smart-alecky—authority."
Philadelphia Inquirer

"Mr. Greenleaf is a real writer with real talent."
The New Yorker

"His dialogue is pungent, his observations mordant, his eye for detail concrete and telling. As both witty entertainment, and modern morality tale, THE DITTO LIST is very satisfying, indeed."
Cleveland Plain Dealer

THE DITTO LIST

Stephen Greenleaf

BALLANTINE BOOKS • NEW YORK

Library of Congress Catalog Card Number: 84-40481

ISBN 0-345-32139-1

This edition published by arrangement with Villard Books, a division of Random House Inc.

Manufactured in the United States of America

First Ballantine Books Edition: July 1986

FOR ANN, AGAIN

■ PLEADING

ONE

KNOW he's seeing a woman he's got three children older than, Mrs. Kunsman. . . .

"I know she wears peek-a-boo skirts and no underwear on her boobies. . . .

"I know they're probably doing things that will kill him what with his heart. . . .

"I know she's only after his money, I know your children are upset, I know the neighbors talk, I know all that and more, Mrs. Kunsman, and I have to tell you the same thing I told you the last time you called: there's absolutely nothing you can do about it. You got the house and car and cat and half the assets and two thousand a month and a medical plan plus dental. He got the dog and what amounts to a permit to do the things you tell me he's been doing. And that's all there is, Mrs. Kunsman. The system doesn't let you spank him or send him to bed without his dinner or cover up his girlfriend's boobies. It only lets you take his money and keep his name if you want it. My advice is to forget about him and her and make a new life for yourself.

"I know it's easier said than done for a woman almost sixty, married forty years, Mrs. Kunsman. I know that as well as I know my own name."

Deep within the fifth floor of the Hanford Professional Building, in one of the three windowless rooms that constituted the Law Offices of D. T. Jones, Attorney and Counselor at Law, Juris Doctor, Professional Corporation, Certified Specialist in Family Law, Available Day or Night, D. T. Jones who was all those things put down the phone, then reached across his littered desk and pressed a button on his cassette deck and silenced Willie Nelson in mid-lament. Then he glanced at the clock on the wall beside the framed photograph of John and Robert Kennedy he had purchased at a flea market for a buck from an Armenian exactly six years and six days after Jack had been shot in Dallas, the portrait marking generally the last time D.T. had felt an expression of optimism was warranted about anything remotely governmental, which included nearly everything, when you stopped to think about it.

The clock read 8:45. D.T. swallowed a dwindling chip of Cloret, unbuckled his thirty-two-inch belt, unzipped his thirty-four-inch slacks, stuffed the ends of his crewneck T-shirt and the tails of his oxfordcloth button-down back below his waist, then redid his slacks and donned his size thirty-eight long side-vented blazer with the missing sleeve button and the cigarette burn above the left side pocket, snugged his challis necktie more firmly around his fifteen-inch neck, and forced the slightly frayed cuffs of his thirty-six-inch sleeves out of sight with a shrug of his narrow shoulders with the protruding clavicles that had provoked a giggle in every woman who had ever seen them. Dressed the way he had dressed for twenty years, he walked to the door and went into the neat, bright realm of his outer office, the domain of his secretary, Bobby E. Lee Merryweather.

Bobby E. Lee took one look at his boss and shook his tight black curls, then slid a three-inch stack of file folders across the desk. D.T. eyed the files and then eyed Bobby E. Lee, who was, on that morning as on all mornings, so impossibly pretty that the back issues of the magazines on the coffee table across from his desk, even the ones with Burt and Loni on the cover, were never touched by the waiting women. "How many?" D.T. asked him.

"Seven."

"Problems?"

"Not that I've heard."

"Same time, same station?"

"Roger."

"Then let the Friday Fiasco begin," D.T. proclaimed with the only grandeur that the day would bring. "I may be gone for the duration,'' he added, as his head pulsed to the legato beat of his hangover.

"Oh, no, you won't,'' Bobby E. Lee countered. "You've got three appointments. You told me I could schedule them. If you want to cancel, call them yourself.''

D.T. waved off the challenge. "If I'm not back by two you know what to do.''

Bobby E. Lee shook his fluffy head again, this time with resignation. "The flu or Chicago?'' The words rose like gulls, above a bog of sour disgust.

D.T.'s pose became theatrical. "The flu, I think. One can recover more quickly from the flu than from Chicago, and one must always allow for recovery in the unlikely event that one discovers a place he actually wants to be or a person he actually wants to be with.''

"You're real bad today, aren't you, Mr. J? You always talk like an Englishman when you're hung over real bad.''

"Accurate as always, Bobby.''

D.T. scooped the pile of files under his arm and left his office. After a glance at his watch, he walked the two blighted blocks to the former grade school that now sheltered the southside division of the county court, through air that was already too warm and wet to please anything but fish and joggers, past the squat, concrete-block offices of bail bondsmen and tax preparers and lawyers even lower on the professional ladder than himself, around the panhandlers and prostitutes who knew him well enough to wave, then leave him alone.

He was running late. Judge Hoskins' clerk was closing the door with a liver-spotted hand as D.T. trotted down the marble hall toward Courtroom Two. "Hold it, Walter,'' D.T. called out. "Can't start the show without the star.''

Walter's flesh trembled around his laugh. "If it's you, D.T., it must be Friday already.'' A pink smile broke the gray ceramic of Walter's face, which then mended itself gradually.

"Friday it is, Walter. How's His Honor today?''

Walter rolled his eyes. "How's he ever? Best you watch your step. He's still grumping about the one that speechified on that guru, what's-ever-you-call-him, Maha-I-don't-know-who. The judge don't like speechifying, D.T. Not on Fridays, he don't.''

Walter's Gulf Coast accent acted on D.T. like a feather. He placed his arm across the fat man's shoulders. "No problems today, Walter. You have a good weekend. Reno?''

"You bet," Walter said as he passed D.T. through the door before he closed it. "Hundred and a half for baby's new shoes last Sunday. Keno at the Grand.''

"Quit while you're ahead, Walter. That's my advice to keno players and married women."

Walter ignored his counsel. "Who you like in the feature, D.T.?" he whispered.

D.T. shook his head. "Half the field's scratched, so it's a sucker bet, Walter. You got a better play at keno."

"I hear you talking, D.T.," Walter said, a grin again separating his pulpy lips. "I got just one question. Who you got *your* money on?"

D.T. smiled. "Mama's Buns at eight to one. But you're on your own, Walter. I don't recommend the action."

"I been on my own since I was ten, D.T. Begins to look like it'll be full time."

Walter waved and moved toward the chair directly below the judge's bench. Once there he would serve as everything from a bouncer to the custodian of admitted evidence to the nearest human target for Judge Hoskins' rubber bands on the frequent occasions when the expressway justice became strewn with man-made obstructions and the judge was moved to shoot at something.

D.T. slapped Walter on the shoulder as he passed, turned right at the second row of benches, and slid across the empty pew, looking all the while at the seven women who faced and watched him, their eyes locked on his and therefore sliding as he slid, their expressions midway between a plea and a barely stifled wail. His clients. Fodder for the Fiasco.

Appropriately, they sat like prisoners. Shoulder to shoulder, dress to dress, nylons to nylons, and dread to dread, they occupied the entire left portion of the back row of the courtroom, waiting patiently, all just as Bobby E. Lee had instructed. Bobby E. Lee issued wonderfully lambent instructions, but in one way each of the women had strayed. Hair too stiff, lips too red, cheeks mottled from the use and abuse of makeup, they all had tried hard to be something they were not and in the process had masked the one thing they all unquestionably were— young and undeserving of what they had endured in marriage.

D.T. had seen each of them for thirty minutes, a degree of client contact considered insanely bloated by most other practitioners in his specialty. One such, Randolph Q. Spivey, Esquire, boasted he had reduced his clients' claim on him to an average of seventy-two seconds. His goal was forty-five, at which time he would, according to his accountants, be earning one hundred and twenty thousand dollars a year. Net.

Of course it was not a perfect world. Even in D.T.'s practice most of the actual work was done by a secretary —forms filled out, questions asked and answered, cautions issued, script rehearsed, assurances conferred, and, most important of all and therefore the first in time, the entire fee obtained up front. At each of these tasks Bobby E. Lee was far more proficient than D.T., so the client suffered not at all from the arrangement. For his part, D.T. mostly listened—a high percentage of women came to him primarily to publicize their predicaments and to be told, emphatically and repeatedly, they weren't crazy to think what they thought and feel what they felt. Then he asked questions designed to discover how in the world the woman had managed to get herself into the fix she was in. Only then did he explain, if she asked, how she could get out of it and what it would cost her and why she couldn't pay on credit.

"All set, ladies?"

D.T. eyed them one by one. Seven heads nodded, seven mouths stayed silent. D.T. quickly reviewed the files, then read off seven names and received seven nods in Pavlovian return.

Their stories were as interchangeable as their gestures. All of them had been married in their teens, all were barely literate, all worked at menial jobs involving food and could at any moment be replaced by workers in the country illegally, and all were married to raving assholes

—drunks, addicts, or cretins who were in jail or in debt or in the next state in what they thought was love with a woman other than the one they had promised to cherish until death.

But the women were human as well as forsaken, and thus there were differences among them. Each had her own story, her own pet of anguish that accompanied her everywhere, the leash a chain of sorrow. One had a brother with a blood disease that was killing him, whom she visited every Sunday in a hospital a hundred miles from where she lived, fighting off drunken mashers on the Trailways every mile of the way. Once she had been almost raped in the toilet at the rear of the bus. Twice a guy had barfed all over her nice clean frock. Another of the women was married to a guy who made her wear Frederick's of Hollywood costumes whenever they went to a party, ones that displayed an expanse of her breasts not always excluding the nipples. And one was leaving the next day for Alaska to work as a cocktail waitress in a town near the pipeline where she'd heard a girl with a good body and a friendly smile could earn five hundred a week in tips without having to do anything but stand on her feet for eight hours and listen to stories about the girl back home. And if she was willing to spend some time on her back as well, she could get rich quick if she wasn't supporting a habit. And one of them had caught herpes from her husband who had earlier caught it from her sister, and one was going regularly to AA, and one was worried because her last period had lasted two weeks and she didn't know why and couldn't afford to hire a doctor who would tell her, and on and on. For over a year, D.T. appeared in court on behalf of five such women every week. He loved them all, and wished he could lavish them with riches, introduce them to swains, bathe them in oils, dress them in silks, shelter them from future sadness, all of which would be within the power of the thing he wished he was: Sir Jones. Knight Errant. Brave and Stalwart. Champion of the Miswed. But instead of silks and oils, on every Friday in the most definitely unfantastic atmosphere of the city's civil courts, D. T. Jones would obtain for his clients the minimum legal judgment available to women of their station—a Default Divorce.

No alimony, no property settlement, no nothing, usually. Only the silent disintegration of a vow, to be memorialized six months hence in a humdrum legal form, with appropriate boxes checked and blanks filled in and notices and warnings printed in boldface at the bottom, entirely unsuitable for framing.

"Remember your lines?" he continued.

Another seven nods.

"Answer 'yes' unless I rub my nose," he reminded. "Then answer 'no.' Right?"

Seven nods.

"You'll do fine. Just stay here till I call you up. We'll probably be last, so relax. In an hour you'll be free from the biggest mistake of your life. Then you can go make another one just like it."

Because he had already started sliding toward the center aisle he doubted they could hear the last, but he didn't care if they had. Recidivism in the domestic relations business was as rampant as in crime, and was far less excusable, since for a woman a year in a bad marriage was far worse than a year in jail.

D.T. walked to the bar of the court, nodding to the few lawyers he knew and liked, ignoring the rest, and read through the divorce court's calendar for the day—the Ditto List, Bobby E. Lee called it. As always, the table of civil strifes amused him: *Crater* v. *Crater; Winthrop* v. *Winthrop; Koleski* v. *Koleski, such* v. *such; so on* v. *so on; etc.* v. *etc.*

D.T.'s ladies were last on the Ditto List, as he knew they would be. Judge Hoskins was disgusted by D.T.'s practice and made no secret of it. On the contrary, the judge frequently made a prayer of his distaste, asking a higher power for deliverance from D.T. and settling for putting D.T. off as long as he could by relegating him to the bottom of the calendar, which meant D.T. would waste a lot of time waiting his turn, time for which he would not be compensated, monetarily or even otherwise, as the judge well knew. At times Judge Hoskins refused to call D.T.'s cases at all, explaining that enough was enough, that he would not have his weekend ruined by knowing participation in assembly-line justice.

Part of the reason for his enmity was that Judge Hoskins was Catholic, which meant that in his eyes D.T. made his living abetting sin. Another part was that the judge had never himself been married, and thus assumed divorce to be a blame-ridden event and wives to be the only conceivable source of it. Still another part was that the judge was an arrogant ass who mistakenly felt he was qualified to be sitting on the state supreme court rather than in the family law department of the southside division. All of which should have disqualified him from domestic matters if not the entire spectrum of jurisprudence, but which, despite numerous official and unofficial complaints to the judicial council, seemed to mean that Judge Hoskins would hear nothing *but* domestic matters until the day he died. Actually, D.T. had a degree of sympathy for the embattled jurist. D.T.'s practice depressed him too, at times, until he made himself remember that the assembly line was what, more than anything but John Marshall and the Bill of Rights, had made America great.

There were at least a dozen matters ahead of him on the Ditto List, so when D.T. heard Walter's gavel rap to proclaim the arrival of the judge he went out into the hall to wait. Attorneys and clients scurried past him on all sides, on their ways to courtrooms where fates other than divorce awaited them. D.T. paid them no mind. Other branches of the law no longer existed for him. He hadn't appeared in court on anything but a domestic case in years. He hadn't, in fact, had a client who wasn't a woman in the throes of a matrimonial earthquake in over eighteen months. This drift toward specialty—divorce work—and subspecialty—wronged wives—was accidental as far as D.T. could tell, the product of a series of good results and the word of mouth they fostered in the network of desperate women that operated, like a conjugal Resistance, in all areas of the city.

"Hey. D.T. Remember me?"

D.T. moved from under the hand that plucked at his shoulder like a shrike and looked back at its owner.

"Jerome. How the hell are you?"

"Great, D.T. How about you?"

"Adequate at best. What brings you down to the wild

side? You're still with Bronwin, Kilt and Loftis, aren't you? The law of the rich and their many irritants?"

Jerome Fitzgerald smiled uneasily, patted his razor-cut, adjusted his horn-rims, and glanced quickly at the people milling within earshot. When he remembered he was nowhere he visibly relaxed.

Jerome's clothes betrayed his mind. His shirt was white and his shoes were shined, and his suit lay on him like a tan. A pristine inch of handkerchief protruded from his breast pocket, a campaign ribbon from a bloodless war. His glow was fluorescent; his posture martial. "My sister was in a fender-bender," he explained. "Her trial starts today. I'm here to hold her hand."

"Who's her lawyer?"

"Lester Farnholtz."

"You'd be better off holding her pocketbook."

Jerome's smile undulated beneath his too-sharp nose. "Always with the joke, D.T. Just like in law school. It kept you off the law review, you know. That attitude."

"I know, Jerome, and I thank God for this attitude every day of my life."

"Come on, D.T. *Everyone* wanted to make law review."

"Just let me say this about that, Jerome. We traveled in such different circles that yours was in fact a square."

Having mistakenly assumed that time had pressed out the wrinkles in D.T.'s personality, Jerome looked for an exit of physical or conversational dimensions. "So what are you up to these days, D.T.?" he asked, lacking a semblance of interest in the answer.

"I specialize in the consequences of lust, Jerome."

Jerome frowned. "Divorce?"

"Dissolution is its current sobriquet, my man, although like you I eschew it as a pulseless modernism. Dissolution, from the Latin *dissolutatus,* meaning *fed up.* How about you? You and Kathy still knee-deep in marital bliss?"

Impossibly, Jerome grew more funereal. "We split up three years ago, D.T."

"Oh? That's too bad. I always liked Kathy. Who was her lawyer?"

"Well, I was, I guess. I mean, the *firm* sort of handled

the whole thing. Made a nice arrangement for both of us."

D.T. laughed. "How's she getting along on food stamps, Jerome?"

"Don't be ridiculous." Jerome reset the already impeccable knot in his tie.

"She still in town? There's a remedy or two for that kind of ethical obtuseness that I'd like to apprise her of."

"Now, D.T.," Jerome said, and started to move away. But for some sudden reason D.T. wanted him to stay.

Jerome Fitzgerald had been one of the students he most despised in law school, one of those who had always known they wanted to be lawyers and had always known why—money and power and deductible vacations. No cause, no principle, no reformist zeal, just a respectably lucrative job. Less pressure than medicine, more fashionable than real estate or insurance, less risky than wildcatting or drug dealing. D.T. had once overheard a girl ask Jerome to name his favorite novel and movie and symphony. The novel was *The Robe;* the movie *Spartacus;* the symphony *The Grand Canyon Suite.* Yet Jerome provoked a certain fascination in D.T., an awe of his ignorance of doubt, of his seamless self-confidence, of his assessment of a scrambled world in such simple forms and rules that he could doubtlessly vote Republican, belong to the ABA, drive a car that cost as much as a house, and, in his racy moments, make snide remarks about divorce lawyers and liberal politicians and people who slept in doorways and ate free food.

"Hang on a minute, Jerome," D.T. urged. "What else you been doing for the last twenty years? You made partner yet?"

"Of course."

"What department?"

"Litigation."

"Really? Don't see you down here in the trial courts much. Never, as a matter of fact."

"Most of our work is in federal court."

"Yeah? Like what?"

"Oh, antitrust. Commercial litigation. Securities fraud."

"Yeah? Which side you on? The frauder or the frau-dee? As if I didn't know."

Jerome hitched up his slacks and searched again for a path that led away from where he was. "How many jury trials you had?" D.T. probed, conscious that he was close to pillory.

"I . . . I'm not sure. I don't keep count."

"Come on, Jerome, How many?"

"Uh . . ."

"Five? Ten?"

"Well, none, actually. Most of our matters settle be-fore trial, of course. All of them, actually. Protracted litigation is so . . . expensive."

"Right, right," D.T. agreed. "Expensive and scary, too. Right? I mean, there's always that chance the old jury foreman will stand up and look you right in the eye and say, 'Jerome, my man. You fucking *lose*.' Right? I do a little litigation myself, as a matter of fact. Not fed-eral, of course. No big deal. Just who gets the kids and who pays the rent and the orthodontist. So let's have lunch. Huh, Jerome?"

Jerome adjusted his tie again. "Sure, D.T. Next time you're uptown give me a call."

"Next time I'm uptown I'll have taken a wrong turn," D.T. said. "But I *am* eager to reminisce about the good old days. Like, remember that multiple-choice exam old Hardflood threw at us in estate tax?"

Jerome smiled and fingered the Coif medal that swung from his watch chain like a soggy sock. "God, yes. What a total incompetent."

D.T. laughed and slapped Jerome on the back. "You can say that again. And remember how often you looked over at my paper? Huh? At least a dozen times, as I recall. God, that was a scream, wasn't it? The way you cribbed your way through that one?"

"Hey. Wait a minute, D.T. I never. . . ."

D.T. turned his back and went inside the courtroom and sat in the row in front of his string of frightened ladies.

Judge Hoskins was especially snappy as he moved through the calendar, which meant things clipped along at just below Mach two. Witnesses and attorneys were cut off in mid-word. Judgments were uttered before requested. Silences were castigated. "*Blutz* v. *Blutz*," Walter finally called, and looked at D.T. and grinned.

"Show time," D.T. whispered to the women behind him, and then stood up. "Ready, Your Honor."

He turned back to the row of women. "Mrs. Blutz? You're on. Relax and enjoy it. The court will set you free."

He allowed the trembling woman to precede him down the aisle. When they reached the counsel table he whispered for her to leave her gum with him, a stunt she managed with a minimum of notoriety, then directed her to the witness chair to the right of Judge Hoskins' elevated throne. D.T. placed his pile of files on the counsel table and looked into the immaculate scowl of the Honorable Willard Hoskins, Judge of the Circuit Court.

"How many this morning, Jones?" Each word was dipped in what the judge would have called justifiable vitriol and what D.T. would have called unearned pomposity.

"Seven, Your Honor."

"All defaults?"

"Yes."

"No husbands popping out of the woodwork today, demanding jury trials? No children suddenly announcing a preference to live with Daddy in Tahiti? No last minute allegations of spousal abuse or incestuous assault?" The judge rolled his eyes and rubbed his nose.

"No, Your Honor." D.T. bowed in chastened humility before the court's unchallengeable rectitude and rolled Jerlene Blutz' Doublemint into a ball and stuck it to the underside of the counsel table.

"You may begin."

Begin he did. Questions of name, age, address, length of marriage, length of residence in the state and county, venue established, jurisdiction established, judicial system engaged. Then the high hard ones, in the language of a statute thought by the legislature and its advisors to be an advance in the sociolegal approach to crumbling domesticity—"Have you and your husband experienced irreconcilable differences during your marriage, Mrs. Blutz?" Why yes, that's just what we've experienced,

Mr. Jones; irreconcilable differences. A whole mess of them, too. Just that kind. "And have these irreconcilable differences led to the irremediable breakdown of your marriage, Mrs. Blutz?" You took the words right out of my mouth, Mr. Jones. That's just what they led to, the what-you-call-it breakdown. Bang. "Petition for interlocutory decree of dissolution granted. Next case."

Five more times D.T. observed the ritual, and the staging and the script were flawless. "And have you and your husband experienced irreconcilable differences, Mrs. Rodriguez?"

"What is that? I no understand."

"Have you and your husband had problems? Arguments?"

"Fight? You mean do we fight?"

"Yes."

"*Si*. We fight. It José's fault. Tequila make him loco."

D.T. began to sweat. "Fault is not at issue here, Mrs. Rodriguez, as we discussed. Now, have these differences with your husband led to the irremediable breakdown of your marriage?"

"The furnace is what break down. Is that what you mean? The furnace break down and so I no pay the rent and the landlord he come put a paper in the door that say we got to leave by Sunday and I talk to woman at the neighborhood center by the laundromat and she send me to Legal Aid and they tell me to come here today and so here I am and I say we no leave. Huh? Is this when I say that? *We no leave!*"

"Mr. Jones."

The judge's voice awakened the dead and deeply buried. "Unless I miss my guess the young lady is here to defend an unlawful detainer action, not to petition for the dissolution of her marriage to the excitable José. There is undoubtedly another Rodriguez in the building, detailing her marital woes in response to questions about the furnace. Perhaps if you *interviewed* your clients, Mr. Jones, these travesties would not occur. I suggest you give it a try. In the meantime, I suggest you point *this* Mrs. Rodriguez in the right direction. I also suggest, no, *advise*, that if this happens again in *my* courtroom you will immediately be jailed for contempt and the bar association will be notified of the way in which you conduct your practice. Such as it is. Court is adjourned.''

As Walter rolled his eyes and scurried after the departing jurist, D.T. picked up his files and whispered some words to the witness and guided her to the master calendar board, then directed her to Courtroom Six, where *Watson* v. *Rodriguez*—Unlawful Detainer—was scheduled for hearing. Then D.T. looked in the appropriate places for *his* Mrs. Rodriguez. Not finding her, D.T. left the building. Another day, another dollar, another slap of shame. D.T's only consolation was that no one except his ex-wife had ever called him anything he had not already called himself.

■ TWO

PROBLEMS?" Bobby E. Lee raised a brow as D.T. came through the door. "You've got that look."

D.T. dropped the files on Bobby E. Lee's desk. "Problems indeed. But I don't seem to be able to blame any of them on you."

"You never can," Bobby E. Lee replied truthfully. "What was it this time?"

"An overabundance of the surname Rodriguez."

"So no Chicago and no flu?"

D.T. nodded. "Judge Hoskins depresses me so much I can't do anything but work. What do we have?"

"Two dittos, plus one non-usual."

"And the lad with the scarf and earring?" D.T. dared a glance toward the couch.

"He's with me. We're off to lunch."

"Didn't it hurt to stick that diamond in there?"

"I suppose, but then Tod's rather into pain." Bobby E. Lee placed the cover over his typewriter. "I may be late getting back. I have to buy Daddy a birthday present."

"I thought you and Daddy weren't speaking."

"We aren't. I'm going to get him some bikini underwear to remind him why."

Bobby E. Lee smiled a trifle fiendishly and closed the drawers of his desk, then plucked his satin jacket off the rack, motioning for his punctured friend to follow. The pair exited the office with the flair of those who see themselves as *objets d'art*.

For the hundredth time, D.T. started to wonder about Bobby E. Lee, but as usual he stopped himself before his speculation became risqué. Bobby was a good secretary and a good person. It was all D.T. needed to know, all he trusted himself to know as well. The rest was Bobby's business. Still, D.T. felt uneasy, as though there was some continuing obligation he was not fulfilling. He guessed it had to do with Bobby being homosexual, and with his own nonspecific responsibility for the jokes about fags and queers that befouled the air without his protest, with his apparently congenital sense that he should somehow make it better. For Bobby E. Lee. For everyone. Of course, a concrete obligation did exist. D.T. was more than a month in arrears in paying Bobby's salary.

D.T. glanced at the empty waiting room, then straightened the already straight copies of *Cosmopolitan, Vogue, People, US, Self, Shape,* and *Mad* that littered the coffee table. Whistling tonelessly, he emptied the ash-tray and threw away the wilted rose that Bobby E. Lee had picked in the park on his way to work. Happy to be momentarily a janitor rather than a lawyer, he wished he would not have to imagine, whether in a few minutes or a few months, how the women he had freed at the Fiasco that morning would ensnarl their lives again.

He entered his private office and took off his coat and hung it on the rack. The small refrigerator in the closet contained only a slice of swiss cheese the size of a domino, a can of light beer, and a magnum of French champagne, the latter received in lieu of a more fungible fee from a client with a flair for the unusual and a brother in the booze business. As the result of his second honeymoon—embarked upon with his ex-wife after only ninety-seven days of marriage—D.T. hated both the French and their champagne and so was waiting for a suitable occasion on which to present the magnum to Bobby E. Lee.

D.T. took out his buck knife and cut a sugary dollop of mold away from the cheese, then downed it. The bottom drawer of his desk yielded half a roll of Lifesavers and a quart of Bailey's Irish Cream, a Christmas gift from the member of his poker group for whom D.T. was in the nature of a perpetual annuity. The liqueur washed away the lingering dust of cheese, the beer washed away the lingering film of candy. The mechanics of sustenance accomplished, D.T. pulled his time sheets from the credenza behind his desk and made notations appropriate for the morning's activity, calibrating and quantifying his most recent humiliation.

D.T. rarely performed a professional service that was payable on an hourly basis as opposed to a flat fee, so the time sheets he prepared so meticulously were invariably worthless. But there was always, he frequently told himself and occasionally believed, a chance that an initially routine matter would burgeon into a great litigious engine that would unearth someone, somewhere, who could be directed by an appropriate court to compensate D.T. for each and every minute of his time, at an approximate rate of two dollars per. Then he could live the way half the lawyers he knew were living—from the proceeds of that one big case, a sinecure that had fallen into their undeserving laps like a starling struck by lightning and had nevertheless generated, despite their persistent lassitude and seamless incompetence, a fee of an outrageous and easily sheltered six figures.

In the meantime, D.T. used the time records as raw data from which to calculate a flat fee that would yield him a reasonable return for services rendered and at the same time keep the unfortunate ladies coming through the door at an approximate rate of three per day. The last time he had run the numbers it had come out thusly for a default divorce, the staple of the Friday Fiasco:

> Bobby E. Lee—Intake interview, forms completion, telephonic instruction re court appearance: 30 minutes @ $25.00 per hour = $12.50.
>
> D.T.—Client interview and forms review: 35 minutes @ $75.00 per hour = $43.75.
>
> D.T.—Court appearance: 15 minutes @ $75.00 per hour = $18.75.
>
> Expenses—Filing fees, service of process, etc.: $75.00.
>
> Total time and expenses = $150.00.
>
> Surcharge for overhead and unforeseen difficulties, tantrums, wails, interruptions, consolations, reconciliations, etc.: $150.00.
>
> Surcharge for inflation: $50.00.
>
> Discount for socioeconomic character of clientele and ex-

istence of storefront law firms that advertise on billboards and compete on price: $150.00.

Net total: $200.00. Flat rate for default or uncontested divorce. Entire amount payable in advance unless alternate arrangements made prior to initial interview. Subject to change without notice. Frequently subject to reduction, occasionally subject to waiver, a gesture followed inevitably by regret and self-reproach.

D.T. shoved the papers away from him and thought again about what had happened in court. Running into Jerome Fitzgerald after all these years reminded him how differently his own life had evolved from the course he had envisioned during the turbid days of law school. Had he known anyone to whom he could have been truthful about such things, he would have confessed during his freshman year that he believed himself a fermenting mix of Perry Mason and Clarence Darrow, a nascent champion of lost causes, reviver of trampled liberties, master of the sine qua non of the trial lawyer's art—convincing anyone of anything. But after he had gone into practice on his own—against the advice of everyone he knew and a lot of those he didn't—the clients who came his way all possessed totally prosaic difficulties, dilemmas that, while they involved the basic passions and requirements of life and therefore invoked D.T.'s empathy and an invariably unprofitable expenditure of his time, did not attract the kind of publicity or renown that would bring more glorious causes to his door.

Mildly injurious dog bites, trivial slips and falls, evictions, credit hassles, change of names—the clients trooped in and out of his office like files of captured soldiers, asking little, getting less. His silver tongue tarnished by life's relentless ambiguity, the major Perry Masonish mystery in his practice soon came to be whether he would be able to pay Confederated Properties the exorbitant rent for the suite of offices that, he insisted as a point of pride, be at least one storey above the street and occupy at least one more room than the nearest branch of Legal Aid. So, twenty years after his dreams of glory and eminence had vanished as steadily as a salt lick in a stockyard, here he was, not quite envious of others, yet not quite satisfied with himself, pursuing a profession whose moral component was detectable only with the aid of a microscope or a philosopher.

D.T. swore at the law and at Judge Hoskins, made a resolution to change his life in some respect as yet unspecified, and took a sip of Bailey's. While his cheeks swelled with liquid candy, the bell above the door to the hallway tinkled briefly and a few seconds later the bell on Bobby E. Lee's desk chimed to match it. D.T. walked to the file cabinet and extracted the form headed Petition for Dissolution of Marriage and the accompanying Confidential Counseling Statement and Property Declarations and laid them on his desk. Then he picked up the phone and called a number he had called once a week or more for the past three years.

"Conway residence."

"May I speak to Mrs. Jones, please?"

"Mrs. Jones ain't Mrs. Jones no more, she Miz Conway back again, and besides, she out." The voice paused and experienced metamorphosis. "Whom shall I say is calling?"

"The one still stuck with the name of Jones. How are you, Mirabelle?"

"I's fine, D.T. Didn't recognize you voice. Been drinking lunch again?"

"Not a drop," he lied. "Where's her loveliness?"

"Jazzercise, she call it."

"She turned hip in her old age?"

"Not so's you'd notice, D.T. She still buying them tunes like they play in the supermarket. She be back by four, I expect. Take her another hour to recover, you got anything strenuous in mind."

Her laugh made D.T. laugh. "Jazzercise. Is that dancing, or what?"

"Jumping like a toad on a hot rock is what it look like. She all the time practicing with a nappy-headed man on the TV sounds like my niece Lucille."

"Have her call me, will you, Mirabelle? I'm at the office. My picture still on the piano?"

"The day it ain't, I let you know."

"How's Heather?"

"Sweet as a sugar lump, like always."

"Give her a squeeze for me. Tell her I'll see her to-morrow."

"You bet I will."

"Take it easy, Mirabelle."

"You, too, D.T. Wish you'd come around here more. You an amusing man, especially when you had a few belts."

"See you soon," D.T. said, and thought for a mostly pleasant minute about his ex-wife and for a wholly pleasant minute about his daughter, then hung up and pulled out of his In Box the small stack of freshly typed statements that Bobby E. Lee had left for him.

They were the bills about to be sent to clients whose obligations had not been entirely satisfied in advance of D.T.'s services, despite his sworn policy to the contrary. D.T. reduced the amount due on the ones whose recipients either could not pay or for whom he had done less than either of them expected, and increased the amount due on others for whom both the results and the ability to pay were exalted. He went through them quickly, abashed as always at having to make his living by dunning women. When he had finished, he ran a quick total on his calculator, multiplied the result by 45 percent, which was roughly the coefficient of collectability in his practice, and applied the product to the outstanding balance on his note at the Citizens Bank and Trust. A drop in the proverbial and gargantuan bucket of his debt.

When the lady in the next room had been waiting long enough to suggest her prospective attorney was a man of frantic and colossal accomplishment, D.T. went out to retrieve her. As he approached the couch she put down her outdated *Vogue* on the exact spot from which she had obtained it and rose to meet him.

She was forty, perhaps, laboriously neat and hyper-alert, as though applying for a job for which she was unqualified. Her hair was short and shaggy, the color of collies, a tattered curtain across her forehead. Her brown eyes were outsized and ill-defined, doubtlessly sculpted with one of those long hairy tools promoted on TV. She was tall and slender, simply dressed and slightly sexless, careful. The ceramic glaze over her eyes would have caused some to wonder if she were drunk or drugged, but

D.T. saw that look every day. His clients wore it like a mandala.

The woman wiped her hand on her slacks, then extended it toward D.T. along with a firm smile. D.T. smiled back. Her name, she said, was Mareth Stone. After a minute of greeting and small talk while they walked to his private office, her firm rein of intellect upon emotion led D.T. to suspect she could serve as an exemplar of his First Principle of Modern Matrimony—at any given point in any marriage, the wife is more intelligent than the husband on any subject of importance.

As she took her seat, D.T. glanced at the metal indicator in the top drawer of his desk. She was divorce client number 998. He was fast coming on a landmark. He clicked to the next digit and closed the drawer, uncertain whether he was cheered or depressed by the number of scalps he had accumulated.

He offered Mareth Stone a drink and a cigarette and she declined them both. He mentioned the weather and an event of current controversy and she had interest in neither. He looked her over carefully and obviously and she neither squirmed nor preened. She made no effort to seem devastated or blasé. At which point curiosity drew him out of his doldrums. After twenty years he still wondered what had finally killed their marriage.

"So, Mrs. Stone. What seems to be the problem?"

"I seem to need a lawyer." Her lips didn't quiver and her eyes didn't leak. Unusual, but not unprecedented.

"What makes you think so?"

"I've been served with divorce papers. Haven't I?"

She reached into her bag and brought out an unsealed manila envelope and handed it to him. On it was the word "Divorce," written with savagery in what he suspected was her hand.

He removed the contents and scanned them quickly. "So you have," he said. "Your husband's lawyer is the best in the business, by the way, present company excepted. Was it a surprise?"

"Totally." She closed her bag and clasped her hands and adopted the clueless expression she seemed determined to wear no matter what.

"He hadn't moved out, hadn't found the secret of life

in the form of a controlled substance or a teen-age swami or a woman half his age? Hadn't smacked you on the nose? Nothing?''

"Nothing. At least nothing that conclusive." Her lips disappeared momentarily and he guessed what curled them against her teeth was fury.

"Where is he now?"

Her narrow, charmless face seemed to harden by the moment. "I have no idea."

"When did you see him last?"

"This morning at breakfast."

"And he said nothing about this?"

"Not a word. And not a word last night, when we made what I foolishly assumed was love."

The disclosure was not premeditated and its candor seemed to alarm her. D.T. thought it possible she had never previously made public acknowledgment of her own participation in the sex act. The memory of profaned embrace jellied her eyes, but only momentarily.

"I'm sorry," she said, after but a single sniffle.

"Don't be." She was so quickly composed D.T. began to worry that she had bent her demeanor so unnaturally it would eventually shatter.

"I never thought it would happen. Not this way. I always thought we could work it out, I guess. I had all these little *speeches* ready, for when he wanted to talk about it." She laughed dryly. "He seems to have skipped that stage."

D.T. leaned back in his chair. "I was struck by your phraseology, Mrs. Stone. It seemed to suggest that perhaps you considered filing for divorce yourself."

"I . . . well . . ."

He maintained his easy smile. "I imagine ninety percent of married women have considered shedding their spouse at one time or another, Mrs. Stone. It's not a sin. Or even silly."

"We've had some problems," she conceded finally, "though I was never certain he realized it. I suppose this means he did." She gestured toward the papers she had given him.

D.T. decided to thrust for the rot. "Did these problems, as you call them, ever send you to another man for solace?''

Her eyes swelled like baking muffins. Her fingers curled. ''Of course not. No. Not that it's any of your business.''

D.T. sat up straight and held up his ringless hand. ''Let's get one thing clear right now, Mrs. Stone. If you want me to represent you in this matter then absolutely *everything* in your life is my business, from your bowel movements to your taste in millinery. If you don't buy that, I suggest you go find some lawyer in a fifty-man firm who makes a quarter of a million a year and thinks that means he knows everything he needs to know about divorce work even though the only one he's ever been involved with is his own.''

D.T.'s anger surprised them both, and they both stayed silent while it cooled. When she spoke again, Mareth Stone was frowning, still leery of discussing private matters with a man who looked like an assistant basketball coach at a religious college somewhere in south Georgia. ''Everything I tell you will be confidential, won't it?'' she asked, her voice smaller, more youthful and entreating than before. Which immediately made him like her. Which made him glad.

''It will unless you break the confidence by telling someone else. Or unless you're using me to commit a crime or you tell me you intend one. Or unless you refuse to pay my fee and I have to sue you for it. Okay?''

She nodded.

D.T. got comfortable in his chair. ''Is he a bastard?''

''Chas? No. You mean Chas?''

''Chas? Jesus.''

She smiled. ''Short for Charles. When I married him he was Chuck. And he isn't a bastard, exactly. Ambitious and insensitive, yes. And maybe a little bit stupid.''

''Does he gamble?''

''No, not that I know of.''

''Booze? Drugs?''

''Don't be silly.'' Her back stiffened as she sensed the implication might eventually pass through her husband's character and splash on hers.

''Then who's the other woman?''

"There *is* no other woman."

"Eight to one there is, the way it's gone so far. So indulge me. If she exists, who is she?"

Mareth Stone frowned and pulled a cigarette from her purse and lit it with trembling fingers, her second hint that the day was an anomaly. "I don't know who it would be," she said finally. "I don't think Chas has the energy for an affair any more, if you want the truth. His money saps his strength."

D.T. stood up and began to pace the room, beginning his examination. The client chair creaked as she twisted to keep him in view. "An affair's their last gasp, sometimes. Like a fish jumping out of the boat."

"Is it important? Who she is? *If* she is?"

"Not really. Not right now. Are there children?"

"Two. Eight and thirteen. Cristine and David."

"Is there money?"

"Now there is. Chas has been quite successful, if money is the measure."

"Was he rich when you married him?"

She shook her head. "He had to borrow money to buy the ring." She looked down at her hand, at the thin gold band that lived there. "He kept wanting to buy me a diamond after he made his money," she mused quietly. "I kept thinking it was important to keep wearing the ring he gave me when he proposed. When we were poor and struggling. I guess it wasn't important enough."

She cried silently. D.T. had long ago learned better than to try to interfere. "How much do you want?" he asked when she stopped.

"What do you mean?"

"Come now, Mrs. Stone. I'm sure you know something about the law. You're entitled to half the assets accumulated during marriage, and if there wasn't any money in the beginning all the assets you have are presumptively marital. Unless he inherited a bundle or unless you have money of your own."

She shook her head. "Neither of those."

"Did you live together before marriage?"

"Why?"

"That can increase the marital period and entitle you to more money."

She sighed. "We were very proper. Apparently even that was a mistake." She fingered her hair absently. "It's very difficult for me to think of this in terms of money, Mr. Jones. I mean, I know I have rights, and I want to assert them, but it's like putting a price on fifteen years of life. Of love. And I always believed love was priceless." She started to smile at the cliché, then to say something else, then stopped and closed her eyes.

"In this jurisdiction love goes for about two hundred bucks a month per year of marriage, Mrs. Stone," D.T. said, loosely calculating an alimony formula employed by at least one judge in the southside division. "What does your husband do for a living?"

"He's an investment advisor."

"With a firm?"

"He has his own business."

"What's his income, roughly?"

"Eighty thousand last year. Or so he said to someone. Lately, most of what I know about Chas has come through eavesdropping. And of course he might have been boasting."

"How do you contribute to the business?"

"Not at all, I suppose. At least that's what Chas would say."

"Never entertained any clients?"

"Only a few hundred. I've made barrels of paté in my day." She smiled sadly. "And I just *hate* paté."

"Never packed his bag for trips or drove him to the airport at six a.m.?"

"Several times. Yes. I get the point, and I do feel entitled to something . . . *tangible* out of all this. I mean, it's not that Chas doesn't have enough for both of us."

"Good," D.T. said. "I may not get you what you're entitled to, but I can get you enough to keep you off relief and make him afraid of going on it." He walked to the file cabinet and opened the second drawer from the bottom. "I keep a bottle of brandy on hand for sipping upon the birth of an attorney-client relationship, Mrs. Stone," he lied. "Will you join me?"

She looked at him over her shoulder. "I . . . is this customary?"

"Customary drives a Mercedes and works down-town."

"Well, I suppose it's all right. Somehow I thought you would be much more . . . somber somehow."

"Probate lawyers are somber; divorce lawyers are clowns. Death is serious business; the rest of it's a joke."

D.T. poured into polished snifters. They both drank, eyes on each other, exchanging the silent promises that are the consideration for future services.

"I'm going to ask you some questions now, Mrs. Stone," D.T. said as he refilled her snifter and put away the bottle. "To advise you properly I must have honest responses. If I sense you're passing counterfeit, our relationship shall terminate, the brandy notwithstanding. Understood?"

"Of course."

"Incidentally, my meter, as they say, is running. From here on, each hour I devote to your welfare will set you back a hundred bucks. I hope to defray most if not all of it through a court-ordered contribution from your husband when the matter is finally concluded, but that, of course, is contingent. You are and will remain the primary obligor."

D.T. watched carefully for her reaction. A hundred an hour was his penultimate rate. Mrs. Stone would have been charged more only had she proved herself, upon the initial interview, to be despicable.

The stated fee, such as it was, seemed not to faze the woman. She asked if he wanted a retainer. He considered momentarily whether any other client had ever used the word.

"One thousand dollars, please," he said.

"Will you take a check?"

"I will take beads and trinkets."

She wrote on the negotiable rectangle with no more thought than she would give to the purchase of bulbs from the blind. Watching her do it was more fun than D.T. had had since Cheerio came home at twelve to one and he'd pulled square with his book for the first time in the decade.

When she presented him the check he read it carefully, noting the baroque script, the designer imprint and coloration of the paper, the elegant face amount. "I notice this is drawn on your individual account," D.T. said. "What kind of balance do you maintain?"

She shrugged. "A few thousand. Sometimes less. Why?"

"Any other accounts in your name alone?"

"I . . . no. I don't think so."

"How about your family? Parents? Are they still living?"

"Yes."

"Wealthy?"

"No. Not at all."

D.T. nodded. "Listen to me, Mrs. Stone," D.T. said as he placed the check beneath the corporate seal of an enterprise that had once cost him half his net worth and thereby convinced him to abandon corporate law. "This case already has a certain smell to it, the smell of one that will go to trial and appeal, so listening to my questions will be good practice for things to come. First, how long have you been married?"

"Fifteen years."

He positioned himself in front of her. His eyes grabbed hers and held on. "Do you love your children?"

"Yes. Of course."

"Why?"

"What?"

"Why do you love them?"

Once again her decorum stumbled aside. She plucked at her clothes and twisted her legs and inspected her nails. It was the one he always hit them with, the mothers, and it was surprising how few of them had an answer ready. It was grossly unfair, but it was his first and best sense, often, of their behavior under fire.

"I'm their mother," she stuttered finally. "I mean, well, mothers love their children. It's . . . it's nature."

"The hell it is," D.T. snarled. "I had a client wanted me to peddle her kid for a sixty-eight pickup and she'd throw in diapers and a sleeper on the deal. So let's not wax misty about motherhood. Why do you love your kids?"

Mareth Stone stiffened. A bulge appeared over the hinge on her jaw. "Because they're *neat*, that's why.

Because they make me laugh and cry and want to hug them. Because they teach me things. Because they're the only thing of consequence I've ever done on my own, the only nice things I've made since the days when I went to Bible school and wove lanyards and drew pictures of Jesus with finger paint. Is that enough, Mr. D. T. Jones? And what the hell does D.T. stand for, anyway?"

D.T. watched her dab her eyes while he wondered when she had last sworn at a total stranger. "Doubting Thomas," he answered. "And that will do just fine. Question two. I see from the Petition your husband wants the kids. Do you think he's serious?"

She sniffed and thought about it. "Probably. He said he would fight me for them once, when we had a quarrel. And I think he will. I think he needs for me to come out of this a loser in as many ways as possible."

"I have to warn you then, the law no longer prefers mothers to fathers in custody cases; the sole standard is the best interest of the child. I also have to warn you that in a majority of cases in this state, when the father is serious about wanting custody, he gets it."

"You must be joking."

"I'm afraid not. The good news is that most judges ignore the law and try the case as though the husband has the burden of showing the mother is unfit."

"That's good news?"

"It gets messy, if that's what you mean. Also, if it's a true custody fight then you have to go to mediation. It's the law."

"What's that?"

"You and your husband get together without your lawyers in the presence of a mediator—not a lawyer or judge but a lay mediator—and try to work out a custody arrangement."

"Does it work?"

"If the parents can simmer down long enough to negotiate a deal. If they both have the best interests of the kids at heart. And if the mediator is competent and the lawyers don't come in afterward and mess it up and if the kids don't object to the deal. Among other things."

"You don't sound optimistic."

D.T. shrugged. "It works or it doesn't. If it doesn't, we go to trial. Now. Why did you marry your husband?"

She frowned and grew angry again. "Will I be asked this in court? Somehow I doubt it."

"I doubt it, too. So why did you?"

"Do you really want to know, or are you just playing with me?"

"I want to know. I only play with women after hours," he added, hoping to keep her mad.

She thrust her jaw as though it were a cudgel. "Chas was the first man who made love to me. I believed what my mother told me—that sex without marriage was a sin. I wanted the sex so I took the marriage. Neither one of them turned out to be as good as I thought."

"So it was convention and nothing more, is that what you're saying?"

She paused long enough to recall an emotion that had blazed its brightest fifteen years before. "Oh, Chas is not an ogre. He's charming, or he was. For some reason he decided he wanted me so he did what he thought it would take to get me—flowers, poetry, picnics, presents. And I bought it all. I truly loved him, in the beginning."

"And last night, when you were making what you thought was love, as I believe you put it? Did you feel the same way?"

She shook her head.

"Why not?"

She gathered herself for an answer that would have meaning. "I'm not sure I can tell you what happened," she began. "I just know that a few years ago life began to be very hard for me. The things I had enjoyed for ten years didn't seem to be enough any longer."

"Things like what?"

"Mothering. Cooking. Playing bridge, playing golf, playing house . . . playing. It was as though I'd been given a blood transfusion; my personality changed completely." She paused and sighed, weary. "But then I suppose you've heard all this before. I mean, if I know anything at all about myself it's that I'm not unique."

"My memory's so bad it doesn't matter whether I've heard it before or not. Go on."

"Well, while I struggled to find out how to deal with

those new feelings, Chas was no help at all. Which wasn't surprising, I guess. I mean, this is a man whose idea of communication is to leave me a list of things that need to be done that day. This is a man whose idea of sentiment is a box of Bavarian mints on our anniversary. *Every* anniversary.'' She shook her head. ''I didn't expect him to *give* me meaning, but I didn't expect him to get in the way when I went after it myself. But Chas took it as an insult that I wanted to do something besides make him happy. Whenever I talked with him about what was going on inside my head he just made fun of me. Called me a libber and all that. Made jokes to his buddies. I see now that he was a little bit scared of what was going on, and I know *I* was. There certainly weren't any easy answers, I don't mean that, but I think he could have *tried,* you know. Worked with me. Talked to me. *Listened.* I don't know. . . . Last night, when he climbed onto me, I saw such *contempt* in his eyes.''

She began to almost cry, then forced herself to stop. ''When I began to really look at him I realized that since the day we married Chas hadn't learned one single thing that wasn't connected directly and solely with his precious business. I mean, in the beginning I was his project, so he made me happy, but then I wasn't a project any longer, money was, and so all his attention went to that. I realized Chas had absolutely no concern for other people, that he felt the world owed him both wealth and a clear conscience, and he was enraged at whatever he thought was an obstacle to either, whether the income tax or a disgruntled client or a wife who wanted him to contribute to charity or teach their children the Golden Rule or discuss the meaning of life. Do you need more, Mr. Jones?'' She raised her chin defiantly. Her breaths came in gasps.

''That's fine for now,'' D.T. said, ever so calmly. ''At some point we may want to add more, shall we say, unsavory aspects of his character to that list. Now tell me about your affair.''

''*What* affair?''

''Come now, Mrs. Stone. I've been in this business since the Kennedy administration. Women who've slept around give off signals.''

"What signals?"

He shook his head. "Trade secret. So tell me about it."

She fidgeted uneasily. "Will *this* come out at trial?"

"Right now you're in a better position to judge that than I. Who's the lucky man?"

She paused, then blinked, then lowered her head and yielded. "A friend's husband."

"How long ago?"

"A year plus a little."

"How many times?"

"Twice, if you mean sex. A dozen times, if you mean talk."

"Does your husband know?"

"No."

"Are you sure?"

"I . . . no. I suppose not, given this morning."

"Would your paramour have any reason to side with your husband in your case? To testify against you?"

"No. . . . I don't know. He never had anything good to say about Chas, but then why would he, in the circumstances?"

"Would he lie for you in court, if you asked him to?"

"Yes. I think so. But I never would."

D.T. closed his eyes against her innocence. "Do you plan to marry him?"

"No."

"Does his wife know about the two of you?"

"I'm not sure. She seems . . ."

"Then she knows. How does she feel about your husband?"

"She hates his guts. I think."

"Why?"

"Because she isn't cute or rich and Chas absolutely ignores women who aren't cute or rich." She looked down at herself. From her expression she saw nothing cute there, either. She looked up at him. "Can I go now? I just hate being here. I *hate* it."

"Why?"

"Because it's so *common*. Every woman I know is divorced. I was so *determined* it wasn't going to happen to me. But apparently I'm about to join the pack." She laughed. "Do you suppose it's anything like Brownies?"

D.T. shrugged. "I don't know about Brownies, but it's not the worst pack in the world to be in. I mean, some women watch Donahue every morning and others drink whiskey."

Mareth Stone only closed her eyes. "I do both," she said. "What does that make me?"

D.T. took a deep breath and looked at the woman for whom life was about to become a brawl. "Where are your children, Mrs. Stone?"

"In school. Why?"

"Which school?"

"Country Day. *Why?*" Worry polished her forehead.

D.T. pushed his telephone toward her. "Call them. Make sure your children are still there."

"What are you saying? Do you think Chas has done something? He *wouldn't*."

D.T. held up a hand. "I have no idea whether he would or wouldn't, I just know that divorce can get to be the stinkingest, slimiest thing you can imagine, and it can get there fast. I know that men whose wives have cooked their food and washed their socks and licked their cocks for twenty years will suddenly try to cut them off without a penny and see to it they spend the rest of their lives in a welfare line. And I know that a hundred thousand fathers kidnap their kids every year and a hundred thousand mothers spend the rest of their days looking for them. Or vice versa. Call the school."

She looked at him oddly. "You take all this personally, don't you?"

He met her eyes. "Do I?"

"I think so. I'm surprised."

"So am I. Call the school."

D.T. waited while she placed the call and enjoyed her relief when she learned that the children were there. D.T. whispered to her to instruct the school to keep them inside until she picked them up, which she did. When she hung up she looked at him fearfully. "Is there a place you can take them for a while?" he asked.

"I don't know. My parents aren't good with them, not

at all. My friends seem at odds with their own so much, I don't know. I'll have to think."

"After you pick them up you should go to your bank and take all the money out of all the accounts you can lay your hands on. I mean *all*. Plus you should empty all the safe deposit boxes and get a new one in a different bank and put the stuff in it. Okay?"

"But is that fair? I mean . . ."

"In this business fair is first, Mrs. Stone. Besides, my guess is you're going to discover your husband has beat you to it and the accounts will be empty. So be prepared."

She lowered her head. "It's like preparing for war, isn't it, Mr. Jones?"

"That's exactly what it's like, Mrs. Stone. And your husband is already marching through Poland so we've got to get busy."

"I didn't think it would be like this, somehow," she said quietly. "Not us."

D.T. nodded. "The whole world thinks it's an exception. I felt the same way when I was drafted. It lasted till I got shot. There's one more thing."

"What?"

"Call a locksmith and change the locks on your house. Then search it for any kind of business papers you can find. Deeds, stock certificates, anything having to do with property. Eventually I'll want to know everything you own, you and your husband I mean, so start getting together anything that will help. Do you have a stock broker or does your husband handle it?"

"My husband."

"Do you own any real property besides your home?"

"A cabin at the lake."

"Call your realtor and tell him your husband is not authorized to act for you in any way. How many cars do you have?"

"Three."

"Take the one you're driving and park it in a long-term garage. Take a cab home and use the second one. I assume your husband drives the third."

"Yes."

"How much do you need a month, Mrs. Stone? To

support you in the manner to which you've become accustomed?''

She folded her hands and closed her eyes for a long
time. ''I've never really thought about it. The money was
just there. For whatever I wanted.''

''Three thousand? Four? Ten?''

''Three, I should think.''

''We'll go for five. Has your husband ever hit you?
Slapped you around?''

''No. What do you think he is?''

''A man who didn't have the guts to warn you he was
about to break your life in half. Do you sniff coke, Mrs.
Stone?''

''You can't be serious.''

''Why not? It's evidently replaced milk as the world's
most perfect food.''

''No. Nothing like that.''

''Well, we all have sins, Mrs. Stone. What are yours?''

She laughed uneasily. ''This is sort of like church, isn't
it?''

''This is nothing like church. How about it?''

''You first.''

''Me? I bet sports with money I don't have. I lie to my
clients when they need it and sometimes when they
don't. I cheat on my girlfriend almost as much as she
cheats on me. Let's get back to you.''

''Well, I cheat, too, as I said. I spend lots of money on
worthless trinkets to punish Chas for neglecting me. I
drink too much sometimes, and am honest when I
shouldn't be except when I pretend to like people I can't
stand. Does all that mean I won't win my case?'' She was
almost giddy, momentarily forgetting what losing her
case would mean.

''Hell, lady. In this office that makes you a saint. Now,
how do you feel about your husband right this minute?''

''How do you mean?''

''I mean if he comes around next week and talks nice,
brings you a box of mints, apologizes for taking all the
money, and offers to stick his cock in you again, what
are you going to do? Think about it.''

It took her three seconds. ''I'm going to cut the
crooked son of a bitch off and fry it up for breakfast.''

D.T. clapped his hands. "Hot damn, Mrs. Stone. I think we're about to have some fun. Here. Sign these forms."

"But they're blank."

"Not for long."

"Is that legal?"

"Don't worry about it." He gave her his pen.

After scratching out her name, Mareth Stone stood up and shouldered her purse and looked at him. "Do whatever has to be done, Mr. Jones."

"Lucky for you that's my Golden Rule, Mrs. Stone," he said, and then leaned back in his chair. "Right about here I usually tell my clients to relax, to leave it all to me, that everything will be all right. But I don't think I'm going to tell you that."

"Why not?"

"Because I'm afraid you might believe me."

"But I'm fine. Really."

"That's what I mean. You don't even know what's happened to you yet. Some time or other you're going to crash. It may be tonight, it may be a year from tonight. You'll feel alone, cheated, wronged, guilty, worthless, and ashamed, and you'll be a little bit right about all of it, but it won't help. You'll be very depressed, so depressed you can't move, can't get dressed in the morning, can't eat, nothing. One of my clients stayed in bed for twelve days. Pissed and shit and everything, right there on the old Posturepedic. Luckily they found her before . . ."

"I won't do anything like that. Good Lord. I . . ."

"Let me finish. When it happens, friends can be a help. So can family. So can I, a little, and I know some people who can help you a lot more. Counselors. Support groups. Shrinks. You can call me any time. Here's my card. Put it by the phone. Call me day or night. I mean it. Okay?"

"Okay. But I don't do things like that, Mr. Jones. I really don't."

She was so convincing he knew better than to believe her.

■ THREE

MARETH STONE left the office just as Bobby E. Lee returned from lunch. Their eyes absorbed each other, their lips, similar shades of umber, smiled. After she had gone, D.T. returned to his office, took Mrs. Stone's check from his desk and endorsed it, then took it out to Bobby E. Lee. "Deposit this in the office account and draw one payable to yourself in the same amount. How will that leave us?"

"You're still a thousand light."

"She's a paying customer, Bobby, and she looks to be in need of some heroics. We should be square in a month."

Bobby E. Lee looked through the glass door thoughtfully. "Figured she was," he said, and stuffed the check into the single pocket of his skin-tight shirt. "But be careful, Mr. J. When things tighten up, that kind throws in the towel."

D.T. started to object, then stopped. Bobby was too often right about the nuance of personality. His sense of which clients had firmly decided to divorce and which were only window-shopping was unerring, as was his sense of which of them needed tact and which a rather brutal shove. D.T. often wondered what he would do without Bobby E. Lee. The answer was always distressing.

D.T. went back to his office and reviewed the monthly statements once again, reducing three more of them in light of the affluence of his most recent client. The statements ready for the mail, he changed the cassette in his deck and let his blood squirt to the beat of Doug Kershaw

38

while he noted on his calendar the day that morning's interlocutory decrees would become final. On that date, six months hence, Bobby E. Lee would send each participant in the Friday Fiasco a single red rose along with a certified copy of the final judgment of dissolution. Half the time the envelope and the flower were returned. Addressee unknown. No forwarding address. Starting over elsewhere.

D.T.'s phone rang. When he picked it up he was greeted warmly by his only ex-wife. "Jazzercise?" D.T. said after she had said his name.

"Keeps me trim, darling. I had to do something since I stopped having sex on a regular basis."

"Oh? Religious reasons?"

"More aesthetic, I would say. Middle-aged bodies are so untidy. Present company excepted, of course. I always liked your body, D.T. It was your mind I couldn't handle." Her laugh reminded him of engines.

They had been married over six years of wrangles, jousts, and contests, during which D.T. had failed to adjust to her money and she had failed to adjust to his misanthropy. Now they had been divorced over three years of weekly phone calls. Over that time, talking to Michele about subjects they had been too insecure to discuss while wed had been D.T.'s close-to-favorite moments and, he hoped and suspected, his ex-wife's as well.

"So how are you, D.T.?" Michele asked as she always did.

"Good-to-better, Michele. How about you?"

"My yeast infection cleared up so I'm fine and dandy and looking for love."

"Glad to hear it."

"How was the Friday Fiasco?" she asked.

"About average."

"That bad?"

"Afraid so."

"Why do you keep on, D.T.? I know you've had offers from other firms. Landon Towers was telling me the other night that he's been trying to get you to go in with him for over a year. They must have thirty lawyers now."

"Forty-five."

"Which means someone else could take care of your damsels in distress and you could do something dignified, to say nothing of remunerative."

"Landon Towers wants me to do bankruptcy work. Ever spend an hour in bankruptcy court, Michele? Compared to it, *Queen for a Day* was a noble enterprise. Besides, the Friday Fiasco's as close as I'll ever come to participating in the forgiveness of sins." He shifted gears and hoped she would follow, stifling her instinct to reform him. "You still getting married?"

"I suppose so. Are you still going to give me away? You're the only one there is, you know."

"I'm perfectly happy to give you away, Michele. Just not to George."

"Yes, well, we've been through *that*, haven't we?"

"Yes, we have."

George was, among other things such as the owner of a wholesale fabric business, about to become an exemplar of D.T.'s Second Principle of Modern Matrimony, the one which states that in a modern woman's second marriage, the husband has the backbone of a grape. "To what do I owe the pleasure of your call, D.T.?" Michele asked sweetly. "Thursday night poker leave you short again?"

"Yes, as a matter of fact."

"A nonpositive cash flow over the near term, was, I believe, the way you put it last time."

"Something like that."

"How much?"

"A thousand would be fine."

"And where would that put us?"

D.T. didn't have to think; the figure was stamped on the fore edge of his mind. "Seventeen-five," he said "I've got it all down in my ledger."

"How CPAish of you. Shall I mail it?"

"I'll pick it up tonight around six," D.T. said quickly. "Just leave it with Mirabelle, why don't you? Then I won't have to bother you."

"Oh, you don't bother me, D.T. Not any more. In fact, I don't know what I'd do without you."

"Me, either."

"I wasn't speaking in the financial sense, D.T."

"Me, either."

"Liar," she charged, then paused that pause and D.T. steeled himself. "You know, D.T.," she went on softly, "I told you the day we divorced that we could still have sex whenever you wanted. Do you remember?"

"Sure."

"So how come we haven't? Just out of curiosity."

"I don't know," D.T. mumbled. "Maybe because there are only about three things I do regularly that keep me above the creatures that live in the slime and I think that's one of them."

"What are the other two?"

"The Friday Fiasco and there used to be something else but now I can't remember what it is. I guess there are only two."

Michele laughed. "Well, I'll forgive you for not treating me like a call girl, D.T. But I won't forgive you if you start treating me like a branch bank."

"No danger of that, Michele. I hardly ever have dreams about branch banks."

"Do you really dream about me, D.T.?"

"Sure."

"What do we do?"

"Things."

"Old things or new things?"

"Both."

"How exciting. Will you tell me about them some night? In all their throbbing details?"

"Sure."

"When?"

"Soon."

Michele paused. When she spoke her words were round as plums. "You don't have to be afraid of me any more. You know that, don't you, D.T.?"

"I know that the same way I know I can't get VD off a toilet seat, Michele."

She laughed again. "You're not all bad, D.T. Not all bad at all. Maybe I'll see you this evening. George isn't picking me up till eight."

"Maybe so," D.T. said, immediately planning how to get hold of the check without encountering her. Michele on the phone was one thing; Michele in her sixteen-room mansion dressed for dinner at a restaurant that didn't open for lunch or bother to list its prices was something else again.

"Are you still seeing Barbara, by the way?" Michele asked as he was about to say good-bye.

"Yep."

"She's good for you, you know."

"So she tells me."

"Do you want some advice?"

"No," D.T. said quickly. "I'll pick up Heather at ten tomorrow. Dress her for the out-of-doors."

"Oh?"

"Zoo."

"God, D.T. Do you know how many times she's been to that pitiful zoo? The monkeys think she's a cousin from L.A. Give her a break."

"The museum of natural history?"

"That's just a zoo that died, D.T."

"Planetarium?"

"Last month, with the enrichment class."

"Aquarium?"

"You know she hates fish. Alive or cooked."

"Art museum?"

"At her age?"

"Why not? Indoor dress. Ten sharp. Take it easy, Michele."

"Easy's the only way it comes when you drive a Rolls, D.T."

Michele's trouble was that she believed it. D.T.'s trouble was that it seemed to be true.

Bobby E. Lee stuck his head in the door. "A Lucinda Finders is here. Better get the tissues out." The door closed without further explanation.

D.T. looked at his watch and decided to hurry the day to its conclusion. After putting Mareth Stone's papers in his Out Box, he went to fetch a client that Bobby E. Lee had only to lay eyes on to know was swaddled in a story that would in a very short time erupt in tears on the other side of D.T.'s battered desk.

She was young, too young to be married or divorced, too young to be seeing a lawyer for any reason. She was also pregnant, and too young to be that, as well. Beneath a hood of blonde curls she looked at him bravely, with a sunny, shadeless face that not many years ago would have sucked many a boy into puberty before his time and would now cause many a man to assume she had been created solely for his pleasure.

Her blue eyes skipped quickly over D.T.'s face, to see if it was going to be as bad as she feared. "Hi," she said simply, and stood and walked toward him on triangles of wood that made her thighs seem hydraulically propelled. D.T. bet himself she had first had sex when she was fifteen, and had no idea then or now that there were people in the world who thought it wicked to partake at such an age.

He took her hand and bowed. The girl inhaled with surprise, as though she had feared herself untouchable. She had somehow outgrown her skin and her clothes as well, her blouse so taut across her breasts and belly he feared its buttons would soon be missiles. D.T. had an urge to laugh, mostly because he sensed there would be nothing else to laugh about till she left his office.

As he released her hand he noticed her little finger was bent unnaturally, twisted, then frozen in an arc. When she saw him notice it she rubbed the finger on her stomach, then hid it behind her back. D.T. glanced at Bobby E. Lee, who shook his head out of what D.T. guessed was pity.

"Come in and sit down." D.T. said. "Can we get you some coffee?" When she passed him he saw that her flesh was as white and flawless as her slacks, which were tight enough to line her crevasses.

"No, thanks," she said when she was seated.

"A Coke?"

"No. Really. I'm fine." Her twang was of the type that came often out of D.T.'s radio, accompanied by steel guitars and backup singers and words of rue or longing.

D.T.'s stomach began to burn. He looked in the wide drawer of his desk for a mint but found only the number 999. He pushed the little metal counter to 1,000, which confirmed his sense that the girl was somehow special, a carrier of curse or blessing. "What's your name again?" he began, with something leaden in his heart.

"Lucinda Finders."

"Where you from?"

"The valley. Reedville."

"What do your parents do?"

"Farm. Onions, mostly. Some beets."

"But you live in the city now?"

She nodded. "Come after high school with my girl-friend Ruth. Went to beauty school for a while but it didn't take."

"Why not?"

"Them chemicals they use made me swell up."

The words reminded her of her current condition. She looked at her stomach and didn't seem happy with what she saw. He expected her to reach for the tissues but instead she reached in her purse for a pack of gum. As she unwrapped a stick of Spearmint her crooked finger curled away from the foil in a silly parody of elegance. D.T. asked her how old she was.

She got the gum chewed to where she wanted it. "You got a bathroom? I'm sorry, but I got to pee every two minutes since this baby come along." Her statement was simple fact, uncomplicated by embarrassment.

He smiled and pointed toward the door across the room. She left him and closed the door behind her. He heard musical, flutish sounds, then the rush of water. When she came back her hair was combed.

"How old are you?"

"Twenty-one."

"You look younger."

"Everyone says that. Don't know why, unless it's 'cause I stay out of the sun."

D.T. took a breath and held it, reluctant, gripped by his frequent feeling that his job had become uncouth. He exhaled a breeze that caused the curls that framed her face to flap. "Well? What seems to be your problem, young lady?"

"I need me a divorce." Her lips tightened down on the words, providing them with splints.

"How long have you been married?"

"Eight months and three days.'

"Not long."

"Long enough, I guess." She tried and failed to become flip. "There ain't a waiting period, is there?"

D.T. shook his head. "Are you sure about this or are you just thinking about it."

"I'm sure," she said, sounding surer than D.T. had ever been of anything.

"What's your husband's name?"

"Del. Delbert Wesley Finders."

"Where is he now?"

"Home, I guess. We got a trailer in a park out on Simpson Boulevard."

"Where are you staying?"

"My sister's place."

"You want to go back to the trailer?"

"The trailer's Del's."

"Not necessarily. We can probably order him to vacate if you want to."

She shook her head. "Marilyn's is okay. For now."

"Is it in the city?"

"On Sixty-fifth Street. Out by the Century Mall." She told him the number.

D.T. knew the area. It was a sad sheet of lower-class whites with no jobs, no money, and no sense of anything except that they were sinking out of sight of anyone but the government. More of his 999 clients than he could count lived out there. "What happened between you and Delbert?"

"You mean why do I want the divorce?"

D.T. nodded and waited. He wished he was somewhere in public, where private woe would not be uttered. He decided not to see any more clients on Fridays. Not on top of the Fiasco.

Lucinda didn't answer for a moment. D.T. sensed she was reviewing the entire eight months and three days of her marriage, weighing its merit, deciding once again whether it was right to be where she was, do what she was doing, say what she was about to say. "Del beats up on me sometimes," she murmured finally.

"More than once?"

She nodded.

"Why?"

She shrugged. "He gets drunk. And imagines things."

"Things like what?"

"Oh, that I talked to a guy at a party too long. Or let someone look down my dress. Stuff like that." She twisted with embarrassment. Guys must have been looking down her dresses for years, but it was not a thing she would have talked about or even thought was vile.

"Did Delbert do that to your finger?"

She held it up. "This? I guess. Yeah."

"How long ago?"

"Day after we got married."

"Why?"

"He claimed I danced too close with his brother at the reception." Her grin made the maiming seem a silly bit of mischief.

"Have you talked with anyone about all of this, Lucinda?" D.T. asked.

"Just my sister."

"She told you to leave him?"

"She told me not to marry him in the first place."

She said it as a joke, and D.T. smiled stupidly, to accommodate her. She had already joined that half of all women who will be assaulted by their mates, but perhaps she was one of the lucky ones, who would escape before it could get far worse. "Have you talked to anyone else? A doctor? The police? Anyone?"

She shook her head.

"Has Delbert ever been in trouble with the law?"

She frowned, quickly angry. "How'd you know that? Has he talked to you, or what?"

D.T. shook his head. "I've never laid eyes on Delbert, Lucinda. If we're lucky I won't have to. It's just that most men who drink a lot sooner or later get in trouble with the law. What did Delbert do?"

"Beat a guy up."

"Bad?"

"Hit him with a pool cue and cracked his skull. Del got two years' probation."

"He still on probation?"

She nodded.

"He got a job?"

"A welder, when he works."

"Pretty good money in that."

"I guess. Del has trouble staying on with anybody steady."

"He do anything else? Hobbies? Other jobs?"

"He fishes some. Hunts. Fixes cars. Draws some pictures, too. Of cars, mostly. And me, before I got like this."

"How about you, Lucinda? You have a job?"

"Waitress, is all."

"Where?"

"Pancake House."

D.T. fought an impulse to ask her to leave, to walk peaceably and quietly out of his life, to spare him. Instead he zeroed in. "Is Delbert upset that you left him, Lucinda?"

"I hope to shout."

"What'd he say when you told him?"

"Well, for one thing he said if I don't come home he'll kill me." She arched her back and thrust her lip the way her pregnancy had thrust her breasts and dared him to doubt her. D.T. didn't doubt one word.

"Do you believe him?" D.T. asked.

"I believe he'll try."

"You don't seem very frightened."

She shook her head. "I can handle Del. I mean, I can't keep him from beating on me if he's a mind to, I guess, but I can talk him out of murdering me, I think. Anyhow, it's not what he'll do to me that's worrisome." Her eyes lowered again.

"Then what?" D.T. resisted his desire to take her hand again, for fear she would misinterpret him. She was not a girl for whom holding hands would mean anything but a prelude to unwanted sex.

"It's the baby," she said softly. "I'm afraid for my baby. I'm afraid it might be dead."

"What did he do?"

"When I told him I was moving out, he punched me in the belly. Said I might go but I couldn't take his kid with me. It hurt real bad for a while. I threw up and stuff.''

"What did the doctor say?"

"I ain't seen a doctor."

"Why not?"

"My sister's against 'em. Says God's will is what it comes down to, doctor or no. She's got this new religion since she left home."

"You have to see a doctor, Lucinda. Right away. There's a free clinic not too far from your sister's place, or I can give you a name. He might come by your sister's house if you can't get to his office."

She shook her head. "Not the clinic. The doctor, maybe. I can probably sneak away, maybe later, when Marilyn goes to church. Who is he?"

D.T. gave her the name and address of his doctor. "Have you ever heard of a place called the Spousal Abuse Victims' Environment? SAVE, it's called."

"No."

"They help women who've been beaten by their husbands. Talk to them. Get them medical treatment. Find them a place to stay, sometimes. I think you should go down there."

"I don't take welfare, Mr. Jones."

"Christ. This isn't welfare. Farmers got crop supports, lawyers got professional incorporations, doctors got Medicare, this is just something for *you*. *Go* there. Let them help you." D.T. realized his words were shrieks. Taking it personally. He watched her shake her curls.

"I think not. Thanks all the same." She had become prim, a woman from another age, with principles to match.

"Please? It's free. It won't cost anything."

"No. I can't. I couldn't never go back to Reedville if I did something like that and my daddy found out. Now, I come here for a divorce. Can you get me one or not?"

"I can," D.T. said slowly. "I can do that. God help me, I can do that just fine." D.T. pulled some papers toward him. "First, we have to decide how much property there is, so we can list it on the . . ."

She stopped him with the crooked finger and the hand it sprang from. "I don't *want* no property. Just a *divorce*, like I been *saying*. Del don't have no property anyway, not that's paid for, except maybe his tools."

"We could claim half their value, Lucinda. What kind of tools are they?"

"*No*. Now, this girl at the Pancake House told me she heard you were pretty good at this divorce business, but if you keep on I'm going to have to go look up someone else. Not be rude or nothing, but . . ."

"Okay. No property. But on Monday I'm going to get a restraining order that will direct Delbert to stay the hell away from you. In the meantime, I think you should go somewhere he won't think to look if he decides to try to see you again."

"I'll be fine at Marilyn's, Mr. Jones. Don't worry."

"I do worry though, Lucinda. I worry about a lot of things, and drunks like Delbert who like to beat women are one of the things I worry about most. *Please* go somewhere else. The cops aren't much help in cases like this, you know. They only show up after the damage has been done and unless there's a restraining order in effect they don't do much but tell everyone to calm down. And I can't get an order before Monday. You're on your own over the weekend."

"I'll be fine. Really. Though I appreciate the worry." Her fingers wriggled among themselves like worms, the littlest of them stiff and dead.

D.T. leaned forward and drew her eyes to his. "If you see Delbert around your sister's place you let me know, Lucinda. After Monday there'll be a restraining order filed, prohibiting him from threatening or assaulting you, or even coming around your sister's place. If he does, he's committed a misdemeanor and the cops will arrest him."

She smiled. "And let him out an hour later."

"Probably. But whatever happens, don't let him in your sister's house. Not unless someone else is there. Someone who can handle Delbert."

"Aren't many who can handle Del, Mr. Jones. Seen plenty who tried and wished they hadn't. Del loves to fight." She smiled proudly, to D.T.'s disbelief.

"You know, Lucinda, by assaulting his wife Delbert has committed a felony, and undoubtedly violated his probation, too. You can send him to jail if you want. Might make life a lot easier."

She stood halfway out of her chair. "I don't want that. Don't you do *anything* like that, Mr. Jones. I mean it. I married Del knowing he was mean when he drank, and I tried to change him and couldn't, and so it's my fault as much as his it's come to this. Plus if you knew what I had to put up with back home before Del took me off you'd know what I owe him. I just want it so me and the baby are free of him, and that's *all*."

He made himself say it. "He'll hit you again, Lucinda, if he gets the chance. They always do. He can't do it if he's behind bars."

"*No,* I told you. I'm beginning to believe you got some sort of hearing problem, Mr. Jones."

D.T. leaned back in his chair and looked at the ceiling. It looked like a game of connect the dots. He wondered what would emerge as they were connected. He was afraid to find out, just as he was afraid to contact the police or the family bureau on Lucinda's behalf, afraid to go behind her back to places that could help her.

"Okay," he said, still not looking at her. "A divorce you want, a divorce you'll get. No more; no less."

She nodded. "How much money do you want?"

"Fifty dollars? I'll need a hundred more later on."

"Okay." She opened her purse and gave him cash. "You need more you tell me. I been saving tips. Now what goes with this deal? What do I got to do?"

"Not much," D.T. answered. "First, I file the petition for dissolution. That's this top form. Then I have the sheriff serve a copy on your husband."

She frowned. "Does it have to be the sheriff? I'd as soon it weren't the sheriff."

"Okay. I'll use a process server. Then Del has thirty days to respond. You think he's likely to oppose you? If you don't want any of his property?"

"He might, just for spite. Will it cost him money to go up against me?"

"Not necessarily. He could file on his own. So could you, for that matter."

She shook her head. "There's things I can do and things I can't. This is one I can't."

"Okay. Once his response is filed we set a date for a hearing. If he wants custody of the child we maybe take his deposition to see what he claims against you, if anything. Then we go to court and if you win you get an interlocutory decree and six months later it's final and you and Del are one no more."

"How about the baby?"

"We'll ask for exclusive custody. It'll be hard denying him visitation rights, though I'll try to make them contingent on the presence of a third party."

"I don't care about a visiting, just so he can't take it away with him and has to leave when I say."

"He can't take it away unless he gets custody, Mrs. Finders, which he won't unless there's some basis for deciding you're an unfit mother. Is there?"

Her eyes shot him. "There is not one single bit of it."

D.T. smiled. "I didn't think there was. How much alimony do you want to ask for?"

"None."

"Jesus, I . . ."

"*None.*"

"A dollar a year? So we can modify it later if circumstances change or . . ."

"None, I said."

"Okay, okay. You probably couldn't get much, anyway. Child support? You *have* to get child support. The Pancake House won't support both of you, tips or no tips."

"How much could I get?"

"Two or three hundred a month, maybe, if Del gets a job and we get the right judge. When we get assigned one I'll tell you more specifically how it looks."

"A hundred's all I need," she said simply.

"I'll ask for three. We can always take less. But I have to warn you only a third of divorced mothers actually receive any child support even though there's a court order that says they're entitled to it, and the ones that do get some usually don't get the full amount they're supposed to. But we have to try, okay? For the baby?"

"I guess."

"On average a woman's income drops seventy percent in the first year of divorce, Mrs. Finders. What I'm saying is that things are probably going to be pretty tough for you financially for a while."

"Things have been tough for me before. I don't need much."

"But now you'll have a baby."

Her eyes flashed. "I'll take good care of my baby, Mr. Jones, don't you think I won't. Now, what else do you need to know?"

He accepted the rebuke. "How about your house? Did you own or rent the trailer?"

"Own, if you can call it that. We put a thousand down. It was all Del's money, so you leave it be."

"Cars?"

"Just Del's. A fifty-one Ford he fixed up. I'd never take that."

"You're being foolish, Lucinda. I have to tell you that."

"I've been foolish before, Mr. Jones. Likely I will be again. You just do as I ask. I just want me and Del to be back where we was on the day we met."

D.T. shook his head. "That's one place I can't put you, Mrs. Finders."

She frowned. "Why not?"

D.T. pointed at her. "One reason is that little tyke in your womb. Another is that every man you meet from now on is going to have to do one thing that men haven't had to do for you before."

"What thing is that?"

"Prove he's not Delbert Finders. Do you see what I mean, Lucinda? You're not the same person you were when you first met Del, so don't try too hard to pretend you are."

She nodded and thought about it. "We done now?" she asked after a minute.

D.T. nodded. "Just sign these." He pushed some papers to her and watched her laboriously execute them. Then she stood up and offered him her hand. He held it as long as he could without alarming her. Then he said what they all wanted him to say, that it was going to be all right. Then she left the room.

D.T. listened for the door to tinkle, then went into the outer office and told Bobby E. Lee he'd been wrong about the tissues, that as far as D.T. could tell the girl had never shed a tear in her life over her own predicament.

Bobby E. Lee shook his head. "I didn't say they were for *her*," he said.

■ FOUR

AFTER Lucinda Finders had disappeared down the long dark hall outside his office, D.T. returned to his desk and leaned back in his chair and put his heels on the file folder closest to the corner. Her fertility fixed in his mind, her history fresh in his gut, D.T. tried to imagine what the future would hold for her and the baby. Impoverished, unskilled, alone. The world, not kind to such, demanded fealty a proud person like Lucinda would refuse to pay. She reminded him of the statement he often made when drunk and holding forth—that the single greatest gift to mankind would be an inoculation against fecundity, effective for precisely twenty-five years, to be administered to all babies at birth, regardless of race or creed or color. Lucinda also reminded him of a statistic that haunted him: one-third of all murdered women are murdered by their mates.

Bobby E. Lee would call Lucinda an Atomic Lover— one of those women who do everything right in a marriage yet still get burned, who love too hard, overlook too much, undertake a too-extensive rehabilitation of their mate, and in return receive brief minutes of pleasure isolated between long days of abuse and neglect. It loaded their men with guilt, that worshipful endurance, and the men often beat them bloody to evade or somehow to deserve it. Psychology 101. Bobby E. Lee thought Atomic Lovers were the saddest people on earth. And Bobby E. Lee claimed to be one of them himself.

D.T. picked up the telephone and dialed his bookie Sol. Mama's Buns had come from twelve lengths back to win at eight-to-one, which put D.T. almost a thousand to the

54

good. He hoped Walter had followed his tip. Still, he was five hundred down for the month, many thousand down for the year. He should quit gambling. It had cost him a quarter of his income over the years, had provoked at least one IRS audit and, after a particularly persistent streak of ill fortune, a telephone call from Las Vegas that could only be termed terrifying. But he wouldn't quit, he knew, not as long as he had an income and a bookie, because gambling was his one indulgence that yielded a quick and certain judgment. When he won at trial the victory, though always sweet, always had its price—delay, expense, anguish, the unseemly if not illegal gambits that litigation so often required of him. So despite his losses he craved the wager more and more, its purity, its definition, its lack of nuance, its rush. He shrugged and replaced the phone and flipped through the latest issue of *Flannery's Football* for an early look at the NFL.

A minute later the intercom buzzed and Bobby E. Lee announced his final appointment. "It isn't a ditto, is it?" D.T. asked. "I don't want any more dittos this afternoon."

"Non-usual," Bobby E. Lee said simply.

"But what?"

"Who knows? She looks like a cheerleader. Maybe someone stole her pompons."

It was far too late in a far too depressing day to stage his usual charade of sedulity. Instead, he tossed aside the football book, dropped his heels to the floor, and went straight to the waiting room.

"This is Miss Rita Holloway, Mr. Jones," Bobby E. Lee announced, emphasizing the title. "Your final appointment for the day. I'll be leaving now," Bobby E. Lee added quickly. "Have a nice weekend."

"You, too," D.T. said, then remembered the diamond in the lunch companion's nostril, then envisioned the two men about to couple, then stopped himself.

When he turned toward the couch he saw a small woman looking at him eagerly from behind the undisturbed row of periodicals. She was short and dark and wore grey slacks, white sandals, and a yellow knit top that billowed around her shoulders. Her smile exposed a perfect row of teeth. Her skin was the color of the leather purse that lay beside her; her hair was a fixed swirl of black meringue. Her quick black eyes made D.T. feel like a somewhat loathsome specimen.

When she had learned all she could from a glance the woman crossed the room and stuck out a hand so small it seemed a technological triumph of Oriental origin. "I'm pleased to meet you, Mr. Jones," she said easily, the words crisp, the gesture accomplished. D.T. swallowed her hand in his and she squeezed with surprising strength.

D.T. was immediately on edge. He was used to serving the distraught, not the capable. "Come in, Miss Holloway," he managed. "May I get you some refreshment?"

"No, thank you. But please help yourself."

D.T. let her precede him into his office, then turned and watched as Bobby E. Lee lifted his jacket off the coat rack, draped it across his shoulders, and sauntered to the door. When he reached it he turned back and saw D.T. watching him. He shrugged a wordless disclaimer and opened the door and entered his other world.

D.T. entered his office and took his seat and watched as the eggplant eyes of Rita Holloway took in his lair. What she saw mostly were books, law books numbered and stacked in tiers, text books arranged by subject, special books inside an antique glass case, including the leatherbound set of novels given to him by his ex-wife, all of them written by men about women—*Moll Flanders* and *Clarissa, Madame Bovary* and *Anna Karenina, Sister Carrie, Ruby Red*, and *The Easter Parade*.

After sweeping through the books her black eyes lingered over the tousled heap on his library table, the detritus of a brief in progress, the issue a divorced wife's right to abort her child over the father's objection and offer of custody and support following birth. Her forehead wrinkled at the peculiar pen-and-ink drawings on the wall—Michele's essay into a Germanic style of political art, inspired by Watergate, the Vietnam War, and the death of Doctor King. Her lips pursed at the distinctly residential furnishings, possibly because they had been donated to D.T. by a client who, after a long period of living alone, had remarried at age fifty and acquired a spare set of almost everything and who seemed to believe that wood should be veneered to look as much as possible like cream sauce. Her nostrils narrowed because among and around it all were the piles of old briefs and current case files, *Racing Forms* and *Sporting News*, legal newspapers and bar journals, a fishless aquarium, a broken bust of Brahms, and the thises and thats of twenty years of talking to people about troubles that were so bad they were willing to pay a slender stranger to solve them. And then the full lips smiled, and Rita Holloway stood up and went to inspect the stimulus more closely.

It lay atop a file cabinet, a small diorama, exquisitely crafted, a western town, laden with detail from the Silver Dollar Saloon to the tiny horseshoes in the tiny forge in the tiny blacksmith's shop at the end of the tiny street. Michele had found it at a model railroad show and had presented it to him on the first anniversary of their divorce, adding only one detail to the extant perfection. At each edge of town she had placed a sign, and on it in the tiniest script decipherable she had written two words: Split City. When Rita Holloway read the words she laughed.

"Souvenir?" she asked as she sat back down.

"E Pluribus Unum."

"What are the others?"

"I have a drawer full, most of them unmentionable."

"Oh, go ahead and mention them."

He matched her grin and shrugged. "A pair of panties ripped off to reveal a legally irrelevant contusion. A wrist bandage unwrapped to reveal the scabs of a bungled suicide. And, let's see, a pencil drawing of the distinctly peculiar conformation of a husband's penis. A purposely punctured diaphragm. Pornographic snapshots. Love letters. Suspiciously stained handkerchiefs. Credit card receipts from Nevada whorehouses. And all kinds of other stuff that one client or another thought had something to do with why they were in my office."

Rita Holloway was chuckling happily when he finished. "An interesting life."

"Occasionally."

"What made those little holes in the floor?" She turned back to look at them.

"Golf cleats," he said, stimulated in spite of himself

by the interest she seemed to take in what he supposed was his life.

"But you shouldn't have done that. It'll cost a fortune to replace that parquet."

D.T. shrugged. "At the time it was indispensable to my immediate well-being to hit a nice crisp wedge shot. Not being at a golf course seemed an inadequate deterrent."

Her black eyes widened. "Did you hit it?"

"Yes."

"What happened?"

"The ball lodged between Volumes 238 and 239 of the *Pacific Reporter*."

"Do you always do impulsive, destructive things like that?"

"Only on my good days."

She frowned and considered his remark more closely than it deserved. An earnest person, apparently one of the rare ones who believed there were things to be learned in the world if you paid attention. When she started to say something D.T. put up a hand to stop her.

"Why have you come to me, Miss Holloway? I assume you're married, in which case you shouldn't be calling yourself Miss. Not yet. Creditors don't like it."

"I'm not married," Rita Holloway said simply.

"Then how long have you lived with him?" he asked, exasperated because it was only a palimony case and Miss Holloway seemed smarter than that. There were good reasons to live with someone out of wedlock, but not if you expected some sort of financial settlement at the conclusion of the relationship. And since such relationships always concluded, it meant living together was still a man's best friend, *Marvin* v. *Marvin* notwithstanding.

"I don't live with anyone but my dog," she said, surprising him again. "His name is Toledo. He's half Husky and half wolf and he's very mean when I want him to be," she added, smiling momentarily once again, completely unmean herself from the look of it. Non-usual, Bobby E. Lee had called her. Yes, indeed.

Miss Holloway brushed back a delinquent hair, then folded her hands and stored them on her lap.

"Why the hell are you here?" he asked. "If it's about Toledo, I have to tell you I don't defend dog-bite cases."

"Oh, I know that, Mr. Jones. And Toledo doesn't bite, he just looks like he's about to. You're a divorce lawyer. Right?"

"Right. The question is, why on earth do you need one?"

"Oh, I don't."

He made a fist and struck his desk. "Jesus Christ, Miss Holloway. I've just been mauled by the Friday Fiasco, and interviewed a woman whose husband presented her with divorce papers the way he would the ketchup and another whose husband tried to abort her from outside the womb, and here you are, cracking wise, playing mystery games. What the hell is it? You a reporter or something? Reporters are the only ones I know who smile like that, like they own the world and have it trained to shit on paper and beg for food."

Finally the smile was gone. "I don't think that was called for."

"Probably not, but then what is?" D.T. was certain he should have been contrite, and equally certain that he was perversely not. He stared at her until she spoke.

"I'm not a reporter, Mr. Jones," she admonished. "I'm a nurse. I'm here about one of my patients. I've been smiling because everything I've seen so far indicates you might be the right man. The one who'll take the case."

"What case?" D.T. asked, the question shoving hard against his better judgment.

"Maybe I'd better start from the beginning."

"Maybe you had. In the meantime, I'm going to have a drink. Care to join me?"

"Sure."

"Scotch?"

"Fine."

D.T. got glasses from the credenza—the everyday ones—a bottle from the file cabinet, and ice from the freezer, and mixed the drinks. Each watched the other as they took their medicinal gulps. "You may begin," D.T. said.

"First tell me what the D.T. stands for."

"Delirium Tremens," D.T. said. "Now let's get on with it. If you need a refill just touch your nose with your tongue."

"How did you know I could do that?"

"Can you?"

She convinced him.

"I imagine that's a big hit on the terminal ward."

"As a matter of fact, it is."

He sighed. "Please don't tell me about death, Miss Holloway. I'm sure you know a lot about it, but I'd really rather not hear about death at the moment."

Rita Holloway nodded briskly. "It's life I'm here about. A rather spectacular one, at that."

"Explain."

She got comfortable and gathered air, a tidy package of concern. He hoped to hell it wasn't medical malpractice. If it was he'd refer it out. Tempting, though. The plum he'd been waiting for, maybe. But he was too old for malpractice, too old to learn the medicine, too old to bluff the insurance monsters. He'd refer it out. Preferably to someone who would kick back half the fee.

"I'm a practical nurse," Rita Holloway began. "I work in private homes mostly, old people, invalids, that kind of thing. I have a regular list of clients, usually about ten, that I look in on at least every other day. I'm good at my work and I'm well paid, well enough so that two of my ten are taken on a *pro bono* basis."

D.T. nodded, unease developing like a chancre as he wondered if he were in the presence of a special being. God, he hated people who were able to do good effortlessly, whose impulses were charitable, not selfish. He had once represented an ex-nun who was becoming an ex-wife. She had made him feel septic for months. He was cured only by learning she smoked dope.

"One of my current patients is a woman named Esther Preston," Rita Holloway continued blithely. "She lives on Eighty-sixth Street. She has no family. She's about forty-five and she has multiple sclerosis. She lives her life in a wheelchair and she's the most wonderful human being I've ever met."

The encomium reverberated among the books, was confirmed by silence. D.T. looked to see if the statement was a joke or a ploy. It seemed neither, but Miss Hollo-way's purpose was already in part accomplished. Al-ready the crippled woman was a shadow on his brain.

"That's quite a statement," D.T. said finally.

"It's inadequate. As you'll discover when you meet her."

"*If* I meet her," D.T. reminded. "What's her prob-lem?"

"You mean besides an illness that keeps her on the brink of collapse? You mean besides a life that makes it impossible for her to work, or go out for lunch, or shop? You mean besides an illness that no one understands, that can kill or leave her at almost any moment? That makes her wear *diapers,* for God's sake? You mean be-sides all that?"

D.T. sighed. "Yes. Besides all that. Unfortunately, I'm not a healer in any sense that would apply to her."

He watched Rita Holloway reassemble the composure she had arrived with. "I'm sorry," she said finally. "It's not your fault. It's not anybody's fault, and I shouldn't try to imply it is. There's a book out now that even lets God off the hook for things like this, so I guess it's just life. What a *poison* it can be sometimes."

D.T. stayed silent, wondering who Rita Holloway re-minded him of, finally remembering. A girl named Debo-rah Glasston. His date to the junior prom. President of this, secretary of that, decorator of every sock hop in the history of his high school. What he remembered most was after the prom, when he'd driven to the accepted spot for such things, how she'd laughed at him when he'd slid his hand onto a silk-encased portion of her anatomy. It was one thing to be refused on the ground that a moral prohibition must not be breached. It was another to un-wittingly participate in farce. He wondered where Debbie was now. He would have eagerly bet his bookie she was divorced.

"Esther's problem is money," Rita Holloway contin-ued. "She has none. Her savings are gone, her disability won't pay her bills, her rent's been raised, her medicine's gone up along with food and everything else she needs to survive. She's even told *me* not to come back, that she can't pay me any more."

"Why don't you make her a *pro bono* case?"

"I offered to, of course. She refuses to hear of it. She won't take charity. From me or anyone. Meals on wheels, visiting nurses, none of it."

"How bad is her disease?"

"Almost totally debilitating. She's confined absolutely to the chair. She has little physical strength, although some days are better than others. If she has to fend for herself, sooner or later she'll exhaust herself totally, and fall and break a hip or fracture her skull or worse. I just can't stand to think of it. I really can't. It's why I came to you."

D.T. shrugged in the face of two beseeching eyes. "I'm still wondering how I fit in," he said. "Is she married, is that it?"

"No. But she was."

"How long ago?"

"More than twenty years."

"Divorced?"

"Since 1965."

"So what does that have to do with anything?"

A sound emerged that D.T. eventually decided was from the grinding of Miss Holloway's strong white teeth. "Her ex-husband is a doctor. He's a well-known gynecologist, in the most visibly prosperous medical group in town. They're in the new Health Sciences building over on Crestwood, maybe you've seen it."

D.T. nodded. "Quite a building."

"The doctors own it themselves; that is, Dr. Preston's group does. They then lease to other doctors, laboratories, pharmacies, and what have you. They also own two nursing homes. They're even building their own hospital, I hear. All very fancy taxwise, you can be sure."

"Oh, I'm sure of that, Miss Holloway. What I'm not sure of is what you want from me."

"May I have another drink?"

"Sure."

"Do you get mean when you drink, Mr. Jones? Or depressed? Or hostile?"

Her questions seemed sincere, but he lacked answers that would match. "Sometimes yes, sometimes no, and sometimes when I get any of those it's an improvement."

"Then why don't you have another one, too?"

He fixed the drinks, making hers a light one. There were things inside Miss Holloway that he guessed should stay there.

"It's like I told you," Rita Holloway said after her first sip. "Mrs. Preston needs money or she'll end up in a state institution. The only place I can see it coming from is her ex-husband. I want you to figure out how to get some from him."

"They were divorced, right?"

"Right."

"Did she instigate it or did he?"

"He did."

"They had a property settlement agreement, right?"

"I suppose so. Yes, I think she mentioned it."

"And he paid everything he was supposed to pay, right? As far as you know?"

"Yes."

"Are there any children?"

"No."

"And Mrs. Preston doesn't claim the doctor owes her anything, does she?"

"I—"

"Does she?"

"No."

"And in fact he *doesn't* owe her anything, does he?"

"No."

"He's just a deep pocket. Isn't that about it? Mrs. Preston needs money and he's got some and you think he ought to give some to his ex-wife out of the goodness of his heart or, failing that, out of an order from some benignant court. Isn't that about it, Miss Holloway?"

"I'm not a child, Mr. Jones. You needn't speak to me that way." She placed her half-empty glass on the desk.

"I admire your gall, Miss Holloway. That's about all I can say."

"He's a *millionaire*, Mr. Jones. A society physician who makes a fortune peeking into velvet-lined vaginas. Is it *right* that he should live like that and his wife should wither away in an institution?"

D.T. sighed. "She's his *ex*-wife, first of all. And second of all, what I do doesn't have anything to do with *right*, it has to do with *law*. The concepts meld only occasionally. So far you haven't told me anything that would give Mrs. Preston a legal basis for glomming onto her husband's money."

"But there must be *some* way. A loophole? An exception? Aren't lawyers always coming up with things like that?"

"Tax lawyers are. Divorce lawyers do well to file in the right court and show up on the right day. And to recognize their clients when they do." D.T. stood up and walked to his golf bag and pulled out his wedge.

"Another urge, Mr. Jones?" Her words nipped at him like rats.

"I'd like to help you, Miss Holloway," he said, taking his stance, beginning his waggle. "But this isn't a Legal Aid office or a charitable foundation. So far I don't see either a case or a client who could pay my fee."

"What *is* your fee?"

"On a matter like this? Seventy-five dollars an hour."

He heard her gasp behind him. "You must be joking. I thought you were supposed to be . . ."

"Cheap? That *is* cheap compared to what Doctor Preston's lawyer would charge him if I filed some kind of suit. Which I'm not going to do."

"Would you just see her? Please? Just see her and ask about her divorce? Maybe there's something there. Nathaniel Preston's such a bastard, there *must* be something."

Ignoring her frenzy, D.T. took his swing at the phantom ball. His shoulders turned fully, his left side cleared nicely, his finish was high, the sole of the club scraped the pitted parquet with just the faintest whisper. He envisioned the ball, high and arcing, spinning away from his perfect pitch, landing six feet beyond the hole and sucking back, coming to rest inside the leather, a gimme birdie. D.T. was smiling until he looked again at the urgent woman perched on the edge of the chair across from his.

"Does she even know you're here, Miss Holloway?" he asked softly.

"No," she said, matching his tone and lowering her eyes.

"If you'd told her beforehand she would have told you not to come, wouldn't she?"

"Of course. But don't you see? That's exactly why you should *take* the case. She's so proud, she won't do things for herself. We have to do them *for* her."

"How many lawyers have you been to before me?"

"Why . . ."

"How many?"

"Six."

"Big firms?"

"Yes."

"And they all refused?"

"Right."

D.T. dropped the wedge into his bag. "That's the first thing you've said since you've come in here that makes me want to take the case."

Rita Holloway stood up and went to his golf bag and pulled out an eight iron and waved it awkwardly but carefully. "Did you really hit a real golf ball in here?"

"Yes."

"Could I try?"

"Sure."

He took a ball from the enormous leather bag and placed it in the exact center of a square of pristine parquet. "Is this the way?" she asked as she positioned herself.

"Close enough."

"Here goes."

"Watch the ricochet."

She skulled the ball across the room at a height of six inches. It skipped off the floor, hit the spine of a volume of *American Jurisprudence,* and rebounded directly toward her. Had she not hopped quickly out of the way it would have crushed her knee. She looked calmly at D.T. "Will you see her?"

D.T. went back to his desk. "I can't solicit a client, Miss Holloway. It's called barratry and that's what it would be if I went to see Mrs. Preston without an invitation. If you can persuade her to give me a call, then I'll go by her house. But no promises beyond that. I don't think she has a case, and if I still think that after I've talked with her, then that's it. Period. Understood?"

"Yes. Can I be there? When you see her?"

"No."

"Why?"

"There are about six reasons, none of which I'm going into. Where I *am* going is home. I suggest you do the same. And besides. I don't think she'll call."

Rita Holloway pointed the sole of the eight iron at his chest. "You don't know me very well, Mr. Jones. I make my living overcoming obstacles. I give enemas to blocked bowels, and physiotherapy to dead muscles, and closed chest massage to stopped hearts. She'll call within a week."

Somehow, D.T. believed it. When he showed Rita Holloway to the door he felt better than he had all day, which wasn't saying much but was saying something. When he wondered at the reason he decided it was the prospect of encountering someone even more wonderful than the not at all unwonderful Miss Holloway.

FIVE

AFTER dusting Rita Holloway and her principal from his mind, D.T. called his ex-wife and told her he didn't need her money after all, thanks to Mama's Buns and Mareth Stone.

"Don't tell me you picked a winner and turned up a paying customer all in one day," Michele said, laughing.

"Clients. They're called *clients* in this business. And yes. I did. Turn one up."

"Congratulations. So what are you and Barbara doing this weekend?"

"I don't know."

"Which is exactly your trouble."

"What's my trouble?"

"You never plan. You never take *charge*. You just drift along until something happens, which it doesn't very often, at least not to you. Are you still watching television five hours a night?"

"Only when there's nothing on."

"How can you waste your *life* like that, D.T.?"

"It's not waste, it's preservation. Sitcoms prove that my clients aren't the world's most foolish creatures and sports prove there's still one unpredictable public undertaking left in America."

Michele made noises with her tongue. "Poor Barbara."

"Poor me," D.T. countered.

"Why you?"

"Have you seen what's on TV these days? They've not only eliminated all traces of intelligence and wit from the medium, they seem to be proud of it. Still, it's only very bad when it's trying to be very good."

"I wouldn't know, darling," Michele cooed. "The last time I watched TV was the night you cut your tongue on my earring. But I'm happy about your horse and your new client. Really, I am. You're so grouchy when you're insolvent."

"Speaking of solvency, Michele, have you ever heard of a society doctor named Preston? A gynecologist? He's supposed to run with the blue bloods so I thought perhaps you'd met, maybe at one of those Interesting People lunches you go to."

"Now, D.T.," she admonished. "I've heard all I need to hear from you about my luncheons. As it happens, I do know Nathaniel. Why?"

"What's he like?"

"An arrogant boor. Given his profession it goes without saying, doesn't it?"

"Is he married?"

"Yes. She's quite young and quite lovely. They appear to have what is known as an Understanding."

"You mean he sleeps around?"

"That's only half the story."

"You ever partake?"

"Don't be ridiculous. The only doctor I ever slept with acted as though he was looking for a place to attach an electrode. I've never felt more irrelevant in my life."

D.T. smiled at the image. "Does Preston have money?"

"Loads."

"Know anything about his background?"

"Not a thing, D.T. Why? Has Natasha Preston actually engaged you to sue the good doctor for divorce? Has the fun gone out of the relationship? Why, society will veritably *convulse* with the significance of it all." Her low laugh gurgled marvelously.

"It's nothing like that, Michele. But mum's the word, okay?"

"Sure, D.T. You know me."

"I do know you, Michele. I really do. It's one of the few accomplishments of my middle age."

"By the way, D.T. Do you remember those leather

knickers you gave me for my birthday back in the dog days of our marriage?"

"Sure. What about them?"

"Well, leather's come back with a vengeance, and I can't find them anywhere. You didn't take them, did you?"

"Why on earth would I take your knickers?"

"As a souvenir, maybe?"

D.T. laughed. "I've already got a couple of souvenirs, Michele."

"Like what?"

"Like a scar in the shape of a fingernail on my left buttock. And like that poem."

"What poem?"

"Remember the night I proposed? And gave you that ring I bought for a buck at the carnival? You gave me a poem."

"God. That thing? I'd forgotten all about it."

"Want me to recite it?"

"Spare me. Please."

> "Some days your faults are strengths,
> Your parts forever shifting in my mind.
> Hate, pride, always near,
> But you I can only love,
> The whole of you, to me.
> When I am lost in your parts,
> You find me with a word or touch,
> You crystalize and are whole again.
> One feeling replaces many;
> Love is all I know."

Michele sighed. "There was even more, wasn't there? How embarrassing."

"I think it's great."

"Good-bye, D.T. May you be stricken by permanent poetic amnesia."

D.T. closed the file cabinet, locked the safe, doused the lights, and drove to his apartment.

It was one of eight identical units inside a box glued precariously to the side of a hill that rose out of the middle of the city like a wart. He had selected it because he hated freeways, basements, lawnmowers, home repairs, and the thought of not being able to walk away from it all on a moment's whim. And because it furnished a guard and a security system that forewarned of clients prowling after hours. After parking in his assigned slot and removing the mail from his assigned box, D.T. opened the apartment, fixed himself a drink, and took the mail to the deck that opened off the living room.

The view was of the industrial portion of the city, a steamy and disheartening cauldron by day, a surreal mix of light and dark by night, at this hour uninhabited and ominous, somewhat like his brain. D.T. spent much time on the deck, wondering, musing, imagining—constructing apocalyptic conclusions founded on inadequate information, erotic fantasies dependent on impossible coincidence, heroic comportment demanding nonexistent energy and resolve. It was his only hobby besides betting —bending the future in his mind, sculpting it with the aid of booze and solitude and the accumulation of a personal history he needed often to evade. Lately his undirected thoughts seemed inevitably to drift to the fiftieth anniversary of his birth, which lay in wait for him, four years into the heaving sea of his future, like an iceberg ready to sink his simple ship without a trace.

After half his drink was downed D.T. began to wonder about Lucinda Finders. She gave off the stench of victims, of those too perfect in ignorance and allure to survive in a world that feasted on such traits. A lot of Lucindas found their way to him somehow, women fated for disaster despite their precautions and often their predictions. Some seemed actually to seek it out, to thirst for pain, to change only its source, never its frequency. For others, like Lucinda, misery seemed merely unavoidable, the fate of one designed and built as a receptacle for cruelty. Perhaps such women existed as a reminder to the rest of us that we can never be sure things are truly all right, never be sure that we are, at long last, safe. He didn't know about that, but he did know he would have to be careful with Lucinda, would have to beware both her body and her lot.

Then there was Mareth Stone, determined to treat divorce as she would treat a root canal, just another irritant to endure without affect. But she was of the old school, by her own admission, a woman who would need to believe herself an unmatched mother. Because she was human, there would have accumulated mounds of evidence to the contrary, incidents of rage and hurt and sloth that would suggest she was not perfect at all, but rather was unfit to continue doing the only thing she had done with pride for years. She did not seem like one who would bear up well under the attack that her husband and his lawyer could mount. That was Bobby E. Lee's prediction, at least, and Bobby E. Lee was seldom wrong about human inclination.

As the moon arrived early in the sky and was made fuzzy by the smog, D.T. began to look for leverage in what Mareth Stone had told him, something to trade in return for the kids when the bargaining began. The only thing he could come up with was money, the standard sacrifice of alimony, support, or property in return for exclusive custody of the children. But he sensed that in this case money would not be enough. He would need an edge, a smudge on dear old Chas. He made a note to see Mareth Stone again, and soon.

Rita Holloway. Vivacious. Bewitching. A surrogate for an angel if he could believe her. Nothing good lay down that road either, at the very least a vat of wasted time and money. He regretted even agreeing to see Esther Preston, regretted even more what candor would require of him when he did—telling her he was powerless to help, that life was not fair to anyone he knew except perhaps Michele, that she should try to make the best of what she had. As if she hadn't made better of it already than he ever could were their burdens reversed. Caked with soot and sweat, D.T. finished off his drink and dreams.

The mail was feeble, as usual. Slick magazines full of untrustworthy diatribes; a solicitation from yet another political action committee, this one bewailing the Klan; a report from Oxfam America on the starving children who were so ubiquitous as to suggest they were a hobby of the Lord's; a bumper sticker that read, in ashen script, *Roses are red, violets are blue, After the bomb, They'll be dead, too.* And a bill from the phone company with an accompanying flier proclaiming lower rates to Mexico and Brazil.

D.T. tried and failed to think of someone he knew in either country. He thought maybe one of Michele's old boyfriends had come from Rio, the slick-haired one who'd shown up at midnight one evening in a chauffeur-driven Bentley and tried to persuade Michele to go off with him to Nepal. Michele had given him a brandy and declined. But that was it. D.T. had never been to either place. His vacations, such as they were, consisted of a week in Arizona during the last days of the Cactus League season, with a stop at the Grand Canyon along the way to buy beaded moccasins for Heather, then a second quick trip to the southwest for the big meeting at Ruidoso Downs, where he would inevitably lose twice his foresworn limit. The more he thought, in fact, the more he realized he hadn't reached out and touched someone except to put the touch *on* someone for as long as he could remember. He went to his bedroom and took a shower, changed into Levi's and loafers, went to the kitchen and poured a second drink, considered and rejected the pile of dirty dishes in the sink, then returned to the deck.

The humid air still broiled the city. What wind there was seemed to have an alkaline origin. The apartment below was being readied for a party to which he hadn't been invited. Somewhere a basketball bounced interminably. The summer status was firmly *quo*. His phone rang to confirm it.

Except for Barbara and Michele, all the likely callers were present or former clients, all fine and pathetic women possessed of needs he would be incapable of gratifying given the day and the hour and the wellspring of their problems. As always, he would recommend perseverance or counsel forbearance, and hang up hoping catastrophe would not result from what he did or didn't say.

Mareth Stone spoke rapidly, panting like a puppy. "You were right. He took all the money, Mr. Jones. Everything."

"Even the balance in your individual account?"

"No. There's still that."

D.T. gave thanks for the soundness of Bobby E. Lee's

salary payment. "I thought he might pull something like that. Tell me exactly what you found."

He made notes on the back of an envelope as she spoke. "He didn't get the children, did he?" he asked when she had finished.

"No, thank God. They're here with me."

She was close to tears, more from the betrayal than the embezzlement. "It's still not impossible that he'll make a try for them. So, like I said before, take whatever precautions you can."

"Okay." Her voice was the size of pearls in oysters.

"And remember what I told you in the office. On Monday go down and change your individual account to another bank. Take everything of value out of your house that he hasn't gotten to—jewels, cash, securities, whatever—and put them in a new safe deposit box. Make a list of all the property you and your husband own, including what he's already taken—antiques, works of art, gold coins, insurance policies, anything. Try to put a value on each one, how much you bought it for and what it's worth now. On another sheet start listing your expenses. Rent, utilities, food, clothes, laundry, medicine. Everything you spend each month, entertainment and recreation included. Make a separate list for before and after the divorce. Also list any unusual expenditures you and your husband had. If you went to the Bahamas every winter, list it. If you got a new Cadillac every spring, list it. Also list all the debts you know about. Understand?"

"Yes, but what good will it do?"

"As you observed, we're going to war, Mrs. Stone, and in war you learn as much about the battlefield as you can. So call me Monday and tell me how you're coming."

"I'm nervous, Mr. Jones. The only other time I felt like this was rush week."

"This will make rush week feel like a Tupperware party. We're talking nitty-gritty here, Mrs. Stone. And I do mean money. Men like your husband don't yield their money peaceably, which means among other things if there's anything about your moral standards I should know, put it on the list as well. You're not a call girl on the side, I trust."

"Don't be silly."

"You'd be surprised," D.T. said, then decided not to go into it. "On Monday I'll go in for an order that will get you temporary support and I'll also try to prevent your husband from touching the marital assets while the case is pending, but I'm afraid it'll be too late. When they spring a surprise like this they've had prior advice and made protective moves ahead of time. Half the assets have probably been transferred to the Bahamas by now, but we'll do what we can."

"What else should I do? I mean . . ."

"Just leave it to me, Mrs. Stone. Relax. See friends. Explain things to the kids. Talk it over with your parents, let them know you may need financial assistance for a while. If anything strange happens, call me right away. We'll try to end it all as soon as possible. Okay?"

"Okay."

"That's the spirit. Remember, you can call me any time, day or night. I mean *any* time. I'm usually up and about at three in the morning anyway, so don't be afraid you'll wake me. Some of my best advice has been given at three a.m." And some of the worst, he thought but didn't say. "Do you need back the money you gave me?"

"No."

"Do you want the number of a divorced women's support group? Or a psychiatrist?"

"No. I'm fine. I just want to get this over with. How soon can we go to court?"

"Months from now. Sooner, if it's a real custody battle, since they have preference. Don't underestimate the fight we've got on our hands, Mrs. Stone. Just by being in court you're tainted, at least in most judges' eyes. Plus your husband has a good lawyer. So don't think it'll be easy. It'll be the hardest thing you've ever done."

She didn't say anything for so long he thought she'd hung up. "I'm better than my husband at almost everything, Mr. Jones," she said at last. "Chess. Tennis. You name it. For fifteen years I've always let him win. Every time. But not now. Not *this* time." She hung up before he could praise her.

On the way back to his drink D.T. flicked on the radio and caught the last eight bars of Barbara Mandrell's latest. He tried to read the week's *Time* magazine but the words passed his eyes like a string of stock cars in a tight draft at Darlington. The moon ascended. The twilight deepened, pink to purple. The purple came from the cloud released by a Mexican volcano. He'd read about it. He read about a lot of things. Too damned many things. Bliss keeps company only with the ignorant, as the moralists and their lawyers were the first to recognize.

The tepid air finally began to cool. Mosquitos buzzed his face. The people down below activated their electrostatic bug zapper. ZZZZT . . . ZZZZZT.Altering the ecological balance for the benefit of cocktail guests. D.T. slapped at something that was sucking blood from his hand, doing a bit of altering himself, and went back inside the apartment.

He turned off the radio and turned on the TV. News. Tom Brokaw, talking about death. Five straight stories about death—wars, wrecks, typhoons, murders. D.T. had almost died once. Allergic reaction. Breathing difficulty, raging pulse, dizzy spell. Quite a scene. Embarrassing to all concerned. Now he was determined to die conveniently. In bed, preferably, or perhaps while strolling in front of a funeral parlor with a pillow under his arm. The strange thing about it was that he hadn't cared. People always asked him how it felt, and while he always lied and said he was desperately frightened, the truth was that his primary emotion was that he didn't give a damn what happened as long as something happened pretty quick. That had been while he was still married to Michele. His guess was that he would care even less if he were imperiled again today. God forbid. But then that was the problem with God. He didn't forbid nearly enough.

Roger Mudd was talking about a political scandal involving drugs. D.T. was totally uninterested in drugs, as he was in anything that didn't require skill or intelligence to accomplish. He turned off the television and called his girlfriend Barbara.

"Well," she said. Aggressively neutral. Like India and Dan Rather.

"Well, what?"

"What's the program?"

"I don't know," D.T. admitted. "What do you want to do?"

"Oh, no you don't, D.T. I picked last time. The sailboat. It's not my fault you barfed."

"There's a good movie at the Ritz."

"War movies are boring."

"Mose Allison's in town."

"I'm not in the mood for blues, particularly *white male* blues."

"We could drive up to the lake and rent a cabin and lie around in the sun and smell each other's sweat."

"The last time we did that we lay in bed reading Dashiell Hammett novels and you talked like Humphrey Bogart for a week."

"I can't go to the lake anyway," D.T. remembered. "I have Heather tomorrow."

"Want me along?"

"I don't think so. Whenever she sees you she asks me if we're married yet." D.T. could have bit his tongue.

"And what do you *tell* her at such times?" Barbara's words weighed tons.

"I tell her, no. We aren't."

"Do you say why?"

"No."

"I thought not," Barbara said, then scared him with a silence. "Bernie Kaplan invited me to go wine tasting tomorrow," she went on finally, her words flat enough to skate on.

"Are you going?"

"It depends."

"On what?"

"On what we do tonight."

"Oh. Well. Dinner, for sure."

"Where?"

"Wherever you want."

"No, D.T."

"Chinese?"

"No."

Mexican?"

"No."

"Burger King?"

"Jesus, D.T."

"I just wanted to see if there was a pattern there. Apparently not."

"Don't start with me, D.T."

"Italian? We'll eat Italian. Linguini, fettuccine, Lamborghini."

"What's Lamborghini?"

"A car."

"Italian is fine, D.T. What then?"

"After dinner, you mean?"

"Yes."

"After dinner. Well, dancing. How about dancing? That place with the big bands. Swing. How about that? 'One O'Clock Jump.' 'Stompin' at the Savoy.' "

"Very good. Then what?"

"Then . . . back here? I'll make Bananas Foster? Or strawberry daiquiries? Or hot buttered rum? Depending on the temperature?"

"Can we sleep naked on the deck?"

"Well, it's kind of dirty. The deck, I mean . . ."

"*Can* we?"

"Sure."

"I mean really *naked,* D.T."

"Sure. No problem."

"Shall I bring my oil?"

"Why not? Oil. Great."

"Lemon or cherry?"

"Whatever you want."

"*Lemon or cherry?*"

"Lemon."

"See you soon," Barbara said.

When he hung up he was semi-aroused, as he frequently became during one of their spats. In Barbara's view, physical activity was infallible pharmacopeia, a certain cure for everything from corns to cancer, and sex was the most effective medication on that sweaty shelf. Thus the best way to reconcile after an argument was to engage in a particularly lusty evening, with each of them giving and taking more than they had previously dared. So he always knew what to expect, was uncertain only of what he could deliver. Barbara was a Toscanini of the bedroom. She knew and was proud of it, having reached that distinction through a combination of theoretical research and hands-on experimentation. She exulted in aids and devices, would try anything once and most anything twice to be sure they'd done it right the first time, even things that came through the mail from places in Denmark or New Jersey. One thing she wouldn't do was absorb pain, an inhibition which sometimes bothered her but bothered D.T. not at all, since her stance allowed him to thankfully mimic it. Also, she wouldn't fellate him. Not because she found it vile, or because she had never previously performed the act, but because sometime after her marriage and before her first date with D.T. she had decided oral sex was a symbolic deed, the chief metaphor of woman's place in an oppressive world, and thus his every entreaty along those lines had been rejected. This one bothered D.T. quite a bit.

For his part, D.T. felt vaguely immoral in any position other than the missionary and during any act that wasn't at least theoretically procreative. He didn't know why, and he didn't really care, since he was able to suppress those inhibitions almost at will, with the aid of a little booze or a period of abstinence in excess of a week. Deep down, he recognized that he had never enjoyed sex quite as much as he had in the days when copping a feel in the drive-in was the highest achievement of his art, and the pimply prying faces in the vehicles that surrounded his gave even rudimentary fumblings an air of daring he had never been able to duplicate, not even the time he and Barbara had made love in a pup tent at noon in June at a reserved campsite in the middle of Yosemite National Park.

Much of the time D.T. did not have to move a muscle during their reconciliatory trysts. Indeed, the crucial muscle had always moved itself, thank the Lord, as if it were Barbara's puppet and not his own appendage. Thereafter, he had simply to hang onto his erection for as long as possible, by thinking of people and places without the slightest erotic content—Des Moines, say, or Meryl Streep. Sex, too, was rather like a war. The Crimean came to mind.

Despite the fever of making up, their penchant for reaching a disputatious stage two minutes into their every conversation convinced D.T. that he and Barbara would eventually devour what was good in their relationship and leave only the bad, eating the heart and leaving the choke. In his office, D.T. encountered many a couple in a similar set, men and women who defined their relationship solely by the degree of their anger, for whom only argument ignited conversation, only violence begot sex. Still, if he and Barbara were in fact doomed, they would both survive the crash. Barbara could survive anything short of happiness, and D.T., well, he spent so much time lying to his clients he knew exactly how to counsel himself.

He went outside and swept the deck, then tugged the mattress off the spare bed and wrestled it to the space he'd cleaned, then draped the rail with sheets to shield the mattress as best he could, though he knew of no specific eyes to shield it from. It might be like the drive-in, he realized. His cock swelled slightly in his pants and he adjusted it for comfort. Then he went inside and used television to calm him down.

Friday night. *Washington Week*. Second-guessing the politicians. *Wall Street Week*. Games for the rich, the only losers the amateurs putting up the money for the pros to play with. Then the network garbage. *The Dukes of Hazard*. *Dallas*. *Falcon Crest*. The decline of civilization as reflected in its amusements. The Greeks got Lysistrata and Agamemnon. We get J.R. and Luke Duke.

The phone rang again. How he hated the pit it dug in him. "Mr. Jones?"

The voice was birdlike, not possibly in peril. His muscles momentarily retired. "What can I do for you?"

"My name is Esther Preston, Mr. Jones. We've never met. However, a young woman named Rita Holloway apparently went to see you on my behalf this afternoon. Do you recall her?"

"Yes. Of course."

"Her visit was entirely unsolicited by me, as she tells me she disclosed."

"Yes." D.T. tried to think of who she sounded like. Doris Day? No. More like the youthful Katharine Hepburn. Gaily cynical. Firmly self-deprecating. Slightly tipsy.

"I very much do not want to waste your time, Mr. Jones. However, I have a problem. Miss Holloway is currently ensconced on my divan. She has already called her young man and broken her engagement for the evening. She is about to embark on a search for linen, in order to make herself a bed. She threatens to remain until I agree to see you. I hope you understand that she means what she says. She is a very determined woman." There was a pause. "Also a delightful one."

"I agree. On both counts."

"Then I'm afraid we must arrange a meeting. So that Miss Holloway can resume a normal life."

"When would be convenient?"

"My time is entirely unburdened, Mr. Jones. Any time you wish. I assure you it will take no more than a minute to confirm what I'm sure you already suspect."

"What's that?"

"That I have no case at all against my former husband."

D.T.'s mood flip-flopped. For reasons unclear to him, he felt a need to be encouraging. "We'll see," he said. "I have to be in your neighborhood tomorrow evening. Perhaps I could stop by around six?"

"Of course."

"Until then."

"I'll look forward to it."

He replaced the phone but his mind retained her, spun with imagined portraits—gentle, handsome, serene, and maternal. His thoughts floated freely, until he realized he had imagined everything but the central fact of Esther Preston's being—the disease that wracked her body and the chair in which she lived her life. The phone rang once again and he was grateful.

"Hello?" he said.

"Ah . . ."

"Yes? Who is it?"

"Is this Mr. Jones?"

"Yes . . . Who is it? Michele? Barbara?"

"This is Lucinda Finders, Mr. Jones. I, ah, seen you this afternoon? At your office?"

"Sure. I remember. How are you?" he asked, knowing from the sounds that scraped his ear that she was far from fine.

"Not so good, I guess." She coughed or something like it.

"What's the matter?" D.T. began to sweat a toxin.

"Del was here."

"Where?"

"My sister's."

D.T. couldn't recognize her next sound. Its source was clearly agony, its product an otherworldly whistle. D.T.'s bowels loosened then cramped. "Is it the baby?" he asked. "Did he hit your stomach again?"

"Not there. My face, I think . . . can you get a broken face?"

D.T. couldn't bring himself to answer. "Was he threatening you if you didn't stop the divorce proceedings?" he asked instead.

"Uh huh."

"What did you tell him?"

"I told him to get out of my life."

Of course she did. Her courage was a trophy he only dreamed of. With it, he could have conquered Everest. Without it, he lived in fear of calls like this.

"It's my fault, Lucinda," he said. "I should never have let you go back to your sister's. Is there anywhere else you can stay? Somewhere Delbert doesn't know about?"

"I don't know of any. We, I mean I, ain't got many friends. Not since I come to the city. My girlfriend went back to Reedville to work at the cannery."

"How about the Spousal Abuse Victims' Environment? Remember I mentioned it this afternoon? The places they put you are absolutely secret. I don't know where they are myself."

"No. I told you."

"But you can't stay where you are. He'll be back."

"I'll make out, Mr. Jones. I just think I'd best see a doctor about my face. Maybe you could call your friend? If you're not too busy?"

"Of course." His mind spun. "Here's what we'll do. Let me make the call, then I'll pick you up and take you to see the doctor. At the hospital or his office, wherever he wants. Okay?"

"I couldn't let you do that. The bus runs right near here. I got a pass and everything."

"I insist, Lucinda. I'm just sitting here watching morons on TV. What's your address again?"

When she told him without further protest he realized how damaged she must be. "I'll be there in twenty minutes," he said.

D.T. hung up and put on his coat. When he called John Faber, his doctor, he got an answering service. He left his name and a message that conveyed his urgency, and asked the girl at the service to have the doctor leave a number where he could be reached when he called in. Then he drove to Lucinda Finders' sister's house.

It was a single-story bungalow of post-war plainness, complete with mulberry tree and cyclone fence and a lamb lying in plastic, precious peace on the front stoop. All lights in the house were out. D.T. tapped tentatively at the door, wondering if after hanging up the phone she'd done the thing he would have—fled blindly until something stopped her.

The darkness swallowed his knocks. He tried again and waited, looking from time to time for Delbert at his back. "Mr. Jones?"

Her voice crept to him from behind the black screen that was a foot from his nose. "Lucinda? Is anyone here?"

"Just me."

A light glowed suddenly above his head and immediately attracted moths. The screen door opened. She stood on the border of light and dark, and he assumed the streak across her face was shadow. Then she stepped toward the light and he saw that it was blood.

The right side of her face was a balloon of red and black with a creeping stripe of yellow. Her left eye was an involuntary wink. Blood had caked below a nostril. "Are you okay?" he asked insanely.

She nodded and it hurt her. She drew air noisily. From within a wince she suggested that they go. "Del might come back," she explained. "And Marilyn might not let me go off with you if she gets back and you're here. She thinks men are bad for me. I think I'm kind of broke up," she added, touching her face.

"Come on," D.T. said, and took her hand and led her off the stoop. "Did he have a gun?"

"Not that he showed."

"What did he hit you with?"

"His hand."

"What did he say, exactly?"

"He asked if I'd seen a lawyer yet. When I told him I had, he asked me who it was. I wouldn't tell him. He spit on me. Then he hit me. Twice. He would have done it more but he heard a siren somewheres and took off. He said he'd be back if he ever got served with papers."

So. She had been beaten at least in part in defense of his anonymity. D.T. tried not to believe her but couldn't, no more than he could shun the obligation her chivalry created.

He opened the door to his car and helped Lucinda inside, as conscious of touching her luscious body as he was conscious of being the proximate cause of her hurt. "I'm taking you to the hospital. Is that okay?"

"I guess. I don't know if I can pay, though. I only got twenty dollars. But I got more coming the end of the month."

"Don't worry about it."

When they were inside the car, D.T. handed her his handkerchief. She took it from him and looked at its laundered whiteness and placed it on the seat between them, then pressed her fingers to her nose. Her breathing gurgled like a drain.

On the way to the hospital, D.T. stopped at a phone booth and called the answering service. The doctor had left a number. When D.T. called it a woman answered. D.T. asked for Dr. Faber. The woman giggled. "Poopsie? You want Poopsie?" A minute later Poopsie grasped the phone.

D.T. explained the situation. His friend said he'd meet them at the hospital in fifteen minutes, with neither reluctance nor inebriation in his voice. D.T. thanked him and apologized for the intrusion and suppressed an observation about the etymology of Poopsie.

"No problem," Dr. Faber said. "But Christ, D.T. How many *is* that?"

"Four or five."

"What happened to the one who swallowed bleach?"

"She's okay. She moved to San Bernardino with a guy who digs wells."

"Jesus, D.T. You get some characters. But why do they always fall apart on Friday night?"

"Booze," D.T. said, then hung up.

When he got back to the car he pulled the keys out of the ignition and went around to the back and opened the trunk. Among the driving junk was a cardboard carton containing shag balls, a swimming suit, towel and jockstrap, a ball glove, and a camera. He pulled out the camera, checked it for film and batteries and flash attachment, then put the camera behind his back and went to the passenger side and asked Lucinda to get out for a minute.

"What for?"

"Surprise," he said.

He snapped the first one as she was scrambling out of the car, before she knew what he was doing. "Hey. What'd you do that for?" She put a hand over her face and started to get back in the car.

"It's evidence, Lucinda. We might need it."

"To do what?"

He shrugged. "Who knows what's going to happen. But this is the best record there is of what Del did to you tonight. Let me take another one."

"No."

"Come on. Please. I won't use it unless I have to. Remember your baby," he added cruelly.

"No. My looks is all I got."

She turned from him and got back in the car. He stood where he was and when she lowered her hand he pressed the shutter again. The flash exploded both the night and his honor. He told her he was sorry and put the camera back in the trunk and got behind the wheel and pulled quickly into traffic and drove the route that would get them to the hospital in the shortest time.

Beneath a starless sky he turned left and then right and found himself on a lonely stretch of road that crossed the fringe of the industrial area he had recently been viewing from the relative security of his deck, which lay somewhere above them, behind a forest of smoke stacks and storage vats and warehouses that from the look of them housed monsters. He drove as fast as he dared. Beside him, Lucinda Finders breathed in whispers, as though she plotted vengeance. He guessed she was as angry at him as at her mate.

The road was poorly lit and marked, virtually unused. D.T. was afraid he might simply drive off into a pole or a ditch in the gloom, and Delbert's crime would seem to be his own. Squinting, he searched out the ancient center line and followed it as though it led to grail. When he felt the first bump he thought a tire had blown. Then it bumped again and he almost lost control of the careening vehicle.

"What the hell?" As he wrestled the steering wheel, Lucinda looked through the rear window of his Ford.

"It's that other car," she said.

"What other car?"

"The Dodge back there with its lights off. It's ramming you." She paused. "I think it's Del."

"What? Are you sure?"

"It's not Del's regular car. But he can steal one in a minute and this is the kind of thing he'd do. He's warning me to keep away from you."

When the car smashed them this time the rear wheels lost traction and he had to swerve to bring the car in line. The tires screamed the way he wanted to.

Their assailant was a black blob in his mirror, sparked occasionally by a source of useless light, a generic horror. They were as far from help as they could get and still be in the city. A lonely pickup passed them going the other way, oblivious.

The car behind them honked, then banged into them again. D.T. fought the wheel with slippery hands. Hot sweat rolled into his eyes and seared them. "Do you think he's trying to kill us?" he asked, hating the girl because she had generated the danger that pursued them, hating himself for his craven question.

"No," Lucinda said. "He's just funning. I was with him once when he did this to a guy that hustled him at pool. If he wanted to run us off the road we'd already be there. Del's a good driver." She might have been at beauty school, discussing hair.

D.T. laughed tightly at her praise of the devil who pursued them, then pushed his accelerator to the floor. The car barely responded. He pounded the wheel with his fist and looked about for saviors.

And as suddenly as it had appeared the car was gone. The mirror framed only the odd comfort of darkness. He thought he heard the sound of wheels spinning on gravel, and guessed Del had turned and gone the other way, done with sport and warning.

"We should go to the cops." D.T. slowed the car and breathed deep breaths and felt the clamor of his heart.

"No. Please?"

"The man's nuts, Lucinda."

"No, he ain't. He just wants me back."

"It's more than that. He's violent and he can't control it. He's a danger to society. To you."

She was quiet for a minute, then her hand lit like a butterfly on his arm. "Maybe he is what you say. But I married him. And I loved him when I did. And he's the daddy of the thing that's kicking inside my belly. I just couldn't live with the idea I had my baby's daddy put in jail."

His thoughts unvoiced, D.T. drove to the hospital and helped Lucinda through the emergency entrance. A nurse guided them to an empty room. When D.T. told her Dr. Faber was on the way she left them alone amid the steel and gauze and glass that seemed too pure to be a remedy for anything so savage.

The lights in the room were brighter than the sun. Beneath them, Lucinda Finders' face ebbed and flowed with color. Her cheek and lip were larger than before, laughable and cryable at once. When the door swung softly shut behind the nurse, Lucinda began to cry. "I ruined your whole night. It's just I didn't know where else to go." Her words nudged each other comically.

D.T. put his hand on her shoulder and felt it buck. "It's okay. Really."

"It's just . . . he *scared* me this time. He really scared me." She seemed deeply interested in the emotion, as though it were a first encounter.

"He would have scared anyone," D.T. told her. "He scared me plenty in the car. Let me call the cops, Lucinda. So they can revoke his probation and put him away."

"No. I can't do that. I just *can't.*"

"But why not? Look what he *did* to you."

"Don't you see? I *married* him. If I put him in jail it means I'm just a stupid country girl who married a drunk and a jailbird both. I don't want that scratching at my mind. I just *don't.* I'd sooner be in jail myself." She sobbed silently, belly and breasts and battered cheek all bobbing to the rhythms of her sadness.

When Dr. Faber arrived he shoved D.T. out the door and closed it. While he waited, D.T. watched them wheel people past on gurneys, each of them apparently dead or quickly dying. He felt increasingly light-headed, and when one of them screamed in abject terror, he thought he was going to faint. He was seeking a passage to the medicine of the out-of-doors when Dr. Faber emerged. D.T. asked him how she was.

"Broken nose," he said. "I packed it. Cleaned the abrasions. She'll be all right, I think. Unless he hits her again. She really took a shot. The police been called?"

D.T. shook his head.

"Why the hell not?"

"She won't let me."

"Well, *I* sure as hell can do it."

"I wish you wouldn't," D.T. said quickly. "She'd think I tricked her. I'd never see her again. Neither would anyone else who could help her."

Dr. Faber frowned. D.T. sensed he should explain, but couldn't seem to manage it. "Did you check on the baby?" he asked instead.

"I listened for a heartbeat and found one. She still has some pain but I don't think its source is uterine. I *think* she has an ulcer. If she'd let me run some tests I'd know for sure."

"She doesn't have insurance, I suppose."

"Nothing. And this hospital won't admit her without it, either. Maybe she could try the county."

"She won't," D.T. said. "Is there anything special she should do right now?"

"Just stay out of that bastard's way," Faber said, then

patted D.T.'s shoulder. "Hang in there, champ," he added, then left. D.T. went back inside the room.

Lucinda Finders' face wore different colors, medicinal hues that glowed more vibrantly than blood or bruises. White stuffing sprouted from her nostrils. She was looking in a mirror. "Don't look at me," she ordered. "I'm horrible." Her hands rose to hide her face. "Can we go?"

"Sure."

"He was real nice. What do you figure I owe him?"

"He'll total it up later. I'll let you know."

"I'll have to pay on time," she said, lowering her eyes.

"Don't worry about it."

D.T. guided her to his car and drove away from the hospital. He felt suddenly vital and content as though he had cleansed her wounds himself.

"Hey," she said after a few blocks. "Where we going?"

"My place. You're staying there tonight."

"I can't do that."

"Sure you can."

"But—"

"It's the only place I can think of that's both free and safe. So don't argue. I won't listen."

She was quiet the rest of the way. When she entered his apartment she squealed, a reaction never previously provoked by his quarters. "I *love* chairs like that," she said, looking at the imitation Eames. "Can I sit in it? Just for a second?"

"Be my guest."

"Is that real leather?"

"I don't think so."

"I bet it is. I bet everything *in* here is real. Can I look around? Just a little?"

"Help yourself."

His bed wasn't made and the sheets were stained from Barbara's menstrual seep and the bathroom looked like a jaundiced hair factory, but what the hell. He watched her prowl, pleased at pleasing her with his poster-sized photo of Heather on skates and his collection of Pez dispensers and his hole-in-one trophy. When she came back from the bedroom she asked if he'd ever been married.

"Once," he told her.

"Did you get divorced?"

"Yep."

"Is that her picture on the bureau?"

"Yep."

"What's she laughing at?"

"Me."

"Did you want to or did she? Divorce, I mean."

"She did, at first. Then I agreed it was a good idea."

"Does it still hurt?"

He though about it. "Actually, it does. It still hurts quite a bit. I guess if I'm lucky it always will."

"Do you have a girlfriend?"

"Oh, my God."

D.T. ran to the bedroom and dialed Barbara's number. It rang twelve times. He hung up and dialed again. No answer. Wine tasting with Bernie Kaplan. An early start. D.T. swore and kicked at the pile of underwear and socks that smoldered beside his bed, then picked them up and put them in the hamper and straightened the covers.

When he got back to the kitchen Lucinda was washing the encrusted dishes that grew out of the sink like succulents. "You don't have to do that," he said.

"I know."

She worked through the stack with incredible speed. D.T. hunted up a dish towel and began to dry as she plucked plates from the steaming rinse. Their hands touched frequently as they exchanged the crockery. Each time they touched they smiled.

When she had finished, Lucinda went out onto the deck. "Look at the stars," she exclaimed. "What's that one, do you think?"

D.T. looked. Along with his life, the sky had momentarily shed its blemish. "I think it's Venus. A planet."

"Really? Like the earth?"

"I think so."

She noticed the mattress. "Do you *sleep* out here?"

"Sometimes." He thought of Barbara and her oil. And of Bernie and his wine.

"Are you going to tonight?"

"No."

"Can I?"

"Sleep here?"

"Uh huh."

"Sure. If you want. But you're welcome to the spare room."

"I'd rather sleep under the stars. If it's all right. I never done that before."

"Fine with me," D.T. said. "Would you like something to eat? Or drink? Anything?"

"No, thanks. I'm okay."

"Did you have dinner?"

"Sure."

"I'll bet you didn't."

"Well . . ."

"I'm going to make you something."

"What?"

"A surprise. You can watch me if you want, or you can stay here with the stars."

D.T. went into the kitchen and made Bananas Foster, his single confectionary accomplishment. Lucinda hurried back and forth between the kitchen and the deck, enthralled by what she saw from each location. When they'd finished eating she embarrassed him with praise. Then D.T. persuaded her to take an aspirin. After he persuaded her to go to bed he got a pillow and a blanket for her, then went back to his room and tried and failed to sleep.

When he checked on her an hour later she was wide awake, staring at the heavens as though the stars were sonnets. She had pulled the sheet from the rail and wrapped herself within it. Beneath its dingy drape she was naked and unselfconscious, as though she could not possibly arouse him. As a result, his loins wriggled warmly, thrilling and disgusting him. When she saw him looking at her she smiled. "It's so pretty," she said. "I could stay here till I die."

Abashed, D.T. asked if she needed anything else. She said she didn't. Then she thanked him once again. He went to bed and slept and didn't wake till morning, more protected than protector, temporarily cured of every single thing that ailed him.

, Lucinda Finders, hereby swear and affirm that,

I am over the age of eighteen and have been a resident of this State and County for more than six months. I am the Petitioner in the above-entitled cause, and I make this declaration in support of the motion for temporary restraining order which is served and filed herewith.

On December 24, 1982, I married the Respondent herein, Delbert Wesley Finders. I am pregnant by Delbert, and am expecting our child in November of this year. I am seeking a dissolution of our marriage on the ground that irreconcilable differences have arisen between us, which have led to the irremediable breakdown of our marriage. I am also requesting exclusive custody of our child, plus child support in the amount of three hundred dollars ($300.00) per month. I wish no alimony.

Because of his past behavior toward me, I fear that if Delbert Wesley Finders is not restrained by this Court, he may inflict serious bodily harm upon me and upon my unborn child. Delbert Wesley Finders has struck me many times over the course of our marriage, beginning with the day after our wedding when he broke my little finger by biting it almost clear through. At other times he has punched me, and pushed me down. Once he held my head under water when I was in the bathtub till I almost drowned. Another time he held my hand over a candle till it began to burn and stink. I still have a scar from that time, plus I have three scars on my face from being hit by Del. Every time he hit me it was because of something he imagined I did, not something I really and truly did do. Also, every time he hit me he had been drinking.

When I told Delbert Wesley Finders I was going to leave

him and file for divorce, he threatened to kill me if I went through with it. Two nights ago he came to the house where I was staying. He was very drunk and he hit me and broke my nose and again threatened to kill me if I didn't drop the divorce case. He only stopped hitting me because he thought the cops were coming.

Delbert Wesley Finders is an expert hunter and owns at least three guns—a rifle, a shotgun, and a pistol. He practices shooting a lot. I have seen him kill a rabbit from so far away you could hardly see it. He also owns a bunch of knives, and carries one on his belt almost all the time. He gets in fights a lot and is very strong. I have never seen any man get the best of Delbert Wesley Finders in a fight, and I have seen many of them hurt very bad by going up against Del, even with chains or knives. Because of this I believe Del is very capable of hurting me and my unborn baby, and I believe he will hurt us again if we keep on with this case. I would like this court to order Del to stay away from me and the baby until this case is finished.

I declare under penalty of perjury that the foregoing is true and correct.

———————————————————
Lucinda Finders
Petitioner

Law Office of D. T. Jones

by———————————————
Attorney for Petitioner

* * *

I, Mareth Hartwell Stone, hereby swear and affirm that,

I am over the age of eighteen and have been a resident of this State and County for more than six months. I am the Respondent in the above-entitled cause. I make this declaration in support of the motion for temporary restraining order and for temporary support which is served and filed herewith.

On August 27, 1983, my husband, Charles Rawson Stone, served me with a Summons and Petition (Dissolution) in the above-entitled cause. Prior to that time, I had no notice, formal or informal, that Petitioner contemplated proceedings to terminate our marriage.

On that same day, after receipt of said documents, I visited various banks and financial institutions in the city and discovered the following:

1. Petitioner had withdrawn all funds from our joint checking account, in an approximate amount of five thousand dollars ($5,000.00), all of which is the marital property of the parties, and transferred said funds to an unknown location.

2. Petitioner withdrew all funds from our two joint savings accounts, in an approximate aggregate amount of thirty thousand dollars ($30,000.00), all of which is the marital property of the parties, and transferred said funds to an unknown location.

3. Petitioner removed the entire contents of our joint safe deposit box, including many items of value such as jewelry, gold coins, stocks and bonds, of a value well in excess of one hundred thousand dollars ($100,000.00), all of which is the marital property of the parties, and transferred said items to an unknown location.

4. Petitioner removed, at some time prior to the morning of August 27, 1982, certain objects of art and other things of value from the marital home, of an aggregate value well in excess of fifty thousand dollars ($50,000.00), all of which is the marital property of the parties, and transferred said items to an unknown location.

I am informed and believe that Petitioner has appropriated and concealed additional items of marital property and, unless restrained by the Court, will appropriate and conceal many additional items of said property, all to my present and future jeopardy. I am informed and believe that the marital estate of the parties is in excess of one million dollars. By his acts, Petitioner has deprived me of access to any such property with the exception of the marital home which I still occupy, to my great financial jeopardy. I believe Petitioner has taken these steps to punish me for some reason unknown to me, and that unless restrained by this Court I believe Petitioner will attempt to punish me further. I believe Petitioner may take steps to remove our two children from my custody, not in their best interest but only as a further means to punish me for my unknown and nonexistent transgressions. I believe such conduct would be extremely harmful and frightening to the children, and that Petitioner should be ordered to stay away from the children and myself until an order for reasonable and restricted visitation can be entered by this Court.

I declare under penalty of perjury the foregoing is true and correct.

Mareth Hartwell Stone
Respondent

Law Office of D. T. Jones

by_____

Attorney for Respondent

D.T. flicked the rewind button on his dictating machine and listened to the whir that marked the completion of the morning's work, then ejected the cassette and tossed it into his Out Box on top of the rough draft forms and executed blank copies which, when filled in by Bobby E. Lee on Monday morning, would be filed and served and would send Mareth Stone and Lucinda Finders on their way to join the 40 percent of married women who had been judicially severed from their mates.

D.T. enjoyed the office on Saturdays, at least on those days he was not so horny he longed to be home watching *Soul Train*. The phones were still and the courts were closed and the clients were drowning their troubles in *Bugs Bunny and the Road Runner* or the hair of the dog. Alone at his desk, surrounded by tiers of tomes that contained all the law that had ever been uttered by the courts of the nation, D.T. felt part of an important continuum: the Ditto List of Time.

He could almost hear the old cases talk to him—the arguments, pleas, and judgments of the ages—all up there on the shelves, waiting to assist him, whispering. Once in a while he took down a volume just for fun and read a favorite hallmark. Maybe *Willan* v. *Willan*—the wife who pulled the hair and tugged the ears and shook the beard and kicked the legs of her crippled husband, day and night, swearing and pestering, all to make him screw her. Held by the court: since the husband always submitted to her demands, no matter how reluctantly, he had condoned the wife's behavior and no legal grounds for divorce existed. Or *Devine* v. *Devine*, action by a wife against her mother-in-law to enjoin and restrain her from interfering with the marital relations of the wife and the defendant's son. Held by the court: case dismissed because the requested injunction prohibiting the mother-in-law from communicating with her son would be impossible to enforce. Or *Pavlicic* v. *Vogtsberger,* in which a seventy-six-year-old man whose "bankbook became Sara Jane's favorite literature" sued the twenty-six-year-old Sara Jane for the return of the money and property he had lavished on her in expectation that she would become his bride. Held by the court: "To allow Sara Jane to retain the money and property which she got from George by dangling before him the grapes of matrimony which she never intended to let him pluck would be to place a premium on trickery, cunning and duplicitous dealing." Or perhaps his favorite, *McGuire* v. *McGuire,* wife of sixty-six suing husband of eighty for support and maintenance. The court finds the following facts established: wife worked in the fields, did outside chores, cooked and attended to household duties for over thirty years. Husband had given her no money for the last four years and had not taken her to the picture show for twelve. They belonged to no organizations. The house had no bathroom or inside toilet, and no kitchen sink. The furnace didn't work and the car didn't run and the husband refused to remedy any of it despite his wealth. Held by the court: since the parties were not living apart the husband was supporting his wife in the legal sense and the purpose of the marriage relation was being carried out.

As he sipped his coffee, D.T. thought of how reluctant Lucinda Finders had been to elaborate on her months of fear and furor with Del as the two of them had shared some underdone scrambled eggs and overdone toast at breakfast that morning. She had awakened before him, and showered and dressed. When he went to the deck to check on her, she was sitting stiff-backed and -legged, staring at the industrial expanse that spread away from her like a tattered doormat on a rainy day. "You can hear birds," she said when she saw him.

Hair tousled, flesh puffy a bit from sleep and a lot from the assault of the previous night, Lucinda had provided a catalogue of Del's abuses only because he had insisted to the point of inquisition that she do so. When she had finished, he dutifully warned her that Del would be incensed when he saw the divorce papers, told her that serving Del with a restraining order was indispensable to her safety, and explained the legal and practical obstacles to an absolute warrant of her welfare. "There's not much to stop him from doing what he wants to do," was how he'd put it. Yet she had urged him to go ahead. Despite the fright; despite the wounds.

But now he had become reluctant. What if Del exploded again when served with process? What if he came after them, tracked them down, threatened them with harm if the divorce wasn't stopped? What if he himself had to live for weeks as frightened as he had been the night before, as his car was reeling down a dreary road?

But what was the alternative? From the minute Lucinda entered his office it had become impossible to guarantee her safety or his own detachment from her fate. He could only guarantee her status, establish her legal right to keep Delbert at bay. He laughed. The law was such a shell—the hospitals were filled with women possessed of just that right. D.T. frowned and put Lucinda's papers on top of the pile, for Bobby E. Lee to do first thing, then turned to Mareth Stone's ghost-written statement.

She had suffered a less physical but no less brutal blow as she had discovered item after item that her husband had purloined prior to announcing his intent to end the marriage. As she had listed the missing treasures over the phone, D.T. began to wonder what she had done to provoke his ambush. Her affair, perhaps, but the reaction seemed extreme. To nail it down, he would have to take a deposition from Chas Stone. A grilling, under oath, officially sanctioned. D.T. leaned back and began to plot its outline—questions, answers, objections, quarrels with opposing counsel. A cross-examination, one of the best things he did besides worry.

His imaginary inquiry ended only when the phone rang. "Mr. Jones? This is Ida Casting." D.T. suppressed an oath.

Ida Casting was a client of some three years past. A world-class egoist. Fifty-plus. Grotesquely overweight. Unilaterally emotional. Devout to the point of madness. Totally mystified by the hand that God and her husband had dealt her. Personification of his Third Principle of Modern Matrimony—that on the wedding day the bride is always more beautiful than the groom, and twenty years later the situation is always reversed. D.T. asked Mrs. Casting what he could do for her.

"Carl has missed the last three payments, Mr. Jones. My letters are returned as moved, no forwarding. I *told* you this would happen after he missed the first one, but you advised me to wait. *Now* look."

"Take it easy, Mrs. Casting. Where was Carl living when you heard from him last?"

"San Diego. He went down there with that . . . that *tramp*. He claimed he had a job with the Navy."

"Does he have relatives there?"

"The only relative he's got is a sister. She lives in Tacoma. A heathen, if you want the truth."

"Aren't we all," D.T. muttered. "Are you working, Mrs. Casting?" he asked more loudly.

"How can I?"

"How do you mean?"

"Surely you remember my arthritis. Now I've got the shingles on top of it, despite what that upstart doctor says. I doubt I'll ever work again." Her sigh was a siren.

"That's too bad."

She accepted his sympathy as an initial installment. "I want you to go to San Diego, Mr. Jones. Today. Monday at the latest. I want you to find Carl and tell him he has to pay what the judge ordered or he'll go to jail."

D.T. breathed deeply. "No, Mrs. Casting. I can't do that. It would cost you more than Carl owes you for me to do that."

"Then what am I to do? You're my lawyer. You can't just leave me *destitute*."

D.T. smiled bitterly. At certain stages of the attorney-client relationship the client frequently confused D.T.'s obligations with those of the departed husband. "Call the district attorney's office, Mrs. Casting. Ask for the support enforcement unit. They'll get the information they need, then forward it to their office in San Diego and the people there will go to work finding Carl and obtaining payment. It's a great program."

"How much does all that cost?"

"Not one red cent."

She paused. "I'd rather you took care of it yourself, Mr. Jones. I don't trust government lawyers."

"Well, let's see. It will cost at least two thousand dollars for me to go down there, Mrs. Casting, just for my time. Plus expenses. I'll catch a plane the moment I receive your check."

"But . . ."

"Have a good day, Mrs. Casting," D.T. said, then reluctantly added a further sentence. "If they don't find Carl in a few weeks you give me a call and I'll tell you where to go for some temporary help for food and things."

"I don't care to . . ." Mrs. Casting began, and D.T. hung up because anything he could possibly say to her he had said to her many times before.

D.T. turned on the radio immediately and dialed the Giants game. Hammaker versus Niekro, from Atlanta, first inning. D.T. put in a quick call to his bookie and put twenty on the Giants at seven to five, then leaned back and thought of days when he had hit the curveball well enough to consider signing with the Giants for a five-hundred-dollar bonus and spending the next summer in Lodi-sweating and shagging fungoes and dreaming of glory. He'd passed it up, of course, convinced by his alcoholic high school coach that he wasn't good enough to make it to the majors. But what if . . .?

The telephone rang again.

"Mr. Jones? Elizabeth Atherton speaking. You represented me six years ago, though I'm sure you've forgotten."

"Yes, Mrs. Atherton. How are you? I remember you well." And with affection, he might have added, since it was true.

"I'm quite well, Mr. Jones. And you?"

"Fine."

And why shouldn't she be well, D.T. thought. She was attractive, and healthy, and she received thirty-five hundred dollars a month from her workaholic ex-husband, thanks to a rather inspired negotiating session during which D.T. suggested that Mrs. Atherton was prepared to offer evidence that her estranged husband "dallied regularly with young Negresses." An effective ploy when your antagonist is a national committeeman for a political party. And a gamble, since Mrs. Atherton knew nothing at all about the detective D.T. had hired or his extensive and expensive report on the whores her husband frequented on the Sunday afternoons he was supposedly golfing near the sea.

"I see Michele frequently, Mr. Jones," Mrs. Atherton went on. "I hope you two are still friendly."

"Very, as long as there's a telephone between us. Now how can I help you?"

"Well, I don't know how to begin. It's quite peculiar, Mr. Jones. I'm not at all sure what it means."

She seemed befuddled in a way he did not associate with her. "What *what* means?" D.T. asked.

Mrs. Atherton paused dramatically. "I haven't heard from Mr. Atherton since our settlement, Mr. Jones. I hear *of* him, of course, and see his name in the papers from time to time, but until yesterday there was no communication at all between us except for the monthly check I receive from his accountants."

"What did he do yesterday?" D.T. prompted. The Giants had men on first and third in the top of the first. Clark up. You have to get to Niekro early.

"He sent me flowers."

"What was that?" Clark fouled out to Chambliss.

"Mr. Atherton sent me *flowers* yesterday, Mr. Jones. A dozen white roses. It's what he used to send when we were courting."

"Was there a card?"

"Just his business card. Signed. No message."

"Was it your birthday? Anniversary? Anything?"

"No. I thought of that, too, of course." She paused. "What do you think it means, Mr. Jones?"

"I haven't the faintest idea," he said as a sadness creeped over him that was caused by more than Davis grounding out.

"But what should I *do?* I mean, is it illegal for him to do that? Oh, of course it isn't," she added, spiking her own nonsense.

"Does it matter, Mrs. Atherton?"

"I don't know." Her voice seemed small, tired. "He must be up to *something,* don't you think?"

"Maybe yes, maybe no. Maybe he was simply overcome with nostalgia. Maybe he remembers you fondly and wanted you to know it. You were married for what, thirty years?"

"Thirty-two."

"Sit tight, Mrs. Atherton. See what happens. It'll probably be something nice."

"If that's your advice, Mr. Jones," she said, rather primly.

"That's my advice as a man, Mrs. Atherton. Not as a lawyer. *De minimus non curat lex.*"

"What was that?"

" 'The law does not concern itself with trifles,' " D.T. quoted. "So far, that's all this amounts to, isn't it? A rather touching trifle?"

"I suppose so," Mrs. Atherton conceded after a moment. "Am I as pathetic as I think I am? I am, aren't I?"

D.T. laughed. "You have a nice day, Mrs. Atherton. If anything else happens, you give me a ring."

"Thank you. I was foolish to call. For some reason it just made me highly nervous to know that Mr. Atherton was actually *thinking* about me after all these years. I'm afraid that doesn't say much for my sense of worth, does it? Perhaps I'm not as recovered as I thought I was."

"I think you're fine," D.T. told her. "Hang in there."

He replaced the phone. D.T. spent the majority of his time doing what he had just done: hearing the unspoken; answering the unasked. By now he had done it all, could program a robot to replace himself. One day someone would do just that.

With women like Ida Casting, paralyzed for years by an unalterable resentment, beset by a specific problem, D.T. could usually deflect her frustration away from her ex-mate and toward the bureaucracy of welfare or law enforcement, where it would be absorbed by the delay and inefficiency that lurked in systems. Ironically, in cases like Ida Casting's, the system often worked quite well, since the uniform enforcement of support laws was increasingly effective in tracking down absconding, defaulting husbands and making them pay up.

With women like Mrs. Atherton, he could only hold her apprehension up for what it was—a groundless reaction to the harmless, even generous, act on the part of a man she once had loved. Not as easy as it seemed. Many women retained their husbands in their minds for years after their divorce, sparred with them continually over imagined insults and fabricated neglects; expected them to call, to appear, to threaten, to abuse. The more absent the men were, the more expected they became, the women never quite accepting what the law had ordered them to accept—that they were blameless and yet alone, and that the law could impose that fate upon people like themselves.

For some women divorce was a triumph, a liberation, a new beginning. But not for the ones who called him on Saturdays, the ones who buzzed about him like flies, years after both his services and his patience were exhausted. He simply did what he could for them, which was to answer his phone and offer his sympathy and concurrence and refrain from suggesting they were nuts.

He shut off his office machines, locked the safe and the door, and drove the three miles to his ex-wife's mansion, a sixteen-chambered block of neoclassic granite at the end of a gauntlet of ever-more-imposing edifices, most of them apeing the residences of royalty. Their daughter Heather, eight, brown-haired and -eyed, exquisite not only to him but to others, waited for him on the portico beneath the soft black wing of Mirabelle's thick arm.

"Hi, Daddy," Heather said as he strolled up the walk.

"Hi, honey." D.T. found himself seeking in Heather's twitching limbs a body language declaring she was truly glad to see him. Each time he visited he suspected Michele of employing the previous week to sabotage him in their daughter's mind, out of some posttraumatic desire for vengeance. And each time he eventually realized that if Heather's image of him was marred, then he himself had provided the adulterants to accomplish the deed twice over, that Michele had neither the need nor the desire to worsen what he was.

Heather's creation and abandonment were the best and worst of his deeds, and Heather was now old enough to know it. For more than a year he had resolved to sit down with her and talk candidly about the divorce, to find out what she truly thought about it, to explain and justify his act. But he had never done it, in part because he was afraid that what she thought about it might be something quite close to the view he held himself, in part because he feared the opposite might be true—she had adjusted so nicely to his absence that any justification he offered would be of purely historical interest, if at all. So he pretended divorce was something yet to be invented, and tried very hard not to think of Heather solely in terms of what he had done to her.

D.T. squeezed Heather to him, then kissed her on the forehead, which was as nice as kissing custard. "How are you, Mirabelle?" he asked over his daughter's ribboned head.

"Jus' dandy, D.T. You looking like your old self, too."

"Close enough."

"You take good care of my little glass teapot today, you hear?"

"Don't I always?"

"Jus' 'cause something always been happening don't mean it's gonna keep on. I learned that much from Leroy."

Leroy was Mirabelle's ex-husband. D.T. had handled the case as a favor, which meant he knew enough about Leroy not to want to know more. Leroy reduced the species. "Ready, honey?" he asked his daughter.

"Ready, Daddy."

Heather trotted toward his car, skipping lightly, causing her short print dress to hop high above her knobby knocking knees. "God, she's cute," D.T. said to himself. A moment later he found himself fearing, as he always did at his first glimpse of her on these visits, that she would one day end up on the other side of his desk, bemoaning a decade or more of life.

"She love you a whole bunch, D.T.," Mirabelle said behind his back. "Don't you do nothing to change that more than you done already."

He looked at the fat black woman. "If I do, you get Leroy to shoot me down."

"Don't you worry, I will," she said, then cackled. "He

be pleased to do it, too." D.T. kissed her cheek and went off to join his bouncing daughter.

He drove directly to the museum of modern art, peppering the air with his standard list of questions along the way. In response, Heather told him about school, her words tumbling over each other like clowns: Mrs. Nobish was okay, but her breath smelled like rotten peaches and she liked to pinch arms; her favorite subject was social studies because they were learning all about Indians and Indians were rad; all boys but Timmy Fredericks were nerds, but Timmy she liked because he gave her his dessert every noon because Timmy already had six cavities even though he brushed his teeth even after lunch; she had started taking ballet after school on Tuesdays and Thursdays, she just loved it, her teacher was totally awesome, and she hoped D.T. could come by and watch her dance sometime. Huh? Would he? And all the time she was talking D.T. wondered how long it would be before Heather had nothing at all she cared to say to him, about her own life or his or anything. His own adolescence, D.T. remembered, was a half-decade of sullen silence.

The museum occupied a partially restored Victorian mansion near the center of the city. The antique appointments that decorated the old house set off the collection of mostly derivative modern paintings primarily by mocking them. D.T. paid the small admission fee and accepted the free brochure and basked in the congratulatory smile of the blue-haired volunteer at the front desk, then followed Heather into the warren of little rooms in which the art was arranged by the nationality of the artist.

They walked rapidly for a time, through Spain, the Netherlands and Italy, looking at one thing and then another thing that was frequently a lot like the first. Heather trailed her small palms over the more robust pieces of sculpture, and paused briefly before the more heroic canvasses, and admired the few kinetic assemblages, but she had nothing to say about any of it until they reached one of the three rooms devoted to Americans, this one occupied entirely by the work of extremely lesser-known Expressionists. "How come there's no people?" Heather asked suddenly as she stood in the exact center of the room with her hands on what would one day be her hips.

"Well, it's early," D.T. explained. "I'm sure there'll be more visitors pretty soon."

"No, Daddy. I mean in the *pictures*. How come there's no *people* in them?"

D.T. glanced around the room. They were alone, so it was all right to lie or be foolish or even wrong. "Well," he began, "some of these *are* pictures of people. They're just different *kinds* of pictures. They're called Expressionists, these painters. Abstract Expressionism, is what this kind of painting is."

"What's that mean?"

"Well," D.T. foundered, remembering the days when he had stubbornly waded through Rosenberg's criticism, determined to learn enough of the lingo to be a factor at cocktail parties. Now he recalled nothing remotely salient. "It means the painter tries to express what's *essential* about a person, what the person is really *like*, without actually painting exactly how the person *looks*. See, like over there. That picture's called 'Nude Number Nine.' You know what a nude is, right?"

"Jeez, Daddy. Michele paints nudes all the time."

"She does? Who . . . ? Well, this painter thinks he's captured the real meaning of the nude he's painted by making those stripes and swirls. He thinks you can understand what's important about that nude by looking at the design and color."

"But, Daddy. I can't even tell if it's a man or a woman."

"Maybe the painter didn't think that was important, whether it was a man or a woman. Maybe he thought other things were."

"Things like what?"

"Well, see those swirls? They're kind of wild, aren't they? Crazy. Maybe that's what's most important about that nude. That it's a crazy person."

"I think it's kind of important whether it's a man or a woman, Daddy." Her lips twisted with a scorn that would one day wound any male who faced it.

"It usually is important, sugar, I agree. But maybe not this time."

"Daddy?"

"What?"

"What's the most important thing about you?"

"That I'm your daddy, of course."

"Really?"

"You bet."

"That's not what Michele says it is."

"What does Michele say it is?"

"Michele says you're not happy. She says you're very sad because you're not what you wanted to be when you grew up and that *that's* the most important thing about *you*."

D.T. reeled away from his daughter and toward an imitation Calder. "She does, huh?"

"Is she right, Daddy? Are you sad all the time?"

"No, honey. I'm not sad all the time. I'm not sad right now. I'm *happy*. In fact, you tell Michele I'm just as happy as she is."

"Are you sure?"

"Sure I'm sure. Why did Michele tell you that, anyway?"

Heather knit her brow. "Because I asked her why you never came to see both of us together and Michele said it was because I made you happy and she didn't. She said almost everything in the whole world but me makes you sad, and you work so hard because if you stopped working you'd just start thinking about how sad you were. Is that right, Daddy? Does Michele make you sad? Is that why you got a divorce from us?"

D.T. moved to where he could drape an arm across the thin ledge of his daughter's shoulders and draw her to him and at the same time hide the hand that wiped his eyes.

His thoughts bludgeoned him as they moved through the rest of the silly museum. Finally, the excursion ended in the tiny gift shop. D.T. offered to buy Heather a print to hang on the wall of her room. She clapped her hands and looked through a pile of them and selected an El Greco. When he asked her why she picked that one she said it reminded her of him. Quickly, he asked where she wanted to go for lunch.

"Can we go to McDonald's? Please? Pretty please?

Michele *never* lets me go to McDonald's. Can we? Huh?''

D.T. reviewed every single thing he had ever heard about the place, then concurred, determined even at the risk of nutritional imbalance to deliver something more than Michele for once. Better anything than a mimic or a bore. They got in the car and found some arches that were golden, like the day.

They filled themselves noisily, amid scores of others exactly as happy as themselves. As he watched Heather eat something called a McNugget, D.T. again marvelled at her existence, then despaired at the sociological likelihoods that lay ahead of her. She was such a complex stimulus to him. The morning of her birth he had cried with pleasure for the first and only time. The night of her raging fever he had looked to God as something other than a source of blame. Yet since the divorce he had easily convinced himself that Heather was better off by his absence, that greater proximity would have surely infected her with one of the several afflictions that caused him to drag through life as though his brain were a burden, not a tool.

''Daddy?'' Heather asked, her mouth full of McNugget.

''What, honey?''

''See that girl over there? By the plant?''

''Yes.''

''Her daddy tried to kill himself. Do you know how?''

''How?''

''He cut himself on the arm and almost all his blood ran out. So they put some back in before he died.''

''Who told you that?''

''She did.'' Heather extended her arm. ''Guess who gave me this watch.''

He sagged with relief at the *non sequitur*. ''Who? Michele?''

''Nope. George.''

''It's a nice watch.''

''It's okay. Jill Anderson has one with a diamond on it. And Timmy Fredericks has one with a whole *computer* in it.''

He chuckled at this demonstration of the foolishness of

wealth. "How do you like George, Heather? Do you and
he have fun?"

"Sure. Lots."

"What do you do?"

"Oh, things."

"What kind of things?"

"Go places."

"What places?"

"The zoo. The movies. The park. Places like that."

D.T. sighed. It seemed he had an understudy.

George. The wedding wasn't that far off. Maybe he
should try to do something about it before it was too late.
Maybe he should talk to George, to make sure his visitation rights would not be restricted. Or maybe he should
keep his smart mouth shut.

"What are we going to do now?" Heather asked after
her last gobble of an ordinary cookie made divine by its
packaging.

"I don't know," D.T. admitted. "What would you like
to do?"

"Can we go see Barbara?"

He thought of Barbara and of Bernie. Tasting wine;
perhaps tasting each other. "Not today, honey."

"Why not?"

"Barbara's busy."

"Doing what?"

"Retaliating."

"What's that mean?"

"It means she's out of town. How about a movie?"

"Which one?"

They talked it over. Heather opted for a special effects
monstrosity she had seen six times previously, each with
a different adult. Out of things to ask, afraid of what
might be asked of him, D.T. abandoned two and a half
hours of his judicially allotted parental opportunity to the
creators of a glorified cartoon with less story line than a
single panel of *Family Circus*. By the time the closing
credits wound across the frame of his vision he was fran-
tically planning their next activity.

Outside the movie house, the sun squeezed his eyes
like oranges and their juice threatened to spill down his
cheeks. He grasped his daughter's hand and led her to

the car. "You want to ride around a while?" he asked. "Go out in the country and look at some cows or something?"

"Can we go by the lake?"

"Sure."

They drove for miles, gazing upon the bucolic edges of the city in what D.T. hoped was a rapt silence rather than an enervating boredom. They saw crops growing and animals feeding and solitary people working at what they worked at every day of their lives. D.T. began to think of seeking out a place to buy. An acreage. Trees, grass, maybe a creek or a pond. He would grow sunflowers, grapes, berries; make his own wine. Heather would spend all summer with him; they would have time to really get to know each other. He could get a goose for protection, a goat for milk, chickens for eggs. Maybe even a black-faced sheep, just for fun, and a dog for Heather. Excited, he glanced at his watch and reluctantly headed back to town, his wake strewn with future plans.

"Daddy?" Heather asked as he approached the house.

"What, honey?"

"What do you do, exactly?"

"You mean my business?"

"Uh huh."

"I'm a lawyer. You know that."

"Michele says you help people get divorces."

"That's true."

"That doesn't seem like a very nice thing to do, Daddy. Why don't you get a different job? Why don't you start doing something nice?"

"Like what?"

"Like, ah, making ice cream, maybe? Timmy Fredericks' daddy makes ice cream."

"Ice cream causes cavities."

■ S E V E N

I LIKE it when we go places, Daddy," Heather had said after he'd returned her. "Even that funny museum."

"I do, too," he'd responded. And smiled. And hugged her. But their day had ended in a stillness cured only by Mirabelle's heavy voice and embracing flesh, a stillness that failed to mask D.T.'s relief at being able to deposit the responsibility for Heather's future on the lovely portico of a lovely mansion in a lovely neighborhood in which he did not reside. With a kiss, a pat, and a predictable pang of guilt, D.T. had left his only child to grow another week without him.

Now he searched out house numbers in the fading light of evening, numbers pasted to facing rows of bungalows that ranged from crumbling slums to elaborate objects of residential art. It was what the realtors would call a "transition" neighborhood, in which storybook colors and precisely planted flowers vied with shattered windows and rotting shingles to see which would claim the block. D.T. had grown up in a similar neighborhood, amid a similar struggle, in a house that fell somewhere between the extremes of care he was driving through.

His parents had been neither idlers nor artists but workers—his father a grocer with his own store and thus his own prison, his mother a seamstress whose stitches had gathered the pleats and tucks of every formal gown in a town that rarely had a call for formality beyond the New Year's ball at a club that refused membership to coloreds and to Jews, a club to which his parents did not belong. Both of them had spent far more time trying to raise up those beneath them than to climb to those above.

Now his father was dead from a stopped heart and his mother lay bedridden with a broken hip, dependent upon people other than her only child for everything but breath. Some day soon he would have to visit her again. Some day before she died he and she would have to share, for one last time, a room and a past and the prospect of a future that would surely disappoint them. Perhaps that was the precise definition of middle-age: when you were as worried about your parents as you were about your offspring.

He stopped at a sign, calculating that Esther Preston lived in the next block. The visit with her would be a painful waste, and she would end up believing that he had somehow cheated her by not being what she needed. It had happened to him before, with clients to whom he was useless but strained to be otherwise.

He hesitated longer than necessary at the stop sign, then spurted rapidly ahead and parked in front of the appointed number. By the time he got out of the car he was feeling better. Perhaps his visit would not be hopeless after all—perhaps in Heather's lexicon it would be defined as something nice.

The Preston house had a blue composition roof and red siding that had begun to blister. It was so small it seemed suitable for a prize in a board game. An ornamental olive tree grew into ten feet of space beside the front walk. Along the foundation were marigolds and zinnias and, at the corner, a box elder bush. The lush lawn seemed extravagantly tended, given the purported handicap of the occupant.

D.T. pressed the bell and waited; pressed it once again and waited longer, and began to hope he had acquired an excuse to leave. Then the door opened noiselessly and he lowered his eyes.

She was sitting in a wicker wheelchair whose yellowed woven back arced above her like a halo. Hands folded, eyes raised, lips smiling, she seemed without affliction but for the narrow band of cloth that passed above her eyes and lashed her head to the high back of the chair. She was younger than he'd pictured, thin and frail. Gray streaks marbled her brown hair. Her flesh bore the etch of age, but her kinetic lips and eyes diverted him from the sags and wrinkles that advanced on them.

"Mr. Jones?" she asked through the smile.

D.T. nodded. "Mrs. Preston, I presume."

"Of course. Won't you come in? And it's Esther. Please." Her voice was firm but slightly slurred, as though she were fatigued or flirting. Her dress was candy-striped and festive. She unclasped her fingers and seemingly without effort rolled herself back out of his way. The tires of the ancient chair were as black as licorice and were crumbling like cake.

He entered her house. The air was viscous with the scents of starches. D.T. was reminded of his father's store, his mother's kitchen. "Please follow me," Mrs. Preston said, and pushed herself easily into the living room. She seemed to sail before him, as though she were only an idea.

The living room was only slightly larger than the foyer. The ceiling was low and gray, the walls an eggshell white. Here and there little wooden niches gleamed of varnished pine and sheltered knick-knacks. The bulb in the center of the ceiling sparkled starlike through cut glass. The floor was polished hardwood. Strips of rubber runners crossed it like canals of black water.

There was a single place for him to sit, a speckled horsehair divan with doilies pinned to its arms. Across from the divan were an iron floor lamp that had once burned oil and a round marble-topped table with a book and a box of tissues on it. Between the table and the lamp was space to park her chair.

D.T. sat obediently on the divan and saw Mrs. Preston watch him with what looked very much like amusement. "May I get you something, Mr. Jones?" she asked. "I have coffee and lemonade and some cookies I baked this morning."

He began an automatic refusal, based on his dislike of eating in the presence of strangers, particularly from his erratic lap. Then he looked into her hazel eyes and changed his mind. "Lemonade would be fine," he said. "And maybe a cookie."

"How about two?"

"What kind are they?"

"Oatmeal."

"How about three?"

"That's better," she said with a quick laugh, then rolled out of the room like a charioted princess.

D.T. looked around, intrigued as always by being left alone in another person's house. Mrs. Preston had ringed herself with a pocket universe, edited to suit her tastes. There were dried flowers in vases and live violets in pots and a hollowed stone which served as an ashtray. The drawings and photographs on the walls offered birds, animals, stars, sunsets, snow-capped mountains, white-sand beaches, whales. The recessed niches were hives of sculptured miniatures—a brass bee, a porcelain rabbit, an iron frog, a pewter stag, a walnut stallion, and a plaster figurine of someone who looked a lot like Mozart. In the bookcase closest to him were a tiny leatherbound edition of Shakespeare's plays and prosaic odds and ends that ranged from *Pride and Prejudice* to *Fear of Flying*. Most prominent of all was a framed color photograph of the cathedral at Chartres, so precisely focused it seemed something beyond even the ken of God. Next to the cathedral, perhaps as evidence of Mrs. Preston's unbound psyche, was a small reproduction of Lautrec's gay and naughty Moulin Rouge, a line of girls with ruffles flying. D.T. smiled and began to relax. It seemed a place where he could do no wrong.

Gradually he noticed the adaptations. A device on the front door permitted opening and closing with an arm instead of fingers. Chrome rails were attached at various places to the walls, above the paths of rubber pads. The sturdy frame of an aluminum walker hid in the corner behind the bookcase. Long looped cords hung like nooses from the lamps. D.T. changed position and looked at his watch. He'd been in the precise and utile little house only five minutes.

When her wheels brought her back to him they made no noise, and he was caught thumbing through the heavy scrapbook that lay on the coffee table in front of the divan. All the clippings were photographs from magazines and newspapers, some glossily vibrant, others faded and yellowed with age. Each was of a ballerina, leaping and twirling or bowing and posing, all elegant and lithe and mesmerizing.

"My scrapbook," Mrs. Preston said with twitching lips. "I began it when I was thirteen and my life was dance. I saw no reason to discontinue it just because my life became far less glorious than my dreams."

"You mean your disease?"

She laughed and shook her head. "I gave up dance long before sclerosis came along. I'm afraid I lacked the courage to test myself against the art."

D.T. put the heavy book back on the table. When he looked at her again she was inspecting him carefully. His eyes quickly strayed from hers.

"Please don't be embarrassed, Mr. Jones," she said quietly. "I'm really not as ill as you probably suspect. I have very little pain, in spite of how I look. Other than the irritants of slurred speech and some occasional edema and diplopia, my problem is simply strength. I have none much of the time. But even though my body no longer functions well, it does function. One just has to anticipate its eccentricities." She laughed in two syllables. "At one time I thought MS had been visited on me because I had wanted to dance too desperately. That it was punishment for my lust to be not as other beings."

"And now?"

"Now I see it simply as a fact to be accounted for." Her slippery voice was suddenly hollow. "There are so many facts to be accounted for in life, aren't there, Mr. Jones? I'm sure you encounter many of them in your practice. Perhaps even in your private life."

She raised her brows and he nodded uneasily, thinking once again of Heather and feeling the way he always felt in the presence of the handicapped—unworthy of his health.

When she saw his look she immediately constructed a soothing aspect, like so many of the afflicted her function not to be cheered but to cheer. "Here you are," she said, and rolled toward the coffee table. "Please take the tray."

He lifted the tray from her lap and placed it in front of him, noticing in the process the suction cups on its underside. On it were a tall glass full of ice and pulpy pinkness and a small china plate, hand painted with roses, supporting three cookies of the diameter of hockey pucks. D.T. thanked her and took a bite.

"A bit too much vanilla, I'm afraid."

"Couldn't prove it by me," D.T. said, and moved to cookie number two.

"You really needn't rush, Mr. Jones. Unless you have another appointment."

Mouth full, D.T. shook his head. "I'm not rushing, I'm just eating," he mumbled. "You're not the first to confuse the two."

She nodded happily. "Of course, there really *is* no need for you to be here. Other than the rather extortionate demands of Miss Holloway, that is."

"Well, my social life for the week has already come to pass. And this is the best cookie I've had since 1954. Where is Miss Holloway, anyway?"

"She's seeing a patient. She said she'll be back to check on me at eight. She said she would only believe you'd been here if you left a card behind."

D.T. took out his wallet and removed a business card and flipped it to the coffee table. "So much for my presence," he said. "If she still has doubts you can show her the crumbs I seem to be spilling all over your floor."

"Don't worry about it. Please."

"Okay, I won't," D.T. said. "Do you look after the place yourself?"

"The interior, yes. Outside, I have a wonderful neighbor who keeps things looking marvelous. I don't know what I'd do without him. Of course his efforts to please me seem to have backfired."

"How's that?"

"He's made the place so attractive the landlord has increased the rent substantially."

"They tend to do that," D.T. said, then swallowed the dregs of the second cookie. "Which bring us to why I'm here, I believe."

"Yes," Esther Preston acknowledged. "It's quite simple, though, I'm afraid. My ex-husband is well and entirely rid of me, Mr. Jones. He performed all of his obligations under our property settlement agreement if not our marriage contract, and he has gone on to what appears to be, from the things I read in the papers, a dazzling life. I have no claim on him nor do I wish to pursue one." Little lines sprouted above the set of her thin lips, bloomless stems of purpose.

"Do you have a copy of the settlement agreement?" D.T. asked her.

"Yes. Somewhere."

"Could I see it?"

"I suppose so. It's in the bedroom, I think. I'll get it for you."

"Can I help?"

"No. Everything is within reach, Mr. Jones. One learns to do that quite quickly."

She rolled away again, and D.T. took advantage of her absence to finish off the lemonade and the final cookie. When she came back she handed him several sheets of legal-sized paper, stapled at the top and signed on May 21, 1965, by Mrs. Preston and her former husband. There was no indication what lawyer if any had prepared the document.

D.T. flipped quickly through the pages. "Did you have an attorney?" he asked.

"No. It didn't seem necessary. Nat and I discussed it and I felt I was being treated fairly."

"Who prepared this agreement, then?"

"My husband's lawyer. The firm is Bronwin, Kilt and Loftis, I believe. A large one downtown. The particular attorney was a man named Grusen. He was a friend of Nat's. He died some time ago, I believe."

D.T. remembered his chat with Jerome Fitzgerald of the day before. Jerome the litigator, partner in the same firm. D.T. examined the agreement a bit more closely.

The form was basic and familiar. After reciting the facts of the marriage—nine years, no children—and the prior division of personal property to mutual satisfaction and the remaining marital estate of the parties—a home of an approximate equity of six thousand dollars plus unnamed assets of a total value of twenty thousand dollars—the agreement provided Doctor Preston would assume existing debts and Mrs. Preston would receive quit-claim title to the house plus a single lump-sum payment of six thousand dollars plus alimony in the amount of two hundred dollars per month for a period of two years in final settlement of all claims by Mrs. Preston against her husband. Not generous, but not quite unconscionable, particularly for the year in question. About what he'd expected, which meant virtually hopeless. He looked up at her and thought he saw uncertainty in her eyes.

"May I ask you some personal questions?" D.T. asked, determined to do something, unsure of what.

"Of course." The guileless eyes shone brightly.

"How much money do you have right now?"

"Savings?"

"Yes."

"A bit over nine hundred dollars. Plus the interest that will be paid at the end of next month."

"Any other assets?"

"Nothing other than the things you see around you. All of them valueless except to me."

"Do you have any family?"

"No."

"Any investments at all?"

"No, other than the savings account."

"How much did you get when you sold the house you lived in with your husband?"

"Eight thousand net to me. All of it and then some went for medical bills."

"Is that why you sold it? To pay medical obligations?"

"Yes."

"Have you worked since the divorce?"

"For a short time. I had a job in a bank during my marriage and after. In fact that's the way I first discovered that my illness was something other than a lingering cold. I could no longer operate a calculator accurately."

"And since you got MS you haven't worked?"

"No. I made one effort some years ago but it was far too embarrassing for all concerned. My employer was a friend, and he was willing to keep me on, but only out of sympathy. I was entirely useless to him as an employee, as I would be to anyone."

"Do you receive Social Security?"

"Disability. Yes."

"How much is that?"

"Four hundred and twenty-nine dollars per month."

She smiled sadly. "I have just received notice that my status is about to be reviewed. The result may be termination of my benefits." She paused. "A woman I know recently had her benefits eliminated because the department decided twelve years after she got MS that she was not truly disabled after all. They suggested work as a watchperson in an art gallery. She is appealing the decision, but the Legal Aid people are not encouraging," she added bleakly. "Of course Legal Aid itself may vanish soon."

"A sign of the times," D.T. said.

"So it seems. I assume her former benefits will go for bombs and bullets. She can't dress herself, button a button, zip a zipper, anything." Her words seemed more puzzled than angered, as though she truly wished to understand how such a thing could become the way of the world without anyone stopping it.

"When is your review?" D.T. asked.

"Next month."

"What day?"

"The tenth."

"At the Federal Building?"

"Yes."

"Do you care if I come by and watch?" D.T. asked.

She knew his intent and smiled. "I can't accept your charity, Mr. Jones, but thank you."

"But you won't make them arrest me if I show up, will you?"

"No. I won't do that. But I hope you won't. The accomplishment I cherish most is that I am not a burden to anyone. At least not yet."

He had embarrassed them both and wished he hadn't. "Do you rent this house?" he asked, more brusquely than he'd intended.

"Yes."

"How much?"

"This month it was two seventy-five. Next month it will be three hundred and fifty."

"A big bump."

"Yes."

"Who's the landlord?"

"A real estate corporation."

"Crescent Development?"

She raised her brows. "How did you know?"

"They own half the rental units in this area. They've raised the rent on all of them." D.T. sought and failed to come up with an adequate circumlocution for his next question. "Do you need regular medication?"

"Irregular. Valium for spasticity; belladonna for . . . bodily functions."

He reddened. "How much does it cost per month?"

"Thirty dollars, perhaps, in the good times. But it goes up quite regularly. I've lost track."

"Food?"

She laughed. "Do you mean do I eat? Yes, I'm afraid I must."

"How much?"

"As little as I can." Her smile was brazen. "One so wants to remain svelte."

"How much money per month on food?" he insisted.

"Fifty dollars, if I'm careful and if I don't have too many visitors."

The cookie in D.T.'s belly turned to stone. "I don't mean to grill you, Mrs. Preston," he said quickly. "It's just that I'm trying to get some idea of what you need to live on."

"I understand, Mr. Jones. You simply need to know the exact extent of my wretchedness." She smiled again to help him.

"Utilities?"

"Seventy dollars in winter. Less in summer."

"Do you have air conditioning?"

"If I had air conditioning I would not require you to remain as uncomfortable as you clearly are, Mr. Jones."

"It must get a lot hotter than this in here," D.T. said, loosening his tie and collar.

"Many plants cannot survive in it, I've learned to my sorrow." Her chin jutted a bit, a charge of pride at being more enduring than a fern.

"So you get a bit over four hundred a month in disability, and next month it will cost you at least seventy dollars more than that just for basics."

"If nothing goes awry, yes. Lately, though, many things have seen fit to malfunction." She chuckled easily.

"My burners don't work, so everything I eat is baked or broiled. You'd be amazed how ardently one can long for fried food."

He was in fact amazed, but by her unflagging good humor, not her appetite for french fries. It was what so many dramatists missed—those who specialized in miasmic vision—that it is at the very bleakest moment that the highest wit occurs.

"You put him through medical school, didn't you, Mrs. Preston?"

She rolled backward a foot in surprise. "How did you know that?"

"Just a guess. Exactly when were you married?"

"His last year of undergraduate school, at Christmas. 1956."

"What were you doing at the time?"

"I was a year older than Nathaniel so I already had my degree."

"In what?"

"Economics, with a minor in dance. I had a job with a bank. A pretty good one, actually. An analyst in the trust department."

"And you kept it till he was through with med school?"

"Yes. Plus a year of internship and another of residency."

"Did he have money? Family money?"

"No. Neither of us did."

"Was he bright? Bright enough to get scholarships and such?"

She sighed. "No. Not in that sense, he wasn't. Nathaniel was consistently in the bottom third of his class. He could have been higher but he preferred sociology to etiology."

"You mean he was a party boy."

She smiled at the memory. "Nat's true genius was in getting others, me included, to do his bidding without expecting a corresponding favor in return. He was impossible to say no to, which I suppose accounts for our marriage. But why are you asking me these questions, Mr. Jones? What do they have to do with anything?"

D.T. sat back down on the divan and leaned toward

the woman in the high-backed chair with wheels. "There are some cases that have been filed recently by women in circumstances somewhat similar to yours, Mrs. Preston, in which it has been claimed that a wife who puts a professional man through school has an interest in the fruits of his degree that continues beyond the termination of the marriage. Do you understand what I mean?"

She frowned. "You mean I might be able to claim a portion of Nathaniel's income each year he's been a doctor because I contributed financially to the attainment of the degree that allows him to practice."

The words were matter-of-fact and rolled easily off her tongue. D.T. could have been talking to a colleague. "Exactly," he said.

"Has this principle been upheld, Mr. Jones?"

"Not that I know of. My research isn't up-to-date, but as far as I know the claim has only been asserted a couple of times, not upheld. There are two or three appeals pending, one in the supreme court of this state, and there is support for the principle in some journals."

"I don't like the sound of it, Mr. Jones, to be honest with you. It sounds slick. It sounds too much like . . ."

"Like a lawyer?" They exchanged smiles. Hers was close to coquettish. D.T. looked at her closely. "What happened between you and your husband, Mrs. Preston? Did you gradually drift apart, or was there a specific incident?"

"You mean, I suppose, was there another woman." She seemed to think about it. "I don't think so," she said finally. "It's not impossible but I don't think so. But that doesn't mean I know what *did* happen. Nat became more and more immersed in his work. His circle of friends widened, mostly to include people who liked to talk investments rather than obstetrics. I suppose it was the usual doctor's wife syndrome, more than anything. Many women found themselves in the same position I was in soon after their husbands began their practice."

"Did the divorce come as a surprise to you?"

"Yes. I probably should have seen it coming but I didn't. But then I'm quite capable of limiting the horizons of my mind. Of shutting out things I don't wish to think about. I'm quite sure I was doing it then with regard to Nat, just as I do it now with regard to other things."

"How long after he went into practice did he file?"

"Two years."

"What was his income then?"

"I recall he made thirty thousand the first year. It was five times as much as I ever made at the bank. And the next year his income doubled. Part of his salary went to buy into the partnership, I remember him telling me. It's the reason he gave for us always seeming to need more money."

"You mean the medical partnership he was in?"

"Yes."

"I didn't see any value put on that interest in the property settlement, Mrs. Preston. Do you remember anything about it?"

"Not particularly. I remember Nat said his interest in the business wasn't worth much."

"How would you say you lived? High on the hog? Frugally?"

"Quite frugally. Nat said we had to get a nest egg built up. So he could go into practice on his own. Of course he did manage to buy himself an Austin-Healey."

D.T. leaned back and rubbed his eyes. "All this brings one other possibility to mind, Mrs. Preston. Do you want to hear it?"

Her hands twisted in her lap. She looked around the room quickly, and then at D.T. "I don't want to lose this house, Mr. Jones. Not if I can help it. I would not enjoy a communal environment, I'm too used to privacy. So yes. I guess I do want to hear it, though I'm sure it won't make any difference at all. It won't, will it?"

"Probably not," D.T. agreed. "But the only possibility is to do some investigation to see if your husband deliberately failed to disclose some of the community assets the two of you owned at the time of the property settlement. If he did, then maybe we could make a claim for half their present value. If it was a piece of art or stock or something, it might have appreciated quite a bit over the years."

"But you're only guessing, Mr. Jones. You don't have any evidence at all that Nathaniel cheated me."

"I know. But I'd be willing to check it out."

"On what basis? Financial, I mean."

"Oh, a twenty-five percent contingency sounds good. If we come up empty you owe nothing. If we get something out of him I get a fourth of it. Expenses off the top."

"Do you have time to waste on something like that, Mr. Jones?"

"Depends on who you talk to," D.T. said, thinking of his daughter. "Do you want me to go ahead?"

She closed her eyes and remained silent.

"You could use the money," he prompted.

"Yes, I'm afraid I could."

"So you're torn."

"I suppose you could say that. My life is in a delicate balance, I'm afraid. As things stand, I'm able to endure it. To find joy, even, at times. But away from this, in a home, an institution, away from people like Miss Holloway, I just don't know. I'm afraid I might . . ."

He spoke into the hushed monument to her dread. "If I find evidence that your husband cheated you will you let me file a lawsuit?"

"I don't know."

"Maybe?"

"Maybe."

"The same if the Supreme Court rules that wives have a compensable interest in their husbands' professional degrees?"

"I suppose so. I'm just not sure."

"But you'll think about it?"

"Yes. I'll think about it."

"I guess we can leave it at that for now," D.T. said. "When you see Miss Holloway again, have her call me."

D.T. stood up and brushed the crumbs off his clothes and tried but failed to catch them. "Let me give you some cookies to take with you," Mrs. Preston said. She disappeared before he could decline, then returned with a small white bag which she handed up to him. "Thank you for coming by, Mr. Jones. It was kind of you to humor me."

"My pleasure, Mrs. Preston."

"You seem like a good man. Are you?"

He looked to see if she was teasing. "I don't know," he said when he saw she wasn't. "I think I used to be, but I don't know if I've kept it up."

She smiled her smile. "Maybe one day you'll be lucky enough to find out."

"Maybe I will," he said. "Now, can I ask *you* a question?"

"Of course."

"Are you really as good as you seem?"

She grinned. "I suppose that depends on exactly how good I seem."

"You seem like Assisi's sister."

"Well, I'm not nearly that. Not by a long shot."

"Thank God," he said, and left with the cookies and something even better—the glimmerings of a cause.

■ E I G H T

WHEN he got back to his apartment D.T. expected to find Lucinda Finders. Instead he found a hand-scrawled note on the kitchen table and an entirely different body—Barbara's—asleep on his couch.

The note was from Lucinda and imparted her thanks for the bed and the breakfast and ordered him not to worry. But the note itself rendered him incapable of following her instructions. He wondered where she was, if she was all right, who she was with, whether it was possible that Delbert had tracked her down and abducted her from the place he'd thought was safe.

Pushed harshly by such thoughts, D.T. searched cautiously through his apartment for the leavings of violence. Finding only signs of his own indolence, he decided what he frequently decided when confronted with his clients' wrecked and scrambled lives—that there was nothing he could do so there was no sense worrying. The sentiment usually survived till three a.m., when he would awaken in the midst of a frightful slice of dream, his client in jeopardy while he looked on helplessly. D.T. swore under his breath and walked to the doorway between the kitchen and the living room and gazed upon his sleeping lover and wondered why he would really have preferred the woman on the couch to be his pregnant client.

Barbara didn't stir as he tiptoed through the house, changing clothes, straightening up, fixing himself a drink. In the process he noticed the little leavings of Lucinda, the empty glass of milk, the crushed and lip-greased filter-tip, the bloody wad of packing she had plucked from her nose and deposited like a cherry atop the coffee grounds in the garbage can beneath the sink. During all his movements, Barbara's breaths floated through his mind like clouds, forecasting a storm. When he retired to his bedroom with his drink and a detective novel she seemed forever lost to consciousness and he found himself hoping she would sleep till morning so he could spend the evening in silence and in peace.

The dying businessman had just asked the private detective to locate his rebellious son when the telephone rang beside his bed. D.T. started at the sound, then quickly dog-eared the page and picked up the receiver.

"Mr. Jones? Hi. It's me. Lucinda Finders. Remember?"

"Of course I remember," D.T. said. "How are you?"

"Fine."

"How's your nose? Any pain?"

"Not too much. Looks sort of like an old banana, though. I hope it clears up some by tomorrow. I got to start looking for work."

"Where are you, Lucinda? What happened to your job at the Pancake House? Has your husband been after you?" The impossible barrage of questions reminded him of the other occasion when he prattled—his first moments with his daughter on his weekly visitation.

"When I called and told the manager I couldn't come in for a few days he fired me," Lucinda was explaining. "But that's okay. I'll find something. I'm pretty good at finding work."

"Where are you, Lucinda?" he asked again.

"I'm home. That's why I called, Mr. Jones. I'm home in Reedville with my folks. So you don't have to worry about me. I just wanted you to know that."

"That's very thoughtful. But are you sure you're all right?" His grip on the receiver softened.

"I'm fine. Really."

"Your folks treating you okay?"

She hesitated. "Sure. Fine." The silence told him more.

"Has Delbert been around?"

"Not that I know of."

"Does he know where your folks live?"

"Sure. We come here for a few days after we got hitched. Del and my daddy didn't get along so we left."

He could imagine the struggle, titanic collisions of prejudice and misinformation. "You let me know if Delbert tries to see you, Lucinda. Okay?"

"Okay."

"I mean it."

"I will. I promise."

"You still want to divorce him, don't you?"

"I guess."

"Good. I'll file the papers on Monday and let you know how things are going and when you have to be in court."

"Okay."

"And if you want to come back to the city you can stay here any time. Till you find a place of your own."

"You're sure nice to me, Mr. Jones. Are you that nice to all your customers?"

"Some," D.T. said, knowing it was a lie, knowing the only ones he truly embraced were cute and simply wounded and would jeopardize nothing he cherished except perhaps his conscience.

They said good-bye. D.T. tiptoed into the living room and checked the slumbering Barbara once again, then returned to his bed and book. Ten pages later, as the detective was interviewing the mother of the missing son, D.T. finished off his drink and went to the kitchen to pour another. Hungry, he looked to see if Barbara had stirred enough for him to ask if she wanted supper.

He dared not eat alone, he knew, for fear she would think him selfish. And he dared not wake her, for fear she would think him unfeeling. So he watched the rise and fall of her T-shirt, admired its taut span between the breasts that rose above her chest like headlands, and wondered if the hands of Bernie Kaplan had recently removed it.

After a sigh he hoped would wake her but didn't, D.T. went back to the bedroom. As he sank to the bed the phone rang once again. He started to pick it up quickly, then allowed it to issue three more yells at Barbara.

"Mr. Jones. I was afraid you wouldn't be home. What did you think of Esther Preston? Isn't she wonderful?"

D.T. propped himself against the headboard and balanced his drink on his belly. In the process, he noticed the Rorschachian stain on the wall beside the bed and tried to remember why Barbara had thrown coffee at him. "Yes, she is, Miss Holloway," he said. "She is just as wonderful as you described." He couldn't come up with it. Barbara was so angry at him so often.

"I don't know how much she told you about her situation—probably not enough—but it is truly desperate. She has this list of state institutions she's been calling to see which ones have openings in case she has to give up her house? She's put herself on *waiting lists*, Mr. Jones. Did she tell you that?"

"I know she's in trouble financially, Miss Holloway. Unfortunately, that's not the issue here. Misfortune seldom breeds its remedy."

"What *are* you going to do for her?" Rita Holloway challenged bluntly. "Did you think of a way to get that pompous bastard to give her enough of his obscene wealth to keep her out of the poorhouse?"

"It's not that easy," D.T. said. "First of all, Mrs. Preston doesn't want to sue him; she doesn't think she has a case. Second of all, as of now she's absolutely right. She has no case at all that I'm aware of."

Silence. "So does that mean you're not going to do *anything?*"

"What it means is that *you're* going to have to do something."

"What do you mean?"

"The only way we'll persuade her to let me file against her husband is if we come up with clear and convincing evidence that the guy screwed her to the wall at the time of their divorce."

"What kind of evidence, exactly?"

"The only claim I can think of that might pay off is one that alleges Dr. Preston had more assets than he disclosed at the time, assets that she would have been entitled to share had a court known of their existence. Fraudulent concealment, is what the lawyers call it. *In re Marriage of Moondick.*"

"What?"

"That's the leading case."

"Sounds good," Rita Holloway bubbled. "Where can we get that kind of stuff?"

"What do you mean 'we,' Florence Nightingale? If

there's digging to do, someone besides me is going to have to do it since I don't have the time, the money, or the inclination to do it on my own hook. So what do you say, Ms. Marple? If I tell you where to look are you ready to start looking?''

She didn't hesitate a whit. ''What do I do?''

''Plan to spend a lot of time at city hall over the next few weeks, for a start. Check the assessor's office, to see if Dr. Preston was the legal owner of any real property back in '65. Also check the recorder's office. They have grantor-grantee indexes, the people there will show you how to use them. See if he bought or sold any property between 1960 and 1965. Also call the secretary of state's office. See if Preston was listed as an officer or director of any corporations in the state at the time. If he was, run the corporate names through the indexes. Check the plaintiff and defendant tables in the clerk's office. See if he got sued for anything or did some suing. Talk to Mrs. Preston. Find out if he had a stock broker or investment advisor in those days. Find out where she and her husband banked. Find out the names of the other doctors in the medical group her husband was in, then find out where they are today. But don't contact them. Just give me the names and current addresses. Also, ask Mrs. Preston if she knows where any copies of their tax returns for those years are. That should keep you out of trouble for a month or two.''

''What are *you* going to be doing all this time?'' Rita Holloway asked skeptically.

He raised his brows. ''Me? For Mrs. Preston? Not a goddamned thing. You let me know if you decide to throw in the towel, Miss Holloway. So I can get in touch with Legal Aid and see if *they're* in the mood for a lost cause.''

''Oh, I don't throw towels, Mr. Jones. I just use them to dry my hands and once in a while to mop up blood.''

He saw a bulldog in his mind, one with a grin like hers. ''Tell me something, Miss Holloway. What is MS, anyway?''

Her voice changed quickly, from urgent yips to a throaty drone. ''MS is a disease of the myelin and the cells that produce myelin. Myelin is the insulation, so to speak, that covers the nerve fibers. When the disease hits, the myelin falls off and is replaced by sclerotic plaques, or a kind of scar tissue. Then the nerves short-circuit, creating a long list of problems of the kind Mrs. Preston suffers from. Half a million people suffer from it.''

''What causes it?''

''That's the problem, of course. No one knows. Current research is centered on the immune system. The most promising recent development is the isolation of the gene that codes for myelin protein.''

''You mean it may be a virus?''

''Yes. Of a type.''

''No cure?''

''No, although removal of white cells from the blood has given some promising indications. But the strange thing with MS is that there is frequently a complete and spontaneous remission. For entirely unknown reasons. Also, of course, there can be a worsening of symptoms, occasionally to the point of death.''

''Nasty.''

''Most. Mrs. Preston is on the bad side of the ledger, unfortunately. What change there is seems in her case to be invariably for the worse.''

''Sad.''

''You don't know the half of it, Mr. Jones. I suppose it was pretty warm in her house while you were there?''

''A little.''

''Heat exacerbates the symptoms of MS. Brings on episodes, as they're called. Spasticity. Incontinence. Weakness. Backache. I'm sure Esther was in a great deal of discomfort while you were there, Mr. Jones, though I'm also sure you never sensed it.''

''No. She seemed quite comfortable.''

''Well, don't be fooled. Euphoria is a symptom of the disease, too, oddly enough.''

''You're kidding.''

''No. Most of the time I think it's a benefit, but sometimes it makes the patients do less than they should for themselves. Esther, for example, won't let me buy her an air conditioner.''

"I don't think that's euphoria, Miss Holloway. I think that's pride."

"Of course it is." Rita Holloway paused, as if to calculate how much truth he could take. "You know what she does almost every evening?"

"What?"

"Reads books aloud. Onto tapes for the blind. You know what she does with ten percent of the money she gets for her disability?"

"What?"

"Gives it to her church. You know what she does every Saturday afternoon?"

"Give me a break, Miss Holloway. If I'm going to represent a saint I'd just as soon not know about it. It might cramp my style."

"I just don't want you to slough this off, Mr. Jones."

"We'll see what we can do, Miss Holloway."

"You bet we will, Mr. Jones. *You bet we will.*"

If only Sol would give him odds.

As he replaced the receiver a groan crawled toward him from the living room. He dog-eared another page and trudged reluctantly to meet it. At times like these, after he had committed what she viewed as treason, Barbara invariably sought either a slashing confrontation or a rending lust. D.T. definitely was not prepared for the former, and just at the moment the latter sounded oddly repellent as well.

When he reached the living room she was sitting up on the couch, the afghan that had covered her bare legs now bunched at her feet, which were shod in grimy waffled running shoes. She rubbed her eyes and shook her boyish head. Given her daily regimen, he kept expecting her to turn cadaverous, but she kept looking like Mitzi Gaynor. He wondered if it was the bean curd or the tofu that did it.

"Hi," she said.

"Hi."

"Is it okay I'm here?"

"Sure. Why wouldn't it be?"

"I saw the note."

"Oh. Lucinda. She's a client. She got beat up by her husband last night. She slept on the deck."

"Where is she now?"

"Home."

Barbara woke up. "You mean you let her go *back* to the bastard?"

D.T. raised a peaceable hand. "No, no. She's with her mom and dad. In Reedville."

"Where's that?"

"In the valley."

"Must be a thousand degrees out there."

"In the shade."

They paused, wondering how to get to where their history dictated they had to go. D.T. didn't feel it was his obligation to explain his failure to pick her up the night before. At least not until she asked about it. The more he thought about it the more certain he was that he was not only blameless but triumphant. He had done something nice; he had saved Lucinda. Of course Barbara doubtlessly felt a similar rectitude. Whatever she had done with Bernie she had done with provocation. Barbara's every breath was the result of provocation.

"Is that where you were?" Barbara asked him suddenly, while he was scripting the impending battle. "When you were supposed to be taking me to dinner?"

"With Lucinda. Right. And Doc Faber. At the hospital. She called just as I was about to leave for your place. He broke her nose. I was afraid he'd killed her baby, too."

"What baby?"

"The one she's carrying. The husband likes to punch at it. I forgot all about you till it was too late. I called about eleven but you were gone. I'm sorry," he added lamely, quickly wishing he hadn't.

"Me, too, D.T. I should have known it was something important."

She had yielded without a struggle. Knowing he was in the right she had acted reasonably, more reasonably than he deserved. D.T. felt his body unwrap with the thought.

Casting about for an appropriate reaction he became a drizzle of apology. "I could have called sooner. I just forgot. It all happened so fast, I . . . On *top* of it all, her husband tried to run us off the road while I was driving her to the hospital."

Her eyes popped. "You're not serious."

"Yes, I am."

"Did you call the police?"

"No."

"Why ever not?"

"She wouldn't let me." D.T. hurried on. "Did you go wine tasting?"

She hesitated. "Yes."

"How was it?"

"Fine."

"How's Bernie?"

"Fine. He knows a lot about wine."

"I'll bet he does. How much does he know about us?"

"Nothing, D.T. You know I don't talk about us. Not outside a structured context."

"Good. I guess."

"We stopped at a nude beach on the way back, D.T." Barbara struggled for a hustler's smile. "Want to see my sunburn? It's in an interesting place."

"Maybe later."

"*Definitely* later." Barbara gave him her lusty look, the one that activated levers in his cock.

"You want something to eat?" D.T. asked.

She shook her head. "We stopped for tempura after the beach. I think I'll go run some of it off. I feel all bound up."

"How far?"

"Three miles, maybe? I'll be back in twenty minutes. Why don't you fix yourself something and when I get back we can play." She stood and faced him and laid her wrists atop his shoulders. "I really am sorry, D.T. I shouldn't have gone with Bernie; I don't even like him. He thinks women are turned on by dirty words and money. So, well, you know how I am when I think you've screwed me."

He knew. She was a walking seismograph, hyperalert to signs of insult and neglect, and since she lived in a world that specialized in those commodities she was always uncovering ample evidence of deeds that required a militant response. Barbara wrote letters to congresspeople and to editors and to the makers of everything from tampons to breakfast cereal, protesting less-than-pristine courses of commercial or political conduct. She asked strangers to put out cigarettes. She urged the obese to run and to eschew red meat. She was a dogmatic evangelist on a dozen subjects. She spent several nights a week at workshops run by women who called themselves facilitators and held degrees from land-grant colleges that somehow entitled them to tell others how to live their lives. She urged D.T. to take bee pollen daily, and to ejaculate as frequently. She held nothing to be as sacred as her body, unless it was her sex.

Barbara ran twenty miles a week and ate only fruits and nuts on weekdays. On Tuesdays and Fridays she pumped iron. On Wednesdays she fasted. She did not shave her shins or beneath her arms but regularly trimmed her pubis. She stemmed the flow of menstrual blood with sponges from some idyllic sea. She took a handful of vitamin supplements daily, and drank steer's blood when she could get it. She read only fiction penned by women and laughed only at jokes that slandered men. She knew six poems of Sylvia Plath's by heart. She thought the accepted usage of pronouns in the language was criminally inspired, and refused to say anything bad or even funny about lesbians. She tried to have sex at least four times a week. She had no objection to monogamy in theory, but she often proclaimed that she knew of no marriage in which the wife wasn't getting regularly raped by her mate. With the possible exception of the day her tubes were tied, her own divorce—which D.T. had handled a year before he began to handle more of her —was the touchstone of her life. She thought D.T. was a truly special man in a world full of macho creeps, except on days when she thought he was the biggest chauvinist asshole who ever walked the earth. Still, he thought she wanted him to bend his knee and risk a second ditto.

In spite or because of all that, most of the time D.T. thought he was in love with Barbara. She was not at all his type, but that was exactly her charm: she was like no woman he had ever known. Perhaps it was admiration more than love, because what he thought of mostly when he thought of Barbara was the way she wrestled life, fought it tooth-and-nail, demanded that it yield to her every whim. If he was continually amazed at what she asked of her life, he was even more amazed at what it often conferred on her. Barbara demanded friends and got them, demanded independence and got it, demanded pleasure and got that, too. She demanded wisdom and knowledge, respect and equality, and by God she got all that as well. Barbara's wars were fought for others, not herself.

As a by-product of all this, D.T. yielded to most of her demands by rote—he discussed abstractions that he hadn't considered for years, traveled to socially significant places he would never have thought to visit by himself, read obscure little tracts on frightening little subjects that held no interest at all until he involuntarily managed to learn something specific about them. As Barbara bettered her own life she bettered his as well.

But still. She was so strong, so sure of herself, so ceaselessly demanding, and so, in some respects, wrong. Their fights on the occasions he refused to submit in theory or in practice were ferocious, made all the more so by her lack of self-deprecating humor and by her uncritical acceptance of the modern mumbo-jumbo that offered the simplest of answers to the most complex of problems, usually at the expense of the male component of the dynamic. One of their fights would one day consume their relationship, D.T. was certain of it. What he was not sure of was whether or not he cared. He could still remember the night Barbara, her warrior credo diluted by two joints of potent pot, had tried in tears to tell him how it felt to be a woman in a world that was ordered and administered by men who not only wanted from her only what was debasing, but who could also beat her to a pulp at any time they chose. By the end of her soliloquy her tears were matched by his.

Barbara hitched up her satin running shorts and tugged down her cotton shirt and walked out the door, calves knotting, butt bobbing, her body as eager as a colt's. Running made Barbara both fit and horny. It made D.T. asthmatic. Unfortunately, Barbara had not yet quit trying to make him a partner in things more strenuous than sex.

D.T. went back to the kitchen and opened a can of Campbell's and, eventually, boiled it. While it simmered to tranquility he ate three Ritz crackers and a soft banana that had been subliminally suggested to him, perhaps, by Lucinda's description of her nose. He wondered how she was faring out there in Reedville. He wondered what she would have done if he had joined her naked on the deck beneath her blanket and the stars, whether she would have laughed or cried or opened her arms and fucked him. He had never screwed a client, not while she was a client, at least, and in this he differed from almost all his colleagues. Perhaps it was time he joined them. Perhaps his life was now too grave for ethics.

By the time the soup was cool enough to sip, Barbara was back, letting herself in with the key he'd given her the night they had first made love, which was the night they had first met socially, at a fern bar across the street from the courthouse where, Barbara had later confessed, she had lain in wait for him with mischief on her mind and lied outrageously about her car's malfunction and her fear of entering her apartment unescorted. Both that night and since, she got exactly what she wanted.

She stood behind him and watched him ease the soup into his mouth. Barbara was as steamy as the Campbell's, as odorous as an onion. Heat rose off her like a medicinal vapor. She waited patiently till he finished. "I need a shower," she said as he slurped the final slurp. "Come with me."

He shook his head. "I'm still hungry."

"Come on, D.T. We haven't showered together for months."

"Not tonight, Barbara. Please?"

"Come on. You don't have to do a thing. I'll do both of us. I'll use that glycerin soap I gave you. Come on."

She tugged him out of his chair. He banged his shin on the table leg. On the way down the hall she tugged roughly at his belt. By the time they reached the bathroom he was stumbling over the trousers that had fallen to his calves and were serving as a hobble. Coins spilled from his pockets and chimed like the bells of Krishnas as they skittered across the floor.

As he hopped on the cold tile, Barbara peeled off her soaking shorts and shirt and, wearing only panties darkened by sweat in back and by the equilateral shadow of her pubis in front, turned on the shower and adjusted the temperature to suit her, which was within a degree of scalding.

D.T. dallied, struggling out of his pants, trying to tug his trousers over his shoes, finally starting from floor level and working up, beginning with the brogans. He was still in his underwear when Barbara turned away from the hissing shower and peeled away her panties. Then she stretched his shorts beyond his cock and pushed them to his ankles, and raised his T-shirt off his head.

He was always leery when she stripped him. He was not of notable endowment, and Barbara who weighed and measured everything else about him, from his taste in music to the objects of his charitable bounty, must have weighed and measured his cock as well. And doubtless found it wanting. Thankfully, she had never mentioned it. Blessedly, he lived in a culture that decreed that women display their breasts and men secrete their cocks, at least in circumstances short of the carnal or the uronic.

The shower curtain slid smoothly over its rod, releasing sodden smoke that was the stuff of deviltry and witchcraft. Briefly, he thought of cannibals. "Come on," Barbara said, and stepped into the tub and disappeared in the cloud of steam. "D.T.," she warned from within when he failed to follow.

Cupping his genitals to keep them from becoming cooked, D.T. clambered in to join her. Gritting his teeth against the solid swords of water, pulling the curtain shut behind him, darkening the shower into a London fog, he waited for instructions.

"Turn around."

He did and felt her hands slip easily over his back, their kneading surges oiled by a scented soap Barbara had ordered from a catalogue of imported erotica. Within a minute he was drugged by her firm ministrations of his torso, by the assault of the shower, by her delicate probing of his soapy ass. He felt like home-baked bread, hoped that Barbara would soon eat him.

"Now the front."

He turned again and watched the sudsy water find its way around the bulges of her body and drip like albino urine from her pubic brush. As he gazed on her, she soaped him thoroughly, beginning at his chin and neck. When she reached his waist she sank to her knees onto the flowery non-skid appliqués on the floor of the tub. She lingered on his genitals, her work efficient not seductive, causing D.T. to wonder not for the first time if she found them foul.

"D.T.?" Barbara's voice slipped through the cheering shower like a whispered secret.

"Hmm?"

"What's a scrotum?"

"What?"

"What's a scrotum? Bernie said something about his scrotum today and I wasn't sure what he was talking about. I was going to look it up, but since you're here . . ."

D.T. reached for her hand and guided it. "This."

"The balls?"

"No. The sack."

"Oh."

"What brought up the fascinating subject of Bernie's scrotum?"

"He got hot sand all over it."

"Dangerous, those nude beaches. Warning: May be hazardous to your scrotum."

He looked down into Barbara's smile. "See my sunburn?" she said, and raised a breast. Below the deep brown of her normal tan, the pink white circle around her aureole peered at him like a bloodshot eye. He winked back. They played with each other longer.

"Does this hurt?" Barbara asked, squeezing.

"No."

"This?"

"Yes. God." He curled.

"Is that what happens when you get hit in the balls?"

"That. Worse."

"Why does it hurt so bad?"

"Who knows? As an aid to propagation of the species, probably. A function formerly held in high regard."

"Is this where sperm comes from?"

"I think so."

"Don't you know?"

"I think I do."

"Why are there two?"

"Fail-safe, maybe. Or maybe one for boy babies and one for girl babies."

She pinched something near his knee. "Why does one hang lower than the other?"

"Jesus, Barbara."

"Don't you know?"

"No."

"You don't know nearly enough about your body, D.T."

"I'll get to my body as soon as I'm through with my mind."

Barbara washed his ankles and between his toes and then stood up and trailed her fingers through his frothy and newly labelled scrotum. "Do you still masturbate?" Her face was an inch from his.

"Still?"

"Well, all men masturbate, don't they? I read they did."

"Not all. Most, probably. When they get the time."

"You mean you never have?"

"I didn't say that."

"When's the last time?"

"Last night. And then again this morning."

"You." She poked him, and turned her back. "Do me," she said.

He fished the soap off the floor of the tub and did her, back first, lingering at her favorite places and at his own as well. By the time he was finished they both breathed deeply, through parted dripping lips. "Do you want to do it here?" she asked.

"No."

"On the bathroom floor?"

"The bed."

"Okay, but next time in the tub."

"Sure."

"Promise?"

"Promise."

He took her hand and helped her from the tub. Then Barbara assumed the lead, firmed her grip on his hand, and started toward the bedroom. "Do you want a towel?" D.T. asked her glistening back. She shook her head and increased her speed, her footprints on the carpet like the tracks of Crusoe's Friday.

Still pulling him like a Flexible Flyer, she belly-flopped onto his unmade bed, then turned onto her back and tugged him down on top of her. Once fused, their wet bodies bucked and smacked like printing presses, as though each cell was frantic for a mate. D.T. kissed her, tasted the tang of salt and the fatty paste of soap. His thick tongue slipped between her lips and she closed her teeth until he squirmed, then sucked his tongue until he could taste its root. He backed away and took a breath.

Slithering beneath him, Barbara arranged their bodies so that his prick pressed squarely on the bristly carpet that hid and warmed her sex. He gnawed her neck and ground his pelvis onto her, then ground again, alert to what she wanted, then alert to something else. The sensation was different from the usual slab of fur, a gritty scrape along the shaft of his prick. Sand. From the nude beach. Perhaps the grains that had singed poor Bernie's scrotum. The thought of Barbara and Bernie naked lit him.

He rolled to his side and slid down her body until his tongue could lap her fresh-baked breast. He nibbled lightly at the nipple, playfully, then more roughly, then drew as much of the firm sack into his mouth as it would hold. He made more noises, released it, watched it tremble. As he flicked his tongue at the nipple once again, Barbara's moan erupted over him like a tribal command. He slipped his hand between her legs and separated the pucker of her flesh and buried one finger, and then another, leery for a moment that Barbara would make him stop and trim his nails, as she had the first time he had probed her similarly.

Her sticky inner glue threatened not to let him leave. He nipped at her breasts, one and then the other, while propelling his coated fingers so far into her she hollowed out and gobbled him. As she raised her hips to meet his fistic thrusts, the telephone rang. He disbelieved it until it rang again.

"No," Barbara said.

"I have to."

"No." She clamped her legs around his wrist, double-locking him inside her.

"We've been through all that, Barbara. Something might have happened."

"What's going to happen? You know it's always nothing but neuroses."

Barbara's abandonment of this inconvenient segment of the sisterhood amused him briefly. "That's not the point. I just can't not know."

"Please? Just this once?"

He rolled to his back and cast his free hand in the direction of the intruding instrument. After one misfire he grasped it. "Hello." The word was a demand, not an invitation. Barbara rolled and wrenched his wrist.

"Jones?"

"That's me."

"Jones, the divorce lawyer?"

"Hello, Del."

Barbara swore softly and released him. He rolled to his side, away from her and toward the telephone. Behind him, he felt her leave the bed.

"How'd you know who it was?"

"I've been expecting your call, Delbert. I've dealt with guys like you before."

He wondered where Barbara had gone, if she was leaving the apartment, if he should go after her. But more than that he wondered what Delbert Finders was up to, how much he was prepared to risk to get D.T. to abandon his young wife to the hazard of her marriage.

"I know she spent the night at your place, Jones. I followed you from the hospital."

"You must be good at it; I tried to check."

"I'm good at lots of things, pal. You get in her pants? Huh? You roll around on that big belly and suck on them big floppy tits? Huh, Jones? Big Lawyer-Man. She show you how good I taught her to fuck?"

Behind him, Barbara slipped back onto the bed and crawled toward him over wadded covers. His body bounced. A hand gripped his hip and rolled him to his back.

Humming a toneless tune, Barbara straddled him, crouched, balanced on one hand and two knees. Her other hand grasped something round, a jar, a can, something. And she clenched another object, pirate-like, between her teeth. It looked very much like a knife.

"I didn't lay a hand on Lucinda, Del. Which is more than you can say, isn't it? There's a long line of people down at that hospital, Delbert, ready and willing to testify to what you did to your wife last night. Now what the hell do you want?"

Barbara sat back on her haunches, pressed her bottom to his thighs. Freed, her other hand removed the object from between her teeth and joined its mate at the jar. It really was a knife. She wouldn't do anything stupid, would she? Even in fun? The knife dipped slowly toward the crucible.

"The thing is, Lucy don't know what she's doing. She don't want no divorce; she's got no need to get one. I give her everything she needs. Hell, I even give her a baby like she wanted. So the best thing for you to do is tell her to forget it. Tell her to come back home."

"I'm filing the papers on Monday, Finders. You'll be served within a week."

The knife emerged from the jar, laden with a whitish substance. Barbara gazed on the buttery mound as though to read its powers, inhale its scents, then lowered the teeming blade toward his naked chest.

"You best not serve papers on *me*, Jones, not if you want to stay healthy. I'll give you what you got last night and then some. That car of yours ever hits a tree it'll fold up on you like a paper bag. Take 'em a day to get you out."

"You're already on probation, Finders. If you mess with Lucinda or me again I go to the D.A. and have your probation revoked. We'll see how tough you are after a few months in the joint."

"Jail don't scare me none. Cops, neither."

With a single swipe, Barbara buttered his breastbone, the exact center of his hairless chest, with whatever was on the knife. The broad white stripe traversed his sternum and pointed toward his groin. The knife returned to the jar. He sniffed, then cupped the phone and asked Barbara what it was. Stonily, she ignored him.

"Where is she, Jones? She still there with you? You

going to keep her around to service you awhile, like a
whore with your initials on her ass?''

"She's not here. I don't know where she is."

"Crap."

"It's true."

He dipped a finger in the sauce and tasted it. Of course.
Barbara's physic, her balm, next to sex and sweat her
cure for everything that ailed her: yogurt, bran, gorp,
coconut, raisins, whatever else anyone had ever thought
was healthy. She smeared it on everything from ice
cream to mashed potatoes. Now she was smearing it on
him.

The knife returned, the wide line lengthened. With another dip it was at his navel, clogging it. With another it
was at his groin. His body hair occupied the paste like
worms. Barbara paused to inspect her work.

"You talk to her, Jones. Tell her this divorce stuff is
for shit. Tell her she'll be just fine if she comes back
where she belongs. Tell her if she comes home I won't
whip her no more. Tell her that. Tell her from now on I
won't drink nothing but beer. No more pills. No coke.
Nothing like that. You tell her I won't hurt her no more."

"I'm not telling her anything."

"Why the fuck not?"

"Because it would be a lie. Because punks like you
beat their women forever, until someone puts you where
the only woman is a dream."

Barbara wielded the knife again, and this time dabbed
his cock. Again, and yet again, the applications as precise
as pastry, until it was a bright white shaft with a blood
red tip, a beacon or a buoy. She tossed the jar off the bed
and the knife right after it. Crouching again, she began to
lick away the gruel, beginning where she had begun. Her
tongue singed him like a brand, moved teasingly toward
his sex.

Muscles and tendons twitched untouched. His body
arced like a tumbler's. She raised her head and blew on
his groin, hot streaks of air that electrified him, caused
his foot to jerk. Her head moved lower. Like Pinocchio's
nose, as cursed and as untamed, his plastered cock
surged toward her parted lips, its tip as red and close to
bursting as a thermometer on the door to Hell.

"What's that, Mister Lawyer? You say something?"

"I'm through listening to you, Finders. As of tomorrow there'll be a restraining order in effect, signed by a judge, directing you to stay the hell away from Lucinda. You violate it and you're in contempt of court and the cops come looking. You'll be a two-time loser, Delbert. It'll be bye-bye for a long time."

"You best not file those papers, you cocksucker. I'll kill your ass if you do. I got nothing going for me anyway, what the hell do I care if I rot in jail?"

"You feel pretty sorry for yourself, Delbert."

She was going to do it. At long last. As soon as the paste was licked away she would take him in her mouth, do what he had silently willed her to do for months, reward his rectitude. A few licks more. A swallow. Now. In a way she owed it all to Del.

"I'm going to give you something to feel sorry for, asshole. If Lucy isn't back here by tomorrow I'll make last night look like a love tap. I'll mash her up so bad you won't know her from your dog. And if something happens to that little baby she's got in there, well, the blame's right on you, Lawyer-Man. So you just tell Lucy to get her sweet ass back here. Now. Or I find her and make her wish she had. And then I come looking for *you*."

The line clicked dead. He dropped the receiver and twisted to his side, dislodging Barbara from her perch, then curled fetally and closed his eyes.

"D.T.? What's wrong?" Barbara's voice mixed hurt and fear.

"I'm sorry. I . . ."

"Who was on the phone?"

"The guy who beat up his wife."

"Oh."

Barbara curled against his back and began to stroke his shoulder. "Did he threaten you?"

"I guess."

"I'm sorry."

"Me, too."

"Try to forget about it."

Barbara stroked him for long dead minutes. He lay there, smelling a hint of peach, feeling the stiff stickiness

of yogurt and saliva, still afraid. It seemed an age before
she spoke again.

"D.T.?" She mumbled his name and nuzzled his neck.

"Hmm?"

"Can I ask you something?"

"Sure."

"Promise you'll tell the truth?"

"Sure. Maybe."

"Swear to God?"

"Swear to Joe Montana."

"What's the D.T. stand for?"

"De Tumescent," he said, and proved it.

■ DISCOVERY

H E was an hour more than fashionably late. As he climbed the flagstone steps to the tall oak door he again regretted accepting the invitation, and again concluded he had had no choice. The party was Joyce Tuttle's, and she was the only friend acquired during his marriage to Michele who continued to acknowledge his existence.

Joyce had been a helpful confidante to both of them during the long process of their unraveling. She had spent one particularly morose evening alone with D.T., in a bar no one had ever heard of in a place he could never find again, listening to what Joyce called "his side of it"—legitimizing his mistreatment, validating his excuses, accepting his allocation of fault, enduring his wild wallow in self-pity. It had been the one truly rending evening of the whole experience for him, and so he owed her one and Joyce had decided this was it. She had supplemented the printed invitation with a telephone call urging him to come, and he had promised he would, even after learning that Michele would be there, too.

When he reached the door he saw that a document was nailed to it, at eye level, in the tradition of Martin Luther, impossible to miss. When he recognized it he smiled. Joyce Tuttle had just been divorced herself, after a decade of marriage to a marble statue. This was her first postmarital bash, her announcement of a ringless finger, and the document on the door was the official confirmation of her status, signed by the circuit judge, certified by the county clerk. D.T. pressed the ivory bell button. Wriggling inside his best wool suit, shrugging his topcoat higher on his neck to keep the November wind from inching down his back like a stranger's hand, he fought back an urge to flee.

The door was opened by a uniformed maid, who welcomed him and took his coat and directed him to the living room, all without uttering a word of English. He regarded the foyer as a gauntlet, his destination as a cell. He walked toward the white noise of congeniality knowing that most of the people he would soon encounter had advised Michele that she was mad to marry him.

The house was mammoth and contemporary. Christmas decorations abounded, though it was three days to Thanksgiving. The air was scented artificially of pine, and frequently rent by giggles. The gleaming hardwood floors were warmed here and there by rugs from sheep or Persia. Above the enamel walls a fabric made the ceiling look just tilled. Indirect lights cast a glow no less romantic than the slowly setting sun.

Beneath the textured ceiling the furniture was arranged like groups of grazing mammals. Amidst the mammals were their keepers, elegantly garbed and theatrically posed, extravagantly charmed and breathlessly thrilled by whatever they saw and heard and ate and drank, partying till the cows came home. D.T. eyed them bravely from the doorway, planning a tactless evening, knowing the arena he was about to enter demanded skills he had always lacked.

In the far corner a six-piece band played the "Theme from E.T." Beside the band was a bar on which was collected every form of liquor in the hemisphere. D.T. slipped cautiously into the room and sidled along its edge until he could pluck a highball from the bar and seek out a place where he would seem to be a part of something while not being a part of anything at all. As he was avoiding ensnarement by a swag light his hostess found him and offered him her cheek to kiss.

"D.T. I was afraid you wouldn't."

"Accept it as a personal tribute, Joyce," D.T. told her. "You're the only creature on earth who could get me to abandon *Cagney and Lacey* for an evening with these creeps."

Joyce smiled maternally. Her gown winked at him from

several silver eyes. Her hair sported a new coat of platinum, her cheeks a double dose of blush. She was as striking as money could make her, which was pretty damned. D.T. wondered if she was on the make already and if so for whom. He also realized he didn't quite forgive her for not letting him handle her divorce.

Joyce leaned her orange lips his way. As was the fashion, they appeared to be encrusted with dried milk. "Michele's over by the piano," she said, as though it were a secret sought by foreign powers.

"Good. Maybe she'll do 'Jeepers, Creepers.' It's my favorite."

Joyce only frowned. "She wants to talk to you."

"It's no use. I forgot the lyrics."

"Michele and I had a heart-to-heart the other night, D.T." Joyce was bending toward him. Her body gave off more smells than a greenhouse; her breasts seemed outraged by their cups. "I think she wants to get married again."

"I know she does. His name is George. He's a swell guy and I'm giving her away."

Joyce put a hand on his arm. "Not to George."

"Oh? Who?"

"You."

"Me?"

"You."

"You must be kidding. Or hallucinating."

"No. She went on and on about you. She thinks you two could make it work this time. 'Now that we finally like each other' was how she put it."

D.T. sighed and emptied his drink. "A woman who spends two hundred a month on underwear has no business being married to a divorce lawyer who can't keep his bar dues current. All I can say is she must have been having her period. Michele gets nuts when she has her period."

Joyce Tuttle made a face. "Don't be gross, D.T. Just think about it, that's all I'm saying. Keep an open mind."

"Sure, Joyce. An open mind. I guess it's something like an open wound."

Joyce slugged his shoulder. "She's a wonderful woman, D.T."

"I'm drowning in wonderful women, Joyce. What I need is a class A bitch." He rushed to change the subject. "So how about you? You got Harvey's replacement picked out yet?"

Joyce grinned and shimmied, prompting her gown to bat its eyes. "I do have a couple of candidates in mind, as a matter of fact. One of them's right behind you."

D.T. turned and saw an immaculate man of fifty who looked to have just been unwrapped. He had a white head and blue eyes and delicate ears which were listening intently to a woman who had bored D.T. at every single cocktail party he'd attended during his marriage, a woman whose only source of sustenance was a mix of rum and the pain of others. "Good barber," D.T. said.

"Not half as good as his portfolio," Joyce Tuttle said with mischief. "It's too bad I've gotten such a taste for money, D.T. Otherwise you'd definitely be on my list."

D.T. made a silent vow of poverty.

Joyce took his hand and pressed it to her cleavage. "I'd better circulate. If you and Michele get nostalgic, the third bedroom on the right upstairs is ready. But knock first, to make sure Loren and I aren't already *in flagrante*. Loren thinks I'm just the sexiest thing."

Joyce puckered and D.T. tasted her lip-sauce and watched her move through the room with the skill of a quarter horse. A billion cells of pure libido. You didn't see many of them around any more.

D.T. circulated himself, though with a different purpose: that of remaining disengaged. A few eyes met his, and his *outré* image stimulated smiles which died prematurely when the smilers remembered D.T. was no longer among those who had married civility. He passed the bar twice and patronized it likewise. He passed a waitress once and plucked from her tray a crust of something muddied with caviar. After he swallowed it, he coughed.

Moving only tangentially, he drifted toward the band and watched them plod through "Blue Moon" and "The Way We Were." It had been one of his youthful dreams, to be a jazz musician, to live like Miles or Getz or Brubeck, to make new music in a new town on every new night of his life. But he had no gift for improvisation and no discipline to learn the chords well enough to fake it, so he had sold his horn and bought some records and joined the throngs who lived their dreams vicariously.

The band took a break. The sax player nipped something from a pocket flask and winked at D.T. D.T. nodded and moved away, feeling found out.

He was about to complete his third lap of the room when a finger tapped his shoulder like a single drop of rain. He turned and encountered his ex-wife. "Fancy meeting you here, Mr. Jones," she said, smiling warmly, her lips as bright as blood.

He bowed. "You look très swell as usual, former Mrs. Jones," he replied, eyeing the off-the-shoulder drape of the lamé gown that she apparently had only to shrug to be rid of.

"Thank you, kind sir. You look positively Lincolnesque yourself." Above her high cheeks Michele's dark eyes began a game and asked him to play as well.

"It seems life is treating you with its accustomed temerity," he said.

"I can't complain."

D.T. laughed. "No one would believe you if you did."

Michele gripped his upper arm with both her hands and pressed her flank to his. "Let's go in the den so we can talk," she said. "I see you so seldom any more."

"That's the price you pay to keep my hair out of your sink."

Michele squeezed his arm again. Her breast lay like a hot water bottle against his bicep. He let her lead him out of the living room, conscious of the glances that passed over them like shadows and the whispers that followed them like cats.

When they reached the den Michele closed the sliding door behind them, leaving them alone with three walls of books, the aroma of stale cigars, and the heads of several former animals that hung from the walls with the dour demeanor of defeated politicians. Joyce Tuttle's earlier confidence about Michele plotting a sequel to their marriage was punched up on the word processor of his brain. He began to feel warmer than the room.

Michele swept to the rolltop desk and whirled and leaned gingerly against it so as not to tax her gown. "So how are you really, D.T.?" she asked, basking in his inspection, as blithe and perfect at this party as she doubtlessly had been at the same hour with the same people in the same milieu the night before. And the night before that as well.

Michele frolicked five nights a week, and confined it to that number only by rejecting the majority of invitations that came her way. While they were married, D.T. had found himself spending a substantial share of his day devising happenstances that would excuse him from the balls, dinners, cocktail parties, charity functions, soirées, and what-have-yous that made up Michele's normal nights. Based on his increasingly frequent absences from such affairs, the city's social arbiters realized long before D.T. did that his marriage to Michele was doomed.

"I'm really okay, Michele. How really are you?"

"I'm fine. I heard a good joke last night. It's about divorce. Want to hear it?"

"Sure."

She squared her shoulders and clasped her hands. Like all women, Michele worried that she did not tell jokes well. Like most women, she was right. Her expression would have worn well on Lady Macbeth.

"These two old people, man and wife, walked into this lawyer's office and told him they wanted a divorce. The lawyer looked at the man and asked him how old he was. 'I'm ninety-one,' the old man said. 'My wife's eighty-seven.' Then the lawyer asked how long they'd been married. 'Sixty-one years next April,' the old man told him. 'Jesus,' the lawyer said. 'Why on earth are you getting a divorce at *this* late date?' The old man looked at his wife and then at the lawyer. 'We wanted to wait till the children were dead.'"

Michele's hands released each other and her eyes focused once again. "Funny, huh?"

"Crippling. How's Heather?"

"She's fine. She wants a pony for Christmas. Do you think I should get her one?"

"No."

"Why not? I thought a horseplayer like you would welcome an equestrienne in the family. And why don't you ever laugh at my jokes?"

"For little girls horseback riding isn't sport, it's masturbation, and Heather's too young for self-abuse. And I don't laugh at your jokes because they're so often at my expense."

"Come on, D.T. *I* had a pony when I was her age. And they are not."

"You were never her age and you know it."

Michele frowned and slapped her thigh. "I was too, D.T. That was our main trouble, you know. You thought I wasn't human."

D.T. ignored her observation, though not easily because it bore some truth. "Is that why we're in here? The pony?"

Michele shifted position. As she crossed her legs the opposite way her gown divided to reveal a lengthy cylinder of thigh. D.T. found himself remembering what the rest of her was like, the tight thin flesh, the lithe and malleable body that was so eagerly dutiful in matters of sex that D.T. ultimately suspected he had never brought Michele to the point of unfeigned orgasm, despite her elaborate denials on the one evening they had been drunk enough to discuss it. As he stared at his wife—his *ex*-wife—his penis pierced the gap in his shorts and scratched its head on his zipper.

"I was at a dinner party last night," Michele said after a minute. "At Nita Ellerson's. Remember Nita?"

"Vaguely."

"There's nothing vague about Nita. Breasts the size of bathyspheres, which she displays at the drop of an engraved invitation. You always claimed you wanted to take one home as a pet."

"Ah, yes. I seem to recall she offered to nestle my weary head somewhere between them one particularly drunken New Year's. How is dear Nita?"

"Only a shadow of her former self, I'm afraid."

"Illness?"

"Breast reduction. Her designer refused to do any more gowns unless she sliced some off. But Nita isn't the reason I mentioned the party. One of the guests at her little bash was one Nathaniel Preston, Medical Doctor."

"Ah."

"I think I remember you asked me about him some months ago."

"Yes."

"He was extremely interested in *you*, D.T., which he demonstrated by feigning a rather breathy interest in *me*. To my regret, since the good doctor has halitosis of a distinctly camphorish nature. Although I must admit I was tempted to find out what kind of sex turns on a man who spends all day looking into women's organs of generation. Any ideas?"

"Foot fetish."

"Really? And I have such a nice arch." Michele raised a foot and looked at it. "Anyway, not having a set of stirrups handy, I feared I would quickly bore the jerk, but it turned out his real purpose was to pump me about you. He wondered, and I quote, what the hell you were up to."

"Did he, now?"

"He definitely did. So tell me, D.T. What *are* you up to? Did some horrible medical malpractice case walk in and plop itself down on your desk? Are you about to get filthy rich at long last, at the expense of Nathaniel Preston and his errors and omissions carrier? Will you succeed despite yourself, Mr. D. T. Jones?"

D.T. only shook his head. "I'm not up to anything at all, as far as I know."

It was true. He hadn't heard from Esther Preston or Rita Holloway in weeks. Months. Not, in fact, since the day he had appeared at Esther Preston's Social Security hearing and watched the government try to cancel her paltry benefits in the name of fiscal integrity and the MX missile. He didn't even know the result of the hearing, or if Rita Holloway's essay in the detection of hidden assets had borne fruit. He wondered if Esther Preston had succumbed to her sclerosis, or if Rita Holloway had found a more participatory attorney, or if it had all just faded away, as so many grievances do, for reasons ranging from inertia to good sense.

Michele was smiling at him impishly. "The doctor sounded more than a bit upset, D.T. If I didn't know he was a sophisticated man about town, not to mention vaginas, I'd say he was asking me to deliver some sort of warning."

"What kind of warning?"

"To mind your own business, or words to that effect."

D.T. shrugged. "That's exactly what I'm doing, more's the pity. So I'm not going to lose any sleep over it, if it's all right with you."

"I can suggest some other ways for you to lose sleep, D.T. Want to hear them?" Michele patted the back of her newest coiffure, which looked rather like a bat with a missing wing. The diamonds loitering about her hand and wrist spit light at him contemptuously.

"Joyce told me she'd reserved us a room," D.T. said, not saying what else she had said. "But I assumed she'd confused me with George."

Michele laughed quietly. "I don't know why I flirt with you so outrageously, D.T. I guess it's because I know you're immune to it. Are you still seeing Barbara?"

D.T. nodded. "Are you still marrying George?"

They exchanged looks that hinted just a bit of pity. "Life is so amusing, don't you think, D.T.?" Michele asked when the silence made them squirm. "I mean, given a certain perspective, everything is so completely droll. I'll probably regret marrying George as much as people assume I regretted marrying you."

Michele laughed uneasily; her lips curled toward a pout. D.T. said nothing. His penis re-inhabited his shorts. He took his hand out of his pocket.

"Are you coming for Thanksgiving?" Michele asked, suddenly back on beam. "Mirabelle's doing goose. And creamed onions. Black-eyed peas. Mince pie. You know how orgasmic you are about Mirabelle's mince pie."

"I know that. It's George I find less than succulent."

"I can't very well leave him out, D.T. We're going to be married in three months. And besides, he's a nice guy."

"I know. That's precisely the best and worst of him. An evening with George is like an evening with Gerald Ford."

Michele looked momentarily stricken, a condition he had not sought to induce. "I need an escort. D.T.," she said softly, reaching for him with beseeching eyes. "You should *see* some of the men my more bitchy friends have paired me with since you and I threw in our monogrammed towels. The last one left me every nine minutes to phone his mother. The one before that had a lisp and an earring.''

''I can imagine.''

''And George is . . . well, anyway, I think you should come for Heather's sake. She's worried about you, you know.''

''Why?''

''I'm not sure. She just keeps asking me if you're all right.''

D.T. swore, remembering the summer day at the museum. ''Maybe it's because you told her I was the most pathetic creature since Emmett Kelly. Christ, Michele. Why did you do that sad sack shit, anyway?''

Her lower lip stiffened. ''Because it's *true*. You do nothing with your life but burrow away in that wretched little office with your wretched little clients, listening to all that woe. No wonder you're so gloomy. No wonder you live like a monk. Those women have made you ashamed to be a man, D.T. And I think Heather has a right to know. So she'll understand your more neurotic behavior.''

''Bullshit. I'm not *that* depressed, Michele. And I'm not neurotic, at least not when I'm with Heather.''

''The hell you aren't. You're so guilty about our divorce and how you think it's affected her you can hardly look her in the eye.''

''That's not *true*. And I'm *not* unhappy, goddamnit. I *enjoy* my work. My clients need help and I try to give it to them and I feel good when I can. When I can't I get upset, maybe, but at least I *feel*. At least I respond to the pain in the world, Michele. That's more than you can say for the twits *you* run around with.''

''I've never offered my friends as role models, D.T. You know that.''

''You've had it all, Michele, from day one. You peeked out of your crib at that fucking chateau you were born in and you never for a moment had to doubt that there was something important about your life. I mean hell, all that money just *couldn't* be insignificant, could it? Well, not all of us had that advantage. I work my ass off so I can at least be *good* at what I spend ten hours a day doing. So I can *matter* to somebody. It's not much, maybe. And maybe next to Heather it's all I've got. But, goddamnit, I'm *good,* Michele. *I'm the best fucking divorce lawyer in this rotten stinking town!*''

He was shouting, evidently. Someone he had never seen before peeked in the door, looked at him, and closed it, frowning. Michele said something, her hand over her eyes. "The sad thing is, you think it matters,'' was what he thought it was.

D.T. sweated in embarrassment. He turned his back and began reading book titles, the words barely registering in his fevered mind. Michele's capacity to wound him still survived, was a slap for which he was never ever prepared.

She spoke again, the words sunken in apology. "Please come on Thursday, D.T.''

He nodded. Barbara had already invited him to spend Thanksgiving in Visalia with her mother and her brother Bob. Bob was thirty-two and lived at home, grew roses, had asthma, and liked to cook. D.T. very much did not want to go to Visalia and now he had an excuse. Fatherhood. He would endure Barbara's wrath as best he could, which was better every time.

"Tell Heather I'll be there about noon," he said. "If it's too early I'll take her to the park.''

"Thank you, D.T. We'll have a nice time. Maybe you'll even grow to like George.'' She gathered her gown and started toward the door, then stopped, then laughed dryly. "I was going to ask you to take me home tonight. Heather's spending the night with a friend and Mirabelle's at some church thing that lasts till dawn. I thought it would be nice for both of us to be with someone who already knew what to do. I even bought an outfit. But I guess you wouldn't want to participate in anything like that, would you? After what I said.''

He shook his head.

"I didn't think so.''

Michele walked to the door and waved good-bye.

"And no pony," D.T. called after her, but she was gone.

Michele. If she had ever cried, or been visited by despair, D.T. had never seen it. At some time in her life she had simply decided to be happy, so that's exactly and perpetually what she was. She had also managed to avoid the blanket condemnation of the male that was so pathologically common to divorced women, and for that he was grateful, for his sake and for Heather's. Then suddenly, as he thought of his conversation with Joyce and of the behavior of his penis, he began to wonder if he was something more than grateful. He began to wonder if he was still in love.

It was impossible and stupid. Even if it was possible and smart, love was one thing and remarriage quite another. D.T. had long ago concluded that the surprise was not that Michele had divorced him, but that she had agreed to wed him in the first place. Their courtship had been more a daydream than a passion, a free trip to Bermuda won by a couple who only too late learned they had no desire to be in Bermuda at all, that sand and sun gave them hives. All along he had been haunted by the suspicion that he was in the nature of an experiment for Michele, a pool of middle-class attitudes into which she had decided, willy-nilly, to dive headfirst, like a kid at a quarry. Later, when she had found the water far too shallow for enjoyment, and even slightly brackish, Michele had simply climbed out, towelled herself off, and moved toward another pool, without rancor or regret.

Which had been simple enough for her, evidently, but far from it for him. For D.T. it had been yet another thing at which he had not been competent, and worse, a failure at the one thing at which his profession dictated he should be expert. He had agonized over the death of his marriage for months, had berated himself, accused himself, blamed himself, despised himself, then applied the same thoughts to Michele. She wanted him to risk all that again? He thought not. Indeed, he knew not. Didn't he? He smiled. Michele and Barbara. For one, life was so benign as to be a gracious gift. For the other, life was so adverse as to be a vital struggle. And D.T.? Somewhere sadly in between.

As he started toward the door it slid slowly open. He expected Michele to walk through it, to apologize, perhaps to renew her invitation to a romp. Surprisingly, he found himself ready to accept. It would be one of those sins that didn't count, like speeding on the freeway. But the person who came through the door was male, a stranger. D.T. resisted the impulse to run after Michele and let her take him home.

"Jones?" The man was short and wide, with stunted arms and legs and a voice that rattled windows. His hair was bristly, his complexion a wash of reds.

"I'm Jones. What can I do for you?"

"My name is Nathaniel Preston. I think we should talk."

D.T. gulped back a burp. "Maybe we should."

Preston closed the door and strode to the center of the room, advancing until they were separated only by a globe.

"Why are you investigating me, Jones? What the hell are you up to?" Preston's hammy hands clenched and then relaxed. In the cuffs above them were links of gold nuggets the size of normal knuckles. His tone was as heavy as his brow. D.T. suddenly pictured him with a metal flashlight, squinting, squatting, peering between a woman's legs and sneering at what he saw, a Rolls-Royce mechanic servicing a Ford.

"I talked with your first wife a few months ago," D.T. began. "She told me some things. I decided to look into some other things. All very preliminary and informal."

"Preliminary to what?"

"A lawsuit, I guess."

Preston crossed his arms above his barrel chest. "Based on what? I don't understand this. Esther and I were married, and divorced. I gave her half of what I had. What the hell else was I supposed to do?"

"You didn't give her half of your degree."

Preston's laugh was swift and brutal. "No, and nobody said I had to. That isn't the law now, and it certainly wasn't the law then. So I don't get it. What's in it for you, anyway?"

"Have you seen your wife lately?"

"Not for years. No."

"You know she has MS?"

"Yes."

"You know she's spent the few thousand she got in the divorce settlement on medical bills and that she lives on a disability payment that the feds are trying their best to eliminate?''

"I didn't know the last. But what am I supposed to do? There are a million sad stories in the world, Jones. Esther's is not the saddest.''

"I'll bet hers is the saddest of the ones of those millions you married." D.T. looked peaceably at Nathaniel Preston. "But then maybe not.''

He thought Preston was going to punch him, and he halfway wished he would, even though the man looked capable of turning his jaw to dust.

"You son of a bitch," Preston snarled, rubbing his fuzzy head with a puffy palm. "It's money, right? Like every lawyer in the world all you want is dough, and you don't care who you have to smear to get it. So how much? To get you off my back for good? Five grand? Ten? How much blood will satisfy you, you goddamned leech?''

D.T. smiled. "I'll communicate your offer to my client. And recommend that she reject it.''

Preston rolled his eyes. "Reject it? What for? You've got no case. You've got nothing.''

"I've got a client who needs a lot more than ten thousand dollars to get her through the rest of her life in dignity, and I'm going to try like hell to see she gets it.''

Preston unwrapped his arms and pointed a stubby finger at D.T.'s sternum. "I'll see you in court, Jones. I'll fight you all the way. You won't get a dime out of me. *Not a fucking dime.*''

Preston stomped out of the room, slamming the door off its rollers in the process. D.T. followed suit after a minute he used to convince himself that Preston's bluster was only bluff.

He retrieved his coat from the unilingual maid and went out into the cold November night feeling surprisingly good, all things considered. Joyce. Michele. The power of a woman to make a man feel young. When he entered his apartment a ringing phone awaited him.

"Hi.''

"Hi.''

"So how was the party?''

"Fine.''

"How was Michele?"

"Fine."

"Did you talk to her?"

"A little."

"About what?"

"Heather."

"What else?"

"George."

"What else?"

"Me."

"What about you?"

"I'm a shiftless bum, is what it comes down to. She despairs of my future."

"You know what I think, D.T.?"

"What do you think, Barbara?"

"I think Michele still loves you. And I think you're still attracted by all that money and all that style. And most of all by what they would give you if you had them back again."

"What would they give me, Barbara?"

"An excuse."

■ TEN

THE morning was as bright as a freshly sliced peach. Its colors lay around him like a scarf, snug and warming yet brittle, foretelling winter. He kicked at some leaves that had colored, fallen, and been blown into a pile at the base of a spindly aspen planted near the edge of the parking lot, at a point just south of the slot D.T. rented for four hundred bucks a year from a municipal corporation under investigation for corruption. D.T. feared the little aspen, already leafless, would soon become lifeless from the fumes it breathed each day. D.T. also feared its carcass would remain in place forever, symbolic of existence, an affront to his every morning. He wondered whether euthanasia was a defense to the murder of baby trees.

The palsied elevator raised him to his floor. He opened the door to his office and stood for a moment, transfixed by the sight of Bobby E. Lee typing words at the rate of ninety-five per minute. "What are you doing on Thursday?" D.T. asked as the shiny ball of type completed another manic whirl.

Bobby E. Lee didn't look up. D.T. repeated his question, then realized Bobby couldn't hear him because of the headset that admitted to his ears only the barely cogent murmurs from D.T.'s latest cassette of dictation.

D.T. walked over and tapped his secretary on the shoulder. Bobby E. Lee removed the foam-covered ear pieces and raised his brows. "What are you doing Thursday?" D.T. asked again. "Are you going over the river and through the woods or anything like that?"

Bobby E. Lee ran a hand through his curly hair. "If you want me to work I suppose I can."

D.T. sighed. "I don't need you to work; I was just wondering if you had a place to go."

Bobby E. Lee smiled. "I do, actually. Phil's parents have invited him home for the first time since the Bicentennial. They said he could bring a friend."

"Phil. Do I know Phil?"

"No."

"New?"

"Quite."

"Congratulations."

"Thank you."

"I didn't like that other guy, the one with the diamond in his nose."

"I know you didn't."

"It showed?"

"It showed."

"I hope it didn't cause you problems."

Bobby E. Lee shook his head. "Tod got high on disapproval."

D.T. inquired no further. "What have we got this week?"

"Well, there's no Fiasco. That's the good news. Judge Hoskins is taking Friday off. The bad news is, tomorrow's the Stone deposition."

"Already? I thought it was next week."

"Tomorrow. It's on the calendar, should you care to consult it."

D.T. absorbed the sarcasm as his due. "Do I have time to prepare?"

"Later today you do. If you don't dally over lunch. Tomorrow morning's that funeral for your classmate."

Heart. Forty-six. In the middle of *voir dire*. A definite harbinger. "Anything else?"

"Two dittos this morning. Routine."

"How do we stand with your salary?"

"Two thousand at the end of the month will get us square," Bobby E. Lee said quickly.

Bobby E. Lee was clearly tired of bearing more than his share of the fallout from the financial incompetence that seared the office. D.T. needed to come up with a

Christmas bonus that would make it up to Bobby, once and for all. But how? Maybe a quick trip to Reno. Or a big bet on the Niners. Or another dip in the well that was Michele.

"I'll try to scrape it up," D.T. said. "Has the copy machine been fixed?"

"Nope. Rental is three months in arrears. They won't come until it's current."

"How about the letterhead?"

"The printer will deliver it tomorrow. C.O.D."

"And in the meantime?"

"Toilet tissue." Bobby E. Lee laughed, then turned back to his machine and spun the platen. "And if you were about to invite me someplace for Thanksgiving dinner, thank you. It was nice of you to think of me."

D.T. nodded. As usual, their eyes zigged and zagged, never met. He went into his private office and sat behind his desk.

The morning mail was piled in front of him, envelopes slit, contents not extracted. He flipped quickly through the jumble: gaudy brochures promoting everything from personal computers to private detectives; the state bar journal, as foreign to his practice as *Scientific American;* résumés from job applicants, one of whom had written him six times, another of whom offered to work for free for six months on a trial basis, a third of whom enclosed an 8 × 10 color photograph of her standing on what looked like the bleachers at Stanford Stadium; an introductory offer from one of the several newspapers that specialized in the hot blood of legal gossip, whispering to the few who cared which firms were breaking up and why and which partner had walked off with the most wealthy and litigious clients. Two of last month's statements returned as undeliverable. Various legal papers that had been filed or served, on him or by him. A motion seeking a thousand dollars in sanctions for D.T.'s failure to file timely answers to interrogatories and for imposing baseless objections to same. A notice that one of his contested matters had been placed on the dismissal calendar for his failure to prosecute the action. A request that default judgment be entered against his client in a suit to collect damages for inter-spousal assault, on the ground that he had failed to amend his complaint as ordered by the judge. And one last item: a note from his process server, indicating he had not yet located one Delbert Wesley Finders and thus had not effected personal service of the petition for dissolution filed by his wife, Lucinda, or the restraining orders obtained by her lawyer, Jones. Reimbursable expenses totalled forty-seven dollars. Payment would be expected before further efforts would be undertaken to locate the subject.

Christ. He thought that had been taken care of a long time ago. Lucinda should have had her interlocutory decree by now. Instead, Del hadn't been served so the case hadn't begun. How had it slipped by him? How about all the others? He supposed there were reasons for them, excuses for his neglect, but he couldn't think of what they were. Bobby E. Lee would know, though. Good old Bobby. The shepherd of his life.

D.T. tossed the relevant documents into his Out Box and tossed the rest of it into the circular file, all but the subtly erotic glossy of the member of the Stanford class of '84. That he pinned to the corkboard on the wall behind his desk, just below the row of Guindon cartoons that had struck him as particularly illuminating of his life.

As he finished with the photo, Bobby E. Lee brought in his phone messages. After glancing through them all, D.T. returned only the most essential calls, the ones from colleagues from whom he needed favors or from clients from whom he needed money. The rest of them, the majority, the ones urging him to action, all those he ignored.

The first call was to a lawyer whose client had not submitted his itemization of the amounts spent for the child's support, leaving D.T. unable to determine who would have the right to claim the kid as a tax deduction. D.T. made a few mentions of past cooperation, a few forecasts of future complications, and extracted the lawyer's promise to goose his client in the ass. The last call was to a woman whose ex-husband had defaulted on the mortgage and left the city without word to anyone, perhaps carrying out a threat that 50 percent of them made at some time or another—to run away, plant a crop, write a novel, fuck the rest of it, the job included; let the bitch pay her own way for once in her life, I'd rather rot in jail than pay her one more dime. D.T. had nothing cheery to tell the woman, and hung up helplessly while she sobbed in strangled squeaks.

After the calls, D.T. fixed himself a drink and plucked a file from the bottom of the high pile on the back corner of his desk and dictated a motion for a modification of separate maintenance and child support, along with the standard points and authorities and a declaration by the ex-wife that her husband had recently been promoted to assistant vice president at the bank, that she was informed and believed that his salary had increased from eighteen hundred to twenty-one hundred a month, and that therefore she should be entitled to an additional one hundred fifty a month for support of their two increasingly expensive sons. A large portion of that amount, if awarded, would go to the boys' video game habit, D.T. happened to know, but what the hell. Divorced kids got a right to play Pac-Man, too. And if the guy was too stupid to keep his promotions secret, well, that was *his* problem.

D.T. flipped the cassette into his Out Box and went over to his library table and tried to advance the current appellate brief-in-progress. This one challenged the constitutionality of a state statute decreeing that the cohabitation of a supported former spouse created a presumption of a decreased need of support. His claim that the Person-of-the-Opposite-Sex-Sharing-Living-Quarters concept violated equal protection and due process standards had less chance than a snowball in Siam. Fortunately he was getting paid for it. The client who was shacking up happened to be sharing the shack with a guy who'd made a fortune in the chocolate business and the woman was suing to keep her ex-husband's alimony level at its dizzying height only because he had once screwed his mistress in their waterbed.

The brief wasn't finished because he wasn't motivated. When he wasn't motivated, legal research held the same attraction as hardrock mining in the month of July. Still, there was a deadline. Something else he had to do.

He was musing over a bet on the Celtics-Lakers game when Bobby E. Lee poked his head in the door once again. "Lunch," he said.

"Already?"

"I'm hungry."

"Okay. Don't book anything for the rest of the day; I have to prepare for the Stone deposition. Where is it?"

"Here."

"Time?"

"Two."

"Has Mrs. Stone called about anything?"

"Not for a long time."

"Has she paid her bills?"

"Yes."

"How much did we get her in temporary support?"

"Three thousand per month."

"Okay. Dine well."

"At Leo's? You must be kidding."

Bobby E. Lee went away, leaving D.T. to his routine. He fixed another drink, then went to the file cabinet in the anteroom, pulled out the Stone file, and took it to his desk. Not much in it, really. Petition and Response. Income and Expense Declaration. Order for temporary custody and support and property restraint after the motion for same. D.T.'s perfunctory set of interrogatories to the petitioner and a basic request for admissions, drawing predictable answers and objections from Dick Gardner, Chas Stone's attorney. He noticed he had attached a subpoena duces tecum to the notice of deposition, requesting production of a host of Chas Stone's business records. Which meant he would need the copy machine. Which meant he would have to pay the bill. He picked up the phone and bet a nickel on the Celtics, taking the points.

Oddly, there had been no corresponding notice of deposition filed by Dick Gardner. Apparently he had no wish to examine Mareth Stone. Indeed, the only document filed by Gardner was a memo to set the case for trial. D.T. had not opposed it, and the trial date had been set for some three months hence. Quick, but why not? Unless there were disasters lurking in the testimony of Chas Stone, allegations and charges that D.T. had not considered. Then he would have to scramble, perhaps beg the court for a continuance, perhaps lie like hell to get it. All in a day's work.

D.T. pulled out a legal pad and started making notes.

While he was crafting the opening questions the telephone rang. In the absence of Bobby E. Lee, D.T. pushed a button and answered it.

"D.T.? Dick Gardner."

"Dick. How are you?"

"Fine, D.T. You?"

"Great."

"The Stone thing still set for tomorrow?"

"Yep."

"Two o'clock? Your place?"

"Right."

"Good."

A silence. The inevitable prelude to negotiation. D.T. could hardly wait.

He considered Dick Gardner a friend, had picked Gardner to be his own lawyer during his divorce from Michele, had once nominated him for president of the bar association, in the days before he quit paying his dues. In a world where there were three kinds of lawyers—those committed to their clients, those committed to the system, and those committed to themselves—D.T. placed himself in category one, and Dick Gardner definitely in number two. Gardner was among that most endangered of species—a generalist, a trial lawyer as comfortable in the criminal courts as he was doing commercial litigation on behalf of a major bank or business that held a mortgage on half the world. He was the one they called when things got sticky and slimy and hit the papers, when the only way out was hardball. Dick Gardner, in other words, was the lawyer D.T. had always wanted to be himself, was the lawyer D.T. would have been had a different kind of person walked through his door and asked for help.

"I had a talk with my client yesterday," Gardner began.

"How uncommonly professional of you."

Gardner chuckled dryly. "He's not looking forward to his deposition. Nothing to do with the case, of course, but it's come at an inconvenient time, businesswise, and, well . . ."

"I know, I know," D.T. interjected. "So what's your offer?"

Gardner coughed and cleared his throat. "Mr. Stone

has instructed me to tell you he's prepared to be very generous to Mrs. Stone. *Very* generous. Much more so than I would advise him to be.''

"Okay, Dick. I'll play the game. How generous is 'very'?''

"Well, we haven't discussed the details, but basically he's talking property settlement of fifty thousand, lump sum, plus the house, plus the newest Mercedes. Plus two thousand a month alimony.''

"How much child support?'' D.T. asked quickly.

Gardner hesitated, telegraphing what was coming. "That's the quid pro quo, of course. Stone gets exclusive custody of the children. With generous visitation, naturally.''

"Naturally.'' D.T. said nothing further.

"Well? How's it grab you?''

D.T. swore. "You know damned well it's out of the question, Dick. Even putting the custody thing aside, the money is ridiculous. And even if it wasn't, no way she's going to give up those kids.''

"It's possible he'd go a bit higher with the property division, D.T. If a schedule could be worked out so it's paid over ten years or so, couch it as alimony so it would be deductible to him.''

"Forget it, Dick. Mrs. Stone's not going to push her kids into the pot. Now, if he's willing to concede custody, and talk sense on the money issues, then I'm certainly willing to listen.''

"Will you mention our offer to your client?''

"Oh, sure, Dick. I'll do that. And you mention to *your* client that we'll settle for four hundred thousand property, plus house and car, plus four thousand alimony plus three thousand child support plus exclusive custody. With generous visitation rights. Naturally.''

Dick Gardner laughed, then paused. "You're not going to like what you're going to hear tomorrow, D.T.,'' he said seriously.

"I don't suppose I will. Prevarication invariably depresses me.''

"Stone's not a bad guy.''

"Sure. That's why he sprang this thing on his wife like a clown with a whoopee cushion. That's why he emptied the bank accounts and deposit boxes before he told her he was bailing out. Christ, he even snatched her jewelry.''

"I didn't advise that particular tactic, by the way,'' Gardner said. "One of his business buddies told him that was the way the game was played.''

"Well, he was right, wasn't he?''

Gardner paused. "I guess he was.''

"At least he didn't snatch the kids. These days that entitles him to a good conduct medal.''

"Have you seen them?'' Gardner asked.

"Who?''

"The kids.''

"No.''

"Beautiful.''

"All kids are beautiful for about ten years. Then they're not kids. What's the point?''

"They could be in a significant degree of jeopardy, D.T. I just thought I'd mention it.''

"Jeopardy from whom?''

"Your client.''

"Oh, bullshit. Why would Mareth Stone endanger her own children?''

"Because she's not well. Based on what Stone tells me, I'd say she was unquestionably antisocial. Perhaps even psychotic.''

"I guess that's why I haven't seen you around lately, huh, Dick? Been over at the med school, doing your psychiatric residency.''

Gardner laughed. "Just trying to help, D.T. I don't expect you to take my word for it.''

"Good.''

"Also, I wanted you to know why I haven't been playing games with this one. We want an early trial and a final determination of custody as soon as possible.''

"So do we.''

"Then I guess I'll see you tomorrow.''

"Right.''

"Buy you a drink afterward?''

"You're on.''

"Who do you like in the Jets game?''

"Whoever's playing the Jets.''

D.T. hung up, supercharged by the taste of combat. Toe to toe with the great Dick Gardner. D.T. was going to whip his ass. He called his bookie and bet a dollar on a junior welterweight he had had his eye on for six months, and another on whoever was playing the Jets, he didn't need to know the line.

The routine dittos came and went, one uttering oaths, the other prayers. When they had gone, D.T. snuck out to the greasy spoon down the block, the one that obeyed him when he declined the special sauce and made the only double-breaded cheeseburger in the state. Then he returned to the Stone file and his note pad, wondering about the fix Mareth Stone might have put him in by leading him to believe she was normal.

In the beginning he had believed them all. Later, he had assumed they all were liars. Now, hostage to experience, he was beyond generalization. He had believed Mareth Stone because it was convenient, as a result had done less than he should have to prepare a defense to the charge that she was unworthy of her children. He should already have talked to friends and enemies, doctors and teachers and preachers, everyone who was in the bleachers as she lived her life. Instead, he had let it slide.

More and more of them seemed to be sliding lately. Maybe because the kind of truth he needed took hard work to uncover. Maybe because it was the kind of truth he liked less and less to learn. Maybe because these days he frequently found himself intoxicated by about three in the afternoon. Maybe, in Mareth Stone's case, because she was rich and confident and thus reminded him of his ex-wife, who needed no help from him or anyone. Clearly it was he who was unfit. Luckily, fitness was a standard lawyers never had to meet once they'd passed the bar.

He went back to the file. The notes he had made after his conversations with her over the three months since she'd first walked through his door—his initial calls so frequent he seemed willing her to have a problem he could solve—indicated she was adjusting nicely to the breakup. When the order was entered giving her temporary custody and support she had brought the children back from her parents' home and continued their lives more or less as usual. She had provided D.T. with the lists of assets and expenses he requested, a description of her children's typical day, a few other odds and ends, and had ended every conversation as soon as was politely possible. As far as he knew she had received no communication from her husband beyond the arrangements necessary to visit the kids. She had never called for help, never for advice or reassurance, never to criticize, never for anything. Each time he had prodded she had insisted life was fine. Which made him uneasy as hell. From just such stuff came ruin.

In a light sweat, D.T. began making further notes for his interrogation. By the time he finished he was thirsty. As he was on his way out the door, plunging headlong for the corner bar, he encountered a pristine apparition that moved toward him down the dingy hall like the ghost of all his former clients, determined to lay him waste.

■ ELEVEN

HELLO, Miss Holloway. On duty, I see.''
She came up short, startled. Reflexively, she raised her attaché case, blocking him. The look on her face suggested she perpetually feared assault. He wondered if all women did. "Oh. Mr. Jones. Hello." She blinked and lowered the case to her side, exhaling enough air to sail a sloop.

"I was just thinking about you," D.T. said.

"Really?"

"I was wondering what had happened to you, and hoping nothing bad had happened to Mrs. Preston."

Rita Holloway shook her head. "She's fine, given her circumstances. Which are pretty much the same as when you saw her. I've just come from there, in fact. Can I talk to you about it?" She looked toward the dark door to his empty office.

D.T.'s eyes followed her glance. "I was about to go have a beer. How about joining me? We can talk there."

She thought it over, then nodded. D.T. took her arm and led her back to the elevator. Three minutes later they were entering the Walrus, inhaling fumes of disinfectant and stale beer, hearing the hush of regulars who had begun their task long before noon, viewing a dispiriting tableau that featured only respect for your troubles. D.T. loved the place. Russ, the bartender, waved at D.T. and shouted. "Who you like on T-Day, Steelers or Lions?"

"Neither," D.T. yelled back. "Boredom in a walk." D.T. looked at Rita Holloway. "We'll have a beer and . . ."

"Whiskey sour."

173

D.T. repeated her order, then led Rita Holloway to a booth near the back, out of earshot of anyone who could still decipher a sentence.

Like a marshmallow in a brownie, her uniform quarreled mightily with her surroundings. As she slid warily into the booth she brushed her hand across the tabletop, then rubbed her fingers like a safecracker, then whistled. "I hate to think what kind of spores are growing in those cracks."

"Bars aren't places to think, Miss Holloway. Bars are places to do the opposite."

They were silent while Russ served the drinks and rolled his eyes and flashed the high sign, all a burlesque indication that he was favorably impressed by D.T.'s companion. After Russ had gone, D.T. drained half his draught. "So," he began. "What have you been up to?" He licked away the itch of foam from his upper lip before she answered.

Rita Holloway's hot eyes flashed in the black of the back of the bar. "You know damned well what I've been up to, Mr. Jones. I've been playing Nancy Drew, just like you told me to."

His fears confirmed, D.T. leaned back against the back of the booth until it groaned. "All this time?"

"Yes."

"Find anything?" He sighed against the answer.

"That's for you to tell me, isn't it, Mr. Attorney-and-Counselor-at-Law?" Her eyes dared him to deny it.

"I guess it is," he said, then said it once again.

D.T. drained his beer as Rita Holloway reached over and pulled her briefcase from the bench beside her, placed it on her lap, snapped its latches, and reached inside and pulled out a sheaf of papers an inch or more in thickness. She closed the briefcase, set the papers on top of it, and squared their edges, making a perfect pile. "I have an abstract," she said. "Do you want to read it?"

D.T. checked his watch, considered claiming an appointment or an ailment. "I don't suppose we could do this on Friday," he said finally.

"No. We couldn't." Rita Holloway looked capable of false imprisonment.

"Okay," he said. "If we're going to do it let's do it

systematically. Before you tell me what you've found, tell me where you've looked."

She picked through her papers and pulled out the fourth sheet from the top. "I have the list right here."

"Read it to me. Just the essentials."

She wriggled to a more comfortable position and took a hefty drink of her whiskey sour, leaving a red smear on the glass. "I examined records in the following locations, for the years 1960 through 1967, to include five years before and two years after the divorce. Here in the county, I went to the assessor's office, recorder's office, treasurer's office, and clerk's office. At the state capitol, I went to the secretary of state's office, corporations commissioner's office, insurance commissioner's office, and the Department of Agriculture."

"Department of Agriculture?"

"I thought Dr. Preston might have owned a farm. Lots of doctors buy farms. For tax reasons."

"Good thinking."

"Most of the records involved a search for real property or for some sort of corporate affiliation." She looked at D.T.

"Right," he said, to please her.

"I also checked the litigation records in the clerk's office, and the motor vehicle records and the records at the Department of Transportation which show ownership of boats or airplanes."

"Jesus."

"Also," she plunged on, "I have the names of Dr. Preston's former medical partners, and the names of the bank and savings and loan he and Esther patronized in those days. I understand banking records can be secured but I don't know how. Also, I have the names of their stock broker and the realtor who sold them the house they bought in 1964." Rita Holloway looked up from her papers, pleased with herself, ready for a fight. D.T. was again amazed at how many people in the world loved a good scrap. And at how few of them were lawyers and how many of them were women.

"How about the tax returns?" D.T. asked.

Rita Holloway shook her head. "She doesn't have them. I asked."

"Too bad," D.T. said. "Now, before we get to the bottom line, tell me. Which of the people you named have you talked to?"

"What?"

"Which of the doctors or the broker or the realtor did you talk to about Mrs. Preston?"

Her back straightened. "None of them. You told me not to."

"I know what I told you, Miss Holloway. And I know that somehow Dr. Preston learned I sicked you onto him. The other night I met him at a party. He asked what the hell I was up to, quote, unquote. I thought he was going to punch me out."

Rita Holloway frowned and gulped her drink. "But I didn't . . . it must have been Janice."

"Who?"

"Janice Cox. I roomed with her in nursing school. She works for a neurologist named Haskell. By coincidence, Dr. Haskell used to be in partnership with Nathaniel Preston, back when he was married to Esther. Later they had a falling-out. It was very bitter, but no one seems to know why."

"And you talked over poor Esther's problem with your old friend Janice."

"Yes. I'm afraid I did." Momentarily, the spunk had gone out of her, leaving her an entirely different creature. D.T. marvelled at the change, then watched her essence grow back as quickly as a weed.

"And you happened to mention to Janice that the shyster you'd prevailed upon to help you out in all this was a sap named Jones. D.T. Jones, to be exact."

She nodded slowly. "What does the D.T. stand for, anyway?"

"Double Talk. Well, you can count on Dr. Preston knowing all there is to know about our little plan to gouge some bucks out of him, Miss Holloway."

"I'm sorry. I didn't . . . I'm sorry."

"He offered ten thousand to settle the thing, by the way," D.T. added casually. "To get me and Esther off his back for good."

"Really? That much?"

"Really."

"Are we going to take it?"

"I don't think so."

"Why not? I mean, that's quite a bit of money. What if we end up getting nothing?"

"If you wanted someone to fold up at the first offer on the table you should have stayed downtown. Preston got to ten grand awfully fast. We haven't even filed against him yet. If he'll go ten now he'll go thirty the morning of trial. Maybe more."

It was more complicated than that—Preston had, after all, sworn not to pay a dime—but he saw no need to mention it. If Rita Holloway hadn't come up with hard evidence of fraudulent concealment, or if the Supreme Court eventually ruled a professional degree wasn't a marital asset or that a claim against the degree could not be asserted retroactively, then he would be thrown out of court on a motion for summary judgment and the ten grand in the hand would have indeed beaten the thirty in the bush. The wages of litigation. The greatest game in town next to a private casino he knew of near his office.

"Besides," D.T. added finally. "The guy seemed awfully upset. I mean, at best we've got a trivial claim if he's as rich as everyone says he is, but he's taking it very seriously. So I think we should play him a little." He smiled. "But of course Mrs. Preston is the boss. You talk to her and tell me what she thinks."

Rita Holloway nodded thoughtfully. D.T. waved for Russ to bring another round. When the drinks arrived Rita Holloway pushed hers away with a frown. "Have we covered all the rocks you've looked under, Miss Holloway?" D.T. asked when Russ had gone.

"Yes."

"So. Did you find any hidden assets? Did Dr. Preston own half of downtown Phoenix back in 1964 and neglect to mention it at the time of their divorce? Have we stumbled onto a treasure trove, Miss Holloway?"

Rita Holloway drummed her fingers on the table, so incensed at his levity she was oblivious to the grime. "Have I looked everywhere there is to look?" she asked.

"Pretty much."

"What if I haven't found anything?"

"Then that about wraps it up."

"But . . ."

"But what?"

"Isn't there anything *you* can do?"

"Like what?"

"I don't know. Talk to people."

"What people?"

"The doctors. The stock broker. I don't know. *Anyone.*" The last word caused two heads at the bar to turn their way, though not for long.

"You're saying you didn't find anything," D.T. said quietly.

"Yes. That's exactly what I'm saying. I didn't find one goddamned thing except some records that listed the little bitty house they lived in. That's it. I had to put up with all those stuffy lazy bureaucrats who had so goddamned many other things to do other than help me and that's all I came up with. Nothing."

She started to cry and hated herself because of it. D.T. could see her face reflected in the curved flank of his beer glass. It seemed to have broken into pieces. D.T. put his hand over the one of hers that wasn't swiping at her eyes. "Hey. It's all right. Come on. It's all right."

"How can I face her, Mr. Jones? I practically *promised* her I'd do something."

"I'm sure she didn't expect a miracle."

"But don't you see? I *wanted* her to expect a miracle."

She cried again, but only briefly, then blew her nose and picked up her research papers and started to put them back in her briefcase. "Why don't you take those over to my office so I can make a copy of them for me to keep."

"Why?"

"Who knows? Something might come up."

D.T. remembered the copy machine was broken. "Better yet," he amended, "wait here. There's a copy service down the block. I'll run the papers down there and get them started. By the time we finish our drinks they'll be copied and you can pick up the originals and be on your way."

D.T. grabbed her briefcase and trotted out of the bar with it, leaving a protesting Rita Holloway and a quizzical Russ behind him. Luckily, the copy service wasn't busy. Also luckily, their only competent employee was on duty. "Xerox down again?" he asked.

D.T. didn't have a Xerox, and what he had wasn't down so much as underfinanced, but he didn't say that. What he said was, "Rush." Then he returned to the nurse in the bar.

She looked at him disgustedly as he took his seat. "While you were gone your friend made a pass at me."

"Did you catch it?"

"Of course not."

D.T. shrugged. "He likes to keep in shape during the off-season."

Rita Holloway started to counter, then paused, then spoke so softly he had to learn forward to hear. "Did I do everything that could be done, Mr. Jones?"

D.T. nodded.

"Will you please keep trying? Will you try to think of something that might work?"

D.T. thought of his ex-wife and his daughter, and of what they seemed to think of him. "Okay. But don't hold your breath. And don't tell Esther Preston I'm about to be her savior, because it's most likely not true."

Rita Holloway stood up and slid out of the booth. He told her where to go to get her papers and she thanked him as she shifted nervously about, unwilling to meet his eye. "I think somehow you're going to find a way to help, Mr. Jones. Is that silly of me?"

"Extremely."

"Well, I hope . . . I just hope, I guess." She stuck out her hand and shook his when he grasped it, then turned and left.

When she had vanished Russ came over to his booth. "New squeeze?"

"Client."

"Yeah? Probably got a big itch down there, now she's not getting it regular."

"She's not that kind of client."

"Yeah?"

"Yeah."

"So excuse me all to hell. What's the matter with you, anyhow? You been about as cheery as a Jesuit lately. You in hock to the book, or what?"

"That. Other things. Who the hell knows?" Or cares, he almost added.

"You got what they call the male menopause, D.T. I read about it in the *Enquirer*."

"Bullshit."

"No. Really. Men get it too, just like the broads. Makes everything seem the shits for about two years."

"Then maybe that's what I've got. Only I've had it since I was nineteen."

Russ chuckled. "So what you got going for you in the courts, D.T.? Class action, wrongful death, Arab divorce, any of that big bucks shit?" Russ picked up Rita Holloway's glass and wiped the table beneath it, then drank its dregs.

"I got nothing going for me in the courts at all, Russ. Nothing but a Ditto List as long as your arm."

"Ditto List? What's that mean?"

"That's the thing about the Ditto List. It's totally, wholly, and always meaningless."

D.T. pushed his way out of the booth and headed for the lot where he parked his car. Halfway there he detoured sharply and went back to his office.

It was dark and cold, a catacomb that bore the bones of a thousand lifeless marriages. He turned on the desk lamp and walked to various corners of the room, extracting academic journals and advance sheets, looseleaf binders and law reviews, and took them to his desk. He read through them slowly, *Family Law Quarterly* and the *Journal of Family Law*, *New Law Journal* and *Practical Lawyer*, *Law & Society Review* and *Current Legal Problems*, even the *Women Lawyers Journal*, as well as more general periodicals that occasionally bore upon his specialty, getting up to date, absorbing the most recent developments in that déclassé branch of the law on which he perched as precariously as a dove on opening day of the season.

He read for two hours, making notes, dictating file memos, applying what he read to his own Ditto List of active cases that he carried like a menu in his mind. "Evicting the Recalcitrant Spouse"; "Bargaining in the Shadow of the Law—The Case of Divorce"; "Nontraditional Lifestyles and the Law"; "Wifebeating: A Psycho-

Legal Analysis"; "Psychology: Impediment or Aid in Child Custody Cases"; "Dilemma v. Paradox—Valuation of an Advanced Degree upon Dissolution of a Marriage"; "Compelling Disclosure of 'Invisible Assets' Upon Divorce"; and finally, "Domestic Relations Litigation—Attorney's Fees," a gift from the current issue of *Trial*. Part of the unending stream of theory, some helpful, much naive, that had accumulated over the six months or so since he had last done the exercise. He read till his head had apparently cracked open, till it all seemed absurd and useless, then drove home, exhausted.

After changing clothes he fixed himself a drink and turned on the television. On the all-news channel a toothsome woman delivered the headlines and somehow managed to soothe him even as she read of riots and economic collapse. As she droned on he flipped through his mail and pulled forth a man's magazine and turned to the centerfold and wondered what was to be learned from such a specimen, whether it was conceivable that she knew as much as her body and her pose implied, whether such knowledge was a step toward perdition or salvation or merely a good time. Then he wondered why Michele had given him a subscription to such nonsense for his last birthday. To induce envy? Or regret? Or a longing for her own far-less-frightening physique?

The all-news became all-sports. Fights from Atlantic City. Bums. D.T. had won his last fight wager, so he was laying off, not pressing his luck. He watched the white guy get beat bloody, then listened to the list of the weekend's football games, calculated his bets, but decided to wait till later in the week to place them, when the spreads, he hoped, would lengthen. He flipped to a reprise of *Barney Miller*. Wojo dressed as a woman, a lure to muggers in the park. His first drink became his second. His doorbell rang twice before he stirred.

She didn't say a word, just shifted her bundle from one arm to the other and blinked at him uncertainly. "Hi, Mr. Jones. Remember me?"

"Sure I do. How are you, Lucinda?"

"Fine."

Her shyness grasped his heart and rubbed it. "Come in, come in," he babbled.

"You sure? I don't want to disturb nothing."

"Nonsense. Everything in here needs disturbing."

She stepped inside and he closed the door. As she passed close to him he smelled a dusty odor that harkened memories he couldn't quite identify. As she waited for him to join her she began to smile and to look from him to the package she cradled gingerly. "What's in the quilt?" he asked absently, guiding her to the living room, his hand resting lightly on the soft pillar of her back.

"My baby."

He stopped short. "Really? No kidding?"

"No kidding." Lucinda giggled and unwrapped her prize.

It was round and red and wrinkled in odd places, fast asleep, awesome. D.T. remembered his first look at Heather, displayed for him by a nurse who held her as casually as a cucumber. His heart raced now as then.

"He or she?" he asked.

Lucinda sat on the couch, as familiar with his rooms as a lover. "She."

"Name?"

"Krystle." She spelled it. "I named her after Linda Evans. You know, on *Dynasty*? She's the most beautiful woman in the world."

"It's a pretty name," D.T. said. "And she's a beautiful baby. Congratulations."

Lucinda showed a blush, as though she'd heisted rather than birthed the child. "Thanks."

"When was she born?"

"Three weeks ago. She come early. I was getting real tired of being pregnant so I climbed up on a chair one night, and jumped off a few times, and the pains come later on that morning."

D.T. was amazed. "Well. How does it feel to be a mother?"

"It feels just wonderful, Mr. Jones. At least it does when I'm not scared to death about it. Seems kind of cheating that men can't feel this same way, you ever think of it that way?"

He had, in fact, but had reached no firm conclusion, birth being as ambiguous as death. After he nodded he asked if everything had gone all right.

"Well, everything went all right for me. But Krystle, she may have some kind of heart trouble the doctor says. It's why I had to come up to the city, to see some specialist about it."

"Have you seen him yet?"

"Yep. This afternoon."

"What did he say?"

"Nothing. He took a bunch of tests and said he had to wait till the results come back. Then he'll call my doctor in Reedville. Then maybe they'll get around to telling me. They had the poor thing all wired up." Lucinda paused and looked down at the child. "Isn't she just all red and perfect, Mr. Jones? Don't seem possible there's anything wrong inside there, does it? Don't seem possible her heart could get broke so soon."

D.T. sighed. "I'm sure everything is fine, Lucinda. They can fix almost anything these days, if it isn't."

As if to dispute him, the baby began to cry. "She's hungry, poor thing." Lucinda hesitated. "Would it bother you if I fed her, Mr. Jones? I mean, I can go if it would. I can't stay long, anyway. I just wanted you to see the baby 'cause, well, I knew you was worried that one time."

"No, no. That would be fine," D.T. said, eagerness heating him like a wind. "Go right ahead. Do you need anything?"

"I got it all right here," she said, laughing marvelously, perhaps to mock him, certainly not to tease.

He watched her lift the hem of her blouse above her massive brassiere, unsnap a flap, and expose a nipple that was stretched to disturbing dimensions by its function. The baby reached for the tit eagerly, closed her eyes, soon sucked noiselessly. Lucinda wore an expression D.T. had seen only on someone in a spell.

Fascination overcame his embarrassment and his yen. He continued to gaze upon the scene even when Lucinda opened her eyes and caught him. "It'll only be a minute," she said, reinserting the nipple as it popped away from the tiny mouth. "Sometimes I wish she'd keep at it longer. I think these things is about to bust."

D.T. was enraptured. Michele's breasts had somehow malfunctioned, and Heather had been raised on bottles and formula and soy-based liquids out of cans. "What does that feel like?" he asked, compelled to say something.

"I can't explain, exactly. It's just so . . . warm. Like when you get a puppy, maybe. And hold him and think he's always going to be there and love you and do what you want him to. . . ." Lucinda's voice trailed off. D.T. wondered what had happened to her puppy. The baby slipped from sustenance to sleep.

"You know what I wonder, Mr. Jones?"

"What?"

"I wonder it tastes like. My milk, I mean." She started to reach down and snap her flap, then looked at him. "Do you know?"

He shook his head.

"I thought maybe you'd had a taste when you had your baby."

"My wife's milk didn't come. Something went wrong."

"Oh." She fumbled again with her clothes. "That's real sad."

"How about you?" he said, the words as thin as his courage. "Do you want a taste?"

She laughed. "They're big but they ain't *that* big."

"You could put some in a glass. Do you want me to get one?"

"I . . . is it bad? To do that?"

"How could it be?"

"Well. Sure. It's just, I been wondering, you know?"

He went to the kitchen and took a goblet from the cupboard, the most delicate he had, and took it to her. She lowered her flap and grasped her breast with one hand while the other raised the glass to the bulging nipple. She squeezed once, and then again, and a thin white fluid leaked forth, accidentally it seemed, and dripped slowly into the glass, its droplets making the only sounds in the room beyond the baby's peaceful wheeze.

She squeezed thrice more, inspecting only her work. "I feel like a big old Guernsey," she said after a minute, not looking at him.

"Everybody needs milk," he said inanely.

When there was half an inch of nectar in the bottom of

the glass Lucinda stopped milking herself and raised the goblet and inspected it. "Kind of funny-looking."

"Maybe you haven't been eating enough grass."

She smiled and looked at him. "Are you sure it's all right?"

"Sure."

She tipped the glass and wet her lips, then licked them, then frowned. "What flavor?" he asked, his sense escaped.

She took another swallow, then extended the glass to him.

"No." Their eyes locked.

"Yes. I want you to."

"No, Lucinda."

"Please? It's the only thing I got to give you."

He took the glass and closed his eyes and drank the smallest drop he could. Its taste barely stained his whirling mind. Mysterious. Chalky. Watery. Warm. Unearthly. "Thank you," he said, and offered her the glass.

She shook her head. "It ain't good enough for seconds."

He took the goblet to the kitchen and started to rinse it out, then put it back in the cupboard instead, just in front of the cereal boxes, where he would see it every morning and monitor the evaporation of its contents into the very air he breathed. Then he went back to the living room.

Lucinda had redressed her bosom and laid the baby on the couch, snug in its lively quilt. Like a wound, a dark stain spread across Lucinda's blouse at the point over the nipple that had fed them all. "Can I get you something to eat? Or drink?" He looked for signs of shame and found none. He wondered what he showed himself.

Lucinda shook her head. "I'm on a diet. I put on a bunch of weight while I was carrying and I got to get it off. Besides, I got to go. I just wanted to come by and thank you again for being so nice to me that night with Del."

"It was nothing. Forget about it."

"Well, I haven't noticed many people in this town going out of their way to help someone. Not without wanting something back they shouldn't have. You're special to me, Mr. Jones. I wanted to tell it to your face.''

D.T. fidgeted, not knowing what to do but thank her. Lucinda rewrapped her child and gathered it in her arms. "So how's your love life, Mr. Jones?" she asked with a twinkle.

D.T. laughed. "Occasional," he said. "How's yours?"

Lucinda shook her head. "Pregnant women aren't in heavy demand down in Reedville," she said. "And besides, I think I'll stay away from that stuff for a while. I had me an epee—"

"Episiotomy," D.T. offered.

"Yeah. Right. How did you know?"

"My ex-wife had one, too. She sat on a doughnut for a while."

"Well, I didn't let them give me one of *them*," Lucinda said, "but I don't feel much like loving, either."

"Which reminds me," D.T. said. "There's a little problem in your divorce case."

Lucinda frowned. "What kind of problem?"

"We haven't been able to locate Del. Which means we haven't been able to serve him with the petition, to get things started. There are other ways to do it, but because Del seemed so wild about the whole thing I wanted to try to serve him personally, to avoid any technical problems later on. You don't happen to know where he's living now, do you?"

"I . . . no. No, I don't."

"Are you sure?"

Lucinda didn't say anything.

"When did you see him last?" D.T. asked, under sudden strain. "Have you seen him since the night he beat you up?"

"Yeah."

"How many times?"

"Twice."

"Where?"

"He come down to Reedville. Him and my brother got in a fight the last time and he ain't been back."

"Did he tell you where he was living, Lucinda?"

"I guess."

"Where?"

"Houston Street. They repossessed his trailer so he got an apartment."

"What number?"

"Twenty forty-two."

"Lucinda?"

"Yeah?"

"Where are you staying tonight?"

"I . . . home."

"It's a long way to Reedville."

She drew her baby to her more firmly. "I know. That's why I got to get going."

"Are you staying with Del tonight, Lucinda? Is that where you're going from here? To Del's place so he can batter you again?" His anger frightened and surprised her.

"I . . . he ain't seen the baby, Mr. Jones. He has a right to see the baby."

"Even after what he did to you?"

"Even after that. I mean, in a way he done it 'cause he loved me. In a way. And he's real sorry about what happened. Really."

D.T. sighed. He could have debated and argued and pleaded, and with some women it might have done some good, but not with this one. "Then let me go with you."

"No. I couldn't do that. No."

"Then wait till tomorrow."

"He works days, Mr. Jones. Night's the only time he's got."

"Goddamnit, Lucinda. I just wish you wouldn't go over there."

She grinned as though he had cautioned against crossing against the light. "I'll be all right. Really, I will."

"I'll be here, if you need to call," was all he said.

"Thanks, Mr. Jones. You're just too nice to me."

"You're easy to be too nice to."

He helped her stand and accompanied her to the door. She waved good-bye and left. D.T. found himself gazing for a long time at the door through which she'd vanished, dreaming dreams that disturbed him.

Two minutes later he got up and went to the phone, raised the receiver and heard the buzz that told him it was working, would transmit a call for help. Then he made himself a sandwich of Skippy and grape jelly and went back to the TV to watch the Monday night game, Cosell off, his thoughts on a kind of violence that wasn't part of games, remembering articles he'd read earlier—"Defense Strategies for Battered Women Who Assault Their Mates"; "Battered Wives' Dilemma—To Kill or Be Killed"; "Conjugal Violence—The Law of Force & The Force of Law." At halftime he went out to the garage, got in his car, and drove to Houston Street.

The number Lucinda had given him was a four-unit box much like his own, cheap and featureless. D.T. parked down the block and walked to the door and checked the mailboxes. None of the names were Delbert's or anything close. He walked around the building along a slab of parking spaces and looked in as many windows as he could. No humans could be seen, just the things they liked to live with, curtains and cats and hanging plants. In the farthest parking place from the street he saw a shiny car, an early fifties Ford, a common rock that had become a jewel. The number painted on the asphalt beneath it was 2.

D.T. went back to his own car and drove nearer to the apartment building and parked again, close enough, he hoped, to hear any screams that might emerge. He rolled down his car window and slumped down in the seat and felt the night air turn cool as the moon rose and the hours passed. No one came or went. One by one, all the lights in the apartment building went out, including the one he watched dejectedly.

■ TWELVE

THE funeral crept over D.T. like a fog, lingering, hushed, insubstantial. The words he heard were senseless, appropriate to no one, particularly not to the man who lay within the teakwood box, the man who had urged, cursed, threatened, and bluffed his way through the city's courts for twenty years, asking no quarter and giving none, sworn enemy of every being who disputed him, whether judge or lawyer or lying mortal. D.T. smiled to himself behind the reverent drone. Ben Styles had been a brawler, feared because he respected only victory, honorable only in his candor, laudable only in his energies. No religion could contain him, though most would try.

The chapel was full, Styles' many clients shoulder to shoulder with the lawyers who hoped to fill his shoes and thus usurp his clients. Joining the long line of hypocrites, D.T. expressed his condolences to the tiny widow. She seemed not to know him from the others fore and aft, though he had met her several times. He wondered if she knew Ben had once discussed with him the financial ramifications of divorcing her. Their immensity had dissuaded Styles from making the move. D.T. recalled Styles' mention of a younger woman. He cast his eyes across the mourners for a conceivable candidate, but found either none or many.

He was on his way out the door when a hand grasped his arm. "Mr. Jones? May I speak with you a moment?"

The man was Carter Mullins, leader of the bar, pillar of the community, paragon. D.T. wondered what strange debt Mullins owed Ben Styles, and how Mullins knew his name. "How are you, Mr. Mullins?"

"I'm fine. A sad occasion, though. Ben was important to the bar, I think."

"How?"

"He stretched the limits of the law, pushed at its edges, reminded the rest of us what it needs to encompass if it is to remain respected. Lawyers like Ben are particularly important to those of us engaged in drafting the new code of professional responsibility, don't you think?"

"I do, indeed."

"I believe you are such a lawyer yourself, Mr. Jones."

Mullins eyed him from beneath a craggy brow. D.T. didn't know what to do so he just thanked him. Mullins nodded, then guided D.T. toward the door.

"One of my partners is on the ethics committee this year; specifically, the Client Relations Board. He mentioned there have been complaints filed against you recently." Mullins looked him in the eye.

D.T. said, "Oh?"

"Apparently the problem is nothing more than a failure to keep the client informed of the progress of the case. Happens to all of us, of course. They don't understand why the machinery of justice must grind so slowly. I don't understand it myself sometimes, to be honest." Mullins chuckled once. "In any case, I thought an informal word might be in order. There's no danger of a formal inquiry at this point, as I understand it. A few status letters to the clients involved will take care of the matter, I'm sure."

Mullins expected a response, so D.T. said, "Right."

Mullins patted his shoulder. "Well, it was nice to see you again, Jones. There's a bar meeting next week. At the Hilton. Perhaps I'll see you there."

"Perhaps."

Mullins moved down the steps and entered a limousine and floated off D.T.'s portion of the earth.

The avuncular bastard. An informal word, was it? A threat, more likely. He could guess which ones had squealed on him. The bitches. Run to the bar association, would they? By the time he was through their cases would be so old the papers in the files would rot.

He seethed during the long drive back to the south side. After parking the car he stopped in the Walrus for a quick one, then went to the office. By the time he was behind his desk his thoughts were off himself and on Lucinda Finders.

She hadn't called the night before, or by the time he left for the funeral. He had fought off an impulse to return to Houston Street, knock on the door to Apartment Two, and see just what the hell was going on in the way of condonation. So as he had no facts as to her behavior, only suspicions, and like a jealous husband he imagined the very worst—that Lucinda and Delbert had once again entwined and that afterward he had punished her for straying and then for coming back.

His mind a tub of Del's malevolence, D.T. buzzed Bobby E. Lee and asked him to bring a sandwich back from lunch. Then he placed a call to Mareth Stone. Her voice still had the protective coloration he remembered, as though, like him, she had learned to beware her phone. D.T. asked her how she was getting along.

"Fine. Just fine."

"No troubles at all? Money? Loneliness? Regret? Revenge?"

"No. Nothing." Her voice was lifeless. "What is it you called about, Mr. Jones?"

"I'm taking your husband's deposition in an hour," he said. "Since you two came to blows at the mediation session, it looks like the thing will go to trial. I just wanted to touch base to see if you'd heard from him at all since he moved out."

"The closest I've come to personal contact is to see him sitting in his Jaguar on Saturday morning, waiting for the kids to run out and jump in and go off and spend money. And of course I cash his check." Her laugh was as dry as the leaves outside. "What do you expect to learn from his deposition, Mr. Jones?"

"Oh, just an update on his personal finances. And why he thinks you're not fit to have the kids."

He had meant to provoke her but she didn't respond. "Mrs. Stone?"

"I'm here. And I'm not unfit, and there's no basis for him to say I am, so you should have a very brief afternoon. Is there anything else?"

"Not at the moment, I guess. When the transcript of the deposition is ready I'll send it over to you so you can tell me what you think of his charges."

"Oh, I can tell you that right now, Mr. Jones. Do you want to hear it?" The tone was as righteous as the words he had heard beside the casket. He sensed Mareth Stone was convinced she could not be hurt by anything her husband had to say. Maybe in the old days, when a woman had to be committable for a court to take the kids from her, but not today. Not in the days of equal rights, which, while most firmly advocated by women, had in domestic relations law come to be of more substantial benefit to men, proving that the product of the union of sex and politics could only be ironic.

He considered trying to enlighten her, but decided it was not the time. "Why don't we wait?" he said wearily. "Why don't we just wait to talk about that later?" He hung up as Bobby E. Lee was bringing him his sandwich.

"Is the copy machine fixed?" he asked.

Bobby E. Lee nodded.

"Is there enough in the account to cover the rental payment?"

"Unless you've been kiting checks again."

D.T. shook his head wordlessly and Bobby E. Lee left him with his pastrami. By the time Dick Gardner and his client arrived, D.T. had forgotten everything but the allegations they were bringing with them.

Bobby E. Lee showed the two men into the private office. They shook hands all around and D.T. cleared a space at one end of his library table, brushing books and papers to the floor in the process, leaving them where they fell.

The court reporter arrived. D.T. had dated her for a time, as had many of the trial lawyers in the city. She was handsome and energetic and solely interested in making money, which she did in abundance because, like D.T., most of her dates patronized her professionally as well. Her name was Phyllis, and from the smile she exchanged with Dick Gardner he was one of her professional and private customers as well. But it wouldn't make a difference in the deposition. Once a lawyer had offered her five grand to substitute a "yes" for a "no." She had filed the original as is, but changed the lawyer's copy to "you're damned right I did."

It wasn't until D.T. switched on the ceiling lamp that the sense of Chas Stone reached him. The man was a template of propriety, theatrically handsome, immaculately dressed, with a chin that reached to Pittsburgh and a forehead that was still undamaged. He used oil on his hair and wore white shirts. His clear bright eyes and his new crisp clothes made both D.T. and Dick Gardner skulkers by comparison.

Stone seemed tolerantly amused at being where he was, above it all and then some. He smiled easily as the introductions were made, more the host than guest, wearing his holy aspect like a sash. His charm dimmed only when Bobby E. Lee entered to take orders for coffee and Chas Stone momentarily found himself the second most beautiful object in the room.

Bobby E. Lee left. Phyllis nodded she was ready. D.T. told her to go ahead. She asked Chas Stone to raise his hand, administered the oath to tell the truth, and they were under way. D.T. assembled his notes and eyed his foes. They seemed at ease and confident. He considered whether to let them remain that way.

"Usual stipulations, Mr. Jones?" Dick Gardner asked.

"To the extent you mean the deposition will proceed according to the rules of procedure for the courts of this state, then yes," D.T. said. "Signing is not waived, however." Dick Gardner nodded. D.T. cleared his throat and continued.

"Let the record reflect the presence of the deponent, Charles Stone, petitioner in the action, and of his counsel of record, Richard Gardner, Esquire. "Have you been advised of the nature of this proceeding, Mr. Stone?"

"Objection," Dick Gardner said immediately. "What Mr. Stone may have been advised is a privileged communication from his attorney. I instruct him not to answer the question. Let's get on with it, Mr. Jones."

D.T.'s smile broadened. "So that's the way it's going to be," he said.

Dick Gardner only blinked. D.T. felt adrenaline snake through him, filling channels long unused. "A subpoena duces tecum was served along with the notice of deposition. Have the requested documents been produced?" D.T. eyed Dick Gardner.

"My assistant will be delivering them shortly," Gardner said.

"Are any being withheld?"

Gardner smiled. "There are certainly ample grounds for objection, Mr. Jones. However, my client has expressed his desire to conclude this action as rapidly as possible. Therefore we have withheld our objections at this time and have produced the material requested. We of course reserve the right to object if further discovery attempts are made by you, and to object at trial should any of these documents be offered as evidence."

"Your cooperation is deeply moving, Mr. Gardner," D.T. said. "Mr. Stone. Previously in this case you answered some interrogatories I sent you, many of them concerning your financial status, both currently and at the time of your marriage to Mareth Stone. Have you any reason to believe any of your answers were incorrect or incomplete?"

Stone exchanged a glance with his lawyer, then spoke under oath for the first time. "No. But I have not reviewed those materials since I first answered them, so I can't be certain. And of course my financial status fluctuates. Lately the fluctuation has all been upward." His voice and his implied net worth drew a glance and smile from Phyllis, even as her fingers kept pressing the buttons on her machine. D.T. wondered if Phyllis confined herself to lawyers who could send her business. He looked at her again and decided she did not.

"If my memory serves," D.T. began, "in the year in which you were married you had just left the Dean Witter office to form your own financial consulting firm, and in that year your income from all sources was approximately fifteen thousand dollars. Is that right?"

"Yes."

"Since then you have been engaged in the same business, and it plus your investments have constituted your sole sources of income to this day? No inheritances, no gifts?''

"Correct."

"And in the past calendar year you earned approximately ninety thousand dollars, from all sources. Is that right?''

"I believe that's correct."

"How are things going for you this year? Better than last?''

"Much. The market has improved substantially, as I'm sure you know, both in volume and in price. This will be a very good year.''

"How good?''

"I can't say exactly.''

"Guess.''

Stone looked to Gardner for an objection but got only a shrug. "It's speculative but I'll allow him to answer,'' Gardner said. "You can guess if you can. By the time of trial the actual figures will no doubt be available.''

"No doubt,'' D.T. agreed. "Mr. Stone?''

"I would say two hundred thousand this year, including capital gains. It would be more if your restraining order hadn't prevented adjustments in my portfolio.''

D.T. looked at Chas Stone closely. The man was not at all embarrassed by his adjusted gross iniquity. D.T. was cheered. A moral disparity always made these jobs easier. "Let's get to it then, Mr. Stone. Shall we?''

"It's what we're here for, I believe,'' Stone said easily.

D.T. took a deep breath. "You are seeking exclusive custody of your children, is that right?''

"It is. Most definitely.''

"Are you willing to accept joint legal custody? In which you and Mrs. Stone have equal say in the way they are brought up?''

"No. I am not.''

"If Mrs. Stone agrees to waive all claims to alimony would you agree that she could have exclusive custody of the children?''

Stone didn't even look at Dick Gardner. "No. I will accept nothing less than my own exclusive custody, no matter what financial considerations might be offered. My children are not for sale.''

"Very noble," D.T. said. "My question is, why do you want such custody?"

"Because I love my children. And because their mother is not fit to raise them."

"I see. I believe we should explore that a little, Mr. Stone."

"I thought we might," Stone answered, and piously clasped his hands. For his part, Dick Gardner clasped his own hands negligently behind his head and leaned back in his chair and smiled the smile of winners on an hourly rate.

"How long have you considered your wife an unfit mother?" D.T. asked.

Stone hesitated. "For several years."

"How many?"

"Three. At least."

"Was there a specific incident that caused you to come to that belief?"

"There were many incidents."

"No one more troubling to you than the others?"

"Well, yes. There was one."

"What was it?"

"The night I came home and found my wife passed out in the living room while the children were upstairs sleeping."

"Passed out?"

"Yes."

"From what?"

"From liquor."

"She was drunk?"

"Exceedingly."

"Are you saying she has a drinking problem?"

"I most certainly am."

"Then and now?"

"Then and now."

"Were there other incidents of drunkenness on her part?"

"Many."

"Such as?"

"Let me put it this way, Mr. Jones. After the incident I just mentioned I began checking on my wife on a regular basis. I found where she kept her secret store of liquor and I monitored it. Over the past three years she has drunk an average of a pint of bourbon a day. Sometimes more. *Many* times more."

"And sometimes less?"

"Not often. Believe me."

"Oh, I'm not the one who has to believe you, Mr. Stone; I'm the one who has to find out if you're a liar. Tell me, this drinking, how did you quantify the amounts consumed?"

"By marking the bottles and the levels in them. Unobtrusively, of course."

"Did anyone else check these levels of consumption with you?"

"Of course not."

"And you never disclosed to your wife what you were doing?"

"No."

"Do you drink yourself, Mr. Stone?"

"No. I believe it is both wrong and foolish."

"And measuring the bottles is the only data you have on the extent of your wife's drinking?"

"Not at all." Stone's expression approximated a vigilante's. "In addition, I followed her for a period of time. She . . ."

"Excuse me. When was this?"

"Back when I found her passed out. Shortly after that."

"You followed her yourself? In secret?"

"Yes."

"Did you ever hire a private investigator to follow her?"

Stone hesitated. "Not at that time. Not with regard to her drinking."

"With regard to what, then?"

Stone's lips stiffened under further injection of rectitude. "Her sexual misbehavior." Stone unwrapped his hands and wrapped them again.

D.T. nodded. "I see. We'll get to that in a minute. Now back to the booze. What did Mrs. Stone do on the days when you followed her?"

"The usual things. Grocery, hardware, other kinds of shopping. That's the way it always began. But every time she left the house she would always stop at a certain tavern on her way home. And remain for a considerable period of time."

"What tavern?"

"The Stinger. A neighborhood bar. An open sore, more accurately. I can't believe Mareth darkened its door."

"Did you? Ever go in?"

"Once. When Mareth wasn't there. It was a filthy, smelly dungeon. The patrons looked like they hadn't seen the sun for years. Or drawn a sober breath."

"Did you talk to anyone there about your wife?"

"No."

"But you assume she drank on these visits."

"I certainly do."

"How many times did you see her go into The Stinger?"

"About five."

"And you stopped following her at some point after that?"

"Yes. I knew all I needed to know."

"Any other incidents of her drinking?"

"At parties, of course," Stone said, no longer trying to conceal the pleasure he took in cataloguing his wife's misfeasance. "She drank heavily at parties in recent years. To my acute embarrassment."

"What parties were these?"

"Just parties with our friends. The Bensons. Weavers. Culbertsons. People like that."

"Are there any particular incidents that stand out?"

"Oh, she sang a stupid song one night, standing on a coffee table. Something vulgar about a whale. And she began to use foul language in mixed company."

"Language like what?"

Stone raised his brows and glanced at Dick Gardner. Gardner shrugged. "Do you really want to know?" Stone asked.

"I really do."

"Fuck. She said fuck a lot. And shit. Those were the main ones. And not only at parties. She used those words around the children, too. And other words like them."

"When?"

"Approximately a year ago."

"How did you first learn of the alleged affair?"

"Alleged? You need not apply that word to anything I tell you, Mr. Jones. I first learned of it when the wife of Mareth's partner in sin told me of it. She learned of it from her husband, who confessed all last Christmas eve, after they'd been to midnight mass."

"Who are these people?"

"Richard Weaver and his wife, Kathleen."

"Have you ever discussed your suspicions with Mr. Weaver?"

"No."

"Or with your wife?"

"No."

"You have only Mrs. Weaver's word for it, then?"

"And my wife's behavior, which was consistent with her participation in a tryst."

"What kind of behavior?"

"She no longer desired a physical interface with me. I had to practically force her to give me gratification. Frequently it was only manual, I might add." Stone became appropriately uneasy.

"Any other facts that led you to believe Mrs. Stone was fooling around?"

"The detective, of course."

"Ah, yes. After you learned of the affair you hired a private detective to investigate your wife?"

"Yes."

"His name?"

"Edward Fellows."

"Did you receive a written report from him?"

"Yes."

D.T. looked at Dick Gardner. "Will you produce it?"

"Privileged," Gardner said. "Work product."

"The hell it is. I'll fight you over it, Dick. I'll be in court tomorrow to postpone the trial till I get it."

"Give us a minute."

Gardner and his client huddled head to head. D.T. went to the outer office to get some coffee. "How's it going?" Bobby E. Lee asked quietly.

D.T. shrugged. "Can't tell. His wife says he's stupid,

and luckily he hasn't said anything to disprove it. I think I may just touch the high points and leave the rest for trial. With the dumb ones it's best to wing it in front of the judge instead of tipping your hand ahead of time, so they can't practice their answers. He claims she's a boozer, though. That one could be trouble. But so far I can't tell if she's a lush or just likes to ease the pain once in a while."

"I hear he's a real prig," Bobby E. Lee said.

"That's putting it mildly. Did Gardner's people bring over the documents for inspection?"

Bobby E. Lee gestured toward a large box in the corner by the coffee table. D.T. went over and pawed through the papers it contained. Business records, mostly. Ledgers, balance sheets, income statements, tax returns, check stubs, bank books. He had asked for detailed records of Chas Stone's business income during their first year of marriage, to get a lock on the financial status at the commencement of the marriage so he could claim half the subsequent accumulation. Gardner seemed to have made a good-faith compliance with the subpoena. D.T. looked back at Bobby E. Lee. "I guess we'll have to copy it all," he said. "You want to do it?"

"No."

"Okay. Take it down to Swifty. Talk to Ralph. Tell him we need it Wednesday."

"Will do."

D.T. went back to the private office.

Gardner was chatting amiably with Phyllis, who in turn was glancing at Chas Stone at every opportunity. Stone seemed impervious. D.T. sat down and asked if they were ready. Three heads nodded and he asked about the detective's report. Gardner shook his head. "We won't release it without a court order, D.T."

D.T. only smiled. "Was her alleged affair with Richard Weaver the only one your wife had, Mr. Stone?"

"I doubt it very much."

"Well, do you have the names of other men she slept with?"

Stone started to answer but Dick Gardner put a hand on his arm and whispered something in his ear. Stone frowned and nodded and spoke resignedly. "I have no names. Not of men she saw prior to the time I filed for divorce.''

"Are you suggesting she's had sexual experiences since you moved out of the house?''

"I am.''

"What information do you base *that* on?''

"A further report by Mr. Fellows.''

"You hired him again to watch your wife?''

"I did.''

"When?''

"The day I left home.''

"How long did he do this?''

"He's still doing it, Mr. Jones.''

Stone's smile was diabolical. D.T. was cheered. Finally he could hate the man. D.T. looked at Dick Gardner. "Will you produce these reports from Fellows?''

"I have urged Mr. Stone not to make them available without a court order, because of the adverse precedent such conduct might create. He reluctantly concurs with my advice.''

"Very well. We'll do it this way. What are the essentials, Mr. Stone? What did the detective think he learned about your wife and Mr. Weaver?''

"Objection. Hearsay,'' Gardner said.

Stone frowned again and whispered to Gardner. Gardner shrugged. "Oh, go ahead,'' he said.

Stone cleared his throat. "Fellows learned nothing about Richard and my wife. The affair had apparently ceased by the time he began his investigation.''

"Did Fellows uncover any other impropriety?''

"I . . . no.''

"How about since you left home?''

"Mr. Fellows has advised me that my wife has been seeing a variety of men, on an indiscriminate basis, at all hours of the day and night, in her house and elsewhere. On some occasions the children have been there when a man has visited, late at night, for purposes which are all too obvious.''

"Do these men have names?''

"Too many for me to recount from memory. None of them were previously familiar to me.''

"They are listed in the report?''

"Yes. Of course, your own client could tell you. That is, if she bothered to learn them."

"Move to strike as nonresponsive." D.T. leaned toward his adversary. "Did the good Mr. Fellows provide you with pictures, Mr. Stone? Or tape recordings? Any other evidence of the activities of Mrs. Stone?"

"No. Only the report."

"Have you contacted any of the men yourself?"

"No."

"Have you yourself spied on your wife at any time since you filed this action, or did you confine yourself to mercenaries?"

"I have done no spying."

"Have you received reports on her conduct from anyone other than Mr. Fellows? From friends or anyone?"

"No."

"Have you yourself engaged in sexual intercourse with any woman other than your wife since the day you moved out of the house?"

"Objection," Dick Gardner blurted. "Instruct you not to answer."

"No," Stone countered loudly. "I *wish* to answer. My answer is no, I have not had sexual intercourse with a woman other than my wife since the day I left home. I am still a married man."

D.T. smiled and leaned back in his chair. There was so much more to be done with Chas Stone, questions of his work schedule, his time spent with the children, his own private behavior, the judgmental swath he cut through his marriage, that sort of thing. But this was not the time to go into it. If he quit now, Stone would leave the deposition confident that his story was unshakeable, that his version of the marriage was etched in stone. Not a bad position for him to be in, all things considered. D.T. decided to wrap it up.

"We've discussed your wife's drinking habits, Mr. Stone, and her contacts, of whatever nature, with other men. Are these the primary reasons you feel she is unfit to have custody of the children?"

"The primary ones. Yes."

"Are there any other reasons? Any at all?"

"Many. Mareth is far too permissive. The children stay

up till all hours. They lack discipline. They never clean their rooms; their table manners are atrocious. The boy never lifts the toilet seat when he urinates, or flushes afterward. Many things of that nature I find highly objectionable, though thankfully curable once they are living with me."

"What else?"

"Mareth's own habits are quite slovenly. The house is covered with dust. The bathrooms reek of urine. The dishes are frequently encrusted with food even though she has the finest dishwasher on the market. Meals are frequently some frozen thing she has purchased for the sake of convenience. That type of thing I find highly objectionable."

"Have you discussed these matters with your wife in the past?"

"Of course, but nothing ever seemed to change. I'm sure the situation is far worse now that I'm not there to supervise, to insist on certain standards. That's why I want an immediate trial. The children must be rescued from that environment, which, incidentally, includes no religious training whatsoever."

D.T. sighed as Stone's fists clenched in front of him and his eyes gleamed like a redeemer's. "You may be sure we will do all we can to accommodate your desire for an early trial, Mr. Stone," D.T. said. "Now, is there anything else about her that is a basis for your claim she is an unfit mother?"

"As I said, there are a great many items. Her reading material, for example. Feminist tracts, with a distinctly anti-male bias. Her attendance at women's meetings, where I'm sure she was urged to have an extramarital affair, to give 'meaning' to her life." D.T. waited for Stone to begin to froth. "Naturally she no longer wears a bra. Naturally she no longer does her duties around the home. In sum, she is no longer the woman I married. Her faithlessness alone is unforgiveable."

"Is unforgiveness the religion you wish your wife to teach, Mr. Stone?"

Stone had no answer and D.T. had had enough. He pushed back his chair. "I think that about wraps it up. Any questions, Dick?"

"None at all."

"Then the deposition is concluded. Off the record, Phyllis," he said, and all of them exhaled as if on cue. "I'd like a transcript as soon as possible," D.T. said as Phyllis collapsed her equipment.

"Wednesday?"

"Fine."

"Anything else?" D.T. looked briefly at each of them. They all shook their heads.

Phyllis packed up and left, her final act an admiring glance at Stone. A few seconds later Stone departed after telling D.T. he was pleased to meet him, that he knew D.T. was only doing his job, that he didn't take his questions personally, that he only hoped D.T. would keep the best interests of the children in mind when he was advising his client. D.T. managed to keep his hands off Chas Stone's neck, made do with a silent vow to smash the bastard when they got to court.

"How about that drink?" Dick Gardner asked.

■ THIRTEEN

TOLD you it would be ugly."

Dick Gardner's eyes oscillated easily in their sockets, taking in the bar, taking in the patrons, taking in Russ, who had just told his latest Polish joke and gone off to get their drinks. Clearly Gardner's lawyer's mind raced even in the Walrus, where the provocative was as avoided as bright light.

"The kid stuff is never pretty," D.T. said. "Lucky for me Stone's a bastard."

"I wouldn't say that."

"I wouldn't expect you to. Till after he pays your bill."

They flashed brief grins, then leaned back to allow Russ to deliver the libations. After he left they raised their glasses.

"Here's to Holmes."

"Here's to Brandeis."

"Here's to sin."

"Here's to vice."

They took deep drinks and tabled their glasses in unison. "Got any hot ones in the fire, D.T.?" Gardner asked him.

He thought of Lucinda Finders. Of Esther Preston. Of the Friday Fiasco. "Nope. How about you?"

"Couple of criminal things. Rape defense: defendant's fifteen, victim's sixty-seven. Coke bust: two kilos inside some tennis balls. Embezzlement. A sexual harrassment. And the usual two thousand or so drunk drivers, bless their souls."

D.T. shook his head. "How the hell can you represent those creeps?"

Gardner smiled easily. "Everyone's entitled to a competent defense, D.T., as all lawyers say and a handful even believe. And you should talk. How can you represent ball-busters like Mareth Stone? She fucked over her husband worse than a mugger, and now she wants half his dough as a reward for making the guy's life miserable."

"It's not even close to being the same. Mareth Stone was unhappy. The marriage wasn't working and Stone wouldn't give her the time of day. It's not her fault she hit the booze and fooled around; your guy drove her to it."

"Hey. My rapist grew up in twelve different foster homes. You think *he* can help anything? So don't give me that deterministic crap. Not about broads like Mareth Stone. She sandbagged him, D.T. She went into the marriage playing by one set of rules, then changed them in midstream and got pushed out of shape when Stone didn't go along with the new little game she invented. Why the hell should he? He wanted a wife and mother and she knew it from day one. It's not his fault the bitch decided those jobs weren't good enough any more. She wouldn't even do his fucking laundry, did you know that?"

Gardner paused for breath. D.T. frowned, started to reply, then held his tongue because what either of them thought about it didn't make any difference and because he never won arguments with Dick Gardner, only bets.

"You ever think about fighting for custody of Heather?" Gardner asked after a minute.

D.T. shook his head. "Michele could offer her about ten million advantages," he said, "each of them with 'Federal Reserve Note' engraved on the top."

"Money can backfire, though. I've seen a lot of fucked-up rich kids."

"Yeah, but Michele's different."

"How?"

He thought about it. "She doesn't think her money makes her better than other people. She's damn glad she's rich, don't get me wrong, but she'd be just as happy if everyone else had as much as she does. Most rich folks wish the rest of us were even poorer, so they could feel all the more exalted.''

Gardner smiled and loosened his tie. ''Michele sounds like quite a lady.''

''She is.''

''Maybe you should have kept her.''

''It wasn't entirely my decision.''

''Bet you miss the kid.''

''Sure I do. But what the hell. It all goes away after a few belts. Or a few more than a few.'' D.T. drained his glass and tried to clear his mind of Heather.

''So why don't you petition for amended custody? Have her live with you every other year or something.''

D.T. shook his head. ''I'm old-fashioned, Dick. I think kids need mommies more than daddys, especially little girl kids. I think it's biological and I think it's a shame the law doesn't see it that way any more.''

Gardner shrugged. ''One thing's for sure. Kids got a lot of pressure on them these days. Used to be, us middle-class jerks proved what big-shots we were with houses and cars and clothes and like that. Now, hell, it's all the kids. Gourmet babies, computer camps, cello lessons. You been to a playground lately? The goddamned blacks are the only ones let their kids be kids any more.''

''Yeah, well, that's one thing about divorce; it keeps you from fucking up your own kid's life.''

''I guess that's one way to look at it.''

''Yeah. I just wish when I looked at it that way it didn't look back.''

Both men smiled. D.T. signalled Russ for a second round.

Dick Gardner spoke after a long moment of melancholy. ''Be nice to have a kid. Something that made it all worth it, you know? For me it's just the trials. Getting some asshole up there on the stand, showing him up for what he is, seeing that look in his eyes when he knows he's whipped. Sure, half my clients are scum—hell, the corporate guys are worse than the hoods. But it's the challenge, you know? Break open the lie, watch it crack and crumble till there's nothing left but truth. And not just any truth. *My* truth. A gunfighter, is all I am. High

Noon, baby. God help me if the world runs out of felons."

D.T. nodded, then scraped the condensation off his glass and wished it was as easy to clear his conscience. Somewhere by the bar a bottle broke and a man laughed.

"Speaking of changes in the law," Gardner said abruptly. "I'm in charge of the continuing education program next month. Recent Trends in Domestic Practice. Want to serve on it, D.T.? Might lure some referrals your way."

D.T. shook his head. "I haven't been keeping up on current trends, Dick. Maybe because so many of them are lousy."

"Come on, D.T. It's mostly beginners at those things. Just out of law school, trying to build a practice. They could learn a lot from you."

"Hell, Dick, I can't keep my letterhead in print, that's how successful I am at this business. I'm in hock to my secretary, for God's sake. The best advice I could give them is to go into something respectable. Like worm farming."

Dick Gardner laughed, apparently assuming D.T. had joked. "How about premarital agreements? Drafting problems and so on?"

D.T. shook his head. "Don't use them. They're a mistake unless both spouses are independently wealthy to begin with, and my clients don't begin that way. Plus, the women always get fucked. If the guy gets rich she doesn't get enough, and if he doesn't he ends up breaching the deal and she has to sue him. We both know who wins when that happens. All us Juris Doctors."

Dick Gardner shook his head. "You're a cheery soul today. What's wrong, your love life turn stale?"

"Lately stale and fresh taste a lot alike."

"You still seeing that, what's her name?"

"Barbara."

"The jock. Yeah. Hell of a physical specimen, as I recall. Must be like the Olympics every night. The thrill of victory."

"The agony of defeat."

Gardner laughed. "What's the matter, the old hose won't stiffen up for you any more?"

D.T. shrugged. "The sex is okay. For me, at least. And I like Barbara. A lot. But it's over. We both know it, too. I guess we're each waiting for the other to blow the whistle."

"If the sex is good then what's the problem?"

"We're in violation of the Fourth Principle of Modern Matrimony."

"Which is?"

"Opposites attract. But not long enough to make plans."

"Opposite how?"

D.T. drank his drink with urgency. For the first time in years he was about to talk to another man about a woman.

"The main thing is, Barbara's a participant and I'm an observer. She sees plots and conspiracies all over the place, but basically she's an optimist. I empathize and sympathize and romanticize and all that, but basically I'm a pessimist. I think my useful life ended about five years ago, that I'm just waiting my turn to die. Barbara, on the other hand, thinks every day it's getting better and better. She's got answers; all I've got are questions. Plus, there's the little things."

"Like what?"

"Oh, like she's absolutely convinced that running umpteen miles a day will make you live longer and that living longer's good. That all would be right with the world if women were exactly the same as men. That groups of women sitting around using words like relating and sharing and feeling and stroking are engaged in something more meaningful than a discussion of the nickel defense or the 24-second shot clock."

"And you're not sure of any of that, right?"

"Right."

"Hell, D.T. Welcome to the end of the century. It's not nuclear war that's going to be the end of us, it's that men and women can't stand each other any more. You think any species ever decided not to fuck? The dinosaurs, maybe?"

D.T. smiled.

"I think it's the broads' fault myself," Gardner continued, "the lib shit, men are assholes, women are saints, working nine to five in a steel mill is woman's greatest goal. But I suppose you disagree."

"Not necessarily. I think lib's off the track, too, in some ways. Putting all their eggs in the ERA basket. Devaluing motherhood. Promoting abortion like a cosmetic. But women have gotten screwed in some ways, and it's still happening. Look at law firms. You could fire a shotgun in every partnership meeting in town and not hit a single woman who isn't screwing the managing partner."

"Yeah, maybe, but so what? Being a lawyer's a piece of shit. Fucking lackeys, is all we are. Women are crazy to want it." Gardner laughed. "Why do you represent all those broads anyway, D.T.? What are you, a traitor to your sex?"

D.T. laughed. "Hell, I don't know. Because I like women, I guess. Better than men, I mean. Men are so damned frightened by their lives—their jobs, their kids, their age, their bodies going bad. Unless they're a month away from discovering a cure for cancer they figure they haven't fulfilled their potential, and then they figure, hey. Maybe I can't cure cancer but I can sure as hell fuck young girls. So that's what they do. Either that or they just crawl inside themselves and watch football till it's over. Women fight for it. Truth. Meaning. Whatever. And when it still doesn't keep their husbands from running off with the receptionist they're devastated. Then the divorce system comes along and screws them to the wall."

Gardner swore. "That's a crock, D.T. I can name a hundred guys dragging around support judgments that are killing them like the plague."

"And I can name a thousand women who live like slaves because they aren't getting one red cent for themselves or the kids from husbands who've been ordered to pay and can but aren't."

Gardner's grin was sly. "You want to know what I think?"

"What?"

"I think you guys who claim you're so fucking liber-

Gardner shook his head. D.T. grew morose by leaps and bounds.

"Want to go hustle up some chicks?" Gardner asked as he finished his drink. "I know this place on the west side where a lot of our type hang out."

"What type is our type?"

"Oh, the ones who were born about the time 'Moon-glow' hit the charts and give head without being stran-gled."

"I think I'll pass," D.T. said. "The odds of two such lovelies being in attendance at the same saloon are astro-nomical."

Gardner nodded absently, clearly eager to get away. "You're probably smart. Know what happened to me the other night?"

"What?"

"I'm in this joint, see, and I spot this halfway decent chick sitting at a table in the corner, alone, dressed to kill, definitely on the make. So I go over. And buy some drinks, and put about a number two move on her, and she responds on schedule. So I ask if she wants to go to my place for a nightcap. Next thing I know this hand is feeling around my crotch. And I get about half hard, and she acts like she's even hotter than I am, and then she says, 'No thanks; I'm in the mood for something a little bigger tonight.' Can you fucking *believe* it? The world's going straight to hell. But fuck it, right?"

"Right. Fuck it."

Gardner stood up. "Hang in there, D.T. Tell the Stone woman she's about to have some spare rooms."

"And you tell Chas he'd better start getting liquid."

They shook hands and parted at the door. D.T. watched Gardner go off to hustle chicks, and quickly hated him. He drove rapidly to his apartment, his mind woolly with drink and with the feeling he had just been party to something a bit unseemly.

By the time he had changed his clothes it was after six. He was hungry, but there was nothing in the refrigerator he hadn't eaten in the previous three days. As he sur-veyed the chilly larder the waxed carton on the top shelf reminded him of Lucinda Finders and the fantastic fact that she had nursed her child in his living room. His lips puckered. He opened the cupboard and inspected the crystal chalice that still contained a crusty remnant of her milk. He picked it up, tipped it, watched one last drop collect in a pearly puddle. He swirled the glass as though it held a priceless vintage, shuddered, then poured the droplet down the drain and threw the goblet in the soggy sack beneath the sink. Then he went to the phone and asked for Reedville.

"Operator."

"I'm trying to locate a girl who lives in Reedville. At least her parents do."

"What are their names, sir?"

"That's just it. I don't know. The girl's married name is Lucinda Finders. I don't know her maiden name. She's twenty-one. She just had a baby. Do you have any idea how I can reach her?"

"I'm afraid not."

"Could you ask around the office there? Please?"

"I'm sorry . . ."

"Please? It's very important. She could be in trouble."

"Just a moment."

The line hummed for a long minute. He imagined a line of women with red fingernails and headsets, exchanging whispered speculations between the calls of lovers and of gossips. Above the hum he listened to his stomach growl.

The operator returned. "I believe the folks you want are named Klinkheim. That's Earl Klinkheim. They have a daughter named Lucinda that just had a baby. One of the girls here knew her in high school."

"Thank you. Thank you very much."

"You're welcome. Shall I put you through to the Klinkheim number, sir?"

"Please."

"One moment."

The phone was answered with a grunt. "Mr. Klinkheim?"

"So?"

"Do you have a daughter named Lucinda?"

"Who wants to know? This ain't Delbert, is it? It damn sure better not be." D.T. began to understand why Lucinda had gone off with the first one who would take her.

"My name is Jones. I'm an attorney. I represent Lucinda in her divorce action. I'm trying to get in touch with her."

"She ain't here."

"Do you expect her later on?"

"I don't expect her ever. Not after what she said to me the day she left. 'Course that didn't stop her from running back when times wrinkled up on her, like I knew she would."

"When's the last time you saw her, Mr. Klinkheim?"

"Three days ago, I reckon." The brusque voice paused, then spoke suspiciously. "Say now. I just got sent a bill the hospital wants me to pay for them yanking out her kid. Now let met tell you. I ain't gonna pay the hospital and I ain't gonna pay *you*, if that's what you got in mind. The day she left the farm was the day she decided to pay her own way. So don't for a minute think you'll get any money outta *me*, Mr. Divorce Lawyer."

"It's nothing like that. I hope you'll ask Lucinda to call me if you hear from her. That's all I want. The name is Jones."

"Heard you the first time." The line went as dead as the man's compassion.

D.T. put down the receiver, thought for a minute, then dialed his process server. An answering machine squeaked and beeped. D.T. left his message: Delbert Wesley Finders could be served with the petition in the case of *Finders* v. *Finders* at twenty forty-two Houston Street. Current balance in the outstanding account of the Law Office of D. T. Jones would be paid in full at the end of the month. Expedited action on the request to effect service would be very much appreciated. D.T. broke the connection and looked up another number and dialed it.

"May I speak to Dr. Haskell?" he asked the woman who answered.

"He's not here. His emergency number is 4295. If you need treatment please call that number or go at once to the hospital." Her voice was uninterested and would remain so for anything less than a federally acknowledged disaster.

"I need to speak to the doctor about a personal matter," D.T. insisted. "My name is Jones. I'm an attorney."

Her voice mellowed not a whit. "I see. He's at the hospital, I believe. The monthly staff meeting."

"Which hospital?"

"Providence."

"Do you know where the meeting is?"

"The conference room, I suppose. That's where it usually is. If there really is a meeting," she added, something more bitter than boredom in her voice. "Are you suing him, Mr. Jones? Is that it? Is he going to be sued for malpractice, on top of all the rest?"

"Nothing like that," D.T. said quickly, wanting very much to ask what all the rest of it was, whether it was like the all the rest of it he encountered in his practice. But he forced his tongue to say good-bye.

He was at the hospital in fifteen minutes. A woman in white who spoke in whispers told him the conference room was on the second floor. When he got there the door was closed, but when he pressed an ear to it he heard voices. He sat in the adjoining waiting area and thumbed through a back issue of *People*. Johnny Carson was divorcing once again. The legal fee would be six figures. D.T. whistled. Nurses, patients, and visitors floated past, speaking in hushed tones.

The hospital grew still, as though everyone had been cured or died. The only sound came from the aluminum coffee pot that burbled occasionally atop a table in a corner. D.T. helped himself. A woman wearing hiking boots passed, reminding him of Barbara and her incessant clamoring for them to do something out-of-doors. The only thing he liked to do out-of-doors was golf, a sport Barbara held in a contempt more appropriate to despots. He wished he hadn't said anything to Dick Gardner about Barbara. Dick would probably try to get in her pants after he left Michele's.

D.T. put down his *People* and picked up a *National Geographic*. African women were still bare-breasted, he was happy to see, and did strange things to their lips. While he was reading of the liberation of Ethiopian tribeswomen the conference room door opened. A group of men and women spilled into the corridor, chatting, clutching papers to their breasts, moving among each other in stuttering bursts of progress like magnified malignant cells.

D.T. stopped the first one who came his way and asked for Doctor Haskell. The man searched the group behind him and pointed toward a rangy figure walking rapidly down the corridor in the opposite direction. D.T. murmured his thanks and hurried after his prey.

"Dr. Haskell?"

The man stopped and turned. His face was close to gaunt, with caves and ridges and vertical lines. His hair had vacated every part of his head save a band beginning and ending just behind his ears. His eyes were small and seemed pink, like his skin. His smile was bogus bonhomie.

"I'd like to talk to you for a minute about one of your former partners," D.T. said, walking toward him.

Haskell frowned. "Which one? I have more former partners than I care to recall."

"Nathaniel Preston."

"Oh. Him."

"Yes."

"Who are you?"

"D.T. Jones. I'm an attorney."

"Malpractice?"

D.T. sensed the question begged an affirmative, that Dr. Haskell hoped Nathaniel Preston was getting his ass sued off. "I do domestic work," D.T. said. "I represent Mrs. Preston."

"Natasha?"

"Esther."

Haskell's eyes widened, puckering his cheeks. "Esther? My God. Esther. I haven't seen her for years. How is she?" Haskell shook his head in wonder, as though they were discussing ghosts.

"Not well. She has MS."

Haskell sighed and nodded. "That's right. She'd just found out she had it the last time I saw her." Haskell closed his eyes. "Poor Esther."

"Literally."

Haskell frowned. "What's this all about, anyway?"

"Is there somewhere we can talk? It'll take a minute to explain."

Haskell looked at his watch. "I guess I can give you a minute. I think my nurse mentioned something about this a month or so ago, come to think of it, that someone had been asking around about Nat. Why don't we go to the lounge."

Haskell led D.T. into a small room at the end of the hall that was more private and more comfortably furnished than the public area. They sat across from each other in soft, tweedy chairs, crossed their legs, prepared to talk. Somewhere something was playing Brahms. "What's Esther's problem?" Haskell asked finally, over the top of a real cup to which he'd helped himself.

"Money."

"How do you mean?"

"Her disease has made it impossible for her to work. She's without savings because of medical expenses. Her only income is a Social Security disability payment, and that may be cut off. She's being priced out of her home, her food, her medicine, her way of life. I'm trying to find another source of funds."

"You mean Nat."

D.T. nodded. "From what I hear he can afford it."

"No doubt about that, although I hear he may be in over his head on the new hospital he's building. But if he's the same old Nat you'll have to pry it out of him with a crowbar." Haskell's fine lips curled.

"Tell me about him," D.T. said.

"Why? How can that help?"

"If I know the kind of man he is, maybe I'll know the kind of approach to take. I'm not necessarily out to file a lawsuit and spend five years in court before Mrs. Preston sees a dime. Maybe I can appeal to his better nature."

Haskell laughed without humor. "Nat has no better nature." With long smooth fingers the doctor pulled a pipe out of his jacket pocket and moved skillfully through the surgical mechanics of lighting it. After several seconds he looked at D.T. through a veil of smoke that made their convocation seem diabolical. "What do you want to know?"

"What kind of man is Preston?"

"You understand I haven't had any but minimal contact with him for years," Haskell began.

"When did your partnership dissolve?"

" 'Sixty-seven, formally. We wrangled a year before that over the terms of the dissolution."

"How many of you were there?"

"Four. Nat and I, plus Ray Millikin and Francis McDonald."

"Where are those two now?"

"Millikin practices in Hawaii. McDonald got sued—he was a surgeon and left behind a clamp. He dropped out of sight the week before the case came up for trial. That was ten years ago. I understand they entered a judgment of a million two against him."

"What caused the breakup?"

Haskell twisted his long limbs. "Personal and professional differences. Let's put it that way."

"I hear the falling-out between you and Preston was fairly bitter."

"You could say that."

"What was the problem?" D.T. asked affably.

Haskell frowned, seemed to experience a twinge. "Nothing that concerns you. A personal matter, between Nat and me."

"Like what?"

Haskell's smile was wan. "He did something unforgivable. I did what I had to do to live with myself afterward. And that's all I'm going to say about it."

"Sounds intriguing."

"If you ask me about it again, I'll leave." Haskell's eyelids drooped, as though he was taking aim.

D.T. held up a hand. "Okay, okay. So tell me some more about Preston."

"He's vain. Ambitious. Only marginally skilled but he's in a field that doesn't call for much. Penurious, at least as far as others are concerned. Cruel. Fundamentally dishonest." Haskell laughed mirthlessly. "All of which explains, I suppose, why Nat is buddies with everyone from the mayor to the archbishop. As far as his practice goes, Nat is an unadulterated misogynist for whom conducting a pelvic exam is akin, and I quote, 'to looking into a sewer through a mink-lined manhole.' " Haskell set his jaw. "How's that for starters?"

D.T. nodded. "You've given me a great reason to nail the guy. Now I need a nail."

Haskell puffed his pipe. "What kind of suit have you got in mind?"

"Well, Mrs. Preston tells me she put her husband through med school. Financially, I mean. Do you know anything to dispute that?"

"No. Esther worked her ass off. She put Nat through intellectually, as well. I think she knew more physiology than he did by the time they were finished."

"Good. There's a slight chance we could claim something on that basis. Recent decisions have been favorable to granting the wife an interest in her husband's degree."

Haskell smiled ruefully. "Every doctor in the world knows about those recent decisions." D.T. recalled Haskell's wife's reference to "the rest of it." One more ditto, coming up.

"What about Preston's finances?" D.T. continued. "Did he have much money when you knew him?"

"Not in the beginning, certainly. They were dirt poor. He bought into the partnership through his draw. But he earned a lot of bucks before he was through. He saw a lot of patients—we all did—and we did quite well."

"What would you say he was earning in '65, when they split?"

"Let's see. That was just his second year of practice, wasn't it? I'd say fifty, maybe."

"At that time did he own any major assets other than their house?"

"I don't remember any."

"Did he speculate? Stocks, commodities, land?"

Haskell chuckled. "Nat was a gold bug. I don't know exactly when it started but he collected coins, jewelry, all kinds of gold. And that was back when it was illegal and only cost thirty-five bucks an ounce. He must have made a fortune if he didn't bail out too soon."

"Tell me this. Do you think the guy would worry much about a lawsuit like this? Enough to pay a significant amount to buy it off? To escape publicity?"

"Not a chance," Haskell said simply. "I think you're wasting your time."

D.T. sighed. "Anything else you can tell me? See, the theory is, if Preston had assets at the time of the divorce that he didn't disclose to his wife, then perhaps she can claim a portion of their current value."

Haskell shook his head. "The only thing I knew about his finances were the things he bragged to me about. But like I said, that was later on, when the money really started to roll in."

"How much of it?"

"The year we split up Nat made a hundred and sixty thousand. His fees were outrageous, but the more he charged the more patients he had. For some reason women love to give him money. And would you believe it? He still owes me five grand on the partnership dissolution."

Haskell looked at his watch again and stood up. D.T. thanked him for his time. They shook hands. Haskell started to walk away, then stopped. "You may waste more than time on this thing, Jones," he said ominously.

"How do you mean?"

"Nat's got a lot of influence in this town. He's made life miserable for a lot of doctors who've crossed him— me included, for a time."

"How?"

"A credentials problem here at the hospital. It's straightened out now, but he could do the same to a lawyer who got in his way. He's wired politically like you can't believe. If I were you I'd leave him alone."

D.T. thanked him for the warning. As he drove home, D.T. wondered where Dr. Haskell went when he lied to his wife about the staff meetings, and wondered if it would pay him to find out.

He was home changing clothes when the phone rang.

"Hi." Barbara churned with cheer. "Where've you been?"

"Playing detective."

"What were you detecting?"

"Evidence of skullduggery."

"Find any?"

"Nope."

"Too bad."

"True."

"Want me to come over?"

"Do you want to?"

"If you want me to."

D.T. hesitated. "What'd *you* do tonight?"

"Made you some carrot cake."

"Thanks."

"You're welcome. Shall I bring it over?"

"I . . . sure."

"Okay, D.T. I get it. So very sorry to disturb you, Your Highness. I wouldn't interfere with your precious solitude for anything. Especially since it's so *productive*."

"It's not precious, Barbara. It's just necessary sometimes. It helps me. . . ." But he was talking to a dead machine.

When he called her back he got a busy signal, a throb that drilled directly for his faithless heart. Head aching, he took an aspirin and a shower. As the water coursed over him he thought of Barbara and the shower they had taken together back in August, of what she did and didn't do to him that night, of their fellatio interruptus by the threat from Delbert Finders. He wondered if Lucinda and Delbert were back together, and what would happen when the process server showed up in the morning. He imagined another assault, this one triggered by his deed.

Maybe he should call off the process server. Wait till he could talk with Lucinda again. Play it safe. Do nothing to anger Del. No. She shouldn't be with Delbert anymore; she should be divorced. D.T. towelled off his back and his conscience. He was looking in the mirror at his receding gums when he thought of the look on Chas Stone's face when he had glimpsed the beauteous Bobby E. Lee, and of what Bobby had said later on. D.T. went back to the phone.

"Bobby?"

"Just a minute." The voice was annoyed, indignant, not Bobby's.

". . . Hello?"

"Bobby?"

"Yes?"

"This is your sainted employer. Sorry to bother you at home."

"It's all right. Crisis?"

"No. It's just something you said this afternoon."

"What?"

"During the Stone deposition you said you'd heard something about Stone before. About his being a prig. Remember?"

Pause. "Yes."

"So how did you hear it?"

Bobby E. Lee didn't say anything. D.T. could hear him breathe. "Do you really need to know?" Bobby asked finally.

"I don't know. Do I?"

D.T. heard whispers he could not decipher, then an oath uttered by the voice that had answered the phone. "A club. I saw Stone at a club. Some of the members told me about him."

"What club?"

"A private club. You wouldn't know it."

"Come on, Bobby. Do I have to spell it out?"

"No, Mr. J. You're a lousy speller, anyway. It was a gay club. Very exclusive, very hush-hush. For the very rich and the very pretty."

"Are you absolutely sure it was Stone?"

"Yes."

"When was this?"

"A year or so ago."

"Was he with someone?"

"Yes."

"Who?"

Pause. "You're going to blackmail Stone into giving up his children. Aren't you?"

"I don't know."

"It's not right, Mr. J."

"You show me a lawyer who always does what's right and I'll show you one who's living below the poverty line. Come on, Bobby. It's nothing personal."

"But it is. You're saying we're automatically unfit to be with children."

"I am not."

"That's certainly the implication."

"Shit, Bobby. Let's lay off the philosophy. Who was he with?"

"I can't tell you."

"Why not?"

"Because the person simply could not survive having his name in the papers in connection with something like that. He'd slash his wrists."

"You're being a little melodramatic, aren't you, Bobby?"

"Life is melodramatic for most of us, Mr. J. It's something you inherit with the rest of it."

D.T. paused. "It wasn't you, was it?"

"No. It wasn't me, Mr. Jones."

"Okay. No names. Where's the club?"

"What are you going to do?"

"Hell, I don't know," D.T. said angrily. "Burn it down. Join up. Who knows? See if Stone goes there again, I guess. Come on, Bobby."

"It's on Billings Avenue. Ten-eighteen."

"Open every night?"

"Only work nights; no weekends. Rich men have wives on weekends."

"Do you still go there?"

"No."

"Any chance my getting in?"

"None at all."

"Okay, Bobby. Thanks."

"I think I think a little less of you, Mr. J."

"That's okay, Bobby. I think I think a little less of me, too."

D.T. hung up and got into a cold and empty bed. He tossed and turned, struggling for comfort, wondering if he should call Barbara and invite her over, wondering what she would do to punish him, wondering how to handle Chas Stone's Achilles heel. He was in the middle of a dream that featured Victoria Principal when the telephone destroyed it.

"Mr. Jones?"

"Ummm. Who's this?"

"This is Rita Holloway."

"What time is it?"

hour. It took her another hour to crawl to the telephone and call me. I don't know how she managed it.''

D.T. looked at the bathroom. The fixtures were white, the wallpaper and shower curtain pink, the linoleum speckled like the eggs of small birds. Little sprigs of dried flowers and little portraits of Victorian ladies ornamented the walls and surfaces. A mound of scented soaps rose off a clam shell by the basin. A mobile of wooden fish swam lazily in the air above the tub, in the center of which was a sturdy plastic chair on which Esther Preston evidently sat to shower.

Beside the toilet, two steel bars had been anchored tightly to the studs, slanting toward the bowl from shoulder height, like the provision for the handicapped in public restrooms. The only sign of the fall was a wadded throw rug in the corner by the tub and an upturned wastebasket made of white wicker. D.T. backed out of the tiny room.

"She hit her hip on the edge of the toilet, I think," Rita Holloway said. "And her forehead on the sink. I just hope it's not her hip. Her bones are so brittle."

"I'm sorry," D.T. said. "She had an overdose of problems already. But I don't understand why I'm here," he went on. "You said something about murder. It was just a fall, wasn't it? Nobody pushed her or anything. Did you just say that to wake me up, or what?"

"Come here."

Rita Holloway edged around him and went into the bathroom and stood beside the toilet. "You know what the rails are for, right?"

"Sure."

"Okay. Pretend you're Esther Preston. Pretend you back in here in your chair and have to get to the toilet without using your legs. Here. I'll put the lid down."

She lowered the fabric-covered toilet lid and backed out of the room. D.T. looked at her. "Go on," she urged. "Just try it once."

D.T. walked to the toilet, turned around, grasped the nearest rail with his left hand and tried to support himself as he sank toward the seat. Immediately his hand lost purchase and slipped down the shiny rail. D.T. lurched to the side, extended a hand to the sink and caught himself, and stood up. He rubbed his fingers together. "What is it?"

"Baby oil, I think. Someone put it on the rails. That's why she fell. She couldn't hold herself."

D.T. closed his eyes and shook his head. "Come on, Miss Holloway. There must be a hundred ways those rails could get covered with some slick substance, and none of them have anything to do with murder."

"I know," Rita Holloway said, surprising him. "Come on."

She flipped off the bathroom light and closed the door. D.T. followed her through the kitchen and into the living room. She walked to the far corner and picked up the aluminum walker he had seen on his first visit. She turned it upside down. "Look at this."

D.T. walked to her side. She pointed at one of the walker's legs, at a point some six inches from its bottom end, just below where the cross support attached. "See the crease?"

D.T. looked where she directed. The aluminum leg was cracked across a third of its circumference, an evil smile in the satin smoothness of the rest of the support. The crack was thin, its edges smooth, the cylinder undented. Perhaps a natural defect, more likely a deliberate slice. "It would buckle with enough pressure," Rita Holloway said. "Want me to show you?"

D.T. shook his head. "I believe you."

"Okay. Now come over here."

Rita Holloway walked briskly through the kitchen to the rear door of the house. "I've spent a lot of time here," she said to him along the way. "I know Esther's patterns. One of the things she does is take the kitchen garbage out every night, just before she goes to bed. So the house won't smell. She goes through this door and down the ramp and over to the garbage can by the corner of the house and back again."

"So?"

"Imagine you're her again. You've got a plastic bag full of garbage in your lap, and you open the door—go ahead—and you push your wheelchair down the ramp, the way you've done it a thousand times."

He decided to humor her. "Okay. Here I go." D.T. walked to the door and opened it.

"Now push yourself down the ramp."

"Okay." D.T. started to take a step.

"Look down."

He looked. There was no ramp. Only a two-foot drop from the kitchen threshold to the concrete slab poured over the ground outside. A woman fell through his mind, a helpless flailing body in a rolling chair that no longer had anything to roll on.

D.T. stepped outside and looked around. The wooden ramp was some ten feet down the side of the house, up-side down, clearly dragged there by someone who knew exactly what he was doing and the havoc he would wreak.

Rita Holloway spoke from behind him. "Can you imagine what would have happened if she'd tried to go outside tonight?"

D.T. stepped back into the kitchen and closed the door. "Any other surprises?"

"Not that I've found." Rita Holloway gave him that look again, the one that had as much as anything gotten him into Esther Preston's life in the first place. "Now do you believe me?"

"I believe someone wants to hurt her, or frighten her, or both. I don't think they're out to kill her, though. None of these little stunts is calculated to do that."

"Not yet, maybe. What if they get worse?"

D.T. ignored the invitation to speculate, remembered instead his encounter with Dr. Preston at Joyce Tuttle's party. "Who do you think is doing it?"

"Her husband, of course."

"Why?"

"So she won't sue him."

"Pretty extreme reaction. She's hardly a threat to his well-being, financial or otherwise. Even if she wins it'll be a pittance. And frankly I don't think she'll win a dime."

Rita Holloway frowned and crossed her arms. "Maybe there's something else involved. Something that might cost Dr. Preston really big money."

"Like what?"

"I don't know. You're the lawyer." Rita Holloway's mouth flipped up in an indication that being a lawyer was akin to being a ghoul.

"I guess I'd better talk to Mrs. Preston," D.T. said. "Which hospital is she in?"

"Providence."

"Do you think I can see her tomorrow?" He looked at his watch. "I mean today?"

"Probably. For a little while. But if she's had hip surgery she won't be in shape to say much."

"Do you know people at that hospital?"

"I used to work there."

"Can you see to it they'll let me in to see her?"

"I suppose so. What are you going to do? I mean, I'm scared, you know? I thought I was going to help her and instead I've—"

"I'm going to call the whole thing off," D.T. interrupted.

Rita Holloway sighed deeply and closed her eyes and nodded. "Good. And no police, right? We just leave it where it is?"

"Right."

"I hate to be so chicken," Rita Holloway said softly, "but I just can't gamble with Esther's safety. I don't have that right."

D.T. nodded his agreement and went into the living room and looked at the scene that had once charmed him and had now become so sinister. Rita Holloway followed him silently, perhaps lost as he was in thoughts of the consequence of bravado, the cost of courage, the allure of swift surrender. "Are you sure you looked for other sabotages?" he asked her.

"As well as I could."

"I think we'd better touch everything electric, to see if they've been rewired to shock her. Also open cabinets and doors, to see that nothing falls out. I guess it would be impossible to tell if any of her food had been adulterated."

Rita Holloway's eyes widened. "My God. I never . . . She doesn't have all that much food. I'll make a list of everything that's opened and toss it out and buy her new."

"That'll cost money."

"I owe her that much and more."

A tear leaked over a lid of Rita Holloway's eye and traveled blithely down her cheek. She crushed it with a swipe of her hand. "Goddamnit," she said, and began opening cabinets and switching switches. "Me and my good deeds."

D.T. did the same. They worked silently and fearfully. Eventually D.T.'s eyes came to rest on the ancient wheelchair that was like a riderless mount grazing beside the bathroom door. Rita Holloway saw where he was looking. "I checked the wheels. They seem okay."

D.T. went over to the chair and stood behind it and pushed it gently to and fro. Its workings squeaked like mice. He pressed down heavily and did the same. Nothing collapsed, although at one point in its movement the chair bounced as though it had struck something. He pushed the chair away and bent down to look first at the spotless floor and then at the rubber tires.

On hands and knees he pushed the chair again. Something glistened and caught his eye. He rubbed his hand over it. "Look at this."

Rita Holloway hurried to his side. A shard of glass, sharp and jagged and thick, perhaps a piece of broken bottle, lay firmly imbedded in the rubber tires where eventually, inevitably, Esther Preston would someday place her hand to stop the wheels that spun beneath it. "It would slice her palm to ribbons," Rita Holloway said.

"We'd better look some more."

They spent a half an hour peering, kneeling, crawling, feeling, searching through the house, finding only a hard-earned luster. When they had looked and re-looked everywhere they trudged back to the living room and slumped, exhausted, side by side, onto the horsehair couch. "I guess it's safe," D.T. said.

"It better be."

"Can you stay with her when she gets home?"

"For a while. Sure."

"I guess I'd better make sure I get word to the good doctor that we're not snooping into his business any more. The son of a bitch."

She closed her eyes and nodded. "Thank you for coming," she said. "I was terribly frightened when I saw what had been done. Now I'm not so scared. I'm mostly mad."

"Good. Just don't do anything about it that would make Preston think we're still after him."

"I won't. Don't worry. I just hate to let him win like this, is all. I wish he'd come after *me*."

"Maybe he will. You'd better watch yourself."

"Let him try. I'll bring Toledo."

"Who?"

"My dog."

D.T. took her hand and kissed it, then left the house and drove slowly toward his apartment. His mind, so thick with sleep when he'd arrived at the little house, now spun with speculations and considerations of the usual type that tortured him when he became the cause of danger. Halfway to his home he veered toward his office.

When he got there it was four-thirty. The rooms were cold and hollow, without solace. The coffee took forever to brew. The furnace gave off the stench of long decay. The box of documents Dick Gardner's man had left seemed to have grown monstrously during the night, its contents to have multiplied like mutants.

D.T. began to paw desultorily through the papers, arranging them by category, slowly absorbing their significance. The drudgery was common to litigation, so common that most successful lawyers now hired nonlawyers to do it for them. It was boring, the chance of spectacular discovery almost nonexistent, the project a gloomy by-product of the independence he had cultivated like a cymbidium for the past two decades. Not unlike the Fiasco.

An hour later a quick calculation told him Chas Stone's investment business had been only marginally profitable in the early years, which would allow D.T. to claim that its subsequent success was due in major part to the marital contribution of Mareth Stone. As the rising sun peeked slyly through the window, D.T. began to check the confirmations of individual investment transactions, to see that the sum was indeed the total of all the parts and also to see what investments Chas Stone had made for his own account.

There were few purchases by Stone individually, conservative issues mostly, utilities and blue chips, bought at moderate prices and held, D.T. wagered, yet today. If he took any chances at all, Chas Stone took them only with other people's money.

D.T. thumbed quickly through a further batch. One of them, and then another, leaped at him from the thicket. Buy orders, executed on behalf of a customer named Nathaniel Preston. D.T. sighed heavily. God did deal in grace, he just dealt it rather late. He finally had a nail. Then he remembered his promise to Rita Holloway, and realized he no longer had a client to be his hammer.

D.T. looked at the trade orders once again. The stocks were in companies he had never heard of. Electronics, by the sound of the names. Two hundred shares of one, three hundred of another. Total investment of a little over five thousand dollars. Made during the final year of Preston's marriage to Esther. Not specifically disclosed in the property settlement agreement Esther Preston had showed him. D.T. pawed quickly through the rest of the papers to see if there were any further transactions on behalf of Nathaniel Preston or any sales of the two stocks Preston had purchased. He found neither.

He looked at his watch. It was not yet seven. No ordinary business would be open, but it was ten on the East Coast and the market was about to open. Any stock broker worth his salt would be on duty. D.T. called the one he had used as an expert witness the few times when the past or future value of securities had become an issue.

"Green and Hastings."

"Paul Brashman, please."

"Whom shall I say is calling?"

"Say it's D. T. Jones."

"One moment."

D.T. drained his third cup of coffee as he waited, feeling his brain begin to curdle from its impact. His eyes seemed salted. He wanted badly to lie down.

"D.T.? How goes it?"

"At a snail's pace, Paul. How about yourself?"

"Great. Volume's at an all-time high and so is the

Dow. Nowhere to go but up, if interest rates stay down. You're in early.''

"Out late. I need a favor."

"Testimony?"

"Research."

"We're the best in the business. What have you got? Hot tip, I suppose."

"Two companies. Clifford Microdata and East Jersey Instruments. Ever hear of them?"

"Nope. Not big board. Are they public?"

"I think so. Or at least they were. Over-the-counter."

"What do you want to know?"

"Just what has happened to them since 1965. In other words, how much an investment of a hundred shares in each of them in that year would be worth today."

"Hmm. May take a while."

"How long?"

"Three, four hours."

"No problem. Give me a call."

"Will do. Tape's kicking in so I got to run. Let's play golf."

"I get three a side."

D.T. hung up on the broker's curse of protest and went over to the couch and stretched out, masking his eyes with his arm. Should he try to persuade Esther Preston to file suit after all? What if the stock were worth a fortune? He'd told her, what, a 25 percent contingency? He could use 25 percent of almost anything. The problem was her safety. But surely she could be protected. Rita Holloway. Toledo. The cops, if necessary. And hell, it was probably coincidental anyway. A kid had moved the ramp as a prank. The glass and oil were merely spills, the walker defective. Even Vivaldi and Doris Day movies seem ominous at three a.m. Maybe he should go ahead and sue.

The next thing he knew Bobby E. Lee was shaking his shoulder. "You have to be in court in half an hour," he said. "I thought I'd better wake you."

"Right, right."

"The Stone transcript came in."

"Send it to Mrs. Stone by messenger, with a note for her to read it right away."

D.T. stumbled to his feet and went into the bathroom and cleaned himself up as best he could, then, smelling of Scope and Noxzema, he donned the shirt and tie and coat he kept at the office for such contingencies and went out to Bobby E. Lee's desk. "What have I got?"

"Jensen. Motion to compel further answers to interrogatories and production of documents."

"Where's the file?"

"Here."

"Magistrate?"

"Yes."

"See you."

D.T. headed toward the door and then turned back. "Sorry about last night."

"It's all right."

"I had to know."

"I know."

"Maybe I won't have to do anything with it."

"Maybe so."

D.T. went to court to waste his time and his client's money, playing the games that judges let lawyers play despite a thousand reasons not to. When he was finished he drove to the hospital. The nurse on the orthopedic ward asked if he was a relative of Mrs. Preston. He told her he was better than her relative, he was her lawyer. The nurse sniffed and frowned and consulted her chart. "She has suffered a concussion and many contusions," she said stiffly. "She still has much discomfort."

"You mean pain."

"I mean what I say, young man."

"I'll only be a minute."

The nurse scratched her cheek. She seemed to have a beard. "I see Rita Holloway has listed you as an authorized visitor."

"Do you know Miss Holloway?"

"She was formerly on staff." From her look she and Rita Holloway were engaged in a blood feud.

"Which room?" D.T. asked.

"Four-nineteen."

"I'll find it."

He took a right, then a left, and pushed open a heavy numbered door. The first bed was entirely shrouded by an orange curtain that hung like a slice of the sun from a circular track in the ceiling. He peeked beyond the curtain and saw Esther Preston in the second bed.

He had expected a cast or traction or some other by-product of trauma, but she was unencumbered, asleep, propped up by the tilted end of the bed. Her hospital gown was imprinted with little pink flowers, her flesh was as thin and substanceless as tissue. When he approached her bed she opened her eyes.

"Mr. Jones. How nice."

"How are you, Mrs. Preston?"

"I've been better, I must admit."

"I imagine."

"But they tell me I was quite fortunate, it could have been much worse. But then that can be said of anything, can't it?"

"Have you talked to Miss Holloway?"

"Briefly. She was here just after I got out of X ray."

"Did she say anything about how you came to fall?"

"I know how I fell, Mr. Jones. I was careless."

"It may be more than that, Mrs. Preston."

She frowned, and grimaced from what he hoped was a source of pain other than himself. "How do you mean?"

"Have you heard from your husband lately, by any chance?"

She raised her brows. "Oddly enough, I have. What makes you ask?"

"What did he say?"

"He asked me to leave him alone, was, I believe, the way he put it. It was more a directive than a request."

"What did you say?"

"I said I had left him alone for fifteen years and I would be happy to continue doing so. But what does this have to do with my falling in the bathroom?"

"I think your husband may have left you some reminders, Mrs. Preston."

"What sort of reminders?"

He told her what he and Rita Holloway had found, and what they suspected. "Are you certain of this?" she asked when he had finished.

"Not completely, no. It could all be coincidental."

"Is there a way to prove whether or not Nat did it?"

"I doubt it. Certainly not without calling in the police."

"I see."

She closed her eyes and sighed. Her thin chest rose and fell beneath the bedclothes. Somewhere down the hall an operatic laugh rang out, then ceased abruptly. D.T. wondered if there was anyone in the next bed, and what they had that needed to be hidden. "Mr. Jones?" Her voice was faint.

"What?"

"What does the D.T. stand for? If you don't mind my asking."

"Dog Tired," he said.

She sighed and smiled.

"I don't think you ought to stay alone for a while, Mrs. Preston. After you leave here, I mean."

She opened her eyes. "You think he'll keep on trying to frighten me?"

"He may. It'll take time to get word to him that we're not going to file any kind of suit."

"But I never intended to sue him."

"I know. This whole thing is my fault. I did some investigating and in the process word got to him that I was checking him out. He didn't like it, apparently."

"What on earth do you think he's afraid of?" she asked, her voice high in wonderment. "How could I possibly be a danger to him?"

"I wish I knew," D.T. said truthfully. "The only thing I can think of is a malpractice case that somehow stayed hidden all these years."

"But how is that possible?"

"Well, if the victim doesn't realize he or she has a claim, then the statute of limitations doesn't begin to run. So if your husband screwed up, and someone eventually died or was badly injured, and there was no reasonable way for that person to know at the time that it was your husband's fault, he could be sued today even though it's years after he saw the patient. Is there anything at all you can think of like that? A patient who was misdiagnosed? A problem delivery he messed up? A miscarriage caused by something he prescribed? Anything?"

"No. Nothing out of the ordinary."

"How about drugs? Was he a user? Or maybe he sold uppers to the kids on the block?"

"I'm sure not."

"Was he an abortionist? It was illegal in those days, I think."

"No. Not that I know of. I'm sorry, but there's nothing at all like that. Of course, I wasn't at his office. I suppose all kinds of things could have gone on without my knowledge."

"Well, I know you must be tired. Take care of yourself, Mrs. Preston. If you need anything, just call. And don't worry. I'll calm your husband's nerves and you won't have any more trouble with him. And Miss Holloway and Toledo will stay with you for a while, just to make sure."

Her lips grew taut. "I had some other plan in mind, Mr. Jones."

"What?"

Her expression was as uncommon as a mask. "I think we ought to sue the sucker. Can we?" Her lips could have cut wood.

D.T. paused to think and wiped his brow. His face grew warm from his quick desire to abet her folly. "We can sue anybody for anything," he said.

"Can we win?"

He thought about the stocks and decided not to mention them just yet. "I doubt it. A small amount, if anything."

"Will you do it anyway?"

"Are you sure you want me to?"

"I am."

"What about the danger?"

She smiled happily. "One advantage of the afflicted is that we can feign a rather flashy courage. Will you do it, Mr. Jones? Please?"

He sighed, suddenly disliking both of them for what she made him do. "I'll file the complaint, and I'll try the case if it gets that far. But that's it. I can't afford to do much more than that with it. Discovery costs money."

"Sounds good to me."

"Let's do this. I'll go back to the office and draft the complaint. You think it over. I'll send my secretary out here with the original for you to sign. If you change your mind you tell him so and that'll be it. No problem. And in fact that's what I strongly advise you to do, Mrs. Preston. Forget it.''

"Oh, I would have, Mr. Jones. If he hadn't done *this*." She gestured at her surroundings. "He's made me dependent again, and afraid the way I used to be during the days when I first learned I had sclerosis. I can't forgive him for that."

"Well, you think it over," D.T. repeated. "By the way, Dr. Haskell says hello."

"Goodness, I haven't seen him in years. How is he?"

"Emaciated."

She laughed. "He would be. Why were you meeting with him?"

"To talk about your husband."

"Oh? What did he say?"

"That he was a complete and total bastard."

"Yes. I suppose that just about covers it." Esther Preston giggled.

"I only wish there was a law against it," D.T. said, then said good-bye.

As he left the hospital and walked toward the parking lot he heard his name called. Rita Holloway was trotting toward him, carrying a small handbag in one hand. "Did you see her?" she asked breathlessly. "I brought her things."

D.T. nodded. "Thanks for leaving my name."

"How is she?"

"Fine. She wants to sue the bastard."

"You must be joking. Did you tell her what he did?"

"Yep. That's what made her mad enough to do it."

"But what if he tries to scare her again? Or worse?"

"You're going to have to stop him."

"Me?"

"I don't think he'd try anything with another person around the house. And there are ways to let you know if someone has been inside while you're gone. So don't worry. We'll figure it out."

Rita Holloway shook her head. "My God. I can't *believe* she wants to go ahead."

"Sure you can."

She looked at him. "I guess I can at that," she said, then started to move around him toward the hospital.

He put a hand on her shoulder. "Have you had breakfast?"

She raised a brow and cocked her head. "No. I haven't."

"Why don't you drop off Mrs. Preston's things, then let me buy you a pancake or something."

Rita Holloway frowned, eyed him oddly, then scratched her nose. "I have to get out of these clothes. I reek."

"I'll meet you at your place. You can change, then we'll hit a little bistro I frequent upon occasion."

"Not the Walrus, I hope."

He laughed. "This one washes their glasses and everything. So how about it? French toast with sourdough? Belgian waffle with blueberry compote? Buckwheats with real maple syrup? Come on."

She hesitated long enough to make him optimistic. Her lips parted in a half-smile. "Why don't we do this? I only live three blocks from here. You come over, and I'll bathe and change, and then I'll make you an omelette that will curl your toes."

"Jack cheese?"

"Sure."

"Onions?"

"Naturally."

"Tomato sauce?"

"Of course."

"You're on."

D.T. went to his car and waited while Rita Holloway took Mrs. Preston's bag into the hospital. She reappeared a few minutes later, waved at him, climbed into a little red Datsun, and drove out of the hospital lot. D.T. followed closely, wondering what he was up to.

Three minutes later Rita Holloway parked in front of a handsome four-plex with a dark stone front that hinted of fortresses and castles. She got out of the car and waited for him to join her. When he was by her side she unlocked the door to the building and went inside and climbed the stairs to the second floor. He followed, admiring the stretch of her uniform across her rump, resisting an urge to swat her. When they reached the second floor she unlocked the door to Apartment Three and stepped aside for him to enter.

He had taken two steps when a thunder of footsteps made him turn. A beast was hurtling toward them, half-husky and half-lion from the look of him; half-crazed as well.

"Toledo. Hi, Toledo. Hi, hi, hi, Toledo. Yes. You're a good dog. Yes, you are. Want some food? Do you? Do you want your breakfast?" Rita Holloway stopped cooing and turned to D.T. "Let me feed him. I'll only be a minute."

She disappeared behind a louvered door and left him in her living room. Its atmosphere was heavy, almost masculine, with dark blue walls and thick stuffed furniture and stalagmites of books and magazines rising off the floor. The couch and loveseat and club chair were paired with a floor lamp, coffee table, and pouf. The TV and stereo were new. The posters were of art exhibits and modern plays. He was comfortable before he thought to sit down.

"Coffee?" she asked as she came back in the room.

"Please."

"I'll get it started, then change, then get after those omelettes. Make yourself at home. I'll only be a second."

She went through the louvered door again, ran water, rattled cans and cookware, ground coffee beans in a machine that brought to mind his dentist. He sat in the club chair, cast about for something to read, settled for *Cosmopolitan*.

"The newspaper's probably down in my box," she called from behind the door. "If you're interested."

"I'll get it."

He fetched the paper and returned to his chair. From the end of the hall down which Toledo had charged came the high sigh of a shower. He exchanged *Cosmo* for the *Tribune*, read an article about Nicaragua, then one about Beirut, then one about the spread of AIDS. He thought of Bobby E. Lee, and worried.

Something in the kitchen whistled. He went through the narrow door and took the kettle off the burner and poured some water into the filter atop the Chemex, onto the fresh-ground beans. The kitchen was so neat it was unnerving. He grabbed a slice of bread from the loaf on the counter and went back to the living room, then wandered down the hall, munching Roman Meal.

The door at the far end was half-open. D.T. pushed it all the way. Toledo trotted out, growling. He gave the dog the remaining crust of bread. After drooling on his hand, Toledo trotted meekly toward the kitchen in search of a second slice. He peeked, saw the bedroom was empty and went inside. The only place to sit besides the bed was the chair beside the dressing table.

The room smelled of talc and roses. The bed was brass, with a flowered quilt and gigantic pillows whose covers featured the silhouettes of bunnies. The blinds were drawn, the morning light made lavender by its passage through the curtains.

As he sniffed something in a crystal cruet, Rita Holloway walked into the room, head bowed, eyes shut, fixing a towel around her hair. The rest of her was naked. After she tucked away an edge she straightened up and saw him. Her hands dropped from her head to her hips.

"Well."

"Well, well."

"Do you always spy on unsuspecting women, Mr. Jones?"

"Only when I get the chance. And only when they're naked and owe me favors."

"I see. And is this where I'm supposed to scream and carry on and make a mad dash for the closet?"

He shook his head. "This is where you're supposed to tell me if you want to make what is known these days as love. With me. Right now."

"Before breakfast?" Her eyebrows made twin carets.

"Since we haven't slept yet, let's look at it as after dinner."

Her smart look faded. "I'm going with someone."

"So am I."

"I think it should make a difference."

"So do I."

She frowned, then crossed her arms across her breasts. "May I take a minute to see if it does?"

"Be my guest. I'll just do my nails."

He turned his back to her, avoided his reflection in her mirror, grasped an emery board, and began to sand his fingertips. The raspy sound masked what he thought might be her laugh. His mind contained a triptych: her tight brown body, plus Barbara, plus Michele.

The mirror was angled so he couldn't see what she was doing. The sounds she made were ambiguous. He finished one hand and began the other.

"Mr. Jones?"

"Yes?" He started to pivot toward her.

"Don't turn around. Are you in the market for a meaningful relationship or a one-night stand? Or morning, as it were. And please be honest."

"The latter, I guess. I've found it best not to go looking for relationships, that they usually hunt you down themselves."

She paused. "See my purse there on the floor beside you?"

"Yes."

"Open it up and get a dollar out of it . . . no, don't look at me . . . go on . . . now put the dollar in your pocket. Good. That makes you officially my lawyer, right? With a retainer and everything."

"I guess it does."

"So you have to keep what happens next strictly confidential, don't you, Mr. Jones?"

"I certainly do, Miss Holloway."

"Then you may proceed."

There were no covers on the bed, only Rita Holloway, naked but for a diaphanous scarf she had draped over the dark and bulbous portions of her body, masking them in silk, stuffing him with lust. He removed his clothes and joined her. Her flesh was wet and warm. He rubbed her flank, then wrapped his arms around her waist, nuzzling her neck. "Is Toledo going to mind?" he murmured.

"Not unless you make me cry."

They fit themselves to each other, found a rhythm, rolled one way and then the other. "Did you know this was going to happen when you asked me out for breakfast?" she asked as she rolled on top.

"I think so."

"Did you turn off the stove?"

"Yep."

"Then I guess we can get right to it."

He told her he'd give it his best shot. Sometime later she uttered what he thought might be a cry, but Toledo stayed away so he guessed it might have been a cheer.

When he got back to his office he began dictating the complaint in the case of *Preston* v. *Preston*. Halfway through, the telephone buzzed. "D.T.? Paul Brashman. I got the dope."

"Shoot."

Brashman cleared his throat. "Clifford Microdata. Small electronics outfit in Southern California. Founded by some IBM refugees. Now defunct. One hundred shares purchased in 1965 is worth exactly zip."

"I figured as much. Same story on the other?"

"Not quite. East Jersey Instruments. Medical equipment house. Small, then hit on a couple of significant advances in prosthetics. Bought by Federal Hospital Supply in '72. One hundred shares of East Jersey is now a five-hundred-share position in Federal Hospital. Current quote: thirty-seven and a half. Market value: eighteen thousand and change. Less commission."

Times three equalled fifty thousand plus. Divided by two equalled twenty-five thousand plus. Times 25 percent equalled seven thousand plus, contingent fee of D. T. Jones pursuant to verbal agreement with Esther Preston. "Thanks, Paul," D.T. said, and hung up.

D.T. added a claim to his complaint and gave the cassette to Bobby E. Lee to type. When it was finished, D.T. sent Bobby off to the hospital and told him he could go home after seeing Mrs. Preston.

That night Bobby E. Lee called him at home for the first time ever. "I talked to her for two hours," he said. "You absolutely *have* to do something to help that woman."

"Well, plunk your magic twanger, Bobby, and make me something better than I am."

Bobby E. Lee hung up.

D.T. floated through the motions of preparing for sleep, his mind full to bursting with Esther Preston and her problems. When he was under the covers he picked up the telephone.

"Dr. Preston? This is D. T. Jones. We met at Joyce Tuttle's? Sorry to be calling so late."

"I have nothing to say to you, Jones. Talk to my lawyers. Bronwin, Kilt and Loftis."

"I have something to say to you, though. Your attempt at terrorism didn't work, Doctor; it just made her mad. So I'm warning you. No more threats, no more sabotage; no more contact with her of any kind. If she suffers as much as a hangnail I'm going to the cops and tell them exactly what you've been up to and why, and I'm going to swear out a criminal complaint against you for assault and endangerment. Do you hear me, Dr. Preston? I'm telling you to leave Esther the hell alone."

"I don't have the faintest idea what you're talking about, Jones, you goddamned maniac. But if you don't leave *me* alone I'm going to ruin you in this town. Believe me. I'll make you wish you'd *never heard my name*."

■ FIFTEEN

"Mr. Jones?"

"Yes?"

"I'm sorry to be calling so early, Mr. Jones. This is Irene Alford. You represent me in my divorce case? We go to court the middle of next month?"

"Of course. How are you?"

"Not too well, actually."

"What's the problem?"

"I . . . it's difficult to explain. My husband keeps calling me. And coming around. At all hours. He's driving me crazy."

"Is he threatening you? Has he assaulted you?"

"No, no, he hasn't threatened to do anything to *me*. It's . . ."

"It's what?"

"It's him. He claims he'll kill himself if I don't let him come back to me, if we don't reconcile. He tells me how he's going to do it, what it will feel like. *Look* like. It's horrible."

"Do you believe him?"

"That he'll really do it? Yes. I think he might. He talks about suicide all the time. He always has, since way before I considered divorcing him."

"If everyone who talked about it actually did it we'd be running short of people, Mrs. Alford."

"I know, but Louis is different. He has this terrific martyr complex. Always the sacrifice, always the burden on his shoulders, always the victim. It's his thing, you know? He's famous for it. It's one of the reasons I decided I couldn't live with him any more."

"Did we get a restraining order directing him to stay away from you?"

"No. You mentioned it, but I didn't think it was necessary. I keep underestimating him."

"I think we'd better get one now. I'll try to have the papers ready to file today."

"That means the police will arrest him if he comes around again, is that right? If I call them and complain?"

"That's about it."

"I don't know if I could have Louis arrested. He's up for tenure this year. My God, if he gets passed over he will *definitely* blow his brains out. . . . Listen to me. I'm making jokes about it."

"Mrs. Alford, calm down. He's trying to make you solely responsible for the failure of your marriage. He will even get you to believe it if you let him. The first thing to do is keep him away from you. The second is to get him some kind of help. Do you agree?"

"I . . . yes. I guess I do."

"Has he ever been in analysis?"

"No."

"Is there a physician or clergyman or another professional he's close to?"

"No. He's very competitive. He has few friends. He's jealous of the *world*. I have no idea who could help him."

"Family?"

"Estranged."

"Okay. I can give you the names of some psychiatrists who are very experienced with this kind of thing."

"You've had this happen before?"

"Several times."

"Have any of them actually . . . ?"

"One."

"How awful."

"Yes. But the vast majority did not. The point is, it's not your fault if it happens. You are not obliged to live with a man you no longer love, not even to save his life. You aren't required to be the solution to every problem he's got. You weren't while you were living together and you're most definitely not now. Understand?"

"Yes."

"You're human, not divine. Right?"

"Right."

"Now these doctors are all in the book. Their names are Dillon, Friller, and Exlerton. The first is a woman, if you think it makes a difference. Also, there's a crisis center which counsels the suicidal. You might want to talk to them yourself, to get their suggestions on how to handle him if he calls or comes around again. And give him their number, if he calls you. In the meantime, I'll talk to his lawyer. I'll tell him we're getting a restraining order and that your husband could jeopardize his career if he doesn't let you alone. Okay?"

"I don't think it will do any good. He's convinced himself he can't live without me. He just calls and calls. I dread the sound of it, the phone. I just *dread* it."

"Hang up. Change your number. Get an answering machine."

"I have one. He used the entire tape on one call. It reminded me of *Hamlet,* for God's sake. That's what he teaches, by the way. Elizabethan drama. He's an actor in his own play."

"You're in his play too, Mrs. Alford, if you go on like this. So don't talk to him. Don't let him in the house."

"Okay."

"Call me if there's trouble. After tomorrow, call the cops. He'll be a misdeameanant if he keeps harassing you."

"I don't know if I could live with myself if I did that, Mr. Jones. I really don't."

"It might be the best thing for him in the long run, Mrs. Alford. That's all I can say. My guess is he's been coddled all his life. It's time for a kick in the pants. Try not to worry," he added, and said good-bye.

Something else to lose sleep over. Another drama that would stage itself above his bed in the wee hours of the morning, no doubt in a violent and tragic guise. The odds were small that the jerk would do it, but they were there; the portion of the population on the fence of sanity or beyond it was fantastic. Now that they were no longer locked away you saw them everywhere, babbling, raving, burrowing through the city like moles, their minds flapping like torn flags. They were pitiful, and helpless, yet in their abandonment and their potential somehow terri-

fying. D.T. swore. He hated how much he found in the
world to fear. He pulled the phone to him and dialed
another number.

"Mrs. Stone? This is D. T. Jones. Did you have a
chance to read the transcript of your husband's deposition?"

"Is that what you call it? It read like a fairy tale to me.
And I do mean grim."

"I need to talk to you about it, Mrs. Stone. Can I come
by this afternoon?"

"Can't we do it by phone?"

"I'd rather do it in person. Say four?"

"I suppose so. If you must."

"See you then."

Good. He would see her house, see how she fit in it,
the way she kept it, see how much trouble she would go
to knowing he was coming. Then some time before the
trial he would drop by unannounced. To see whether she
really was unfit. Not that it would make any difference.
She had paid her fee and he was her boy. In court he
would paint her a blend of Sister Teresa and Father Flan-
agan, Dinah Shore and Jimmy Stewart.

Bobby E. Lee peeked into the room. "Mr. Slater is
here."

"The process server?"

Bobby nodded.

"What's he want? His money?"

"That. Plus he mentioned the Finders case."

"Send him in."

Bobby E. Lee disappeared and a moment later a fat,
ruddy-faced man stomped into the room, sneered at its
contents, and marched to the front of D.T.'s desk as
though volunteering for something risky. His clothes
seemed to be struggling to escape him. A wad of something the size of a pear filled a front pants pocket. A pen
was clipped to the placket of his shirt, its tip out of sight
behind a polyester plaid. The temples of his glasses were
taped at the hinge. "You ain't paid your bill," he said,
making it a proclamation.

"I told you I'd have it by the end of the month."

"I know what you told me," he countered, his puffy
eyes inviting D.T. to make a further promise. D.T. said

nothing. "The Finders guy? On Houston Street?" Slater went on.

"What about him? Is he served?"

Slater's lips curled as though they had begun to fry. "He pulled a gun on me. A fucking magnum. I could have crawled down the barrel and survived World War Three."

"I'm sorry."

"I didn't hear nothing from you about this guy being a cowboy, did I? Huh? Isn't that what I told you: the guy you want served is a fucking gun-toter you tell me up front, right? Didn't I fucking stand right here and tell you that?"

"I didn't know. I'm sorry."

"Yeah, well, the guy looked like he was ready to give me an extra nostril. Most of them don't, you know, look like they'd really shoot the fucking thing. This one did. But at least I don't got to go back."

"Why not?"

"You ain't paid your bill, number one. Number two, there was this broad standing behind him while he was waving his piece at me, tits like my old lady would kill for. Said she was the wife. Said she wasn't going to dump the cowboy after all. Said for me not to come around with no papers ever again. So here they are." Slater tossed the documents on the desk. "Tab comes to eighty-seven fifty for this one alone. I don't get it the end of the month I give it to my collection agency and they smear your name all over town, the credit dentist won't clean your teeth. You get it?"

"I get it."

"One more thing."

"What?"

"Here."

Slater thrust another paper at him. D.T. took it reluctantly. "Which is this, for God's sake? Don't tell me you missed another one."

Slater's grin spread like a run in a nylon. "This is the case of *Dillinghert* v. *Jones*. Complaint for malpractice. Prayer of two hundred thousand actuals, plus a half million punitives, plus fees and costs. Enjoy." Slater's face was one great gloat. He turned and left the office.

When D.T. discovered his mouth was open he closed it, then clutched blindly at the document Slater had handed him and tried to read its crackling pages. It was as Slater had said, a complaint against him, its code as familiar to him as the *Racing Form*.

Words slapped his eyes then vanished, acrobats, tumblers, unconnected to each other. Dillinghert. Jones. Plaintiff complains of defendant and alleges. Client. Attorney. Services for hire. Fiduciary relationship. Breach of trust. Neglect of duty. Negligently and carelessly failed to discover and include. Husband's pension. Property settlement agreement. Lack of due care. Failure to observe standards of his profession. Knew or should have known of said rights. Proximate cause of loss. Present value in excess of two hundred thousand dollars. Punitives. Fees and costs. Such other and further relief as the court may deem just.

Two hundred thousand.

Two hundred thousand.

Two hundred thousand.

D.T. dropped the complaint on his desk. Goddamned military pensions. A new community property right, first accorded women in the state a decade ago, then taken back by the Supreme Court, then awarded again by Congress. Murky area of the law, coupled with a client he could not abide. She had been arrogant and self-pitying, contemptuous of all men and lawyers except her brother, who lived off personal injuries in the state of Arizona and thus was somehow qualified to second-guess him. He'd wanted her out of his office, the way he wanted to lose a bad tooth, and his perfunctory questions had revealed no hint of pension rights or any other rights in her husband beyond those accorded every citizen. As he recalled, the husband had been self-employed at the time, a cabinetmaker, though evidently not forever. Fifteen pension-earning years in a federal armory, claimed the hysterical complaint.

Malpractice. The plaintiff's lawyer was Oswald Blacker, the sleaziest in the city, a snorting symbol of the profession's lack of standards that proscribed anything short of outrage—standards that in fact encouraged the sham and misrepresentation and false promise which were the specialties of far too many practitioners of the trade of Pound and Cardozo. Malpractice. Bobby E. Lee stuck his head in the door but D.T. waved him away. Mal–fucking–practice.

D.T. pulled out his form file and dictated a motion for a temporary restraining order that would direct the almost-tenured Louis Alford to refrain from communicating his design for self-destruction to his wife. The words fell off his tongue automatically: "restrained from contacting, molesting, attacking, striking, threatening, sexually assaulting, battering, telephoning, or otherwise disturbing the peace of the petitioner." What horror the words encompassed, what insignificance the system had reduced them to, the same phrases used by all—from the truly endangered, like Lucinda Finders, to the trivially annoyed, like the client of D.T.'s who had called the cops when her husband stopped by to ask if she wanted to use his opera tickets.

Malpractice. *That* particular word still held its threat. Too bad there wasn't a restraining order protecting lawyers from their clients.

Louis Alford. Suicide. To be or not to be; right, Professor? Let me count the ways. Bite the barrel, the top of the head spattered against the wall. Slash the wrists and go with the flow. Jump off something. No, he would have to feign an accident, so Heather would receive the insurance proceeds he had been purchasing all these years. Drive into a wall. Stumble off a cliff. Inadvertent poisoning. Electrocution. Drowning. Supposedly the least painful, drowning. All tried and true methods, he supposed, though none as comfortably definite as a bullet in the brain. With his luck he would muff it, render himself an invalid, a prisoner in that most abhorrent of conditions— a human unable to flee the noise of other humans. Suicide. The worst that could happen would be to spend an eternity in hell, which couldn't possibly be worse than an hour at a bar association meeting. Suicide. He picked up the phone.

"Harry? D. T. Jones. How's it going?"

"It's a rocky road, D.T."

"All the rocks on your road are diamonds, Harry."

"A vicious calumny. Spread by those who equate virtue with impoverishment. All of them impoverished themselves, I might note. How can I be of service?"

"I got a call from the wife of one of your clients. Mrs. Louis Alford. Ring a bell?"

"A small tinkle, perhaps. The problem?"

"He's annoying her. Calls. Visits at all hours."

"Violence?"

"Not yet. His gambit is a threat of suicide if she does not tuck him back into the conjugal bed."

"Ah. Entreaty number three-oh-two."

"Right. I'm getting a 4359(a)(2) order this afternoon, should you care to waste an hour opposing it."

"You're kidding. For a few phone calls?"

"The guy's a nut, Harry."

"Nonsense. He holds a distinguished position in one of the finest universities in the world."

"Let's say he *almost* holds such a position. He's up for tenure right now. She won't hesitate to call the law on him, Harry. Bye-bye sinecure if she does. Perhaps you should give him a word from the wise."

"What judge?" Harry asked.

"Buchanan."

"I'll think about it."

"Say, Harry?"

"Hm?"

"Ever been sued for malpractice?"

Harry coughed. D.T. could imagine him straightening his silk tie, shooting his French cuffs, adjusting his rolled lapels. "Are you suggesting I've not met my . . ."

"Nothing like that, Harry. I was just asking."

"You?"

"Yep."

"Once," Harry said.

"What happened?"

"My carrier bought me out of it."

"How much?"

"Sorry."

"Exposure, though?"

"Depends on who you talked to. *I* certainly didn't think so."

"Did it get you down?"

Harry paused, longer this time, long enough for him to

have poured a shot of his favorite cognac. "It was like someone cut off my balls, D.T. I wasn't the same man for a while. For quite a long while, actually. Sex life. Tennis game. Everything. It was as though that one transgression had tainted everything I'd ever done."

"What'd you do about it?"

"Worked twice as hard and made three times as much money as I had before. Tried cases I should have settled and took on clients I should have sent packing. All to prove I was a good lawyer, the best, no matter what that damned complaint alleged. I got a little crazy for a while, is what I'm saying. So watch yourself."

"Thanks, Harry," D.T. said. Harry said good-bye.

After grabbing a sandwich at the Walrus, D.T. went to the courthouse, hunted up a judge, and got his order theoretically protecting Irene Alford from her husband but practically useless against anything Alford really had a mind to do. Harry never showed up to oppose him. After the order was filed, D.T. called Mrs. Alford from the courthouse to tell her the police now had a reason to respond to her calls for assistance. He also gave her his home number. His steps to protect her seemed only to make her more depressed. He could hardly hear her speak. After he hung up he drove to Mareth Stone's.

It was a white colonial in the middle of a block of them, its bricks painted to an alabaster gleam, its chimneys red and tall and undefiled by soot, its portico a triumph of Doric solemnity. It was the kind of house husbands think wives adore, and are usually wrong.

D.T. parked beneath the high porch and crossed the veranda and rang the bell. Although his imagination couldn't fit her in the place, Mareth Stone opened the door immediately, her face as fixed and managed as the first time he had seen her. As she led him through the house he tried and failed to find evidence of the sloth her husband claimed was flourishing there. The thing most out of place was himself.

Without looking back, she strode into the living room and sat down, knees locked, hands clasped, feet flat, aggressively demure. D.T. sat on the loveseat across from her.

"A beautiful house."

"Thank you. I plan to sell it after the divorce."

"You keep it up all by yourself?"

She looked at him archly. "My sister comes in once a week to help. I pay her," she added after a moment.

D.T. nodded. He expected her to offer him a drink and he expected to accept it, but she said nothing. "You read the deposition?"

"Yes."

"What'd you think?"

"Predictable."

"How do you mean?"

"I mean he takes things and twists them and makes it look like he's in the right and I'm in the wrong. On everything. He did it our entire marriage, so it's hardly a surprise that he's doing it now."

"I tend to agree," D.T. said. "He's making his case against you by putting you under a magnifying glass that exaggerates only your faults. He's trying to crucify you for being human. Your mistake will be in thinking he can't get away with it."

"He can't, can he?"

"He can if we get the wrong judge. And he can if we don't do our job. Which is to explain away every one of his allegations. Have you got one?"

"One what?"

"An explanation."

She nodded slowly. "My life may be a mystery to him, Mr. Jones, but it is not to me."

"Let's hear it. First, the booze."

She sniffed. "I am not a drunk. I have never been arrested for drinking; I have never passed out. The night Chas referred to I was merely sleeping." She took a breath. "I drink to relax. Not every day, not even every week, these days. Just once in a while. I exercise my constitutional right to take something to make me feel better. My something happens to be bourbon. And I have acted silly at parties because the parties were silly to begin with."

D.T. smiled. "What about the bar?"

"I went in there once to buy cigarettes. It's on the way home from the mall. I saw a girl who used to be a checkout at the market I use. She had become a cocktail waitress. We talked, mostly about our hair. I liked her. I went back a few times. To talk to her about other things. She told me about her boyfriend Dale and her problems with him. They sounded a lot like mine. I learned a few things.''

"Like what?"

"Like saying no. Like putting my foot down. Like taking a whole day sometimes and doing only what I wanted to do. And the most I ever had in there was two drinks.''

"Witnesses?''

"Well, the girl, except she moved to Phoenix with Dale. The bartender, I guess. He's kind of a lecher. I'm sure he'd remember me.''

"I'll talk to him. How about the affair?''

"I told you. One man. One month. Two dirty deeds. That was it.''

"How'd it start?''

"Chas and I had our first big fight. He attacked me savagely. Verbally, I mean; he's a master of verbal abuse. Called me irresponsible. Negligent. Slovenly, that was the one that got me. Slovenly. I moved to the guest room, but it wasn't enough. I needed someone to tell me Chas was wrong. I knew who that someone was. He liked me. He'd told me so in those ways men have—laughing at your jokes, patting your shoulders, fetching your drinks. The next time I saw him I let him know I was available. He was glad to hear it.'' She smiled for the first time. "We cooked up a plan that ended with us meeting by a carefully calculated accident in a downtown hotel. After that we became less elaborate in our schemes. Interestingly, the affair immediately became less fun. Eventually we learned we didn't have what it took to be cheaters, either of us. We went back from whence we came. And Richard confessed all on Christmas eve. I didn't know that before.''

"What does it take to be a cheater?'' D.T. asked.

"It's not what it takes, it's what it doesn't take, Mr. Jones.''

"Which is?''

"The intelligence to realize that once you have experienced infidelity you can never, *ever* experience fidelity again.''

She seemed sad, wanting to say more, but he let it go. "How about since Chas moved out?"

"I've dated. That's all. Nothing kinky, nothing promiscuous. Men have been here, we've talked, they've gone home, none of them to wives, by the way. And none have spent the night. Not one."

"Sex?"

"Rarely. And not when the children were in the house." She smiled again. "They sleep over a lot."

"The rest of it? The mess? The lack of discipline? The sleeping late?"

"Guilty as charged," she said firmly. "I am not a saint. I dislike most household duties. I neglect them at the slightest excuse. I have trouble sleeping, from reasons ranging from anxiety to depression to rather erotic fancies, so I choose to stay in bed some mornings. The children manage quite nicely. Cristine makes far better oatmeal than I do. She puts cinnamon in it." Mareth Stone looked directly in his eyes for the first time. His eyes tried to hide. "Well. That's my confession. What do you think of it?"

"I think it'll have to get a little better by the time we go to trial."

"Better how?"

D.T. shrugged. "I'm not a coach, Mrs. Stone. Some lawyers tell their clients exactly what to say on the stand, but I don't because the training usually breaks down. We'll talk, though. A couple of days before the trial date. In the meantime, make a list of people who'll testify as to your sterling character."

She shook her head. "I won't drag anyone else into this." She grinned crookedly. "Except maybe my mother."

"Mothers are impeachable. Also, I want you to read the deposition again. Let me know if he was lying about anything. I mean a flat-out lie, not an exaggeration. Also, list anything you can think of that your husband did that was not in the best interests of your children."

"Like work sixteen hours a day? Like run the house like a boot camp?"

"That. Other things. We need to show he's not much of . . ."

"A bargain either? Is that what you were about to say, Mr. Jones? You bastard."

D.T. shrugged. "Close enough. It's been a bad day. I'm sorry."

They stared at each other stonily. Then each saw the other's face crumple into laughter. "This is all just horrible, isn't it? This fighting, blaming, criticizing?"

D.T. nodded. "Yep."

"It's like flunking a test. That's what I feel like. Chas flunked me, fired me from the only job I ever had. You know, being married is the only thing I ever really *decided* to do. Everything else just happened. Even motherhood. But I *decided* to marry Chas and now he's fired me. And it feels like shit, like there's this big hole in the world that no one's ever going to fix."

"I know."

He sensed she had finally surrendered, finally decided to be truthful. "How are you really getting along, Mrs. Stone?"

She sighed and closed her eyes. "I don't know. I'm fighting back, at least. I'm taking some classes at the university, seeing some men, seeing some women. My mother has been great, to my total surprise. I've learned things about her and Dad I never ever suspected. People are so good at hiding things, aren't they?"

"Sometimes it's a good thing they are."

"I suppose."

"How about the kids? How are they taking it?"

She frowned. "I'm worried, particularly about David. At first they both denied it was happening. They insisted Daddy would be back any minute. Then they got mad at him. Swore and carried on, and were very protective of me. But now David has started to blame himself. He feels he disappointed his father and that that's really why Chas left. It's very sad. I may have to take him to see someone."

"I can give you some names if you need them."

"Thank you. I'm trying very hard with the kids, Mr. Jones. I think I'm doing a good job. I think I'm getting them through it with as little scarring as possible. And they're helping me get through it as well. We've become

"Hello, Lawyer. I though I told you to keep away from her."

"She's my client. I wanted to see if she was all right."

Delbert grinned, revealing scrambled teeth. "That's where you're wrong, Lawyer-Man. She don't need a lawyer no more. You're out of a job."

"I know. She told me."

"She tell you I been treating her real sweet?"

"Something like that."

Del nodded peaceably. D.T. could smell the leather of his jacket over the sour musk of his breath. "She tell you to stay the fuck away from us? Huh? She tell you I see you again around here I'm going to bust you up?"

"She told me."

The hand on the knee became a fist. The tattoo undulated. His face froze. "I better seen the last of you, Mister. You hear me? Keep your bony ass away from my woman."

"I hear."

The hand slapped D.T.'s shoulder. The extravagant smile returned. "Good. Want a beer?"

"No, thanks."

D.T. looked at him, at the long brown hair gathered in an oddly feminine ponytail, at the single gold loop that dangled from an ear, at the pack of cigarettes stuffed into the pocket of his T-shirt, at the scattered teeth with edges dark with rot, at the beady, yellowed eyes, and imagined smashing everything about him to a pulp. Cleansing the world of Del forever. But though he warred in dreams, he said nothing that could be heard.

"Suit yourself," Delbert said affably. "Guess I better get in there and give Lucy what she's waiting for, which is about eight inches of good stiff dick. Right, Mister Lawyer-Man? Got to let them have their cock, don't we?"

Delbert had made him a co-conspirator. D.T.'s hands gripped the wheel, his teeth made noises against each other, his veins bulged with rushing blood.

The door opened and closed, the dome light flashed on and off, and Delbert was gone into the night, laughing, strutting, clutching beer. D.T. started the car and drove away, refusing to think of what had just happened, thinking only of where he could go. After ten unnoticed minutes he found himself on Billings Avenue.

The address Bobby E. Lee had given him was a darkly gothic structure, complete with parapets and sloping dormers. Its granite facade was blackened by at least a century of the city's soot, its oculus was lit like a cyclops' eye. A limestone fence protected the occupants from prying eyes. The wrought-iron gate was firmly closed. There was a street light on the corner, lights in several windows of the house, but the rest of the world was dark.

It started to rain. D.T. drove past the entrance once, then circled and passed it again, then turned around and parked down the block, facing the gate. As the rain beat cadence on the roof of his car he slid low in his seat and tried not to think of why he was where he was.

Several other cars were parked nearby, all of them expensive. The other houses on the street were as coldly aristocratic as the club. He wondered who lived in them, and whether they knew what was going on behind the spiked pickets of the gate he watched. Did they care? Should they care? Was there any point in caring about anything any more? He cared, sometimes, and what had it gotten him?

Malpractice.

A taxi pulled to the curb and discharged a passenger. Male. Wealthy. Past fifty. Furtive. A while later a car parked on the other side of the street and another man got out and unlocked the gate and went into the house. Then two men came out and drove away together. Then another one, young, trendy, on foot, went in. D.T. watched them all, hoping one of them would be Chas Stone, knowing that even sin was not that simple. After an hour he drove home.

He undressed and turned out the light and got into bed. He tossed and turned, seeing legal words and Lucinda Finders in his mind. He turned on the light and picked up the phone.

"Bobby? D.T. I'm making this a habit, aren't I?"

"It's all right."

"I need something."

"What?"

"A whore."

"But you . . ."

"Not for me. A guy. A gay."

Bobby E. Lee was silent.

"I want to set Stone up. I want him to meet Stone at the club, seduce him, then take him someplace where I can photograph Stone doing things that will make Judge Buchanan apoplectic. I'll pay two hundred bucks. But it has to be a pro. No amateurs. You know anyone? Come on, Bobby, goddamnit. Do you?"

"Maybe."

"Ask around. Let me know as soon as you can."

"I assume if I don't find someone for you you'll look elsewhere."

"You're damned right."

"I'll let you know."

"I could have done it without telling you, you know. I could have just done it."

"I know."

"Well, thanks for your help."

"I don't want your thanks, Mr. J. I just want the money you owe me. Or I report you to the state."

■ SIXTEEN

H E couldn't breathe. Something covered his mouth, something wet, heavy, soft. He struggled, twisting his head, straining to speak, fighting for air. When he raised a hand to his face other fingers forced it back. The weight of another body imprisoned him beneath his sheet.

Although his eyes were open, the room—blackened by the thick drape across his window—allowed only a guess at the shape and danger looming over him. Del? Had Delbert Finders downed the twelve-pack and come to wreak a vengeance that Lucinda had rendered pointless? Would he die only comically, his entire threat to Del previously dissolved by the capitulation of his wife? D.T. twisted his head again, and finally freed his mouth.

"I'm not her fucking lawyer anymore," he shouted. "She fired me, goddamnit."

Hot breath brushed his face. The scents of things familiar—toothpaste, mouthwash, soap—made him want to scratch his nose. He sneezed. The shadowy form that crushed him pulled back and then rolled off, granting freedom.

"Someone actually fired you? How cruel." The voice was not Del's, not a man's.

"Barbara?"

"You were expecting someone else?"

"What time is it?"

"Nine. Sleepyhead. You're hard to wake up."

"Jesus." He struggled to a sitting position. "I thought you were trying to kill me."

Barbara crossed her legs and faced him like a sporty

Buddha from the foot of the bed. As always, her full face was flushed with life. "Don't be so paranoid, D.T. I'm on my way to Visalia. Want to change your mind and come?"

He shook his head. "I promised Heather."

"We could be back tomorrow."

"Sorry. Next year."

She reached over and patted his cock, which was more alert than the rest of him. "Want me to crawl under there and give you something to be thankful for?"

His head still sloshed with sleep, her words had little meaning to anything except the elastic cells she was massaging. "You know how I am in the mornings," was all he said.

"D.T.?"

"What?"

"You aren't sleeping with Michele, are you?"

"No. Of course not."

"Truth?"

"Truth. Why?"

"I don't know. You seem a little less . . ."

"Ardent?"

"Right. Ardent. A little less ardent lately."

"I'm getting old, Barbara. It's not that I *feel* less ardent, it's just that by the time we get around to it, my ardent machine has already shut down for the day. It only works late about twice a month, for some reason. It doesn't have anything to do with you."

"Are you sure?"

"Sure."

"You're out of shape, D.T. Twenty miles a week would make a new man of you."

D.T. refused the bait.

Barbara smiled and released him. "I wish you were going home with me. You know how my mother and I get. We could use a referee."

He knew how they got, all right. Barbara blamed her mother for everything that was less than sterling in her life. Beyond that, Barbara faulted her mother for achieving nothing more notable than wife-and-motherhood; for wasting her life inside a bite-sized bungalow in the suburbs of a town that didn't even have suburbs. More than once, D.T. had sat across a cocktail table from Barbara, and listened to bar chatter while she had railed for hours against her absent mother. In the process she would characterize what seemed to D.T. a rather normal childhood as a spectacle that would have intrigued Dickens and delighted de Sade. And all evening D.T. would struggle mightily to refrain from pointing out that if Barbara had the right to blame *her* mother for her own shortcomings, then her mother in turn had every right to blame *her* mother for *her* own deficiencies, and so on back to Eve, whose only recourse was presumably to have it out with God.

"I may go on up to Grizzly Ridge on Friday," Barbara was saying. "Cross-country skiing. Want to meet me there?"

D.T. shook his head.

"I'll teach you how. I'll have the equipment all ready, so you won't have to wait in line."

She knew him well. "It's not my bag," he said.

"And golf is?" She mentioned the sport with her usual vaudevillian hoot.

D.T. replied in kind. "Finesse and carefully calibrated physical movement. None of this brute strength and witless reflex. It's why I'm such a wonderful lover."

Barbara climbed off the bed and loomed over him like a spectre in a sweatsuit. "Not before noon you're not."

She bent and kissed him, waved, and left.

Barbara. What was he going to do about her? Over the years he had compiled a long list of things no couple should ever attempt if they wanted to preserve their alliance. Camping together more than one night. Wallpapering. Ice-skating. Playing chess. Those and more were often fatal, as were any activities requiring courage on the part of either participant and any sports in which one of the couple was truly expert and the other a beginner. Client after client had traced the initial tremor of divorce to blunders of this type. Yet these were exactly the things that Barbara insisted, time after time, that she and he engage in. To the point where he dreaded hearing her plans for the weekend more than he dreaded the Fiasco.

What he suspected was that Barbara saw him primarily as a reclamation project, a vessel in need of filling with

improvement in everything from his intake of polyunsat-
urates to the timing of his ejaculations. He in turn had
begun to view Barbara as a professional resource. If he
could figure out Barbara then he could figure out his
clients—was the theory; but its converse must therefore
have been true as well—if he failed to fathom Barbara
then he must have been failing, day after clouded day, to
fathom the women who trooped in and out of his office in
the belief that he was qualified to help them. Their relationship was more the stuff of sociology than romance,
the atmosphere of teacher-pupil rather than of friend or
lover. So he guessed he was prepared to see it end with
Barbara, but not for it to be his doing.

He got out of bed, showered, dressed, read the paper.
Thanksgiving. Cute features about turkeys and Pilgrims,
and pious homilies from politicians thankful only for their
own election and the continued secrecy of their slush
fund. Outside, the downpour matched his mood.

He was due at Michele's at noon. The meal wouldn't
be served till five. Much dead time, one of Michele's best
weapons. He wondered what time George was coming.
What on earth would he say to the man? Should he offer
tips? Would they end up comparing notes about Michele's comportment in the bedroom, like frat brothers after
the second mixer? No. George was a better man then
that, and he hoped he was himself.

He poured a second cup of coffee and went out on the
deck, but the rain and the cold air and the immaculately
enervating view quickly drove him back indoors. He
turned on the radio and listened to Larry Gatlin and his
siblings sing about Beverly Hills. He wondered if a year
from now he would be giving thanks that no malpractice
judgment had been entered against him. Or would he be
scrambling through his scraggly assets, trying to figure
out how to satisfy a judgment without going bankrupt.
He wondered about Lucinda Finders, if she was with
Del, if they were having turkey, if they had somehow
managed to become happy. Not a chance. Big Macs and
beer and an inevitable clash. He wondered about Mareth
Stone. She had kids, and holidays were usually endurable
if kids were around. Except maybe Christmas. Christmas
was a predestined anticlimax, even if you got everything

on your list. He remembered the year he had wanted an electric train. He never got one. Not that year, not ever. Maybe he should buy one now. Run it around the office. A whole train of tank cars filled with Baileys Irish Cream. He wondered about Esther Preston and Rita Holloway for so long that he telephoned the little red house.

"Happy Thanksgiving," he said.

"Same to you, D.T."

"How's Mrs. Preston?"

"Fine. I'm about to serve her some cranberry sauce. She's a fiend for cranberry sauce."

"We filed the complaint."

Rita Holloway paused. "At one time I would have jumped for joy. Now, it terrifies me. If anything happens to Esther it'll be my fault."

"No, it won't. It'll be the fault of whoever makes it happen." And more than a little bit mine for not putting a stop to it, he thought but didn't say. "Any sign of someone snooping around?"

"No. Not while I've been here."

"You have my number, right?"

"Right."

"I'll be at this one from noon till about seven. Then I'll be home." He gave her Michele's number. "Do you have someplace to go?"

"My boyfriend's taking me to Antoine's."

"Nice place."

"Yes."

He waited for more about the boyfriend but it didn't come.

"Remember how I told you to mark the door, to see if anyone got in while you were gone?"

"I remember."

Pause. "Your family live here in the city?" he asked, reluctant to cut the connection.

"No. They're dead."

"I'm sorry. Brothers or sisters?"

"No. You?"

"Only a mother. In the Midwest. In a rest home. She's dying, the last I heard."

"I'm sorry."

"Yeah. You think I'm a lousy lawyer you should see how bad I am at being a son."

"I don't think you're a lousy lawyer, D.T. I think you're quite the opposite. You're one of the things I'm most thankful for today, in fact."

"I guess I'd better quit while I'm ahead," he mumbled. "You have a nice day, Miss Holloway. I enjoyed breakfast."

"So did I."

"Do we need to talk about it?"

"Not now."

"Good. Call me if anything comes up."

"I will. Don't worry. Brave is something I'm not."

"Nonsense. Nurses are the bravest of us all."

"I . . ."

"Bye, Rita."

D.T. hung up and fixed a bowl of shredded wheat to tide him over, then turned on the TV and watched the football game. He had a big bet against both the Lions and the spread. Too big. A loss would wipe out the small surplus he had accumulated over the past few months by virtue of a few paying clients and a few successful wagers. Before he was comfortable in his chair the Lions scored. But Sims was out at least temporarily, his bell rung by a linebacker who had anticipated a swing pass and had gotten there before either the ball or Billy. D.T. cracked a beer and checked his watch.

The phone rang. He let it cry unattended, a baby with the colic, as he imagined every person who could possibly be calling and decided he didn't want to hear anything any of them might tell him. They could stew in their own juice, like the turkey at Michele's. If somebody died, somebody like Lucinda Finders, say, well so what? Society worried too much about death, stretched too far to prevent it, emasculated itself to eliminate risk. It had made cowards of us all, shiftless squid who knew no real danger and so found danger in everything, who knew no real triumph and so found worth in the worthless, success in the insignificant, achievement in the trivial. Nothing noble occurred any longer, in a nation where nobility had once been the everyday measure of man. It was so bad that lawyers like himself could amass wealth and fame for doing nothing more than advancing the collapse of civilization by sundering its most basic institution. The Lions intercepted and ran it back for six. Jesus. In a sneak attack, age had rendered him reactionary. The Steelers fumbled the ensuing kickoff.

He wondered if his gambling was a subconscious evasion of success, a deliberate impoverishing of himself so that he could not be accused of profiting from something so ignoble as divorce law. If that was really and truly the reason he bet, then gambling might be the best and not the worst of his activities.

The Lions fumbled. He flicked off the TV and glanced at his watch. The phone rang once again. He grabbed his coat and left his apartment and drove through a storm to his ex-wife's mansion, arriving thirty minutes early, the unanswered phone still a mite in his inner ear.

Michele opened the door. Her eyes widened in surprise when she saw him, her mouth in pleasure. "D.T. How prompt. You must have missed mince pie more than I suspected."

She leaned toward him and he kissed her cheek. She smelled like flowers, tasted like squash. The long red gown that covered her fell as heavily as burlap.

"Sorry I'm early," he said. "I had a sudden attack of depression and figured if I didn't come over now I wouldn't make it at all." He grinned to undermine the words.

Michele frowned. "Are you all right? Do you want to go in the den and talk? Mirabelle doesn't really need me out there, though she pretends she does."

D.T. shook his head. "George here?"

"No. He's coming at four."

"Heather?"

"She's across the street at a friend's. I told her to be back at twelve sharp. I'm sure she'll be here any minute. She's been looking forward to this for weeks." Michele looked at him closely. "Do you want to say anything to me about Heather, D.T.? I mean, about how she's growing up? I worry about what you think, and it's been so long since we've had a chance to really talk."

"I think you're doing a fine job, Michele, if that's what you mean."

"Do you really?"

He nodded.

She examined him intently. "It means a lot to me to hear you say that, D.T. I want you to know that I'd be interested in anything you have to suggest about her. I mean, it's going to start getting tricky pretty soon, you know. Adolescent girls can be a problem."

"Adolescent girls are the world's most febrile beings. Followed closely by middle-aged men who've slept with only one woman in their lives."

Michele laughed and stepped back to allow him into her house. "Just so you know I can use all the help I can get," she said to him over her shoulder as they walked down the glistening foyer. "Want a drink?"

"Sure."

"Scotch?"

"Wine, I think. White. For a change it's not an appropriate day to get smashed."

"I'll bring it to you in the den."

Michele went off toward the kitchen. D.T. made his way past the double doors to the living room and the single doors to the dining room and kitchen. Although he had lived in the house for six years he had little affection for it. It was less a former home than a hotel he had visited once, on a not particularly successful business trip during which he had comported himself less than honorably.

He looked around as he walked, inspecting. The paintings and mirrors and occasional pieces were as he remembered, but the carpet and the colorings were new. Michele redecorated frequently, for no reason that he could see other than boredom and a fondness for tradesmen. The result was not always an improvement, but that didn't seem to be the point. Her decorator was a friend of Bobby E. Lee's, who had spent a year in Paris.

The den was as cozy as he remembered, possibly because he had refused to let the decorator alter it while he had lived there and Michele had evidently continued the tradition. But most of the toys she had bought him during coverture had been removed—the rear-projection TV set, the video recorder, the laser disc player, the quadraphonic music system. He wondered if George had them now, and if George would be willing to sell him the big-screen TV cheap. How she had spoiled him, though his Puritanism had caused most of her largesse to backfire, to stoke not gratitude but a persistent ember of resentment.

He sat in the soft leather chair and put his feet on the soft leather ottoman and waited for his drink. The trinkets he had given her—the calfskin edition of Emily Dickenson, the Steuben apple, the World War I topographic map of the Balkans—all were where he had placed them for her admiration. He wondered if she'd just hauled them out of storage. He walked over to inspect. No dust. No clear evidence one way or another. He returned to the chair and listened to the rhythm and blues that danced from Mirabelle's radio and smelled the smells that were as present in the air as birds.

Michele came in and handed him a glass of Chablis. It was cool perfection, as were most of her possessions, potable and otherwise. She bought wine by the case, at a discount available to no one who needed it.

Michele sat on the tufted leather couch across from him, crossed her legs, looked at him with earnest intensity. She seemed not to have aged a minute since that same look had first captured him, at a benefit auction for a crisis center he sometimes worked with. She seemed always to blend with her surroundings, to be never out of place, even on the days she had visited his office.

His eyes left hers. The painting above her head was an original Sam Francis. He liked it a lot. He liked Michele a lot, as well. He sipped his wine, feeling as buoyant as he had in months.

"So," Michele began.

"So."

"How've you been?"

"Fine."

"Aren't we the jolly twosome, though."

Michele smiled. "Either that or liars."

They laughed uneasily.

"So what have you been doing lately?" Michele asked finally, recrossing her legs, fiddling.

He thought of his slavering pursuit of Lucinda Finders, of his conspiracy to blackmail Chas Stone, of his endangerment of Esther Preston. "Nothing I'm proud of," he said. "How about you?"

She shrugged. "The usual. I help out one day a week at Heather's school. That's fun."

"Doing what?"

"I mostly help the art teacher get the materials distributed and collected. Monitor at recess. Go along on field trips. You know. It gives me an idea of how Heather spends her day, at least."

"Right."

"I'm pleased with the school, D.T. They're doing a nice job."

For what Michele was paying them they should be making Einsteins by the gross. "It's nice you're involved like that," he told her.

Her dimples told him she was pleased. "I'm doing something new with my own art, too. I've gotten kind of serious about it again."

"Good."

"Want to see?"

"Sure."

She hopped up and led him toward the rear of the house, to the servant's room that was now her studio. Much of her old work was on the walls; some he liked, some were of a formlessness he couldn't bear. The piece of sculpture that had been the major focus of her work while they were married—a bronze rendering of an Amazon contorted in unbearable agony—was now headless and consigned to the far corner of the room. He gestured at it. "Accident?"

"Statement."

He raised a brow.

"Not about women; just about me."

She said nothing further. He made his way through scattered cans and jars and tubes of paint and joined her in the center of the room. She stood next to a large easel which was draped with a thick black cloth. "Ready?" she asked.

He nodded.

Michele flipped away the shroud. "Da Daaa."

It was a piece of glass, the size and shape of a window

or a canvass, half-covered with bright paint: abstract, wild, electric. "Glass?" he asked.

She nodded, eyeing the piece critically. "Do you know glass is perpetually melting, D.T.? Did you know that after a period of time all windows are thicker at the bottom than at the top? So with glass I get a kinetic element, but so subtle it will never be apparent in my lifetime. I enjoy not knowing what my painting will eventually be saying. It gives me, I don't know, a link with the future."

"With glass you might get a link but you also might get breakage."

"I know, and I'm sure a few accidents will happen. But in between those times just think how *careful* people will be with my work." Michele's eyes sparkled. "As opposed to the canvasses they toss around so negligently. None of that with the Conway Double Panes."

"Double?"

"I'm going to paint both sides. Abstract on one, photo-realism on the other. You get tired of one you just flip it over, *et voilà*—new mood, new color, new ambiance."

"Sounds good."

"I'm buying a gallery, too, did I tell you?"

"No."

"Downtown. Michele's. Just a small place, so I can exhibit my friends, and me, and maybe some unknowns as well. I think it'll even make some money. Eventually. Joyce Tuttle's going to run it for me."

"I thought Joyce was marrying money."

"That fell through. Seems he was rather seriously into wearing women's clothes."

"I hope the gallery does well, Michele. Really."

"Thanks, D.T. I've got a lot of time on my hands these days, since Heather's in school or at ballet class all day. I don't know, I wanted to start *doing* something, you know? Instead of just *being* something? Does that make sense?" Her wide eyes begged the answer he quickly gave.

"Sure."

"I know a lot of very talented artists who haven't got the gimmick it takes to break into the established galleries, and, well, I think I'd be contributing something, don't you?"

"No doubt about it."

"Do you mean it? Or do you think I'm being silly?"

"It's a very worthwhile project, Michele. Go for it."

She took his hand, inclined her head to his shoulder. He wrapped her with an arm. "I'm relieved, D.T. It's odd that I still need your approval, isn't it?"

"You're not looking for approval, Michele; you're just making conversation."

She paused, and surveyed the studio, and nodded silently, confirming something that seemed important. "Let's go back," she said, and returned him to the den.

They retook their places and regrasped their drinks, then toasted each other silently. "You said something about being depressed."

"Well, you know me. Even when I feel good I get depressed because I'm not depressed."

"Any specific cause?"

"Only my life. It seems to be getting away from me."

Michele's eyes glinted. "Are you succumbing to one of those tiresome midlife crises, D.T.? I would have thought you were more original than that."

He shrugged. "I'm just succumbing. Period."

"Everything all right with you and Barbara?"

"Let's just say everything's the same."

Michele blinked. "I imagine the two of you together, you know."

"Doing what?"

"Having sex."

"You're kidding."

"No. Isn't that *outré?* I keep wondering what she does for you that I never did."

He only smiled.

"Okay, D.T. Is she better in bed than I was? That's what I really want to know." Her laugh was too nervous to make his answer easy.

"She's different, Michele. Only different."

"Different how? Just out of curiosity."

He tried to fend her off. "What makes you curious?"

She shrugged. "I'd just like to think that despite the rest of our problems our sex life was always pretty good."

"It was. No question."

"But not good enough."

"It had a lot to overcome," D.T. said, and kept himself from glancing at his surroundings, then countered her question with one of his own. "How about George? How's he do between the sheets? Not that it's any of my business."

"Are you implying I've engaged in premarital sex, D.T.?"

"Yes." He grinned but Michele didn't match it.

"George is . . . delicate. Tasteful, one might say."

D.T. smiled maliciously. "Too bad."

Michele started to reply but she was interrupted by the arrival of the dervish that was their daughter. Heather scampered to his side and threw herself into his lap and kissed him. He kissed her back and squeezed her. She scrambled off his legs and snuggled in beside him, pressed tightly against his flank by the fat leather arms of the chair. He dropped his own arm across her shoulders.

"Happy Thanksgiving, Daddy," she said while still wriggling toward comfort.

"Happy Thanksgiving to you, honey. How're you doing?"

"Fine."

"How's school?"

"Okay. I'm going to be in a play. Will you come see me?"

"Sure. What's the play about?"

"Germs."

"Great. What else have you been doing?"

"Playing with Katra."

"Playing what?"

"Ms. Pac-Man. I beat her every time."

"What's Ms. Pac-Man?"

"A *video* game. Geez, Daddy. Katra has Atari; I have Intellivision. I think Intellivision's better, don't you?"

"Unquestionably."

Michele stood up. "I'll have to leave you two alone for a minute," she said. "I think Mirabelle needs my help." She winked at D.T. and left the room.

Heather wriggled even closer to his side. Her hair was tied with yellow bows and smelled like lemons. Her skin was a confection. "Are you a happy girl?" he asked her, as he always did.

"Yes."

"No problems?"

"I have to have braces."

"Really? When?"

"A few years from now. My teeth are crooked. See?" She showed him. They were. "What do you know about Thanksgiving?" he asked as she closed her mouth over her orthodontist's future fortune. "Did you study it in school?"

"We studied it *last* year. The Indians and the Pilgrims and that one, what's his name?"

"Squanto?"

"Yes. Him. He showed them how to use fish. Do they still do that, Daddy, put fish in the ground to make things grow? It seems awfully gross."

"They use mostly chemicals now, I think. Have you thought about what you're thankful for today?"

"I'm thankful for you and Mommy." Her face would have converted Mencken.

"I'm glad, honey. You have a whole lot of things to be thankful for, don't you?"

"I guess."

"You're smart, and pretty, and healthy, and you have a nice house and nice clothes, and nice friends, and a mommy and daddy who love you very much. That's quite a lot, isn't it?"

"Uh huh."

"A lot of children in the world don't have all those things, did you know that? Lots of them don't have any of them."

"I know."

"Lots of kids are hungry every day. And sick. And live in the streets because they don't have a house. I just want you to think a little about those kids on a day like this, okay? Just for a little bit?"

"Okay." She turned and looked at him. "But what should I do about them, Daddy? I don't know what I should *do* about those people." Her voice was a tearful plea.

He had blown it again, had tried to do his duty and as

usual it was all more complicated than he knew, and he had caused his daughter needless grief. She had thought more about those kids than he had, and like everyone else she didn't know what to do and he couldn't begin to tell her.

"You don't have to do anything right now, honey. Not a thing. Right now it's only important that you think about them for a minute today, and maybe pray for them, and not pretend they don't exist, like lots of people do. Then maybe some day when you're older there'll be other things you can do."

"Like what?"

"Oh, cast a vote. Write a check. Smile a smile, maybe. Lots of things." He tried to smile himself.

"I have a nice smile. My teacher said so."

"You have the nicest smile I've ever seen."

He squeezed her roughly. Like her mother moments earlier, she tilted her head against his chest. He was miserably ecstatic.

"Will you be glad when George gets here, honey?"

"I guess."

"Is he over here a lot?"

"Sometimes."

"Does he stay all night sometimes?"

"Why would he do that? He has his own house."

"Have you seen it? His house, I mean?"

"Once."

"Is it nice?"

"It's okay."

"Is it big?"

"Not as big as this. Why do you always ask me about George, Daddy?"

"I don't always ask you about George, honey. I just want to make sure you and George are friends, that's all."

"We're friends. Can we *do* something, Daddy?"

"Sure. Why don't you show me your room?" he said. "Maybe we can play a game."

"What game?"

"Whatever you want."

"Donkey Kong?"

"How about Crazy Eights? Remember how we used to play Crazy Eights a lot?"

"Okay," she said, and led him out of the den and up the staircase and into the marvel that was her room. They fooled with toys and dolls and books and records, played Crazy Eights and Donkey Kong and Simon Says, and she beat him at all of them. The next thing he knew Michele was in the doorway, telling him that George had arrived, asking if he wanted to come down. He left Heather reluctantly and followed his ex-wife down the stairs and shook hands with the man she intended to marry in three months. His replacement.

Michele gave them wine and they retired to the den to talk. George had seen a play he'd liked, and a concert he hadn't, and he was intelligent and articulate and amusing in explaining each reaction. By the time dinner was served he found himself enjoying George, as he was enjoying Heather and Michele. They seemed a family already, a happy one, and there was much laughter and affection and good feeling and good food and so it surprised him greatly when Michele got up in the middle of the meal and fled the room in tears.

■ TRIAL

■ SEVENTEEN

JEROME FITZGERALD on two," Bobby E. Lee announced.

D.T. dropped his gum into the wastebasket and pushed a button. "Jerome. How are you and your pension plan?"

"I'm calling about the Preston case, D.T."

"I thought you might be."

D.T. had spoken with Jerome Fitzgerald twice in the three months since he'd filed the complaint against Nathaniel Preston in November. The first was to arrange a time for a hearing on Jerome's demurrer that the complaint failed to plead facts sufficient to state a cause of action. Jerome had cried long and hard at the hearing, arguing that Mrs. Preston had no legally cognizable claim against her former husband, and that even if she had possessed a claim at one time she had slept on her rights to the extent that legal limitations and equitable laches had long ago worked to bar the suit. Jerome had lost on all counts, though just barely, the law and motion judge making clear through a spectrum of scowls and scoffs his reluctance to rule in D.T.'s favor and his confidence that Jerome's points might well prevail after evidence was introduced at trial.

Their second conversation had been a result of Jerome's attempt to take Esther Preston's deposition. On that one, D.T. had bluffed and won. He'd carefully outlined the torment of Mrs. Preston's disease, and supplemented his call with a doctor's opinion, obtained by Rita Holloway from her boyfriend, to the effect that the rigors of a deposition would be seriously harmful to Mrs. Preston's already delicate neurology. When Jerome had persisted, D.T. had threatened to go to court for a protective order that would stop the deposition, armed with a videotape so heartrending it would be guaranteed to convince any judge with tear ducts that the poor woman was not up to it. When even that hadn't been enough, D.T. had threatened to take Esther Preston's predicament to the papers, as illustrative of the plight of the handicapped in a heartless and legalistic world, and of the burden placed on public programs by the failure of private individuals to do their duty to those who depended on them, *e.g.*, the wealthy physician who abandoned his impoverished former spouse to the public dole.

With that, Jerome had folded his tent, had made do with D.T.'s barely relevant answers to interrogatories and his unhelpful responses to Jerome's request for admissions of matters of fact. D.T. had prepared both documents in the wee hours of the night before they were due, with the help of half a fifth of Jack Daniels and a copy of his law school yearbook opened to a picture of Jerome Fitzgerald accepting an award from the regional vice president of his legal fraternity. The award honored Jerome's significant achievements in the study of law, which Jerome had most often accomplished by tearing pages out of assigned journal articles before anyone else had a chance to consult them.

Now it was summary judgment Jerome was after, claiming that the facts of the case were undisputed, that the only questions at issue were legal ones, whether fraud had occurred, whether Mrs. Preston had a legal interest in her husband's medical degree that could be asserted at this late date, whether statutes of limitation and laches barred all claims. Jerome had filed an affidavit of Dr. Preston in support of his motion, seventeen pages of self-righteous disclaimers and outraged assertions covering every phrase of the complaint against him.

D.T. was worried. His case was weak at best, despite Rita Holloway's efforts to improve it through the acquisition of evidence, and if the judge bought the Preston affidavit at face value then D.T. and Mrs. Preston would be tossed out on their ears and the doctor would be off the hook forever. D.T.'s plan, if it began to look bad at the hearing, was to call the doctor to the stand in person, to insist that Preston's evidence be given under oath rather than by affidavit, so D.T. would at least have the pleasure of working the doctor over on cross-examination before final judgment was entered.

But perhaps Jerome would make another settlement offer. The last time they'd talked, Jerome had made a firm offer of twelve-five. Nuisance value, no more. D.T. had rejected it out of hand. Confidently, to Jerome. Nervously, to himself.

"Dr. Preston told me he'd been served with a subpoena for the hearing Thursday, D.T.," Jerome said, his voice thin with betrayal.

"Good," D.T. said.

"But we've filed his affidavit, D.T. There won't be any *need* for live testimony."

"There will be if I have anything to say about it. You can't cross-examine an affidavit."

"But—"

"But nothing. If you prevail with only that pathetic affidavit as evidence I'll be in the court of appeals before nightfall."

"Well, I just wish you'd talked to me before you had him served. Dr. Preston said it was embarrassing to have the sheriff lurking in his waiting room."

"Good," D.T. said again.

"It's dirty pool, D.T. I would have agreed to produce him without a subpoena."

"But this takes the worry out of it, don't you see, Jerome? I mean, if the good doctor shows up Thursday we're all happy, and if he doesn't, the judge issues a bench warrant for his arrest and I don't have to take you before the ethics committee. So I did you a favor, Jerome. I'm surprised with your vast experience in litigation you didn't recognize that."

Jerome sniffed. "I'm experienced enough to know you're flying blind on this one, D.T. If the judge had any sense he'd have sustained my demurrer two months ago."

"Hell, Jerome. You'll be lucky if my countermotion isn't granted."

"Nonsense."

D.T. was tempted to continue sparring but he let it drop. He wouldn't win anything at all on Thursday. The best he could accomplish was simply not to lose. Many lawyers made livings doing no more than that, but doing what other lawyers did was never reason enough for anything.

"What do you hear about the Supreme Court's opinion on the professional degree issue?" D.T. asked. "I know you guys have wires in to the court."

"They're going to ask for re-argument on the measure of value point."

"Yeah? An even split, huh?"

"Sounds like it. Judge Wygant has recused himself, so we see it three-three."

"The opinion should come down by the time we go to trial, though, right?"

"There's no way you can try this case, D.T.," Jerome insisted. "The money's just not there."

D.T. laughed his condescending laugh. "You still don't get it, do you, Jerome? There's plenty of money for me in the case. My overhead wouldn't keep you guys in Bic Bananas and I don't have to hustle clients at country clubs and cocktail parties."

"Well, a trial is just silly, anyway," Jerome persisted. "I've talked to Dr. Preston. He's willing to increase his settlement offer, to avoid the inconvenience of a trial and to give some assistance to his former wife even though he has no obligation to do so."

"How much?"

"You understand this is not an admission of *anything*."

"How much?"

"He'll go to twenty thousand."

"Will he, now?"

"Yes. But I warn you. The offer will be withdrawn on the morning of trial."

"Lump sum?"

"Yes."

"I'll speak with my client and get back to you."

"Will you recommend she take it?"

"No." D.T. laughed, this time genuinely.

Jerome seemed to squeal. "Why *not?* How much will

it *take*, D.T.? I mean, you've never even made a *counter-offer*. I don't get it.''

D.T. didn't say anything.

"It's me, isn't it, D.T.? You're in this case to beat me, and that's all. You don't give a *damn* about your client, you just want to win against *me*. Because I did better than you in law school, I guess. Or because I make a lot of money in litigation and haven't even tried a case. That's it, isn't it? Well, I'm not a fool, D.T. I know you're good in court; I've asked around. But you can't win this one, you don't have a prayer. So maybe you'd better start thinking about how you're going to feel if you lose. To *me*. To someone who's never tried a lawsuit in his *whole entire life*.''

D.T. was still trying to frame a reply when Jerome Fitzgerald hung up on him.

Losing to Jerome. God. As depressing as impotence or even the Fiasco. So maybe he should cave. Twenty grand times 25 percent equals five thousand as his fee. Plus expenses off the top. The equivalent of twenty-five Fiascos. Enough to get him square with Bobby E. Lee and the book as well. A clean slate, at least every slate but the one tacked to the wall of his conscience, the one that hadn't been cleaned for years.

There was something there, was the problem; something Dr. Preston didn't want known. If he could just learn what it was, the settlement potential would increase by a factor of ten, he was sure of it. His money was on abortion. Lucrative and immoral. It fit all he knew about Nat Preston. But how to find out. He leaned back in his chair and closed his eyes and thought until he had a plan of sorts. Then he buzzed for Bobby E. Lee to join him.

"What have I got this afternoon?" he asked as Bobby came in and sat down.

"Three dittos. All candidates for the Fiasco.''

"Call and put them over to next week. I've got to be out.''

"Out where?''

"Just out. The Preston hearing is Thursday, right?''

Bobby E. Lee nodded.

"When's the Stone trial?''

"Tomorrow.''

His heart flipped. "Jesus, Bobby. How did that happen?"

"You've asked the calendar clerk for too many favors."

"How many names on Gardner's witness list?"

"Twenty or so."

"Who?"

"Friends and neighbors, I think. Or former friends. One psychologist you probably should have deposed."

"Have you notified our own witnesses?"

"Yep. They'll be there, maybe, but they're not too eager. I get the impression Mareth Stone isn't particularly well liked."

"How many have we got?"

"Four, is all I could find the day I went out there. She wouldn't give me any names herself, and nobody I talked to was particularly anxious to help."

"Anything at all from Gardner? Settlement offer or anything?"

"Nope."

"How about our client? Any word from her?"

"Nothing."

"You sure it's tomorrow?"

"It's been on the calendar for weeks, D.T. And there's no way you can get a continuance."

"I know, I know." D.T. looked at Bobby closely. They hadn't spoken about the matter since that first phone call, the night D.T. had lurked outside the Billings Avenue sex club, waiting in vain for his client's husband to make life easy for him. Suddenly it was the day before trial. If it went badly, if there was a real danger that Mareth Stone would lose her children, he would need to apply some heat. And Bobby E. Lee held the only matches in town.

D.T. cleared his throat. "You know what I need to ask you about, don't you?" he said softly.

Bobby E. Lee nodded. "I was hoping you'd forgotten. When do you need him?"

"I can string out the trial for at least two days. Maybe three, if Gardner puts on all his witnesses. And of course the custody issue may turn out to be a gambit, and we can trade some bucks for the kids and remove it from contention. But I think Gardner may be serious when he says Stone really wants them, so we'll have to fight. If we fight we have to win. I mean, the minute a client like Mareth Stone loses a head-to-head custody fight then that's the last paying customer I'll see in here, Bobby. The Friday Fiasco will be the high point of the week.''

Bobby E. Lee sighed. ''I'll make some calls. I should know something by five. But it may take a couple of days.''

''Two at most,'' D.T. admonished. ''We should have done it a month ago.''

Bobby E. Lee nodded and stood up. Frowning, D.T. watched him leave the office, then uttered a quick prayer for forgiveness, addressed to whom it may concern.

He was about to leave his office when the phone rang. ''Mr. Jones?''

''Yes?''

''This is Lucinda Finders. Remember me?''

''Sure I do. How are you? How's the baby?''

Her languid voice gave him the shiver it always did, the hint of defiance and connivance and barely stemmed desire. He had not actually laid eyes on her for months, yet she had materialized before him almost daily, in cinematic visions: wrapped like a prophet on his deck, suckling her babe, licking her wounds, enticing him. She had become his succubus.

''I'm fine and Krystle's fine, too, Mr. Jones. She's just the sweetest thing. Sleeps through the night already and everything. We're just so happy with her.''

''We?''

''Me and Del. I went back with him, remember? And I'm still here.'' She tried to sing it, make it carefree and pleasing. But her chuckle died as quickly as it came, leaving nothing but questions in his mind.

''Where are you living?'' he asked her.

''Same place. Houston Street.''

''Is Del working?''

''Off and on. Mostly off.''

''How about you?''

''I'm back at the Pancake House. Manager said some customers was asking for me so he decided to hire me back. Gave me a raise and everything. I only work nights, now. Seven to midnight.''

"Who stays with the baby?"

"Del.''

D.T. was silent.

"He's good with her, Mr. Jones. Really, he is.''

"Excuse me if I don't believe you.''

She didn't respond. He was aware and sorry that he'd hurt her, and wondered if there was a way to hurt her enough to make her leave the man for good.

"I hate to be calling like this, Mr. Jones,'' she began after a minute, the eagerness of her first words now absent from her voice.

"It's all right. I'm glad you did. I've been wondering about you.''

"What I mean is, I hate to ask you what I got to ask you.''

"What do you have to ask me?"

She paused. "Just hear me out first, okay? Before you get mad?''

"Okay."

"Well, you know the day I first come to see you? In your office? When I thought I wanted a divorce from Del?''

"Yes.'' He knew what was coming, knew she couldn't help it, and knew he couldn't make it easy for her.

"Well, you know that fifty dollars I gave you?''

"Yes.''

"Well, Del says since I didn't get me a divorce after all, then I should get that money back. I mean, he's been after me to call you for the longest time, Mr. Jones, and I finally promised him I'd do it. But I just promised I'd ask,'' she added quickly. "I know you helped me that night, and wrote up some papers, and you got a right to keep the money, I know that, but I had to ask. I mean, somehow Del just knows whether I've done what I promised to or not, you know, so . . .''

He sighed. "It's all right, Lucinda. I'll send you the money. Don't worry about it.''

"It's not right, I know that, Mr. Jones. But, well, the hospital's after me to pay for them tests they run on Krystle, and Daddy won't pay the hospital in Reedville for when I had the baby, so we're kind of in a bind right now. Collection agencies calling day and night and all. I mean . . ."

"Don't worry about it, Lucinda," he said again. "Really. You'll have the money by Thursday."

"Well, thanks a whole lot, Mr. Jones."

"You're welcome."

"I meet a lot of girls down at the Pancake House, you know, and the next one I hear say she's looking for a good lawyer I'll sure send her down your way."

He could see them now, fiascos every one, smelling of syrup and burned batter. "You do that, Lucinda," he said. "Now tell me the truth. Are you sure you're all right?"

"I'm just fine."

"The baby, too?"

"Yes. I told you."

"Is Del there now?"

"He's out back working on the Ford. Del's getting better, Mr. Jones. He really is. He don't drink hardly at all no more."

"That's good, Lucinda. But if he starts up again you get the hell out of there, okay? You and the baby. Don't stay around him if he's drunk."

He had injured her again, had blurred her dream. Her words were pinched. "I can handle it, Mr. Jones. You think I can't, but I can. I know what I'm doing. It might not be perfect but it's as perfect as it's going to get. For me."

He made himself leave it, made himself not beg her not to do anything that would make him live forever with the wish that he'd done much more to help her. "You call me if there's a problem, Lucinda. Anything at all."

"I will."

"Promise?"

She laughed. "Promise."

"Give Krystle a big kiss for me."

"I will."

D.T. hung up and went to the outer office and asked Bobby E. Lee if there was fifty dollars in the office account. When Bobby nodded his head D.T. told him to send a check to Lucinda and write it off the books as a refunded retainer. Then he returned to his desk and picked up the phone.

"Oswald? D. T. Jones."

"Ah." The utterance was Oswald's usual wheeze, as though someone were, finally, strangling him.

"I'm calling about that malpractice case you're bringing against me, Oswald."

"What about it?"

"It would have been nice to give me a chance to settle the thing before you took it to court."

"I don't pay the rent by being nice, Jones."

"And it would have been even nicer if you'd just moved to amend the original divorce decree to get more out of the husband rather than coming after me for malpractice."

"The husband's a deadbeat. Why don't you just let your carrier handle it, Jones? I work with that outfit all the time on cases like this."

"I don't *want* my carrier to handle it, Oswald. *I* want to handle it."

"Yeah? So I'm listening."

D.T. paused, listened to Oswald's harmonic bellows. "Five grand," D.T. said at last. "A week from today. You dismiss with prejudice, and that's the end of it."

"Crap," Oswald Blacker said.

"Crap? No, not crap, Oswald. That's the way it's going to be."

"Or what?"

"Or I suggest to a client of mine who's about to shed husband number two that she has quite a nice case against *you* for the way you handled her divorce from husband number one."

"Yeah? How?"

"The final decree was entered exactly nine years and eleven months after the wedding day."

"So?"

"So if you'd waited another month before filing the decree the woman's Social Security insurance benefit would have been maximized because she'd been married ten years. Forty-two U.S.C. four-oh-four. You can look it up."

"Yeah? Big fucking deal. The five grand is out, Jones. I start discovery tomorrow."

"Remember a woman named Darcel McGee, Oswald?"

"Who?"

"Darcel McGee. As in Fibber."

"Don't know the woman."

"Oh, you know her, Oswald. Not as well as you wanted to, but you know her."

"What's that supposed to mean?"

"She's the one you tried to rape. Right on your office floor. When your secretary was out to lunch. She's the one who slapped your face and ran out into the street to keep you from pawing her."

"Bullshit. That's libel, Jones."

"Not yet, it isn't. It'll be libel when Ms. McGee and I take the story to the papers. Luckily, we have a complete defense."

"What?"

"Truth."

"Like hell."

"Okay, Oswald. See you at the ethics committee. The way I hear it, Ms. McGee isn't the only one you've played caveman with over the years. Should be an interesting session, on top of all the other charges that have been brought against you."

Oswald Blacker seemed to forget to breathe. "Okay, okay. Maybe I was a little hasty getting the malpractice thing on file. But you screwed up, Jones. The woman has a case."

"I know I screwed up, Oswald. That's why I'm settling for five grand."

"But that's not enough."

"Oh, I think it is, all things considered. I can make a damned good argument that I turned out to be right in that case, screw-up and all. Check out *Jones* v. *Stevenson* if you don't believe me. That's a different Jones, by the way. But if you still think it isn't enough, you make up the difference out of your pocket, Oswald."

"You must be crazy."

"Nope. Just pissed off."

"I won't—"

"I want to end it right here, Oswald; I want the case out of my life. It's your last chance. If I have to go to my carrier and you drag the thing through court, believe me, I'm going to take you down with me."

"I—"

"Believe me, Oswald."

"Okay, okay. Cash?"

"Cash."

"Next week?"

"Right."

"Okay."

"Bye, Oswald."

D.T. hung up, hoping Oswald Blacker wouldn't check his files for the nonexistent Darcel McGee, hoping the stories he had heard were true, that there were so many Darcel McGees in Oswald's practice that specific names had become irrelevant. He grabbed his briefcase, made sure it was empty, then left the office and drove onto the freeway that would take him to the heart of downtown.

He hadn't been in the center of the city for months, hadn't inhaled its fumes or shivered in its shadows since the evening Barbara had made him take her to a poetry reading by a coven of militant feminists, a reading at which he quickly became aware that his solitary male presence had been an affront to every other listener in the room, so much so that one of them, in fact, had publicly asked him to leave. He had left his defense to Barbara, and she had eventually prevailed, though not without embarrassing both him and his accuser, with the result that he had been able to hear men called rapists, butchers, and assassins and women encouraged to become castrators and celibates, in various metres and metaphorical flights, for two hours and thirty-seven minutes. Now he simply sought a parking lot three levels beneath the tallest building in the city. Getting there made him feel like a mole, meek and sightless and leery of what might be going on above him.

It was noon, and the streets crawled with the deductibly hungry, the compulsively slim, the financially preposterous. The swirl of elegance and purpose made his blazer and gray flannels feel more like Big Smiths. He was out of his element and knew it, and he was scared by what he was about to do.

D.T. hurried across the marble floor of the lobby, past the security guard station and the revolving metal sculpture, and consulted the building directory. Bronwin, Kilt and Loftis, Attorneys, was listed on the thirtieth floor. Jerome Fitzgerald was listed on thirty-two. D.T. got in the elevator and punched the button for twenty-nine.

He shared the cage with a kid from a messenger service who wore gray coveralls and Converse hightops and had a Walkman in his ear, a padded envelope in his pocket, and dreadlocks in his hair. His eyes were closed and his fingers snapped to whatever came through the Walkman. His fingernails were the length of witches'. When D.T. left the elevator the kid didn't see or hear him go.

He knew immediately that he had made a mistake. Floor twenty-nine was too decorated, too plush, too public. There was a reception desk and a waiting area, and the floor he was looking for would have neither, only a bright bare hallway, and closed doors with little black and white signs on them, and people scurrying to and fro as though their lives depended on it. Luckily, the receptionist had her back to him, talking into the phone while whirling her Rolodex. D.T. punched the down button and got back on the elevator and descended to twenty-eight amid another box of lunchers.

This was it, if it was anywhere he could get to, the bowels of the law firm—Xerox room, storage rooms, microfilm room, computer room, supply room, and the room he wanted—the room of current files. He suddenly remembered he had been there once before, years earlier, on one of his first cases, during which he had been stuck away in a musty storeroom for six days, paging through ancient passbooks and account ledgers and check stubs and the like, tracing the marital and separate assets of a man who over the previous fifty years had been married three times and made four fortunes and lost three and a half of them. Eventually, D.T. had been able to prove that the man's record-keeping was so sloppy and his ignorance of marital property law so pervasive that all his separate property had disappeared by virtue of the process of commingling and the various legal presumptions that favored marital rather than separate funds when strict records had not been kept. His client, a former manicurist, now called Maui home.

He strolled down the hall inspecting the signs. The file room was where he remembered. Now to get the one he wanted. If he was unlucky, Jerome would have the Preston file in his office. If he was even less lucky, someone would discover he wasn't an employee of the firm but rather was a spy, and would call the cops. He would spend the night in jail and maybe lose his license. Maybe not the worst of fates, that latter. Maybe a manumission. He took a deep breath and went into the restroom and took off his blazer and folded it carefully and put it inside his briefcase, then loosened his tie, rolled up his sleeves, tucked the case under his arm, and went to the door marked "Active Files."

The girl behind the Formica counter was young and bright-eyed and seemed delighted by whatever was in all those folders on the metal shelves that stretched behind her into another zip code. When D.T. approached the counter she said "Hi" and slid a pad of paper to him. "File Request Form" it said, and "File—Number—Date Out—Date Returned—Name of Requester—Supervising Partner." D.T. filled in all but the number and the date returned, signing the name Ralph Branca as his own and Robert Thompson as the Supervising Partner, then tore off the top slip and handed it to the girl.

She glanced at it with irritation. "Do you know the number?"

"No. I'm sorry. I just keep forgetting." He rolled his eyes helplessly, a nitwit, the firm fool. The girl was incompletely mollified. "What year was it opened?"

"Last year. November."

"Okay. Just a minute. But try to remember the number next time, Mr. Branca. It makes it much faster."

He assured her he would.

She went away. A sweaty minute passed beneath the hum of the central air conditioning and the icy rays of the fluorescent lights that brightened things that should have remained dull. Behind him, the door opened and closed. A man came in, dressed much as D.T. would have been if he'd worked there. They eyed each other. "Wilson?" D.T. asked.

The man shook his head. "Balwell."

"Right. Right. I'm Branca. I think we met at the firm outing last year." They always had an outing. He hoped.

"Right. How's it going?"

"Great."

"What department again?"

"Litigation. You?"

"Estates."

D.T. grinned sheepishly. "I don't even have a will," he said truthfully. "Guess I'll have to do something about that some day."

Balwell frowned. "You certainly should," he said, suddenly nonplussed at encountering someone so cavalier about contingent remainders and *inter vivos* trusts.

The file clerk returned and greeted Balwell cheerily and handed D.T. a folder. He glanced at it, thanked her, said "Let's have lunch," to the estates man, and gathered up his briefcase and left the file room. Back in the restroom he made certain he was alone, entered a stall, locked the door, lowered the seat, and sat down to examine the Preston case from the opposite side of the dispute.

There wasn't much. Legal documents, of which D.T. of course had duplicates. Research memoranda by two associates in preparation for the earlier demurrer and the current motion for summary judgment. Leaden and redundant. Some correspondence keeping Doctor Preston abreast of developments in the case. Brief and perfunctory. And then the file memos and notes of Jerome's conversations with independent witnesses. D.T. flipped quickly through them.

Most contained Jerome's thoughts on tactics and strategy, the trite and shallow memorialized forever. There were comments to Jerome from senior partners, and Jerome's instructions to junior associates, and the usual back-and-forth, repetitive, trivial, nit-picking, fee-enhancing, ass-covering blathering of the corporate law firm. The contents of these memos would have helped him at the hearing, no doubt, but that wasn't what he was after. He was happy to meet Jerome on the field of battle on approximately equal terms. What he wanted to know was what he had missed about Nathaniel Preston—why the man was so reluctant to go to trial, a reluctance that went contrary to his pugnacious personality, according to his former partner. D.T. didn't stop to read until he came to the memos of Jerome's conversations with Dr. Preston.

Their first meeting had simply reviewed the facts of the case—the marriage, the divorce, the property settlement, the passage of time, Dr. Preston's discovery of the investigation conducted by Rita Holloway, the encounter between D.T. and the doctor at the party, the ensuing lawsuit. Nothing new. The same with the next memo. Additional dates and details already known to D.T., except for the doctor's assertion that the shares of East Jersey Instruments had been included in the catchall phrase "other personal property" in the settlement agreement and thus were not concealed from his wife but rather disclosed and shared. A good defense. He wondered if the doctor could prove it.

He kept reading, through two more memos that chiefly chronicled the doctor's outrage at the injustice of it all. He reached the final page. Jerome's notation was at the bottom, following his memo of a routine phone call: "Preston states that under no circumstances should this case be allowed to proceed to trial. When I asked him why he refused to say, merely instructing me to settle on the most advantageous basis possible. I advised Dr. Preston that opposing counsel had certain reasons to wish to see the case tried, even against his client's best interests. I disclosed my personal history with Jones, and offered to withdraw from the case as his counsel. Dr. Preston refused impatiently, instructing me to 'just take care of it.' I feel some apprehension about this case, for more than the usual reason. It is a no-win situation, given Jones' antipathy toward me and my own inexperience at such lower forms of lawyering."

And that was it. No more than a confirmation of his suspicions that Dr. Preston could be had in a big way, and a calming of his fears that he should have taken the twenty grand and run. D.T. closed the file, returned it to the file clerk, got a smile and a wave and a have-a-good-day in return. He retrieved his blazer from his briefcase and his car from its noxious burrow and left downtown as quickly as he could, inhaling the breath of a bus all the way to the on-ramp.

■ EIGHTEEN

T HE house was as conventionally impressive as the last time he had visited, but now the lawn needed mowing and the flowerbeds needed weeding and someone needed to pick up their toys. Still uneasy at his brief larceny from the Bronwin, Kilt and Loftis file room, D.T. climbed slowly to the porch and pressed the doorbell twice, then pressed it twice again. A progression of slow sounds emanated from the house, and the door inched open.

Mareth Stone stood before him, swaying. She looked at him with puzzlement, rubbed her eyes, looked at him again, and gathered her housecoat more tightly around her narrow chest. "Mr. Jones. I'm sorry. I was napping or something." She yawned, masking it belatedly. "What are you doing here, anyway? You didn't tell me you were coming. Did you?"

He shook his head while she struggled to remember whether his presence was foretold. "I just thought I'd drop by."

"Why?"

"We go to trial tomorrow, Mrs. Stone. I think we'd better talk it over. Can I come in?"

She backed up, looking disconcerted. Her housecoat escaped, then was recaptured. "It's a . . ." she began, then shrugged. "Why not?"

She turned and almost tripped over a backpack that lay on the floor like a pet, then shuffled down the hall on deerskin slippers that were speckled with stains and collapsed at the heels. Her housecoat was red and quilted, with a drooping hem. Her hair was tousled. The house

302

smelled of burned pizza or something like it. It took a long time to get where they were going.

Newspapers and magazines and self-help books were scattered like leaves over the living room. D.T. cleared a space for himself beside the latest issue of *Vanity Fair* and sat down. "So how's it going?" he asked.

Mareth Stone rubbed her face and perched gingerly on the edge of the chair across from him, as though she feared it would collapse or she would. "What time is it?" she asked.

He looked at his watch. "Almost four."

"The kids should be home. No. That's right. They went somewhere with Chas."

"Where?"

"I don't know."

"They're listed on his witness list, you know."

She nodded slowly. "He won't dare try to use them. The kids can't *stand* Chas. Especially David." She patted the pockets of her robe and stood up. "You want a drink?"

"No, thanks."

"Cigarette?"

He shook his head.

"I'll be back in a minute."

She slogged from the room as though its floor were mud. D.T. wondered what she had smoked or sniffed or swallowed to get the way she was, then got up and looked around the room.

Dust and dirt and clutter. Bowls of spilling sunflower husks, glasses with dregs in the bottom and stains on the rims, sport shoes, a warm-up jacket, a Nerf ball that seemed to have been chewed. A light-brown something that had once been edible but now was definitely not. He heard her coming and sat back down.

When she appeared in the doorway Mareth Stone was sucking on a cigarette as though it might yield hope. She sat across from him again and stared into his eyes without expression. "Are we going to win?" she asked thickly.

He shrugged. "I learned a long time ago not to make predictions. We've got some problems, I can tell you that."

"What kind of problems?"

"The people we rounded up to testify on your behalf, for one. My secretary tells me they're not exactly eager."

"Shit." She leaned forward to tap her cigarette on an ashtray full of them. "I told you not to talk to those people." She paused to inhale, then released the smoke with words. "The bastards. They spent ten years drinking our booze and eating our food and dipping in our pool, and now that I don't let them do it any more I automatically become unfit to raise my kids. Huh? Well *fuck* them. I told you I don't *want* any witnesses. Just me. *I'm* the one on trial, right? So I'm the witness. Put me in that chair and ask whatever you want."

D.T. looked at her. "I hope you're taking this thing seriously, Mrs. Stone," he said finally.

"I'll tell you how I'm *taking* it, Mr. Jones. I'm taking three Valium a day, that's how I'm *taking* it."

"Is that what you're on now?"

She nodded, then shrugged.

"I wouldn't volunteer that kind of information at the trial, Mrs. Stone. Also I wouldn't take any more tranquilizers, or anything else, till after it's over. Also, I wouldn't swear, or use buzzwords, or get mad, or argue with me or with your husband's lawyer or the judge or anyone else in the courtroom. Also, I wouldn't wear anything weird and I wouldn't volunteer any information that wasn't called for and I wouldn't guess or speculate or surmise. If you don't know, say so. If you don't understand, say so. Can you remember all that?"

"I suppose so."

"Good. For the next two days the only job you want is Mom. No more, no less. So try to sound like one. Have you been working on your story?"

Her eyes seemed smaller, more focused. "I've been working on a hell of a case of insomnia, is what I've been working on."

"What are you going to say about the affair, for example? Your paramour is also on their list, I suppose you noticed."

She nodded. "After Chas left me, Richard wanted to take up where we left off. I didn't. He was furious. God knows what he'll say. Does it count against me that I don't douche?"

Her laugh was raw and morbid. D.T. smiled despite himself. "That's the kind of thing that will sink your ship, Mrs. Stone. Judges don't like smart-ass women, tough broads, cute chicks, or mothers who've gotten in touch with their feelings or actualized their creative potential. They like Moms who are like *their* mom. It may be lousy, but that's the game, and if you want to win it you'd better play by the rules. And if you don't want to win I can call Dick Gardner right now and cut a deal that will make you financially secure for the rest of your life unless you start playing commodities or free-basing cocaine. So what'll it be?"

"I want to win," she said simply. "I'll do what I have to do."

"Okay. Then think over your answers before you give them. Don't blurt any smart remarks. I'm not kidding. The judge is like God in there. If he decides you're a bitch then you're on your way to hell."

"Are you saying I should try to *seduce* him, Mr. Divorce Lawyer?" She batted her red-scratched eyes.

"I'm saying you should convince him you love your children and will raise them with care and affection, reverence and humility, and perpetual good cheer."

"Well, that's true. I do and I will."

"I believe you, Mrs. Stone. But there's one believer to go. He wears a long black robe. I suggest you make him like you."

She nodded silently. There was no sound in the house. He should inspect the rest of it, on some ruse or another, but it would just depress him. And he should wait to see the kids, but he didn't like putting kids on the stand, asking them who they liked best, where they wanted to live, why Mommy was great and Daddy was not. He was especially leery of doing it in this case, since Mommy very likely was something quite short of great, even in the eyes of her children.

"Have you seen the detective hanging around?" he asked into the silence.

"Yes. A few times."

"Have you been discreet?"

She smiled thinly. "Chaste, is closer."

"I hope you're telling the truth. After the trial you can screw the Chinese army if you want to. But not till then."

"Why, Mr. Jones. That *is* what I want. How perceptive of you to notice." She followed the sarcasm out of the room and returned with a drink in her hand.

"I'm sorry," D.T. said. "My remark was out of line. But you can't let me or anything else throw you for the next two days." He gestured toward the drink. "No more than one of those tonight. And none tomorrow or the next day. Besides, booze with pills is stupid."

"Okay, okay."

"Now, I think we should go through your entire testimony, just the way it will be when you take the stand. Then I'll put you through a cross-examination, just the way Dick Gardner will."

"No."

"Why not?"

"No rehearsals. I don't need to *practice* to be a good mother or to prove that I am. I mean, that's what this is all about, right? Well, I've got more experience at motherhood than anyone in that courtroom, including you and Chas and the almighty judge. *I don't need practice.* Just put me on and ask your questions, Mr. Jones. That's all I want, except to go to bed."

"Listen to me, Mrs. Stone. I'm going to tell you an absolute truth, one of the few sure things I know of in this world."

"What's that?"

"If you don't let me take you through the whole thing —question by question, answer by answer—if you don't let me do that, then you're going to lose your case. *And your kids.*"

"No, I'm not."

"I'll bet you a thousand dollars."

Her smile was a stripe of condescension. "Don't be ridiculous, Mr. Jones. I am not going to sit here and play-act with you all afternoon. I'll tell my story when the time comes, and not before. Is there anything else?"

"I have to warn you, Mrs. Stone, that—"

She stood up. The housecoat flapped open, revealing a flannel gown that had aged to translucence. "Consider me warned, Mr. Jones. Now. Is there anything else?"

To hell with it. He'd fought them long enough, the bitches. The ones who thought they were so goddamned smart, who thought they knew it all, who thought no *man* could best them in court, no *man* could make them look the fool, incompetent, immoral, unfit. If Mareth Stone wouldn't let him win, then he could damned sure let her lose.

"Have you crashed yet?" D.T. asked in a red heat as she waited to dismiss him.

"What?"

"Crashed. Screamed and yelled and fallen on the floor and beat your head on the wall and wanted to be dead."

She scowled. "No. I'm fine. I told you. That's not the way I am."

"Good for you."

"Will you please leave now?"

He nodded, knew he was surrendering too soon, no longer cared. "Be at my office at nine sharp. Bring the kids. Be clean and sweet and alert. Pray to whatever you pray to that I know everything about you I need to know."

She closed her eyes. "Why do I feel as though it's Judgment Day?"

"Because that's the day it is."

Still enraged, he drove against the rush hour to his apartment. On the deck with a drink at his side he checked the *Sporting News* and the sports pages from the L.A. and New York papers he subscribed to, then called his bookie and put fifty on the Beavers against the Bruins, because Ralph Miller was Ralph Miller and the game was in Oregon and the California boys just hated it up there. Then as an afterthought he put another fifty on the Spurs against the Lakers because the A-Train had made them whole. When he was finished, Sol reminded him he was four hundred down. D.T. said he knew it. Sol swore and bemoaned his fate. D.T. cursed the collapse of the Chargers, which was what had caused it all.

He hung up and sat silently for a time, weary, convinced of the nightmare that frequently assailed him—that every day of the rest of his life would be exactly the same as this one. When his glass was empty he went to the bedroom and looked up Dr. Haskell's office number and dialed it. The woman who answered asked if it was an emergency. He told her it was. He didn't tell her that the emergency was legal, not medical, and was of his own making.

After several minutes Haskell came on the line. "Dr. Haskell, this is D. T. Jones. I'm an attorney. I spoke to you a couple of months ago about Nathaniel Preston? Your former partner?"

"Yes. I remember. How are you?" Haskell was tense, irritated.

"Fine. I wanted to ask you a couple more questions about Preston."

"What?"

"First, is there any chance at all that Preston was an abortionist back when he first started in practice?"

Haskell was silent for several seconds. "What on earth gave you that idea?"

"Just a hunch. Is is possible?"

"No. Of course not."

"Are you saying you would have known if he had been doing something like that?"

"Yes. I think I would. I was down there day and night."

"Okay, how about drugs? Could Preston have been an addict? Or a dealer?"

"My God, Jones. What are you trying to prove, anyway?"

"Anything I can."

"Are you saying Esther's still going ahead with this trial business?"

"Yep."

"But I thought . . ."

"What?"

"Well, I heard Nat had done something to her. Threatened her, or something."

"Threaten's a rather benign term for it."

"And yet she's still going after him?"

"Full speed ahead. Preston made her mad."

"I *really* don't think that's a good idea, Mr. Jones. If it's only a question of money I can probably help Esther out a little. How much does she need?"

"A million dollars."

"Come on. Be serious."

"I am serious. How much do *you* need to get you through the next thirty years?"

"But . . ."

D.T. hung up and hooked up his video recorder and got out the cassette he ran at times like this and shoved it into the machine.

The tape was entirely of Heather, age approximately one and a half, filmed over the period of months when she was learning to walk and talk. All comic, all marvelous, all his only legacy to the world. He watched raptly in his blackened bedroom, as poisons and acids drained from his body and his mind, as he took silly solace in the fact that he had once done something holy. As Heather was falling into a plant, the phone rang.

"Leaving the office a little early these days, aren't you, sport?" Dick Gardner chided.

"On the track of a surprise witness. Claims to have photos of your client committing unnatural acts with a goat."

Gardner laughed. "One last chance, D.T. Save yourself some embarrassment."

"Hell, Dick. I try to be embarrassed at least twenty minutes a day. Aerobics, you know."

"No time for mirth, D.T. My guy wants to avoid trial if he can. To spare the kids. *He's* thinking of their welfare, even if their mother isn't."

"Save it for the judge, Gardner. Let's get to the in-grown toenail. Does your offer include exclusive custody to Mrs. Stone?"

"Joint. Both legal and physical. The boy goes with Stone and the girl stays with the mother. Or, six months a year at each place, both kids together."

"Two interesting proposals, Dick. I don't know which is more specious. Your man's just in this to save face, isn't he? He wants a legal judgment that he's a great guy. For political reasons. He doesn't give a damn about those kids."

"Come on, D.T. She could lose them both at trial. Mary Poppins she ain't."

"Mary Poppins she don't gotta be, thank God."

"Stone will give her a quarter million plus the house and car."

"What's she going to do with that house without kids to put in it?"

"The way I hear it, she's found a few things to put in it already, and most of them have cocks hanging between their legs, or did when they went in there. I hear *you* were out there this afternoon, by the way. Have a nice chat?"

"He must be pretty good, Gardner. What was he, disguised as a dog turd?"

Gardner laughed easily. "That reminds me of those old Lone Ranger jokes. Remember? 'Tonto, not recognizing the Lone Ranger disguised as a pool table, racked his balls.'"

"Old isn't the only word for that joke, Dick. And the answer is no. No deal without custody. So how many of that warren of witnesses are you really going to call? The shrink?"

"Who knows?"

"The kids?"

"Who knows?"

"The lover?"

"Who knows?"

"You met with the kids today, didn't you?"

"Who knows?"

"Jesus, Gardner. I've had more intelligent conversations with Judge Hoskins, for God's sake."

"He's got the case, did you know that? Clerk called just before five."

"No. Christ. I thought it was Buchanan."

"Buchanan has the flu."

"Hoskins hates me," D.T. blurted.

Dick Gardner laughed. "With good reason, I'm sure. And with that knowledge I hereby withdraw our offer of compromise."

"See you in court, you prick." D.T. dropped the phone, his concern about the Stone case approaching panic.

The more he thought the more worried he got. Hoskins. An angry, impulsive client. A lawyer who'd done less than he should have to prepare his case. An oppo-

nent among the most skilled in the city. Sweat crawled
forth and chilled him. He put away the video equipment
and picked up the phone and called his secretary.

"Bobby? D.T."

"Hi."

"You got anything lined up on Stone yet? I've got to
try to set it up with someone else if you haven't."

Bobby hesitated. When he spoke his voice lagged with
resignation and regret. "I was about to call. You know
the Lakeview Inn?"

"By the golf course. Sure."

"Do you want a tape or just pictures?"

"Just pics."

"You got a photographer lined up?"

"Right. Ready to go."

"Okay. Have him ask at the desk for the key to Room
214."

"What?"

"He asks for the key. The room's already reserved.
He should be there by ten."

"Tonight?"

"Tonight. Tell him to go to the room and get his camera ready and keep the lights out and not make a sound.
No TV, no nothing. Okay?"

"Okay."

"There's a connecting door from that room to Room
212. Have him unlock it right when he gets there. That's
all, just unlock it."

"Check."

"Sometime tonight two people will check into 212. I
don't know what time, probably not before ten or after
midnight. When he hears them come in have your guy
keep his eyes on the connecting door. When the light
under the door goes out, have him count ten and go
through the door and snap two or three shots and then
take off. The bed's against the far wall, the head at the
corner."

"How far from the door?"

"Twenty feet, maybe."

"Okay. It'll be dark, right?"

"Right. He'll have to have a flash or infrared. After he
snaps the pictures have him get out of there fast. The

stairs are at the end of the hall, just around the corner.
Stone might try to come after him, so he shouldn't daw-
dle."

"Who's the guy?"

"No names."

"Trustworthy?"

"As much as anyone."

"He know about me?"

"No."

"How much?"

Bobby paused. "Five hundred."

"High."

"It's what he needs."

"You absolutely sure they'll be there tonight?"

"As sure as I can be."

"How'd you get it fixed so fast?"

"I guess Stone is always ready to play, provided the
arrangements are discreet. As for the room, well, those
of us who are more adventuresome than others, well,
sometimes we need to make a record of a relationship
ourselves, for various reasons. I don't expect you to understand."

"Okay, Bobby. I'm sorry I had to go to you for this,
but I need an edge in this one. I need one bad."

Bobby E. Lee ignored his plea. "Tell your guy to be
on time. And not to leave anything behind."

"Bobby?"

"Yes."

"One more thing."

"What?"

"The guy in the next room with Stone?"

"Yes?"

"It's not going to be you, is it? I don't want it to be
you, Bobby."

Bobby E. Lee hung up without a word.

D.T. went over in his mind the list of people he could
call who might take the pictures, investigators and pho-
tographers he knew of or had used in the past as witnesses or collectors of evidence. There was a score or
more of them, and afterward he would be hostage to the
creep for life, subject to having done to him exactly what
he was preparing to do to Stone. One word, and his li-

cense goes. One word, he gets sued, or jailed, or both. He would have to take care of it himself. That way his trust would extend only to Bobby E. Lee, where it had already resided for years.

Blackmail. That was a first. But it was only a difference of degree, right? Another price of victory. They all did it, one way or another. The personal injury boys solicited clients, the class action boys split fees, the corporate boys phonied registration statements and bought stock on inside tips, the criminal boys bought experts, and each and every one of the boys suborned perjury in every case that had ever gone to trial in the history of the world. So what the hell? The ingrown toenail was that Stone was gay and gays couldn't be parents. Right? Right. Hell, he could do it in open court if he had to, even without Bobby's help. Find one of Stone's playmates and move for amended custody and subpoena him. Put him on and ask him how Stone liked his sex, whether he used K-Y jelly or only a dab of oleo. Any judge in town would feign a faint and give the kids to Mom. So the result was right, the kids were better off, and who was hurt? D.T. went to the hall closet and dug out his good camera, the one with the automatic film advance and the electronic flash. He wound in a roll of the high-speed Ektachrome he had on hand, set the shutter to the flash indicator, opened the aperture as wide as it went, put new batteries in the flash attachment, and aimed and shot his bedroom door. The flash exploded, momentarily erasing the room, permanently erasing his illusions of legitimacy.

He checked his watch. Eight-ten. He made himself a peanut butter sandwich and drank a glass of milk, at one point conscious that it would be his final brush with wholesomeness. Then he stuck his camera in his briefcase and got in his car and drove to the Lakeview Inn and reconnoitered.

It was a large and popular place, modishly decorated, proximate to tennis, golf, swimming, and a trendy shopping mall, perpetually full of convening salespeople, energetic engineers, reuniting high school classes, or dancers who were charitably motivated. The leather lobby chairs were full, the desk clerks harassed, the floor littered with the luggage of the checking-in or -out. The bar off the lobby rollicked with warbled laughter and a banjo that was strummed, not picked. The dining room opposite the bar dripped with chandeliers and ferns. And Muzak maligned it all.

D.T. took the elevator to the second floor, found his room, found the stairs around the corner at the end of the hall, took the stairs to the main floor, and exited into the parking lot through the nearest door. He walked to his car and drove it to a place just outside the exit door, then took his briefcase and walked back to the main entrance and waited in line until he could ask the desk clerk for the key to 214.

The clerk slid the key his way without looking at him. No one else in the lobby seemed to notice him either, not even the woman he briefly wished would do so. Had his face not clashed with his emotions, every eye in the place would have been on him and every voice would have screamed for a cop. He crossed the lobby and took the elevator up a floor, sharing it with a Latin waiter who tended a cart of dishes topped with silver domes.

The elevator stopped at two. He walked quickly to his room, turned on the lights to check the layout, pressed his ear to the wall and listened for soundless minutes, then unlocked the connecting door. Retracing his steps, he wiped his prints off everything he'd touched, turned off the light with his elbow, and took out his camera and lay on the bed to await his victim. Before long, D.T. had convinced himself that he would not be altering history but merely hastening its pace.

He floated gently on time, exercising the skill he had developed in college to think of the erotic when confronted by the dreadful. The only light in the room came from the languid digits on his watch, the only sound from the toneless whistlings of his breath. He closed his eyes and watched the liquid colors that formed behind his lids. He took his pulse and tried to make it race and subside to his will. He held his breath for seventy-six seconds. He unzipped his pants and scratched his balls. He thought of Barbara and Michele, of Heather and Lucinda Finders. He thought of Bobby E. Lee, of how to apologize for this. He heard a sound and wished he hadn't.

Light spilled under the door, a yellow dash of doom,

just as Bobby E. Lee had predicted. Motionless, D.T. listened for words or telltale sounds but heard nothing coherent. Water ran, a toilet flushed, water ran again. Drinks, he guessed. Or drugs. Coke would be good. Amyl nitrite, maybe. Free-basing? Who knew? Who cared? For thirty minutes more he was left to his imagination and his conscience. He cradled his camera like a baby chick and thought of every naked woman he had ever seen.

The light under the door went out. He got up as quietly as he could and went to the connecting door, counting to himself, readying his optic weapon.

On the count of ten he turned the knob. He pushed; nothing happened. He pressed harder, swore silently, then pulled. The door swung toward him quickly, squeaking only when it was open wide enough for him to pass beyond it. He stepped back, then stepped quickly into the other room. He heard vocal rumblings from the far corner, querulous, not yet frightened.

D.T. raised his camera to his eye, aimed for the sound, pressed the button, filled the room with light and lovers, was aware of only generality—their presence and predicament. He kept his finger down, and the motor whirred and the flashes came again and again, blinding him, preventing his sense of who he was shooting, of whether his pictures were anything he needed, or anything at all.

A voice beyond him cursed and ordered him to stop. He retreated, slamming the door and locking it. He grabbed his briefcase and ran toward the stairs, listening for pursuit, hearing nothing but his swollen, throbbing heart and his coward's fleeing footfalls.

Halfway down the stairs he tripped and almost fell. At the bottom he slowed to a homely walk, stepped into the parking area, and encountered a young boy with a sports bag over his shoulder, a racquet under his arm. They eyed each other nervously. D.T. walked on, opened the door to his car, got in, closed the door, inserted the key, turned it. The car started, no traffic impeded him, and he was on the boulevard that led to his apartment before he thought to look back.

Nothing followed. It had all gone perfectly. Perfect, perfect, perfect. So perfect it was bound to fall apart.

When he got home his phone was ringing.

"You the lawyer?"

"Yes."

"You do divorce?"

"Yes. Who is this?"

"The name is Kates. The wife just threw me out. How much you charge to get me a divorce?"

"It depends on what—"

"How much?"

"Two hundred dollars, minimum. Cash up front."

"Fucking asshole bastard."

At the very least.

■ NINETEEN

THE photographs—crisp, shiny glossies, developed and printed in D.T.'s makeshift darkroom—imprisoned Chas Stone and a tawny Aryan lad of about twenty-five, the pair of them snug and naked in the rumpled bed of Room 212 in the world-famous Lakeview Inn, American plan, all credit cards accepted, AAA-approved, group rates upon request. Their eyes were pinkish from the bounce of the flash off the rosy carpet, and the focus was a touch blurred since the darkness and distance reduced the depth of field, but the essentials were there for the looking, preserved on a borderless print.

Stone was covered from the waist down by an electric blue acrylic blanket, a preliminary pose of modesty or enticement, but in the chest and shoulders he was a Carrara bust—hairless, trim, and eager. And his partner, well, his partner had taken care to display himself in all his oiled perfection, from his tapering calves to his stubby, angled prick to his yellow curling locks to his knowing sadist's smirk. He was clearly teasing Stone, and Stone was clearly teased. The pictures wouldn't make *Popular Photography*, or even *Male Muscle*, but they would carry out their function, when and if D.T. had the need and the will to use them. He patted the pocket where they lay, glanced across the courtroom at Stone and Gardner, then looked at the client who he was about to call to the stand in the case of *Stone* v. *Stone*.

He still wasn't certain of his capacities. Hard as he tried to deny it, blackmail was a step beyond the tricks and stratagems he had used before, a step across the edge of felony, the stuff of detective novels and TV. Still, the choice between premeditated crime and ignominious defeat was not an easy one. He thought his scruples had been suppressed over a night of rationalization. He thought he was prepared, in other words, to do what had to be done. But, amazingly enough, he was apparently to be blessed. He could continue to face both the mirror and Bobby E. Lee of a morning because it looked very much as though he wouldn't need the extortionate emulsions after all.

The trial was going well. Freed from the monotony of the Friday Fiasco, Judge Hoskins was tolerably civil, which was all D.T. asked and more than he had figured to receive. Dick Gardner was as good as D.T. had expected him to be, but he was nothing miraculous, nothing otherworldly, nothing that could not be whipped, given a few breaks. And D.T. himself—albeit weary, ill-prepared, and penitent—he himself had been supreme.

Chas Stone had floated to the witness stand like an angel and rested there serenely, an object to be worshipped, on a par with God. D.T. had allowed Dick Gardner to elicit Stone's testimony without interference by way of legal objection, so that by the end of the direct examination Chas Stone had become a star of straitlaced rectitude, beyond the reach of mortal man or even lawyers.

Then, after lunch, the cross-examination. And at its end, just before lunch the following day, Stone had slithered from the stand like a slandered slug, battered, beaten, burdened by a view of himself that would fester like a pustule at the exact center of his soul. As Stone had passed his table on his way out of the courtroom, D.T. had barely suppressed a jeer.

He had made his points one by one, methodically and relentlessly, his tone suggesting, implying, doubting, accusing; his gestures scornful, dismissive, curt. Yes, Stone worked very hard at his job, spent many nights and weekends working or entertaining clients. Yes, he played golf every Sunday. Yes, he played racquet ball every Wednesday after work. Yes, he was a member of a men's club, an athletic club, a business club, and an alumni club and attended their functions regularly. Yes, he traveled at least six times a month, to conventions, or to securities analysts' meetings, or to visit companies whose stock he found attractive. No, he had never attended a PTA meeting or been a scout leader, a Little League coach, a Campfire counselor. No, he had never changed a diaper, mixed a formula, fixed a lunch, made a bandage, sewed a hem, mopped a spill, framed a picture, papered a wall, built a treehouse, constructed a fort, batted a ball, made a costume, pedalled a bike, assembled a dollhouse, or played doctor, cowboys, Indians, Monopoly, Clue, G.I. Joe, or Space Invaders. He thought he had helped David with some quadratic equations, and he knew he had once played in a father-daughter tennis tournament with Cristine. They'd lost their first match. No, she hadn't played much after that, she preferred music to sports. No, he didn't play an instrument himself. No, he had never taken her to a music lesson or his son to ball practice. Yes, he'd been to some baseball games. A few. Three last year. Out of ten or twenty, he wasn't sure. No, he didn't know the name of Cristine's piano teacher or David's coach or the school principal or the math teacher or the guidance counselor. He wasn't sure what book they'd read last, what their favorite music was, which movie star they liked. Cristine had a picture of a singer on her wall once, but it wasn't up there any more, he was pretty sure. Michael Jackson maybe? Was that somebody?

So it had gone, until the climactic incident, disclosed to D.T. by his client during recess called so Judge Hoskins could relieve himself. Yes, David had once taken his father's favorite putter to play with in the yard and had forgotten to return it to the bag. Yes, Stone had only discovered it on the first green while playing with his Sunday foursome. Yes, he had been upset, and had punished David. How? Well, he had made David clean his golf clubs. And wash his golf balls with his toothbrush. And shag practice shots for two hours the next Saturday instead of playing in his Little League game. Yes, there was one more thing. He had beaten David with the putter, just the shaft, across his thighs. Yes, there had been a bruise. Yes, David had run away from home that night, but only for a couple of hours: they'd found him at the mall at midnight, caught by an usher while trying to hide inside a movie house so he could spend the night there. No, the police hadn't been called. No, he didn't think David had been mistreated. Yes, he had spanked David on other occasions. Yes, he believed in discipline and occasional corporal punishment. Yes, when he spanked David he generally used a quirt.

When D.T. had finished, Mareth Stone had thanked him in a whisper and squeezed his hand, her eyes matched bowls of grateful tears. Her pleasure in his work had almost been enough for him to forget the photographs he carried in his jacket pocket like a passport to perdition, though not quite.

The rest of Gardner's witnesses had fared little better. Neighbors, acquaintances, busybodies, they had all seen the Stone family in one stage or another of stress and distress, had all seen Mareth Stone do something improper with her children or something unseemly with herself. One man had seen her retrieve the morning paper wearing only a bra and panties. The neighbor woman had heard her use language that would shame a trucker, had often heard the children crying, though for what reason she really couldn't say, it couldn't have been anything good, not the way they were screaming, she'd never heard anything like it in her life. A woman had seen Mareth get sick at a party that featured Boom Boom punch. A man remembered her saying that she envied him because he was childless and single. All nonsense, all trivial, most of it in a jury case irrelevant. But as the sole trier of fact Judge Hoskins had let it all come in to soil the record, as any jurist would.

The big problems were the booze and the sex, and the only one who could explain them away was Mareth Stone herself. The time had come. Purged of his pique, determined now to win despite his client's rash imprudence, he cleared his throat and called her to the stand, patting her shoulder as she left his side, crossing his fingers as he watched her take the oath to tell the truth, knowing he had no idea if she intended to obey it. He had never begun an examination with more foreboding, not an examination of his very own client. For a moment his voice fluttered and betrayed his fears, then he settled down, as interested as an observer in what she had to say.

He took her through the preliminaries slowly and calmly, cracked a few jokes, smiled a few smiles, loosened her up, made the judge like her or come as close as he could come. He covered the marriage breakup briefly, establishing that she was not the initiator of the action, that she was without rage or rancor, that she was agreeable to liberal visitation rights being accorded her husband despite their past wrangles, that she had recovered from whatever heartbreak the separation had originally caused. Then he took her from being wife to being what she wanted to remain.

Using details she had supplied or he had merely guessed at, he brought out her involvement with her children, reviewed her daily contribution to their welfare, elicited a frank confession of the frustrations and irritants of child-rearing before Dick Gardner could introduce the subject from a different tack, anticipating his opponent's thrusts. All the things her husband didn't know she knew, what he had never done had been done by her, what he believed, she doubted, and vice versa. By the time his initial gambit was concluded he had cast Mareth Stone as Earth Mother, nurse, chauffeur, coach, instructor, pastor, pal. But he knew Judge Hoskins remained to be convinced, was waiting to hear about the affair and about the booze. In spite of the relativistic statutes and decisions and attitudes now littering the law, they remained two vices that could end her reign as Mom.

He went first to the booze, unaware of what she was going to say about it, aware that imprecision and arrogance were the major mistakes of one in her position. Gardner would exploit the slightest opening, magnify the smallest slip, exaggerate the merest frailty. She was as vulnerable as a babe, but Mareth Stone had chosen the course herself. Her fate was where she wanted it—entirely in her hands. D.T. began his questions. Judge Hoskins was, for the first time since Chas Stone had left the witness stand, giving the case his full attention.

She had had her first drink the night after the last day of her freshman year in college, a store-bought Tom Collins mixer heavily laced with rum, a long night of revelry followed by a longer morning of nausea and remorse. She had been able to taste the concoction for years afterward, whenever she came near a potion that hinted of the blend of lemon-lime. She had never drunk rum again, but she had continued to drink socially, before her marriage and after, never regularly, never to forget or anything, only to relax, to feel comfortable and funny and free to laugh and joke and enjoy herself outside the joyless atmosphere her husband imposed upon their home. The pattern changed only when her marriage began to sour as bitterly as that first mixer.

She had drunk excessively for a period of perhaps six months. She admitted it. She regretted it, but it was no longer a problem because she had abandoned the habit of excess because it hadn't worked and because now that her marriage had definitely ended there was no longer a need for whatever it was that liquor had given her. What was that? Oh, a certain anesthetic condition, an insensitivity to her deteriorating marital environment, an ability to delude herself into thinking that all the things that were happening might be sad, and horribly depressing, but they were inflicting no lasting pain.

No, she no longer believed that. There had been much pain, almost blinding at times, and it continued to this day. She had loved Chas once, had wanted to keep her marriage alive, had not wanted to become like all the others out there—the twice-or-thrice-divorced, minstrels of love, wandering from man to man until all men were equally acceptable or not, indistinguishable, tools. She had wanted to succeed, but now that it was clear that she and Chas were through, she could accept it. And make a new life for herself and her children, a process she had already begun.

No, she had never been arrested while drinking, or for being intoxicated in public, or for any other reason. No, she had never been hospitalized or forced to dry out. No, the children had never suffered as a result of her problem. Yes, the problem had been eliminated; no, she had not had to seek professional help to accomplish it; yes, she was fully in control of the situation now. It was simply not a problem. Yes, at about the time she had begun drinking too much she had begun a love affair with another man.

It was not something she had planned or wanted. The

need had just materialized, magically, insidiously, like a virus. Like the drinking, she felt the affair was a result of an expanding desperation about her marriage and her life, of her sense that everything she valued had taken a step back, was just beyond her reach. Basically, the affair was part of her effort to get through an entire week without crying. Over the way she felt, over the way her life was going, over her effort to avoid the conclusion that she had failed at every single thing that mattered.

They had met several times, ten maybe, at first only to talk, to share mutual disappointments and dissatisfactions, to learn enough about each other to decide if they wanted to go to places neither of them had been before. He was a nice man, kind, considerate, patient, sympathetic, understanding. He seemed, for those few days, to be everything her husband was not, though she now knew that was an illusion, a perfection she had seen because she had so badly yearned to see it.

Yes, the affair had eventually culminated in a sexual relationship. But only twice. It had not been what she needed or wanted. It had in fact added to her burden, not eased it, and after the two times she had ended the relationship. Yes, completely. She had never seen the man alone again. That had been almost two years ago now. No, there had been no other affairs during the time she and Chas were living together. Yes, there had been a sexual experience since he had left her. With one man. No, the children had not been in the house at the time. Of course they had not seen the act, good grief, what kind of woman would make love in front of children that age? Yes, she intended to marry again if she found the right man, but she wasn't in a hurry, wasn't desperate.

She loved her children, and wanted them with her, and would be able to support them with an award of three thousand dollars per month in child support from her ex-husband. She was certain the children wanted to stay with her. There had been no serious problems since their father had left home, nothing she couldn't handle. They were all getting along just fine. In some ways, she thought life at home was actually better, now that the discords of marriage had been removed. Was there anything else she wanted to say? Only that she was a good mother, that being a mother was the most important thing in her life, that she wanted to continue loving and caring for and sharing in the lives of David and Cristine for the rest of her life. She begged the court not to take them from her.

"Your witness, Mr. Gardner."

D.T. sat down and Dick Gardner stood up. "Thank you, Mr. Jones. Mrs. Stone?"

Gardner paused, focusing all minds in the room toward him, gearing them for a shift in attitude, for a wrenching of their sentiments. Standing there, slim, tall, the slightest, kindest smile on his lips, even inanimate objects— the flags behind the judge's bench, the long lights overhead, the long benches bearing spectators—seemed subservient to his will, awaiting with pleasure his assault upon the woman who twitched nervously in the chair before him.

"I listened very closely to your direct testimony, Mrs. Stone," Gardner began. "It was quite enlightening. Somewhat contrary to what I had been led to believe were the true facts, however. So . . ."

"Objection. Counsel is testifying."

"Sustained."

"Excuse me, Your Honor," Dick Gardner said. "Mrs. Stone, I'm going to have to go over some of the points you brought up, I'm afraid, to get things clear in my mind. First, during the time you were living with Mr. Stone, that's Chas Stone, the petitioner seated here before me, during that time did you ever have a love affair other than the one with Richard Weaver you described already, Mrs. Stone? An affair that culminated in sexual congress?"

"No. I did not. Only the one."

"Are you quite certain of that?"

"Yes. Of course."

"I suppose you would know, wouldn't you? I mean, it's not the type of thing you'd be likely to forget, is it?" Gardner's smile would have charmed an asp.

"No. It is not."

"Very well. Where do you buy your booze, Mrs. Stone? I mean your hard liquor."

"Why, the store on Calumet, usually. In the shopping center."

"Quality Liquors?"

"I believe that's it. Yes."

"What type of hard liquor do you usually buy?"

"Bourbon. Once in a while."

"What brand?"

"I . . . Early Times."

"Do you ever buy liquor for anyone else? Friends? Neighbors?"

"No."

"Do you buy wine at that store?"

"No."

"Beer?"

"No. Only liquor."

"How much Early Times did you buy last month, Mrs. Stone? In January. Do you have any idea?"

"I don't know."

"Well, you carry an account at Quality Liquors, don't you?"

"Yes."

"How much was last month's bill?"

"I don't recall."

"I see. You did pay it, didn't you?"

"Yes. I'm sure I did."

"Then perhaps I can help you as to the amount. It was ninety-nine dollars, was it not? Ninety-nine dollars and eleven cents, to be exact."

"If you say so."

"How much do you pay for a fifth of Early Times, Mrs. Stone?"

"I'm not sure. Nine dollars, I think."

"I think that's about it. Nine thirty-five, is the current price, is it not?"

"That sounds right."

"So, assuming those two figures for the moment, a little arithmetic reveals that you purchased exactly ten fifths of Early Times last month, isn't that right? Allowing for sales tax of six percent? Ten fifths of bourbon over a period of thirty days. This is correct, is it not?"

"I suppose it is. But . . ."

"Thank you, Mrs. Stone. Do you have any idea how many individual highballs there are in a fifth of liquor?"

"No."

"A good stiff drink has an ounce and a half of liquor in it, right?"

"I guess."

"And a fifth has twenty-four ounces?"

"I haven't the faintest idea."

"Well, assume for a moment that it does. That makes sixteen drinks, times ten fifths equals over one hundred and sixty drinks a month. More than five a day. Right?"

"I don't know."

"Well, if you don't know I'm sure there are others in the room who do."

Gardner consulted his notes. Mareth Stone shrank inside her clothes. "But I've had *guests*. And I . . ."

"Move to strike, Your Honor," Dick Gardner said.

"Sustained. Please limit yourself to answering the questions put to you, Mrs. Stone," Judge Hoskins admonished.

"But there are *explanations*. I'm not a . . ."

"*Mrs. Stone*. Silence. Please."

She bowed her head and bit her lip. When she glanced at him, D.T. made a sign to calm her down. It didn't seem to take. Dick Gardner stood up.

"Now. You mentioned guests, Mrs. Stone. How many different men have you entertained in your home since your husband moved out of the house some six months ago?"

"Objection, Your Honor," D.T. said. "Irrelevant."

"Overruled."

"Mrs. Stone? How many?" Gardner repeated.

"I have no idea."

"Two? Ten? A hundred?"

"I really don't know. Not nearly a hundred."

"It's been exactly seventeen, hadn't it, Mrs. Stone? Seventeen different men in your house, after dark, all at your invitation?"

"I doubt very much that it's been that many."

"I see. Do you want me to read the names? I have a list right here. Thomas Irwin. Lawrence Forsythe. Calvin Cox . . ."

"I . . . no. You don't need to read the names. That damned *detective* did it, didn't he? The slimy bastard. I saw him out there. Acting like I was some sort of animal in a cage. What kind of man are you, Mr. Gardner? That's what *I'd* like to know. Just what kind of man *are* you to hire someone to peep in my windows day and night like a . . . *pervert?*"

Gardner was impervious. "Please confine yourself to answering my questions, Mrs. Stone. You have already had your opportunity to speak on the subjects that interest you. Now—"

"*None* of this interests me, Mr. Gardner. It's boring and stupid. If I could, I'd take my kids out of here right now and never come back."

Gardner glowed. "But of course that's what we're here to determine, isn't it, Mrs. Stone? Who should be the one to take the children home. And quite frankly I'm surprised that you feel this court has no business knowing how many men have traipsed through the lives of you and your children over the six months since their father was forced to leave the family residence."

"Forced to leave? No one *forced* him to leave. He snuck out like a rat, without telling any of us what he was going to do. That's the kind of man *he* is."

Judge Hoskins adjusted his robes and glared. "All right, Mr. Gardner. Mrs. Stone. Let's get on with it. This wrangling is beside the point, as you both well know."

Gardner bowed. "Very well, Your Honor. My apologies to the court. I have only a few more questions, Mrs. Stone. Your kitchen caught fire two weeks ago, didn't it?"

"Yes. How did you know that?"

"While you were preparing the evening meal?"

"Yes."

"But you weren't in the kitchen when the fire broke out, were you?"

"No."

"You were—where?—in the bedroom?"

"Yes."

"Lying down?"

"Yes."

"Asleep?"

"No. Yes. I guess I was. For a minute."

"The children were in the house, were they not?"

"Yes."

"Downstairs?"

"I guess so."

"Now, shortly after the fire broke out the smoke alarm went off, didn't it?"

"Yes."

"But it didn't wake you, did it?"

"Not right away. No."

"The children had to come up and shake you awake, didn't they?"

"I guess."

"They were very frightened, weren't they?"

"For a few minutes, maybe."

"Crying?"

"Yes."

"Screaming?"

"I don't know. Maybe once or twice."

"After the fire was out they wanted to go spend the night with their father, didn't they?"

"No."

"*Didn't* they, Mrs. Stone?"

"One of them did. Cristine. But not David. David would *never* go to Chas."

"You didn't let *either* of them go to their father, did you?"

"No. They weren't serious. They were only frightened by the smoke and the noise."

"Yes. The smoke alarm. It was very loud, wasn't it?"

"Yes."

"My question for you is this, Mrs. Stone. *What had you taken that made you sleep right through it?*"

"You son of a bitch. *Nothing.* I . . ."

D.T. got to his feet. "Objection, Your Honor. Mr. Gardner is being argumentative. Also the question assumes facts not in evidence."

"I wasn't taking one damned thing, Mr. Gardner. *Not one thing.*"

"You needn't scream, Mrs. Stone. I can hear you quite well."

"Your Honor. May Mr. Gardner be instructed to cease his harassment of this witness?" D.T. sank back to his chair.

"Mr. Gardner is within proper bounds, Mr. Jones. The

witness, however, is instructed to cease her outbursts and limit her statements to full and complete answers to counsel's questions. Are you finished with the witness, Mr. Gardner?"

"I have only a few more, Your Honor. Do you have a personal computer in your home, Mrs. Stone?"

"No."

"Your son wants one, doesn't he?"

"He thinks he does."

"Your husband has offered to purchase one for him, has he not, but you have refused to allow it in the home? Isn't that correct?"

"Yes. I don't believe in computers. They're worse than TV. They turn kids into robots. I won't have David destroying his mind with those grotesque games."

"But computers do much more than play games, don't they, Mrs. Stone?"

"That's what they claim, but I've never seen any evidence of it."

"But you've never consulted an expert, have you, to learn exactly what a computer will do?"

"No."

"Do you ever take your children to a doctor? For checkups?"

"Of course."

"Do they have a pediatrician they see regularly?"

"Yes. Dr. Arnoldson. A wonderful man."

"How about a dentist? Do they see a dentist regularly?"

"Yes. Of course."

"The same one or different ones?"

"The same. I forget his name. He has an office downtown."

"Dr. Flynn. Is he the one?"

"Yes."

"Children are supposed to see the dentist—what?—every six months. Isn't that right?"

"I think so."

"When's the last time you took your children to see Dr. Flynn, Mrs. Stone?"

"I don't know. I'm not sure. A few months ago, I think."

"Well, I have Dr. Flynn's appointment records right here. Would you like me to tell you what they say? No? Well, I'll tell you anyway. These records suggest your children haven't been to the dentist for *seventeen months*. That is correct, is it not, Mrs. Stone? You haven't taken your children to see a dentist *for a year and a half?*"

"I don't know. I don't think that's right. It *couldn't* be, I . . . I just don't know."

"Yes, well, perhaps someone *should* know, Mrs. Stone. Perhaps that's why we're here. No further questions, Your Honor."

"Redirect, Mr. Jones?"

D.T. wiped his steaming brow.

■ TWENTY

HE rehabilitated her as best he could, gave her a chance to explain, justify, modify, excuse. She did it well, dispassionately and maturely, but she had been damaged, perhaps fatally. Judge Hoskins eyed her speculatively, as though seeking in her shaded eyes and sunken cheeks a clue to the real woman that was asking him to find her fit, to the woman who lived outside of courtrooms and law offices, to the one that mothered children.

D.T. pressed a hand momentarily over his heart. The photographs seemed to pulse, to be heated by the blood of life. By now each image was impressed on his mind and on his soul as well, stains that might never be removed, even by the bleach of time. He dropped his hand away. Once confident that the pictures were unneeded, he was now convinced they must be used.

"I believe I have finished with my redirect, Your Honor," D.T. said. "But may I have a brief recess before excusing the witness?"

"Make it *very* brief, Mr. Jones. Ten minutes."

Judge Hoskins left the bench with Walter close behind. The spectators scrambled toward water fountains and lavatories, the bailiff blew his nose, the court reporter made notes, and Dick Gardner and Chas Stone huddled at the next table, exuding total confidence.

D.T. motioned for Mareth Stone to leave the witness stand and join him. When she was seated beside him he leaned toward her and spoke in whispers. "Who was it?" he asked.

Her eyes widened. "Who?"

"Lawyers always open their cross-examination with a sure winner. A point they know, sooner or later, they can develop to their advantage. The first thing Gardner asked you was whether you'd had any other love affairs. You said no. You were lying, and Gardner knows it and what's worse can prove it. So who's the guy?"

She didn't respond except by closing her eyes. Beyond her, Chas Stone looked their way and smiled a pitying smile.

"Come on," D.T. urged. "You tried a finesse and it didn't work. They never do. The other side always knows the one thing you think they don't. So who was it?"

She looked at the empty witness stand. "He'd never testify against me. Never."

"Welcome to Never-never land, Mrs. Stone. Give me a name."

"He wouldn't *do* that. He . . . he's not *like* the rest. I *know* he isn't."

"Sure, sure. Well, it's too late anyway, I suppose. But when you see him come into the courtroom you let me know."

She blinked and looked at him. "This is so much worse than I thought it would be. I felt like such an *idiot* up there, a child, totally without control. I had no idea."

"That's called lawyering, Mrs. Stone. Gardner had you in the palm of his hand, a lump of clay. He made you look just the way he wanted you to look, which was pretty horrid. On redirect I got you back in shape a little, but I don't know if it was enough."

She looked at him sadly. "Are we winning?"

"It's close. You're a little immoral and your husband is a lot neglectful. Six of one and half-a-dozen of the other. Luckily for you a tie still goes to the mother."

"Isn't there anything more we can do?"

"Put the kids on."

She shook her head violently. "*No.* I won't let you do that. They shouldn't have to go through something like this. I absolutely forbid it."

"Not the girl. I agree she's too young. But how about David? According to you he hates his old man. He could carry the day."

"No. I won't win that way. I couldn't live with myself."

D.T. shrugged, more convinced than ever that the case could be won only with what was in his pocket. "Anything else I should go over with you before you leave the stand?"

"I can't think of anything."

"Okay. I'll tell the judge we rest."

"Is it over, then?"

"Nope. They have a chance for rebuttal. They can call witnesses to challenge anything you've testified to. So. Like I said. Tell me when lover number two walks in. Maybe we can tear out his tongue." D.T. shook his head. She recoiled as if he had slapped her.

The bailiff put his handkerchief away, the spectators took their seats, Judge Hoskins climbed to the bench and Walter sat beneath him, the clerk gavelled the room to order, the din stilled, the court reporter fit a new stack of paper in her machine. D.T. stood up. "Respondent rests, Your Honor."

Judge Hoskins smiled approvingly. "Rebuttal, Mr. Gardner?"

"A few points, yes, Your Honor."

"Call your witness."

D.T. felt a tug on his sleeve. "He's here." The breath that formed the words seemed to singe his ear. "He *came*. You were right. God, why don't they just tie me to the stake?"

D.T. looked back and cast his eyes across the rows of spectators.

The newcomer wore a placid, peaceful countenance, his rusty face resting atop a muscled, athlete's body. He was dressed casually, as though he were shopping for a battery or a belt. The man—the traitor—seemed entirely incapable of intrigue, which doubtless meant he had been entirely successful at adultery's essential element. D.T. turned back to Mareth Stone.

"Who?"

"Brick Lawson."

"Who else?"

"Chas's best client. Or was."

"Still is, it appears. Married?"

She nodded. "I can't *believe* he told Chas about us. I just can't believe it."

"An hour from now you'll believe anything I tell you, Mrs. Stone, but by then it'll be too late."

"I . . ."

Dick Gardner rose from his chair and spoke. "Petitioner calls to the stand Master David Stone, Your Honor. The son of the parties to this action. Their eldest child."

D.T.'s client gasped and gripped his forearm savagely. "No. He can't do this." Her voice serrated the words, cutting him.

"Of course he can," D.T. said. "I told you he could."

"You have to stop him."

"I can't."

"But it's so . . . so *brutal*. To make David choose between us. I just . . ."

Her voice faded as she watched her son emerge from the crowd of spectators and pass through the bar of the court. He was lithe and fluid in movement, wearing pressed pants, a crocodile shirt, and shoes with stripes. He seemed totally at ease. After he had taken the oath and was seated in the witness chair he even grinned, though not at his mother. D.T.'s gut grew sour.

Dick Gardner smiled at his witness. "Now, David, tell us your full name."

"David Allen Stone."

"Are you the son of Chas Stone and Mareth Stone?"

"Yes."

"Your parents are both in the courtroom, is that right?"

"Right."

"How old are you, David?"

"Thirteen."

"And which one of your parents do you currently live with?"

"My mom."

"And you've lived with her since your dad moved out of the house?"

"Yes."

"But you've seen your dad from time to time since

then, am I right? About twice a week? Sometimes more?"

"Right."

"Now, David, I'm going to ask you a few questions. I'm not going to try to trick you, or confuse you, or anything like that, so if I ask something you don't understand, or aren't certain of, you just tell me—okay?—and I'll try to be more precise. Sometimes I get tongue-tied and don't make any sense. If that happens you just tell me, okay?"

"Okay."

David smiled, he and Gardner buddies. D.T. wondered how many coaching sessions Gardner had conducted, question-and-answer marathons that put David on automatic pilot, that ensured his testimony would be as deadly as a scythe. Perhaps D.T. should go into it on cross-examination, the question of coaching. Perhaps that would be the only thing he would have to work with.

"Now, you've taken an oath to tell the truth, David," Dick Gardner continued. "You understand what that means, don't you, to tell the truth?"

"Sure."

Judge Hoskins glanced at D.T. over the top of his glasses. "Does counsel wish to voir dire on competence?"

"No, Your Honor."

"Proceed, Mr. Gardner."

Dick Gardner's smile would have sold a Chiclet to a Wrigley. "Now, David, I want to ask you a few questions about your life at home with your mom. And I'm talking now about the period of time since your father left and moved to another place, which was approximately last August. Remember?"

"Sure."

"Okay. Now, since that time have you and your mother had any problems?"

"Some. Sure."

"What kind of problems?"

"Well, Mom, you know, sometimes Mom gets a little weird."

She gripped his arm and started to rise from her seat. D.T. was barely able to force her down.

"How do you mean weird, David?" Gardner prompted.

"Well, you know, I mean there's *lots* of things. She yells at us a lot. About nothing, you know? Then other times she doesn't seem to care *what* we do, even things that aren't real safe, you know, like when we take the bus downtown? And then, she gets sloshed, you know? Mom gets wasted every once in a while and Cris and me have to take care of her kind of—put her to bed and stuff, make sure the doors are locked and the furnace is down, that kind of thing."

She broke away like a mustang, rearing to her feet, her mouth spraying spittle. "No! David! Don't you know what you're doing to me? Oh, my God. David. My dear sweet God. How did he get you to do this, David? *What did he buy for you to get you to say that?*"

As D.T. reached for her, Mareth Stone slapped his hand away, then turned and ran blindly from him, upsetting her chair, bouncing from obstacle to obstacle, tripping and almost falling over a spectator's foot just before she reached the door that opened onto the corridor. Nothing stopped her flight, not even the arms of her former lover, which reached for her as she ran by. With a final cry of anguish, Mareth Stone pushed through the door and was gone.

D.T. started to go after her, then stopped and faced the bench. "A recess, Your Honor?"

"Very well." Hoskins looked at his watch. "It's after three. We'll adjourn for the rest of the afternoon. Court will convene promptly at nine. I want testimony and arguments completed by noon. I've scheduled other matters at one. Understood?"

"Yes, Your Honor."

"Calm her down, Mr. Jones."

"Yes, Your Honor."

The gavel banged and the judge was gone.

D.T. looked at Dick Gardner. Gardner smiled ruefully and shrugged. "Sorry," he mouthed, then turned back to his client, who had lost a struggle to restrain his glee. If he had not hated Stone fully before, D.T. hated him fully now. He patted the pictures in his pocket, then looked at the witness stand.

The boy still sat there, his eyes darting with uncertainty. D.T. walked to him. "It's all right, son," he said. "We're finished for today."

The boy nodded bravely, his only other movement the tremble of a lip. D.T. put a hand on his shoulder. David looked up at him through liquid lenses. "Will Mom be all right?"

"Sure."

"I didn't mean to hurt her."

"I know. She knows, too. Don't worry about it, David. Everything's going to be all right. Do you need a ride home?"

The boy looked out at the courtroom, at one chair that was empty and another that was filled. "What home am I supposed to go to?" His voice broke as audibly as his mother's heart.

An hour later, D.T. was back in his apartment. David had left the courtroom with his father. D.T. had asked Dick Gardner if he wanted to discuss a settlement, and Gardner had looked at him and laughed.

After fleeing the courtroom, Mareth Stone had gone home. D.T. had called her, she had answered, then hung up when she heard his voice. He would have to go see her, he supposed, to tell her to be in court the next morning, to tell her all was not lost even though it most definitely was.

His second drink was as tasteless as the first; his TV dinner as tasteless as his drink. When the phone rang he assumed it was Mareth Stone, assumed he would once again be hearing the mournful music of a life awry. Instead, it was Barbara.

"Hi."

"Hi."

"How'd it go?"

"A disaster. Mrs. Stone broke down when they put her son on the stand and he said she was a little weird."

"How do you mean broke down?"

"I mean she ran screaming from the courtroom, never to return."

"How awful."

"That doesn't begin to describe it. Judge Hoskins'

eyes were the size of cue balls, his every prejudice confirmed.''

"Does that mean she'll lose the children?"

"Probably."

"How typical."

"Typical of what, for God's sake?"

"The way women get screwed by the system."

He found himself enraged. "Well, it's not exactly irrelevant to a custody decision that the woman gets so drunk her children have to put her to *bed,* Barbara. I mean, in this case I wish it was, but it isn't."

"I'll bet the kid was lying."

"Christ, Barbara. Every woman in the world isn't Joan of Arc. It was lousy enough without you trying to make it sound like I let my client be chewed up by some kind of domestic relations *conspiracy.*"

Barbara paused. D.T. stayed silent himself, amazed by his outburst and more amazed by his lack of an apologetic urge. "Okay, D.T.," Barbara said finally. "You had a bad day. I'm sorry. You want me to come over? For a little TLC?"

"I don't think so."

"Oh."

"I've got to go see Mrs. Stone and try to salvage something usable in court tomorrow. Then I'm going to bed. I'm shot."

"How about this weekend? Will you go river rafting with me?"

"No."

"Why not?"

"It would be too tempting to drown myself."

"You have to learn to leave your work at the office, D.T. Otherwise you're diffusing your energy, not focusing it. Work hard, play hard. You can't sit around and mope twenty-four hours a day."

"Want to bet?"

"Please come on Saturday."

"No."

"I have to have a partner. For the kayak."

"How about Bernie?"

"If you insist." Her voice was wine gone bad.

"I'm sorry I'm such a continuing disappointment to

you, Barbara. Give Bernie my best. I hope you win the race.''

"It's not a race, D.T.''

"Your whole life is a race, Barbara. And you'll do anything to win.''

He hung up, conscious that the rift might well be permanent, conscious that for Barbara as for everyone, certain truths were unacknowledgeable. He said an egocentric prayer and dialed Mareth Stone, once again wondering what he was prepared to do to win for her.

This time she stayed on the line and let him talk. "Are you all right?'' he asked her.

"Of course I'm not.'' The words were slurred, laced with liquor.

"Are the kids there?''

"No. Chas has them both. Under the circumstances I guess I can't blame him.''

"We reconvene in the morning at nine.''

"I'm not certain I'll be there. I mean, it's over, isn't it? I blew it, didn't I?''

"Maybe so; maybe not. Don't throw in the towel.''

"Just throw up, is that it? Do you understand how humiliating that was? How painful? David, on top of all the rest? With lover-boy Brick just waiting in the wings? Good God. I've tried to think of what I've done to deserve all that and you know what? I can't come up with anything. *I really can't.*''

"I tried to tell you the way it would be, Mrs. Stone. I tried to get you to rehearse exactly what would happen when you testified. I think it would have helped if you had let me do it.''

She swore bitterly. "Oh, yes, Mr. Jones. You did your job. I was warned. Do you have a statement you want me to sign? Something saying you're the world's greatest lawyer? Or maybe you can run an ad in the paper. 'Bitch too dumb to keep children. Goes against lawyer's advice. Loses kids. Loses life. *Loses.*' ''

Her voice disappeared. She had accomplished what she had sought to accomplish: she had made him share her pain.

"Are you going to be all right?'' he asked again.

"Yes.''

"Are you sure?"

"Yes."

"Please don't drink any more tonight, Mrs. Stone. Don't take any pills. Maybe I should find someone to come stay with you."

"Oh, don't worry, Mr. Jones. I'm even too dumb to kill myself. I'll probably even see you in the morning; I'd hate to deprive Chas of an opportunity to gloat. But if I'm not there you have my permission to start without me."

The phone went dead. D.T. wondered what he should do, and decided to do nothing. He took a shower and put on his pajamas and drank some chocolate milk and climbed into bed.

The detective novel on the bedstand seemed suddenly too real to be a tool of comfort or escape. The TV offered dross on the commercial channels, the usual apologia for the British class system on the public channel, PKA full-contact karate on the sports channel, and *First Blood* on HBO. He turned off the light and looked at the shadows on the wall, imagined they were demons, imagined they had come to claim him, imagined he was on his way to hell, where a demon other than himself would be responsible for his sins. He picked up the phone and dialed one of the four numbers he knew from memory.

"Hi. It's D.T."

"Well, hi. How are you?"

"Not too good. Can you talk for a minute?"

"Of course. What's the problem?"

"I'm losing a case in court."

"Oh. Well, you've lost cases before, D.T."

"But this time it's my fault. I screwed up, Michele. I let it slide and now it's too late to salvage it."

"You're only human, D.T. You work so hard, once in a while you're bound to run out of time to do it perfectly. That's the price people pay to get a good lawyer."

"It's a price they shouldn't have to pay, Michele. If they hire me they should get my best. And no one's gotten that for quite a while."

"I doubt that very much."

"It's true."

"Let me tell you something, D.T. I used to think you

were working beneath yourself by doing all that divorce work. And I didn't make a secret of it, did I? Remember how I always had a new idea of what you should do with your life?"

"Vividly."

"Well, I want you to know I've changed my mind. After going through our divorce, and hearing all about Joyce Tuttle's and a dozen other friends' who've been through it in the past year or two, I've decided women are damned *lucky* a man like you stays in the divorce business, instead of moving on to something else. And I've decided you're, well, quite special to have stayed with it despite all the chances you've had to do something more, shall we say, glamorous. So what *I* think is, fifty percent of D. T. Jones is better than a hundred percent of any other divorce lawyer in this rotten, stinking town." She paused. "Does that help?"

He laughed. "Actually, it does, Michele. Even though I know you're lying like a rug. Good night, Michele."

"Good night, D.T."

"How come you're home, by the way?"

"I . . . I just thought Heather needed me, I guess. No special reason."

"Is anything wrong with her?"

"No. She's fine."

"You sure?"

"There's no problem, D.T. I just thought I should be spending more time with her, that's all."

"Kiss her for me, okay?"

"Okay."

"And thanks for the kind words."

"Any time."

"See you."

"See you."

Michele's balm was only temporary. He tossed and turned beneath the covers, struggling for comfort and finding none. The night dragged interminably, pressed on him like a weight. When the phone rang he was grateful. He pressed the receiver to his ear.

"Mr. Jones. Are you there, Mr. Jones?"

"Who is this? Lucinda? Is that you?"

"Could you please come, Mr. Jones? I'm sorry, but could you come? Now? Please?"

"What's happened? Where are you?"

"Houston Street. Please? I don't know what to do."

"Do you need a doctor? Shall I call an ambulance?"

"No. No doctor. Just come."

"Hang on. I'll be right there."

He struggled into his clothes, his mind spattered with calamity. What had Del done this time? To the baby? To them both? That Lucinda was still alive seemed suddenly miraculous. That he was again on his way to help her seemed suddenly foolhardy. He hurried to his car, his mouth dry and fouled by sleep, his stomach a rotting sack, wishing he was someone who didn't do business making others believe he could help them.

The trip to Houston Street was near eternal. When he pulled to the curb across from the charmless apartment building he inspected it for hints of its contents. It was dark, seemingly abandoned by everything but blight, a haunted house. No windows held light, including the one to Apartment Two. He left his car, alert for other sounds, especially alert for Del, wishing he had a gun.

He crossed the street. The building seemed to step to meet him. Somewhere far away a siren sounded. On the next block a hot-rod raced away from a stoplight. He entered the building, hoping what he feared to find had somehow not occurred.

He pressed Lucinda's bell. The door opened immediately, as though she had been leaning against it as a surrogate, awaiting him. He stood in the hallway, peering into the dark apartment, searching for clues to what had been visited upon it. He saw nothing fearsome, heard nothing menacing. Then Lucinda came from behind the door and pressed against him, her head against his chest, her body bucking, her mouth murmuring thanks.

He wrapped her with his arms. "What happened, Lucinda?" he whispered. "What did he do to you?"

Her answer was muffled by his clothing. She seemed to wish to slip inside his skin, to use him as a cave. He squeezed her harder, patted her shoulder, whispered soothing sounds. "Is he still there?" he asked. "Where is he?"

She pushed herself away. Light from the parking lot skimmed off her eyes. He looked for blood but saw none. Her sweatshirt was ripped at the sleeves and neck, though by fashion not by violence. "Mr. Jones. I . . . it's horrible, Mr. Jones. It's . . "

"What is, Lucinda? Come on, tell me. I'm here to help."

"No one can help me now." The words were clear, distinct, as though the thought were new.

"Is it the baby? Where is she? Has something happened to Krystle?"

As Lucinda backed into the apartment he followed her inside. Down the hall behind them he heard a door open, and imagined the eye that nestled in the crack. He closed the door against observers. Lucinda stood in darkness, head bowed, arms crossed. Her voice was raw, as though she had screamed for days.

"He was teasing me. He was mad because I got home late from the Pancake House. One of the girls had a birthday and we went out drinking after work. I called to tell him but he wasn't home. Then when I come in he was already drunk. Worse than he'd ever been. He started teasing me, saying what he'd do the next time I stayed out whoring around and stuff like that."

"How else did he tease you?"

She raised the back of her hand to her nose and wiped and sniffed. "He went and got Krystle. And started tossing her around, up to the ceiling and back. He did it a hundred times, it seems like. Krystle was crying something fierce, and Del was yelling for her to shut up, but he just kept tossing her. Then he took her to the bathroom and dipped her head in the *toilet*. Clear under water. Her eyes were *open*, Mr. Jones. She was looking up at me from under there, begging me to help her. She swallowed some water and started to cough. I thought she was going to die, I really did. I tried to get her back but he just beat me off. Then he took her into the kitchen and turned on a burner and held her over the flame. I could smell her. It made me throw up, Mr. Jones. Krystle's hair got so hot it crinkled up. I thought she was going to catch fire."

"Where's the baby now?"

"Sleeping. In the bedroom. She's all cried out."

"Is she all right?"

"I think so."

"We should have a doctor check her, to make sure."

"Okay." The word was an island, unconnected to anything real.

"Did Del hurt *you*, Lucinda? Did he do anything to you?"

"No. He just shoved me back, so I couldn't help my baby."

"Where is he now?" The question emptied him of all but fear.

He expected anything but what she did. She pointed. "In there."

"The kitchen?"

Her black shape nodded.

He walked, wondering how he would react when Del confronted him, whether he would remain a man till it was over. When he reached the kitchen doorway he stopped and looked for Del, still fencing with his elusive courage.

The room was dark. Its only window was masked by plants and dangling doo-dads and a picture of a cat, its only light was from the halo of a hissing burner. D.T. closed his eyes and opened them and still saw nothing human. He wondered if there was a back door, if Del had simply escaped his crime. He turned on the light and saw him.

Delbert Wesley Finders sailed on a bright red sea, becalmed, incapable of anything, including harm. A carving knife protruded from his chest like a thorn. One hand grasped its handle, a finger curled delicately around the bolster, as though it were a long-stemmed rose. The position was fetal. The eyes were open, as awed as D.T.'s own. The stink was of booze and the heavy sweet smell of puddled blood.

D.T. turned off the light and backed away. The sputtering burner made everything move but Del. He turned around. Lucinda was sitting on the couch, her head dangling into two cupped hands. "How long ago?" he asked her.

"Just before I called you up."

"Did you phone the police?"

She shook her head. "What will happen, Mr. Jones? Will they take Krystle away? Will they give her to the state?" She raised her head and looked at him. He couldn't meet her eyes.

"I don't know, Lucinda. I don't know what they'll do. I think I'd better call the police."

She nodded silently, accepting a fate beyond the ken of anyone alive. A thought occurred to him. "But first I'm going to get you a lawyer," he said, then went to the phone and looked up a number.

The phone rang every fourth time his heart beat. It was answered with a grunt. "Dick? D.T. Sorry to wake you."

"What the fuck is this? Sabotage? You want me to fall asleep in court tomorrow?"

"This is different, Dick. I'm at the apartment of a client of mine, a girl named Lucinda Finders. She just stabbed her husband. She needs a good lawyer. For some reason I thought of you."

"Is he dead?"

"Yep."

"Where are you?"

"Houston Street." He gave the number.

"I'll be there in ten minutes. The cops been called?"

"No."

"Call them. But no one says anything till I get there."

"Okay."

"She got any money, D.T.?"

"No."

"Well, we'll work something out."

"You're making enough off Chas Stone to do this one for free."

"The hell I am."

Gardner hung up and D.T. dialed the number for all the world's emergencies, including ones that aren't emergencies any longer, that are only questions without answers, deeds already done.

■ TWENTY-ONE

WHO'RE you?'' the cop demanded. His brown suit matched his eyes and shoes; his square head matched his manner. "My name is D. T. Jones. I'm a lawyer.''

"A lawyer? Got here pretty fast, didn't you?''

"I'm not a criminal lawyer, I'm a divorce lawyer.''

"Yeah?'' The cop glanced at Lucinda. "She getting a divorce from the stiff? That what this is all about? She decided she couldn't wait for the decree?''

"Not exactly.''

The cop rolled his eyes behind their puffy pouches. "Not exactly. You're beginning to interest me, pal. Who is this broad, anyway? Who's the guy she butchered?''

"Her name's Lucinda Finders. The dead man is her husband, Delbert Finders.''

"Yeah? Let me talk to her.''

The cop took two steps forward. D.T. reached out to stop him. "Not right now. She has another attorney coming. Dick Gardner is his name. He's advised her not to say anything till he gets here.''

The cop grunted. "Gardner, huh? I better make sure the boys don't screw anything up in there.''

The big cop turned away and went into the kitchen, where others of his ilk busied themselves with gathering evidence and taking photographs and examining the earthly remains of the ensanguined Delbert Finders. There were occasional bursts of laughter and an isolated curse, frequent explosions of a flashbulb, murmurs. Once one of the men stood in the doorway and stared for a long time at Lucinda, as though to measure her against her deed. Lucinda was heedless of his gaze, as she was heedless of all else. D.T. tried to do something helpful but could only sit and hold her hand. In another room the baby slept as her heritage lay in wait for her.

"I'm scared, Mr. Jones," Lucinda said suddenly. "I'm scared and I'm cold."

D.T. looked around the room for something that would warm her, saw only a nylon windbreaker draped over the back of a butterfly chair across from the TV. He walked over and picked up the jacket. As he started to drop it across her shoulders he noticed the writing on the back: "Larry's Lounge—Coors on Tap." He swore and tossed the satin shell aside and went into the bedroom Del and Lucinda had so improbably shared.

The bed was mussed, its linen wrinkled and limp and stained, its center springs collapsed. Clothes were scattered everywhere, men's clothes, greased and giving off the smells of garages and grease pits. On the wall above the bed was a stylized rendering of a single word: LOVE. On the opposite wall was an 8 × 10 of Delbert and his Ford. On the tiny dressing table in the corner a jumble of jars and bottles testified to Lucinda's efforts to please her man.

D.T. entered with trepidation, almost stepping on a scant and filmy nightie that lay like a fallen cloud in the center of the doorway. He was more interested in the room than he cared to admit, was unable to stop himself from imagining what must have occurred in it despite all the rest that had occurred between the pair, the flower of sex a miraculous bloom in the desert of the relationship.

The bulb in the lamp on the bedstand was red, the light in the ceiling was on a track that directed it at the center of the bed, the dresser mirror directly opposite was tilted to capture what the light revealed. Del apparently liked to stage his sex, to admire his thrust and ebb, to confirm his wife's impalement. He wondered if Lucinda enjoyed display as well, decided she must, why else would she do it? He was tempted to open drawers and probe the closet, to look for further secrets, but he grabbed a thin blanket from the foot of the bed and returned to the living room instead.

The blanket bore the heavy smell of talc. When he

wrapped her with it Lucinda had no reaction. Excessively appreciated for what he had done for her previously, D.T. was hurt now by her indifference to his need to comfort her.

He was trying to think of something sane to say when Dick Gardner walked in the open door, surveyed the scene, and moved briskly to the couch, the tails of blue pajamas flapping from beneath his short red jacket. If he was tired he kept its leavings secret.

"Is this Mrs. Finders?"

D.T. stood up. "Thanks for coming, Dick." He performed the introductions. Lucinda barely acknowledged her second lawyer's presence. After shaking her hand Gardner drew D.T. to the other side of the room. "She say anything to the cops?"

"No."

"Did you?"

"Only her name and that the dead guy was her husband. And that you were on your way."

"Okay. The woman's in shock. She should go to a hospital. She got any friends in town? Someone who can take her there and stay with her?"

D.T. shook his head. "I don't know of any. She told me once she didn't know anyone here in the city."

"She was married to the guy, right?"

"Right. She filed for dissolution, then called it off."

"She's a sexy little thing. How about the brain department?"

"Ignorant, maybe. Far from stupid. Came from Reedville. Parents don't want anything to do with her, at least her father doesn't."

"This her first marriage?"

D.T. nodded. "The guy's been jailed for assault. A drunk. Typical punk."

"Good. Where's the body?"

D.T. pointed to the kitchen. Gardner told him to stay where he was, then went to see the scene. D.T. looked over at Lucinda. She was blinkless, breathless, as though her soul had gone to join her husband's.

He went to her side. "We're going to try to get you to a hospital, Lucinda. Is there anyone who can go with you?"

She shook her head silently.

"Is there anyone who can come stay with the baby?"

She shook her head again, then suddenly jerked erect. "I want Krystle with *me*. Where is she? *Where's my baby?*" Her voice rose wildly, to a screech that alarmed him. D.T. patted her as he would a startled dog.

"She's still sleeping, Lucinda. She's in the other room. Now just relax."

"What will they do to me? Will they kill me? They kill murderers in this state, don't they? Don't they kill people like me, Mr. Jones?"

He squeezed her arm. "Listen to me, Lucinda. You're not a murderer. What you did was fully justified. You stabbed Del to save your child. That's clearly self-defense."

"I'm guilty, Mr. Jones. I killed him, so I'm guilty."

"Sssh. You're not guilty of *anything*. Dick Gardner's the best lawyer in town, and he'll prove it if he has to. In the meantime, don't say anything like that to the police or to anyone else. Just leave the talking to Mr. Gardner."

He tried to get her to meet his gaze, but she was looking at a place beyond him, perhaps to see how someone who always tried to do right had somehow managed to commit the biggest wrong there was.

Dick Gardner came back in the room and D.T. went to join him. "Any doubt that she did it?" Gardner asked.

D.T. shook his head.

"What'd she tell you about it?"

D.T. told him the story, trying to remember her every word, trying to capture the madness of the evening, the innocence of the girl, the wickedness of the man she'd slain. Gardner absorbed it all, but was not visibly moved. "Where's the baby?"

"Sleeping."

"I want it checked out at the hospital, too. Detailed exam, everything recorded. I'll call a pediatrician I know and have her there."

"Okay."

"The cops will want a matron to go along. Who's going to take her?"

"I am, I guess."

Gardner looked at him skeptically, then shrugged.

"They'll want someone to take formal custody of the kid or the matron will have to take it to social services. You know anyone who'll want it?"

"No."

"Well, she should be out on bail in a few days. If you want to chance it, you can just disappear with the kid at some point, let them track you down, play dumb when they find you, and hope by that time they've let her out on bail. It's not strictly legal, but it's the only alternative to social services if there aren't any relatives around."

D.T. nodded. "I'll do it if I can."

Dick Gardner smiled. "Who the hell's going to teach *you* how to change a diaper?"

"I don't know," D.T. admitted.

Dick Gardner looked over at his client. "What's the story of the marriage? Why'd she want to shed him?"

"He drank and beat her up."

"Lots?"

"Yes."

"Bad?"

"Fairly."

"Arrests?"

"Not for that. Just for clubbing a guy with a pool cue."

"Was she ever hospitalized?"

"Once that I know of. I took her there myself. He broke her nose, messed her face up pretty good. It was while she was pregnant. He also punched her belly. He threatened to do worse if she went through with the divorce."

"So she didn't."

"Right."

"Who was the doctor?"

"Faber."

"A good man, but not a good witness. Too goddamned precise." Gardner eyed D.T. closely. "I don't suppose you got any pictures?"

D.T. smiled, quickly pleased. "As a matter of fact I did. They're still in the camera in my trunk. They're not developed."

Gardner slapped his back. "You old devil-dog. I knew that despite your performance in the Stone case there was some reason people claim you're a good lawyer."

D.T. ignored the jibe. "When I was taking her to the hospital he tried to run us off the road."

Gardner raised his brows. "You're kidding. You saw him?"

"I'll testify to it."

"That's not exactly what I asked."

"Right," D.T. said. "But it's what you want to know."

Gardner only smiled and nodded. "You report it to the cops?"

D.T. shook his head. "She asked me not to."

Gardner thought it over. "Well, partner," Gardner began, slapping him again on the shoulder, "I don't think this little lady has too much to worry about. Battered women have been killing their husbands all over the country, and most of them have been getting off scot-free. It's the modern crime of passion. Been wanting one to walk in my office for a long time. The publicity alone should take care of the fee. Come on. I've got a question I want to ask our charming client."

They walked over to where Lucinda sat. "Lucinda? How are you feeling?" Dick Gardner asked.

"Okay. I'm just cold."

"That's natural, Lucinda. In a few minutes Mr. Jones is going to take you and your baby to the hospital. To make sure you're both all right. Understand?"

"Yes."

"Then, if you are all right, the police will want to question you. So Mr. Jones will bring you downtown to the police station. I'll meet you down there, and I'll be with you when the police talk to you. I may or may not want you to answer their questions. In the meantime, I don't want you to say anything to anybody about what happened in the kitchen. Do you understand that? It's very important."

"I understand. But I killed him. I—"

"No more of that." Gardner's voice would have stopped a train. "Nothing about your husband. I mean it, Lucinda. Agreed?"

"Okay."

"Now. I warn you, Lucinda, after the police question you they'll probably put you under arrest. You'll be entitled to bail, but it will probably amount to several thousand dollars, at least initially. Do you have that much money?''

"Not nearly. I got eight hundred dollars saved up. It's for Krystle to go to college. No one in my family's ever been to college. I want Krystle to be the first.''

She was talking only to herself, as though the past two hours had been erased. D.T. and Dick Gardner exchanged glances. Gardner spoke again, his tone as calming as a cordial. "I'm sure Krystle will do just fine at college, Lucinda, but in the meantime we have to find someone she can stay with until you're released on bail. Are your parents available?''

"No. They . . . no.''

"Brothers? Sisters? Other relatives?''

"My brother got killed on his motorcycle. My sister's born again. She ain't got time for no one but Jesus.''

"Mr. Jones says he'll take the baby until you're released. Is that okay with you?''

She looked at him as though he were a stranger. "You don't have to do that, Mr. Jones. I can take care of her. She won't be no trouble in jail.''

"They won't let you take a baby to jail, Mrs. Finders,'' Gardner said. "It's either Mr. Jones or social services, until they let you out.''

"You already been too good to me, Mr. Jones.''

"Don't worry about it.''

Dick Gardner leaned over his client. "I have one more thing to ask, Mrs. Finders.''

"What?''

"When did you last have your period?''

Lucinda's eyes narrowed, then hardened from the suspicion that she was being mocked. "What? I . . . *what* did you say?''

"When did you menstruate last? What day?''

"I don't know. I don't keep track.'' There was anger in her voice, a stubborn stiffness that hadn't been there all evening. D.T. hoped it meant she was swinging back toward normal, that she had shed the crust of Delbert's death.

"Well,'' Gardner said, "when you do get your period again you give Mr. Jones here a call and he'll arrange for

a doctor to see you, okay? It's very important. The very
first day. Can you remember?''

"I guess so. But why? I know what to do with *that*."

"We'll go into it later. Right now I'm going home and
catch some sleep. Give me a call when you leave the
hospital for the police station, D.T. I'll meet you there.
If she's going to be held for observation, let me sleep till
seven. One way or another I guess I'll see you later on.
Mrs. Stone going to show up in court?''

D.T. shrugged and raised his hand to the lapel of his
coat. The photographs still lay in their wool-blend grave.
D.T. wanted to reach for them, to display them, to knock
Dick Gardner out of his icy confidence, to do what he
had been unable to do in a fair fight in the courtroom—
end the Stone case on terms he could live with. But his
hand held fast while Gardner waved and left the room.

Additional technicians streamed in and out of the small
apartment, the tools of their trade encased in small black
bags. All of them glanced curiously at Lucinda, all admired her looks, all were intrigued by her capacity, and
all swept past her without a word of greeting or consolation. Minutes later two men wheeled in a metal gurney,
disappeared into the kitchen, and reappeared with a body
zippered into a black rubber bag and strapped to the gurney with canvas belts. The gurney's wheels giggled as
they left the building. Beside him, Lucinda Finders said
something softly to herself. D.T. draped her with his arm.

Time took place unoccupied by either of them, was
filled only with the bureaucratic aftermath of violence.
D.T. struggled with words, formed sentences and abandoned them, considered clichés, condolences, catchalls.
Nothing seemed as appropriate as Delbert's death. Finally, the police matron arrived and they left for the hospital.

The matron took Lucinda and the baby in a black-and-
white. D.T. followed in his Ford. At the hospital, Lucinda's dilemma became routine, banal. Lucinda went one
way, the baby another, borne by a hefty nurse. The matron hesitated a moment, then followed after the aide who
led Lucinda.

Useless, D.T. found the waiting area. Its magazines
were older even than his own. One was devoted to cars.

He read it closely, every phrase unfamiliar, every fact a revelation. By the time the matron and Lucinda returned he thought he had learned why he often stalled on his way to work.

D.T. asked Lucinda how she was.

Her smile was wan. "Okay. They gave me these pills. To relax me. I don't think I better be too relaxed right now, though, do you, Mr. Jones? Not if I got to talk to the police."

D.T. glanced at the matron. She bore an odd resemblance to Audie Murphy. "Are you taking her to the station?" he asked.

"That's my orders." Even the voice was husky.

"Couldn't it wait till she gets some sleep?"

"You'll have to take it up with the people downtown. I got to bring her in."

"What about the baby?"

"I do what they say downtown. They want me to take it, I go to social services. That's all I can do." The matron shrugged. Complications. Trivia. "Let's get rolling."

D.T. told Lucinda to stay where she was, then returned to the nurses' station and asked about the baby. He waited while someone was unintelligibly paged. A moment later a young woman in a white coat came up to him, her face narrow with concern. "Are you the police?"

"I'm a lawyer. D. T. Jones. I represent the mother."

"I thought this was Dick Gardner's case."

"It is. I called Dick in on it. Are you the pediatrician he mentioned?"

The woman nodded. Her blonde hair bounced. She seemed far too dainty to deal in anything as unsavory as illness. D.T. wondered if she and Gardner were lovers. "Is the mother in jail?" the doctor asked.

"Not yet. She's here in the hospital."

"But she killed the father?"

"I . . . I'd better not say anything about it. How's Krystle?"

"Fine. There's minor destruction of hair, slight burns on the left cheek and arm, some bruising from the way she was handled. Must have been an ugly scene."

"I'm sure it was. Are all your findings contained in the hospital record?"

"Of course."

"How about pictures?"

"There's really nothing that would show up on a snapshot, I don't believe. In this case words will be more than sufficient. And I'll be happy to provide them." She smiled the smile of an expert witness.

"Thanks for your help," D.T. said. "Is Krystle discharged?"

"Yes. I hope not to social services."

"We'll make other arrangements. I hope."

"Good. Do you do divorce work, Mr. Jones?"

"Yes."

"I think you represent a friend of mine. Rita Holloway? Something about a patient of hers?"

D.T. nodded. "Esther Preston. Right. Which reminds me, I've got to talk to them. We go to court on Friday."

"Rita says you're the only lawyer in town who would help her."

"Well, she hasn't been helped. At least not yet."

"I'm sure you'll do fine." Her smile would have won his heart if it hadn't been previously captured by the evening.

He backed away. "Well, I guess I'd better go. The matron will be sending out the dogs."

"Good luck, Mr. Jones."

"Thanks."

"Krystle's one of the lucky ones, actually. Most of the time when the parents use the child as a weapon the child doesn't come out so good. Tell Mrs. Finders she can get her baby in Room 34. And tell Dick Gardner he owes me some scampi."

D.T. went back to the waiting area. Lucinda was where he had left her, looking at him anxiously. "Where's Krystle? Is she all right?"

"She's fine. She's ready to go. You can get her in Room 34."

"Now?"

"Now. I'll meet you back here."

Lucinda and the matron went after Krystle. D.T. went

back to the nurses' station. "Who treated Mrs. Finders?" he asked the woman at the desk.

She shuffled some papers. "Dr. Lind."

"May I speak to him?"

"I'm sorry. He's in emergency right now. It may be some time."

"Okay. I'll get in touch with him later. Please tell him this is a criminal matter, and he may be called upon to testify in Mrs. Finders' case. His records should be complete."

"Our records are always complete, sir."

"Sure they are."

D.T. went back to the waiting area to call Dick Gardner. He told him they were about to leave for the station. Gardner grumbled fuzzily, but said he would be there as soon as he could. Moments later, Lucinda joined him, clutching Krystle as though she had recently dropped her. "They say she's just fine, Mr. Jones."

The matron was out of earshot so he spoke quickly. "Now, when we get to the station Mr. Gardner will be there to advise you. I don't know how long it will be, or what'll happen afterward, but I think I should just take the baby when we get there. When you're released on bail and can take her back again, you just call and I can bring her to you. How does that sound?"

"Okay, I guess. I just wish I knew what was going to happen."

"I know. I do, too."

The matron beckoned and they trooped to the parking lot and climbed in their cars and drove through slumbering streets toward a meeting with the law.

It was four a.m. D.T.'s eyes felt raw and sanded, his mouth ulcerated, his head submerged. The street lights splayed into fuzzy suns as he approached them. He shook his head to remain alert, then flicked on the car radio. The song was by something called the Clash. His head began to ache.

The police station was strangely calm. The drunks and whores and junkies were evidently processed already, the evening's work complete, the next day's yet to begin, time to do the paperwork. Dick Gardner met them at the door, shepherded them through the foyer to a room empty but for a metal table and three metal folding chairs. When Lucinda was seated and the matron had departed, Gardner looked at D.T. "Everything okay?"

D.T. nodded. "They gave Lucinda some tranquilizers but she decided not to take one yet."

"Good." Gardner looked at his client. "You feel like talking to some cops?"

"I guess. If I have to."

"Well, you have to do it sometime, and I'd just as soon you do it now. That way if you make a mistake there'll be a lot of explanations if we need them. But I may decide for you to keep quiet. We'll see how it goes."

Lucinda shrugged. The baby in her arms gurgled once and returned to Nod. Lucinda looked down at her daughter, then offered her to D.T., the act somehow symbolic. "She's real good, Mr. Jones. She eats almost anything. Carrots and squash are her favorites. But she hates beets, so be careful." Lucinda's laugh became a cry.

D.T. reached out and grasped the bundle. "I'll take good care of her, Lucinda. I'll be real careful. Don't worry. You'll be back together before you know it."

"I know." Lucinda looked at someone else. "We will, won't we, Mr. Gardner?"

"I don't know yet," Gardner said. "Let's go find out. You better go out the back, D.T."

Gardner turned and started to walk away. "Can I talk to you a minute, Dick?"

Gardner looked back. "Sure." They moved toward a quiet end of the hallway outside the interrogation room. "What's the matter, she confess she stuck him for the insurance money?" Gardner's laugh was a muffled rasp.

"The Stone case," D.T. said.

"Yeah? What about it?"

"Here. Hold the baby."

D.T. transferred the child to Gardner and reached into his pocket and drew out the envelope he had carried for two days. "Someone delivered these to the office. Just an envelope. No letter; no nothing."

"What the hell are they?"

"Here. I'll take the baby."

D.T. exchanged the smut for the child. Gardner extracted the contents of the envelope and flipped quickly through the pictures. "Shit. The stupid bastard." Gardner looked at D.T. fiercely. "This smacks of a setup, D.T.; you son of a bitch."

D.T. shrugged. He felt drugged, nerveless. "I don't know anything about it, Dick. All I know is, your guy's gay. And you know Hoskins."

"I know Hoskins and I know you, you prick."

"Hey. Who had a private eye sleeping on my client's porch for six months? Don't play Marquis of Queensbury with *me*, goddamnit."

Gardner sighed. "Okay, okay. When can we talk?"

"Eight-thirty? Jury room across from Hoskins' courtroom?"

Gardner nodded. "Your client know about these?"

"No."

"How about that secretary of yours? Hell, he's one of them too, isn't he?"

"He doesn't know either."

"I'll bet. Christ Almighty. There goes my great victory for the husbands of America. But hey. The fee's not contingent so what the hell. See you, D.T. You asshole."

"See you, Dick."

Before they parted, D.T. reached out and plucked the pictures from Dick Gardner's hand. After they parted, D.T. gave the baby to a patrolman to hold, then went to the nearest restroom and was sick into the foulest bowl imaginable, with a listing wino looking on. Then he reclaimed the baby and went looking for the palace he planned to put it in.

■ TWENTY-TWO

WELL, D.T. Of all people. What are you *doing* here at this hour? Have you taken a paper route to make ends meet?" His amazement was such that he scarcely heard her. "What on earth are you *wearing*, Michele? You look like you're on your way to a black-tie breakfast."

"It's my wedding dress, D.T."

"At six o'clock in the morning?"

"It's the only time I have for a fitting. So what do you think? *Très soigné, non?*"

"*Très.*"

Michele whirled beneath the porch light. Her heavy gown swelled centrifugally, the shiny mint material momentarily leaving its stylish drape to reveal a flash of slender calf. The pirouette complete, Michele gathered up her hem and stepped back inside her house, her silk pumps clattering on the marble floor like a set of plastic teeth.

"Come in, D.T." She squinted. "What's that you're carrying, for heaven's sake? It looks like a baby."

"It is a baby."

Too vain even before breakfast to wear her bifocals, Michele's eyes became two lines. "You must be joking."

"No."

"But . . ."

"Can I put her down somewhere, Michele? It feels like I've been holding her for a week."

Michele dropped her dress and clasped her hair and whistled tunelessly. "But whose . . .? Let's see. The den? While I have Mirabelle hunt up the bassinet? What *did* we do with it? Mirabelle! Could you come down? We're in the foyer.''

Confronted at dawn by her ex-husband with a babe in arms, Michele was as flustered as he had ever seen her, save only the past Thanksgiving. As he backed down the hall—her eyes locked on his treasure—she almost tripped on her hem. She gathered her dress again and this time raised it to her thighs, which came complete with garters. D.T. whistled approvingly.

"A baby," she said again. "I can't believe it. Is it a foundling, D.T.? Did one of your dittos deposit the poor thing on your doorstep?"

He shook his head and Mirabelle arrived to defer an explanation, shouldering her way down the hall like a patron with a pass. "D.T. You up pretty early for a rascal like yourself. Or maybe you just getting in."

"Some of both, Mirabelle. How you doing?"

Mirabelle's big body swayed within her shift, creating tidal waves of fabric. "We all upside down over here, D.T. Never knew a wedding be such a strain on rich folks. It's a wonder they fuss with it."

Michele and D.T. paired laughs. "That package in his arms is a baby, Mirabelle," Michele said.

"A baby! What you doing with a baby, D.T.? You find it? Or you just a tomcat got stuck with the litter?"

"It belongs to one of my clients."

"So what's troubling her? She too busy living fancy to do what she made by the Lord to do?"

"She's in jail, Mirabelle." He looked at Michele. "She stabbed her husband tonight. He was torturing her and the baby. She killed him to stop him."

"My God," Michele said.

"Good riddance to bad rubbish," Mirabelle scoffed. "I bet he a drinking man just like Leroy."

D.T. nodded.

"Mirabelle, where did we put Heather's old bassinet? Do you remember?"

"Third floor. Green bedroom. All that baby stuff in there, look like heaven for midgets."

"Let's set it up. How long will this be, D.T.?"

He shrugged. "I don't know. It could be quite a while

if social services doesn't track me down. Her bail may be too high for her to pay.''

"Don't she have people?" Mirabelle asked.

"Not that want the baby, I guess."

"White folks sure be strange, don't they, D.T.?"

"They do indeed."

"Let's make up a little nursery, Mirabelle," Michele said. "The blue bedroom?"

"White. Too dark in the blue."

"Okay. The white. Bassinet, changing table, playpen. Diapers. Do we have any diapers any more? Did you bring any, D.T.?"

He shook his head. "She likes carrots and squash. No beets. That's all I know."

"We can buy some later today. In the meantime use the linen napkins, Mirabelle. Those monogrammed ones. They're about to be obsolete anyway."

"You just leave this little love bundle to me, Miz Conway. D.T., you give me that child and I fix her up just right, the way I did that sweet Heather before she got too big to be done for. Now give her here, D.T. You all thumbs and you always was. I followed you around for two years, ready to catch what you was about to drop. Now you just give that child to me."

He handed it over.

Mirabelle clutched the baby to her bosom. It seemed to shrink and then to purr. "Now there's just one more thing I got to know," Mirabelle said.

"What?"

"What's this poor child's name?"

"Krystle. With a K."

"My little glass teapot. That's just what I thought. I hope this baby be around here for a long time. Keep my mind off this wedding fuss." Mirabelle eyed her employer. "You think a woman on her second helping would know which fork to use, wouldn't you, D.T.?"

D.T. laughed and Mirabelle snorted with enlarged disdain, then marched off down the hall and began to climb the stairs.

Michele looked at him. "She absolutely adores you, D.T. I was afraid she was going to quit me after the divorce. She kept saying how lazy life was since you left.''

''I miss her, too.''

''Let me get out of this dress, okay? I'd like to talk if you've got a minute.''

''Sure. I'm sorry to unload this thing on you, Michele. I just didn't know where else to go.''

''I'm flattered you thought of me. Now, why don't you go to the den. I'll be back in a blink. There's coffee and rolls in the kitchen. You know the way.''

Michele walked to the stairway and began to climb it, regal in the midst of dawn and complications and a gown that needed work.

D.T. went to the kitchen for coffee, then to the den, where he sank again into what had been his favorite chair. Thankfully, he was too exhausted to appreciate his ridiculous circumstances: his visit to his ex-wife with a baby in hand, his attempted extortion of a settlement from Dick Gardner, his pursuit of a baseless lawsuit against Dr. Preston that would be heard and doubtlessly exposed in open court the very next day. No, the slightest thought caused his head to crack or feel like it, so he tried to become what the chair was—dumb and padded against the world's great weight.

He must have come close, must have been asleep when she poked his arm. ''Daddy. Wake up.''

''Heather. Hi. How are you, honey? What time is it?''

''Seven. I always get up at seven.'' She bounced before him, still a blur. ''Michele says you brought me something, Daddy. What is it? A dress? A video cartridge? What?''

''I didn't . . . Oh. Well, what I brought you isn't exactly a present, honey. It's a . . .''

''What?''

''A baby.''

''A *baby*. You can't have a baby, Daddy. You're not married.''

''I know. It's not my baby, Heather. The father is dead and the mother can't take care of it right now, so I thought maybe it could stay here for a while.''

''Where is it?''

''The white bedroom.''

"What is it? A boy or a girl?"

"A girl."

"What's its name?"

"Krystle."

"*Dynasty*! Neat. Does it wet and everything? I'm going to go look. See you, Daddy."

"See you, honey."

Heather's place in the room was taken by her mother, now barefoot and wrapped in a dressing gown of oriental silks and ideographs. Her expression was of the East as well: serene, alert for nuance. "It's nice to have a baby in the house again, D.T. I often wish we'd made another before we quit. Heather could use a brother."

"I know."

"And you could use a son."

"Well, given how things turned out, maybe it's best we only put one kid through it."

"I don't think Heather was scarred permanently by our divorce, D.T. I really don't. By the time we know it'll be too late, though, won't it?"

"Afraid so."

Michele lit a cigarette. He thought she'd quit, but didn't chide her. "I think Heather should spend more time with you, D.T. Maybe this summer for a month? Before she goes to camp?"

"Sure." He looked around the sumptuous den. "If you think she can stand the change of scene."

"She's not that spoiled, D.T. Really, she isn't."

"I know, I know. I didn't mean she was." He closed his eyes and kept them closed. What he saw was Lucinda Finders on the day she milked her breast.

"What's wrong?"

"I'm tired. And depressed about tonight. She was a special one, Michele. If I could have persuaded her to go ahead and divorce the bastard maybe none of this would have happened. Even if Gardner gets her off she's going to hear whispers the rest of her life. It's funny. I always thought one of the dittos would die, that one of their men would kill them because I was too lazy or too powerless to prevent it. I didn't expect the ditto to be the killer. I'm not sure I know what to do. I'm not sure I'm not happy she killed him."

Michele smiled, tolerating his blasphemy. "Is Dick Gardner her lawyer?"

D.T. nodded. "Why?"

"Oh, he came by here one night. A little drunk and a little horny. He came on rather strong for a guy who wears tweed."

"I'm sorry. That was my fault. I was extolling your virtues to him over a beer one night and he said he might try to take you out. I should have warned you, or headed him off."

Michele smiled her smile. "No harm done. And it's nice to know you still have me on the recommended list."

"Well, at the time I wasn't sure you and George were going to make it."

"Yes, well, it appears that we are, doesn't it? To the altar, at least. Or else I've wasted a fortune on a green dress that doesn't go with anything but wreaths. You'll be there Saturday, won't you, D.T.?"

"If I'm not dead or in jail."

"You sound as if both of those are possible."

He sighed. "It's just that I've been playing things pretty fast and loose in my practice over the past few months. I've been abusing the system and I may OD on it." He sipped his tepid coffee. "But let's talk about more sublime subjects. Where are you going on your honeymoon?"

"George wants Bermuda."

"But *we* went to Bermuda."

"I know. So does George. It didn't seem to matter. I rather wish it had. I have this feeling I'll be slinking around the whole time, trying to avoid the people we saw before. Remember that couple from Baltimore?"

"I thought he was going to crawl inside your bikini for a better look. Not that there was room in there for him."

Michele laughed. "Now, D.T. That's the whole point of going to those places, so you can wear things you wouldn't be caught dead wearing in your hometown. Not that I'm going to be on display this trip. I'm afraid my bikini days are over."

"I don't see why. You look pretty good to *me*, kid."

She bowed. "Thank you, sir, but *you're* the one who's scrumptious. Your Coefficient of Modern Matrimony, right? Or whatever you call it? You're hitting your prime and I'm ready for the glue factory."

"Right. But we're the exceptions that prove the rule."

Then they were silent. Comfortable. Sharing history that was only theirs.

Outside the den were household sounds: Mirabelle, Heather, others maybe. At one time she had kept a staff of four. He remembered stumbling over them regularly, always abashed when he made requests they had to honor.

Heather peeked in the door to say good-bye. Her uniform was a pleated skirt and knee socks and a blouse white enough to be married in. She thought the baby was super, she wanted to keep it for ever and ever. Could they? Maybe? When she had gone Michele looked at him. "Am I making a mistake, D.T.?"

"In marrying George?"

"Yes."

"I can't tell you that, Michele."

"He's no Lancelot, I know that. But I'm no Guinevere, either. I don't know, D.T., I'm just afraid if I get to be fifty and I'm still alone, I'll start doing stupid things. Like those old ladies in Bermuda, with their gigolos rubbing tanning butter all over them like they were ready to put them on a spit? I can't stand the thought of ending up like that, D.T. I just can't."

"You won't end up like that, Michele, married or not married. Besides, George is kind and funny and cultured to boot. Heather seems to like him fine. There's no reason not to marry him."

"Well, there's sex."

"What about it?"

"I like my sex, D.T."

"I know you do, Michele."

"And George, well, it's all a little *oily* for George, I'm afraid. Oh, he's a sport about it, up to a point. But, well, he's not *abandoned* the way you were, D.T. It's like he's following a manual."

"You'll just have to teach him what you like. Barbara does that all the time. My last report card was a C plus. Except for a D in ejaculation. She suggested certain exercises . . ."

Michele was elsewhere. "There are all those *years* out there, D.T. They make us stay alive so *long* these days. Have you ever thought about it? Being alive for fifty more years?"

"Only women live that long. I'll have cancer in a decade."

"You will not." She lit another cigarette, as if she was assuming his risk. "Are you going to marry Barbara, by the way?" she asked when the smoke was flowing.

"I doubt it."

"Why not? You've been going with her for a long time."

"Going. That's just it. We're always going; we're never getting anywhere."

"Maybe it's not her fault."

"It's not a question of fault, it's a question of fact. And the fact is, I can't give Barbara what she wants, which is some kind of clone who'll match her stride by stride, therapy by therapy, fad by fad. And she can't give me what I want, which is I-don't-know-what-but-I-know-I-ain't-got-it."

"Life is mean, D.T. A mean old broad. It reminds me of my aunt. Remember Aunt Wanda?"

"She broke wind at the reception." He laughed and looked at his watch. "I've got to go, Michele. I've got a court appearance at eight-thirty."

"Will I see you before the wedding?"

"I doubt it."

"The rehearsal dinner's tomorrow night. Antoine's. Eight o'clock. You're invited, but I won't expect you."

"Good."

"The ceremony's at ten on Saturday. Plymouth Congregational. Be early, please? I may need an injection. Optimism or something."

"I'll try to score some on the street." They stood up and looked at each other. What he saw in his ex-wife's eyes made him embrace her. "Hey. Relax. The second time's a picnic. All my clients say so."

"They do not," she said, and slugged him on the arm.

"One more thing," he said.

"What?"

"I need five thousand dollars. Cash."

"When?"

"Next week."

"Okay."

"Don't you even want to know what it's for?"

She smiled her lazy smile. "No."

He shook his head. "You're a piece of work, Michele, to quote Frank Gifford."

"Who?"

He laughed and kissed her cheek and left the baby and its temporary palace both behind.

He shaved and showered in a daze that somehow acted as an upper, and made it to court by 8:42. Dick Gardner was waiting in the jury room, looking entirely unaffected by the evening's waltz with criminal procedure. "How's Lucinda?" D.T. asked him.

"Okay. They booked her. I thought for a minute they might not file, but an assistant DA with a cob up his ass showed up and started preaching about the plague of domestic violence, equitable treatment, and such. Apparently he thinks stabbing husbands might catch on, like toga parties and *Flashdance*. Bail is fifty grand, which means her bond will be five. I think I can get it kicked down to ten at the arraignment, but she'll still have to come up with a thousand to spring herself. And I don't advance bail money to clients."

"I may be able to help."

"Never post bail with your own money, D.T. Any criminal lawyer in town will tell you that."

"I don't listen to lawyers," D.T. said. "So how about Stone?"

Gardner smiled ruefully. "Yeah. How about him? You'd think he could have kept it zipped till he got the decree, wouldn't you? Well, let's get at it. I got to monitor a show-up at ten, then hunt up someone who'll say good things about a rapist."

They wrangled for twenty minutes, then sent a message to the judge that settlement was imminent, and wrangled for twenty minutes more. When they finally went before Judge Hoskins neither of the principals was in the courtroom. When they presented the terms of the settlement Judge Hoskins raised his brows. "I'm surprised, gentlemen. I must confess I thought the weight of evidence was the other way. But I guess if the parties agree it's none of my business. There was certainly no proof that either party was unfit as a matter of law. My question is, why didn't you settle this thing two days ago?"

Gardner looked at D.T. D.T. looked back, hoping his face was a fraud. "The ebb and flow of litigation, Your Honor," Gardner said finally. "Mr. Jones proved to be a more formidable opponent than I originally estimated."

Judge Hoskins nodded. "Yes. I was much impressed. Why on earth do you do so many of those seamy defaults, Mr. Jones? They're clearly beneath your talents."

"But not my tax bracket."

"Yes, well, it's a public service, I suppose, though one I must admit I view with distaste."

"I frequently find it distasteful myself," D.T. said, but didn't say that the reason was sitting high above him.

When he got back to his office he called his client. She seemed afraid to speak. "Did he take them away?"

"No. Gardner and I settled the thing. You want to hear the terms?"

"Settle? I didn't agree to settle. What did you do, Mr. Jones? Give up? Did Chas buy you off?"

D.T. took a deep breath. "You get exclusive custody of the kids. Stone gets them two weekends a month plus six weeks in the summers. He pays eight hundred a month per child in support, plus educational expenses through college and graduate school or age twenty-six, whichever comes first. He pays medical insurance and life insurance on the kids, with you as beneficiary till they're emancipated. You get the house, car, and three hundred grand in marital property, payable at thirty grand a year for ten years. He puts enough stock in escrow to cover it. He pays the mortgage and all current debts. He pays alimony of fifteen hundred a month for ten years or until you remarry. After ten years he pays a grand. Plus he takes out an insurance policy that guarantees alimony and child support will be paid even if he pulls a Gauguin. Best of all, he pays me twelve grand in attorney's fees. How's it sound?"

"Are you playing with me, Mr. Jones?"

"No."

"How did you do it? It all seemed so hopeless. You must have sold my soul to the devil." She tried to laugh but it didn't form.

The soul in the devil's pouch is mine, D.T. thought. "Don't ask how I did it," he said. "And don't believe it if someone tries to tell you."

"I . . . it's more than I deserve, isn't it?"

"Probably, but that's justice for you. A zany, wacky concept. Relax and enjoy it, Mrs. Stone. I'll get the agreement to you in a few days. My secretary will bring it by and notarize your signature. You'll get an executed copy to keep for yourself. I hope you live happily ever after, Mrs. Stone. If you have any problems, you let me know."

"I . . . I don't know what to say. I thought after yesterday I was going to lose everything. Now this. It just doesn't make *sense*, Mr. Jones. Are you sure you've told me everything?"

"Everything you need to know. As for what to say, a simple 'thank you' will do. In my line of work I don't hear that much."

"Thank you. And I'm sorry I was so difficult."

"You can do me one favor."

"Yes. Anything."

"Lay off the booze."

"I . . . I'll try. I really will. Maybe I don't need it any more, now that it's over."

"You never did need it, Mrs. Stone. And it's never over, it just slows down once in a while. Maybe you should keep that in mind."

He replaced the phone and leaned back in his chair. The end justified the means, did it not? At least almost? At least enough to let him live with himself? Well, he would have to see. And what the hell. If he could no longer live with himself, he could go and live with someone else. He grabbed the phone again.

"Mrs. Preston?"

"Yes?"

"D. T. Jones. How's it going?"

"Fine, Mr. Jones. How are you?"

Her voice acted on him like Clorox, bleaching his conscience. "I'm off the critical list, Mrs. Preston; temporarily, at least. We have an important hearing in your case tomorrow, and I'd like you to be in court if you can. Do you feel up to it?''

''I do if you feel it will help.''

''I don't know if it will or won't. But I'm going to try to make this hearing a little more than routine, and your presence might convince the judge to let me do it.''

''Then I'll be there.''

''I should warn you, there's some chance you could be called to testify by your husband's lawyer. That's because I'm going to try to call your husband. And actually, I hope he does call you as a witness. You'd destroy him, and I think he's too dumb to know it.''

Esther Preston laughed. ''I'm afraid I have no wish to destroy anyone, Mr. Jones.''

''Truth can be the most destructive instrument on earth, Mrs. Preston. Shall I pick you up?''

''Rita's here. Let me ask if she wants to go. If she does, she can take me.''

''Why don't you put her on?''

The line buzzed momentarily. ''D.T.,'' Rita Holloway said briskly. ''What's happening? My calendar tells me there's some kind of motion in the case tomorrow.''

''Right. The good doctor's motion for summary judgment, trying to throw us out of court. Might be routine, might be crucial. I want Mrs. Preston there. Is she up to it?''

''Did she say she was?''

''Yep.''

''Then I guess she is. This isn't one of her better weeks, but it's not her worst, either. I want to come, too. I'll bring Esther. What time?''

''Nine-thirty. Courtroom Four. Judge McCall.''

''We'll be there.'' Rita Holloway paused. ''Esther told me not to tell you something, but I think I will.''

''What is it?'' He heard murmurs, muffled and indistinct.

''Her husband called her yesterday.''

''He's not supposed to do that.''

''I didn't think so. He offered her some money to settle the case.''

''How much?''

"Forty thousand. He suggested she fire you first, so she could keep it all. She told him he was a child."

D.T. laughed. "The son of a bitch is scared to death of something. But what the hell is it?"

"Dr. Haskell called her, too."

"Yeah? Why?"

"He told her he thought there was a better way than a lawsuit. He told her she ought to talk to Preston herself, to see if she could work something out informally."

"And?"

"And Esther told him she was entirely in your hands, but that she'd mention his suggestion."

"Good for her. I've tried to call you a couple of times," he lied. "You're never home."

Rita Holloway paused. "I've been kind of busy. I . . . things are going pretty well on the romantic side for me right now. So . . ."

"Sure. That's great. He's a doctor, right?"

"Right. He's a nice guy. You'd like him."

"Is his name George, by any chance?"

"What?"

"Never mind. I'm happy for you, Rita. Really."

"He, ah, doesn't know about our . . . breakfast, D.T. Just in case your paths happen to cross."

"I get it. No problem. By the way, Mrs. Preston should look, well, pathetic tomorrow, if you know what I mean. We need every edge we can get."

Rita Holloway's words were cutting shards. "I'll pretend I didn't hear that, D.T."

"Pretend what you want. Just bring the wheelchair."

He hung up. None of them understood how the game was played, none of them. He was like soldiers and cops, isolated by his methods and his skills, welcomed only for his achievements, which were expected to be perfect and unfailing.

He heard a noise and looked up. Bobby E. Lee came in and sat down without being asked. The expression on his face caused D.T. to cringe. "I'm quitting, Mr. Jones."

"For good?"

"Yes."

"Why?"

"You know."

"The Stone thing?"

Bobby nodded. "I . . ."

"That's *over*, Bobby. Spilled milk. The guy was a prick. All you did was make it possible for the kids to stay with their mother, which is where they want to be anyway."

"There's more to it, Mr. Jones."

"The gay thing? It doesn't have anything to do with that, Bobby. Stone's a jerk. Gay or not gay."

"It's not exactly that."

"Blackmail? You didn't do that. I did."

"But I *helped*. And I used what I feel, what I believe, what I *am*. I twisted all that and made it work to harm someone. Maybe ruin their life."

"He's an asshole, Bobby. He didn't deserve those kids."

"Then you should have *proved* he was an asshole, Mr. Jones. You only proved he was gay."

"Come on, Bobby. Forget it."

"I can't. I mean, I can live with what I did, but it'll be easier if I don't have to live any more of my life in this office."

"Bobby, goddamnit. This whole thing is *my* fault, not yours. You didn't do anything, you just—"

"Followed orders?" Bobby's smile was haunted. "That's not a consolation. Good-bye, Mr. Jones. You know where to send my check whenever you get the money. If you could include a letter of recommendation, I'd appreciate it, but if you don't I'll understand."

"Don't do this, Bobby. Please? I can't do what I do without you, Bobby."

"Do what? What exactly is it you're *doing* down here, Mr. Jones? Maybe you'd better think about that."

"I don't dare, Bobby," D.T. said. "I don't dare."

Bobby E. Lee stood up, turned, and left. "Bobby!" D.T. started after him, then stopped, then started after him again. "Wait, Bobby!" But the phone rang, so he returned to his desk. As he picked up the receiver he heard the outer door open and close, the bell tinkling twice to taunt him.

"D.T.? Hi. It's Barbara."

"Hi."

"Is something wrong? You sound funny."

"No."

"Good. You . . . you're not going to like this, D.T."

"Like what?"

"I want you to come rafting with me this weekend."

"Why?"

"As a token of commitment. As a symbol of our connectiveness."

"Why don't we just go cold turkey on symbols for a while? Let's see if we can survive on boring old substance."

"I'm serious about this, D.T. We don't share life experiences any more. The entire burden of the relationship is on me. It's so reactionary. It's the historic pattern. We only do what you want, never what I want. We see your friends, or no one. We talk about your work, or nothing. You're defining me, D.T., and I need to define myself. This river trip can get us started toward an equal, coupleist relationship."

"A what?"

"Coupleist. The joining of equals. A lot of people I network with will be on the river, from the running cadre, the support group, the center for personal growth. They want to meet you. They can show you how to move away from your historic manist bias toward true coupleism. It will be very revealing if you refuse to publish your commitment in this way, D.T. Do you understand?"

"I'm afraid so."

"Now, you'll need a wet suit. You can borrow Bernie Kaplan's; I'll pick it up for you, and . . ."

"Barbara?"

"What?"

"Fuck you and the raft you rowed in on."

■ TWENTY-THREE

RIDING the thrill of battle like a surging wave, D.T. entered the courtroom. Purged of fatigue, charged with anticipation, he moved quickly through the spectators and crossed the bar of the court, his heart pumping at a rate that matched his stride. "Good morning, Jerome."

"Good morning, D.T."

D.T. examined his opponent carefully. As expected, his pinstripe suit was cast from steel—blue, unbending armor. The shirt was starched to match, white and glistening—hairless hide. But the clothes outstripped the man. Sweat glazed Jerome's high forehead, and his bright eyes danced on fat black pillows, dusky half-rings of sleepless worry. When Jerome Fitzgerald raised his briefcase to the counsel table it vibrated as though alive.

"The first one is hell, Jerome," D.T. said affably. "Don't let it get you down."

"I don't know what you're talking about."

"Some guys still barf before every court appearance, even after thirty years," D.T. went on. "For some it never goes away."

"I'm fine, D.T."

"Good. I'm fine, too." D.T. looked back over the courtroom. "Where's your client?"

"On his way."

"Good. Mine is, too."

"I'm going to resist any attempt to have Dr. Preston testify," Jerome announced, his voice too loud.

D.T. smiled. "I know you are, Jerome. That's what makes this all such fun. You're going to resist, and I'm going to resist your resistance. Don't you feel great finally being up against a lawyer who really wants to go to trial?"

D.T. patted Jerome Fitzgerald on the back and went to the other counsel table and spread his papers on it, then glanced at the clock. Both his client and the judge were late. McCall had that reputation. Everything in life was more important to him than what was going on in his courtroom, including his daily fifth of gin. D.T. sighed and leaned back in his chair to wait it out.

McCall had been known to be as much as two hours late for law and motion. If there were ten lawyers present, billing an average of a hundred bucks an hour, then McCall's behavior would cause a thousand dollars of unproductive billings. Multiplied by the scores of judges with similar habits, the figure would offer one big reason why the system had become prohibitively expensive for any but the wealthy who could pay the fees, or the maimed who didn't have to.

Jerome slipped into the chair next to him. "Got a minute, D.T.?"

"We've got more than that, if McCall's running true to form. What's on your mind?"

"Settlement, of course. I can't believe you seriously want to go to trial."

"Why not? I don't have anything else to do next month."

"But the time. The expense."

D.T. shook his head with pity. "See, that's what you guys don't get. It's *my* time and *my* money, and I can spend them on anything I want. I don't need to get a big return on my investment because I don't have partners who piss and moan because they're not making half a million a year off my sweat and blood. I can take any damn case to trial I want to. And this one I want to."

"Forty thousand, D.T."

D.T. raised his brows. "That all?"

"Come on. It's ten times what the case is worth and you know it."

"Sorry."

Jerome's eyelids flapped. "What are you *doing?* Is it me? Is the only reason you filed this case so you can show me up in court? If it is, I don't understand. What did I ever do to you to make you *feel* this way? I don't understand what I ever had that you wanted so badly you feel you need to *punish* me. What is it, D.T.? Tell me, so at least I'll understand what's going on.''

D.T. looked at Jerome with some surprise, surprise at his candor, surprise at himself for not knowing the answer to the question. "It's nothing to do with you, Jerome," he lied finally. "It just has to do with winning."

"Is that all that matters to you, D.T.?"

D.T. only smiled. "Let's see what happens today, Jerome. Who knows? McCall might even grant your motion. Then instead of forty grand I'll have to settle for a Snickers bar and a Myron Floren album."

Jerome frowned. "I'll warn you, D.T. When we win this case my client fully intends to bring a malicious prosecution action against both you and your client, seeking monetary damages commensurate with the losses he has suffered. So consider yourself advised."

"Oh, don't make me laugh, Jerome. That threat isn't even good in small claims court. Grow up and do your job. Leave the threats to the kids who think they work."

Jerome sputtered with uncertainty, then looked up anxiously as Judge McCall entered the room from the door behind the bench.

Both lawyers stood up. The clerk hurried to his place, the court reporter arched her fingers over her machine, Jerome scurried back to his table. The judge sat down and so did all the rest. D.T. heard a noise beside him.

Nathaniel Preston was standing in the center aisle, staring at him furiously. D.T. smiled and waved. Preston mouthed an epithet, then moved to join Jerome.

"Well, gentlemen," McCall began, flipping through the file. "Summary judgment, is it? Any reason why the matter can't stand submitted? I've reviewed the affidavits and points and authorities. They seem satisfactory. No need for anything more, is there?" McCall's puffy features broadened hopefully and his wide smile blossomed, making D.T. leery to erase it.

Jerome stood up. "Jerome Fitzgerald, Bronwin, Kilt and Loftis for the defendant, Your Honor. We stand by our moving papers and are happy to submit the matter on the record.''

McCall nodded and turned his head. "Mr., ah, Jones, is it?"

"Yes, Your Honor. We do wish to present testimony this morning.''

The smile narrowed. "From whom?"

"Chiefly from the defendant, Nathaniel Preston. I wish to call him as an adverse party.''

"Objection, Mr. Fitzgerald?"

"Most definitely, Your Honor.''

"Is the doctor in court?"

"Yes, Your Honor," Jerome answered. "But the plaintiff is not. If Dr. Preston is examined we would want a concomitant right to examine his former wife.''

"Was she subpoenaed?''

Jerome wiped his brow. "No. I assumed there would be no testimony taken.''

"It usually helps to subpoena your witnesses, Mr. Fitzgerald. Mr. Jones? This is really a question of law, isn't it? Whether the woman at this late date has a right to the fruits of her husband's degree? And isn't the Supreme Court about to enlighten us on that point any time now? Shouldn't we just wait and see what happens?''

D.T. stood slowly, plotting a response. "Your Honor, in his affidavit Dr. Preston has denied that his wife was their sole source of income during the time he was acquiring his medical degree. Also, there are other claims. Dr. Preston asserts stock he currently owns in East Jersey Instruments was included in the boilerplate language of the property settlement agreement, even though there is no evidence other than his word to support that contention. Cross-examination on these and other points might well be conclusive, Your Honor, in establishing plaintiff's right to prevail on her countermotion. The examination need not be lengthy. An hour at most. I—"

"Is plaintiff in court?"

"No, Your Honor. But I expect her momentarily. She —"

He heard a voice. The door at the rear of the courtroom opened. Rita Holloway pushed Esther Preston into the courtroom.

It could not have been staged more dramatically. Every eye was on her, every ear was attuned to the squeak of the ancient wheels, every breath paused at the particulars of her misfortune. D.T. moved to the bar of the court and held open the gate, smiling at the most perfect client he had ever had. When she had rolled to a space beside his table, D.T. turned back to the judge. "Mrs. Preston is here, Your Honor. May I proceed to call Dr. Preston?"

Jerome was on his feet, his face reddened as though the air itself was dye. "Your Honor, defendant objects. This is not a trial on the merits, this is merely a preliminary motion. Dr. Preston is a very busy man. To make him waste valuable time giving pointless, redundant testimony is both inconvenient and totally unnecessary. The affidavit—"

"Cross-examination is still the best vehicle in which to pursue the truth, Your Honor," D.T. interjected loudly. "While only an inconvenience to Dr. Preston, this matter is vital to his former wife, who as you can see suffers from a most debilitating disease. Surely shortcuts are not in order in this case, Your Honor. Surely Dr. Preston's time is not more valuable than truth itself."

Judge McCall nodded. "Yes, Mr. Fitzgerald. This court is not run for the convenience of litigants, even medical doctors, though at times it may seem otherwise. Your objection is overruled. As it happens, my calendar this morning is clear. You may proceed, Mr. Jones. But make it brief and material."

As D.T. assembled his notes Jerome and his client huddled hurriedly. Jerome stood up again. "Your Honor, in light of your ruling the defendant hereby withdraws his motion for summary judgment and asks that court be adjourned."

"Plaintiff's countermotion is *not* withdrawn, Your Honor," D.T. said quickly. "May I proceed?"

"You may."

"Then defendant's withdrawal is hereby, ah . . ."

"Withdrawn?" D.T. suggested.

"Yes, Your Honor." Jerome sat back down and faced his client's scowl.

"Plaintiff calls Dr. Nathaniel Preston," D.T. announced, and watched his adversary leave his lawyer's side. As Preston shouldered past him he muttered, "You bastard; I'll get you for this. And if you try to break into my office again like you did last night, you'll be a dead man."

D.T. laughed. "Do you want your statement on the record, Doctor?"

Preston only pressed his lips. D.T. wished he knew what Preston was talking about, wished even more that he knew what there was to do in the next few minutes beyond a sweet but irrelevant humiliation of Nathaniel Preston.

The doctor took the oath and then his seat. Judge McCall, his hands out of sight below the bench, seemed to be engaged in something else entirely, perhaps the crocheting for which he was infamous. D.T. crossed to the front of the counsel table and leaned back against it. "When were you married, Dr. Preston? To the plaintiff in this case?"

"Nineteen fifty-six." If D.T. had been closer to Preston he would have been spat upon.

"At the time of your marriage were you employed?"

"No. I was a student."

"An undergraduate?"

"Yes."

"What was your net worth at this time?"

"Not much. I don't know, exactly."

"Virtually nothing, isn't that correct?"

"Virtually. I had a car. That's about it."

"Your wife had just graduated from college, had she not?"

"Yes."

"And she took a job just before your marriage? At the Western Mountain Bank?"

"Yes."

"In fact her job was the determining factor in your decision to marry; she now had an income that could support you both, isn't that right?"

"I wouldn't put it that way."

"No, I don't suppose you would. Now, you were in medical training for the next seven years, were you not? Including residency?"

"Yes."

"And during medical school you earned not one cent yourself, whether in wages, scholarships, or gifts, isn't that right?"

"Well, I—"

"Isn't that right, *Mister* Preston? Yes or no."

"I believe. . . ." Preston reached for his briefcase and put it on his lap and opened it and shuffled through some papers. "Yes. I guess that's right," he said after a moment.

"You earned two hundred dollars a month as an intern, right? After you left medical school?"

Preston looked once again inside the briefcase. "Twenty-five hundred dollars a year, to be exact."

"And your wife in that year made what?"

"Ah, let's see, sixty-five hundred."

"As a resident what did you earn?"

Preston probed his case. "It's written down here. Forty-eight hundred."

"And other than that, nothing?"

"I guess so. I'd have to consult my notes."

"Well, please consult them."

Once again Dr. Preston reached inside his briefcase and rattled through some papers. "Yes, I had no other income in those years."

"Thank you. And your wife in each of those years was earning between six and eight thousand dollars a year, was she not?"

"If you say so."

"Well, your records don't dispute that, do they?"

"No."

"Okay. Let's move on to something else. You and Esther Preston divorced in 1965, correct?"

"Right."

"You had a lawyer and she didn't?"

"We both had a lawyer."

"The same one?"

"Yes."

"The same firm that represents you here today, isn't that right?"

"Right."

"And that lawyer drew a property settlement agreement? And you and your wife signed it?"

"Yes."

"She got the house, and a sum of six thousand dollars, and alimony of two hundred a month for two years, is that right?"

"Yes. I believe so. I'd have to consult the agreement."

"Do you have a copy?"

"Yes."

"Then please consult it."

Preston opened the briefcase once again. "Six plus the house and alimony. That's right."

"Now," D.T. continued. "What was that six thousand dollars supposed to represent?"

Preston shrugged. "How should I know?"

Jerome stood up. "Objection. Calls for a legal conclusion."

"You're a little late, Mr. Fitzgerald," Judge McCall pointed out. "As I understand the law of evidence, the objection is supposed to precede the answer. Overruled."

"Thank you, Your Honor," D.T. said. "Come now, Dr. Preston. You understood that the six thousand was to represent a portion of the marital assets, didn't you?"

"I did. Yes."

"And by this time there *were* some marital assets, were there not? You were in the second year of your practice, after all."

"I suppose there were some."

"And your income the first two years of practice was, what? Do you remember?"

"Not without my notes."

"Please consult them."

The briefcase came and went. "I earned thirty-one thousand the first year. And fifty-two the next."

"Calendar year?"

"Yes."

"Net of business expenses?"

"Yes."

"And exactly which assets were divided to give Mrs. Preston that six thousand dollars? Do you have any idea?"

Preston smiled savagely. "I certainly do. I gave my lawyer a list of everything I owned. He divided it up. The house plus the six thousand was exactly half. Which was everything she was legally entitled to."

"Do you have that list with you?"

"Yes. I just found it recently, in some papers I had in storage."

Preston brought the briefcase back to his lap, fished around in it, brought out a sheet of paper, and proffered it. D.T. stepped forward and took it from him. One glance showed him the East Jersey Instruments stock was listed, along with various savings accounts and other minor assets. Alongside the items were value amounts, and half the total was six thousand and change. The interest in the house was in lieu of further alimony. A common practice in those days. D.T. swore under his breath, knew if he raised his eyes they would be slapped by Preston's grin.

He looked at the list again. There was no date, no signature, nothing. It could have been written yesterday, forged, manufactured solely for purposes of this hearing. But evidence of such chicanery would be scientific, not producible at this stage of the litigation. Besides, D.T. sensed no forgery, sensed that the list was genuine, sensed that he was screwed.

He flipped the paper to the table and glanced over at his client. She seemed to sense it, too, the sinking of their most promising claim, their status now reduced to litigious nuisances—beggars, cheaters, frauds. D.T. sagged inwardly at what he'd done to her. He turned back to the witness.

"An interesting document, Mr. Preston. Totally self-serving, of course, and totally inadmissible, since it was not produced for my inspection in response to my request for all such documents in your possession or control." D.T. turned toward the judge. "Your Honor, Mr. Preston seems to have a great many papers in that briefcase of his, and many of them seem to relate directly to the issues in this case, to contain material evidence of the facts at issue. He has referred to those papers repeatedly, and the one document he produced from it is something withheld from plaintiff though clearly called for in our discovery.''

McCall shook his head to clear it. "What's your point, Mr. Jones?"

"I request permission to examine the entire contents of the briefcase, Your Honor."

Jerome Fitzgerald leaped and screamed. "I object, Your Honor. A totally inappropriate invasion of privacy. An outrageous request."

"Nonsense," D.T. said calmly. "That briefcase clearly has nothing to do with Mr. Preston's medical practice; it has to do with this lawsuit. I request leave to examine the papers he has collected and brought to court to aid him in his testimony, and to arrange for copying those that are relevant, which I suspect is all of them."

"A fishing expedition, Your Honor. Totally beyond the proper scope of discovery." Jerome's face was as white as his shirt.

D.T. laughed. "Mr. Fitzgerald apparently learned the law of evidence watching Perry Mason, Your Honor. There is nothing inappropriate in fishing inside a briefcase from which relevant documents have been extracted in order to determine whether other of its contents may lead to the discovery of admissible evidence. If nothing else about his testimony is true, it is certainly true that Mr. Preston has demonstrated that the contents of that briefcase are very likely to lead to just such materials."

"Let me see it." Judge McCall gestured toward the case. Preston frowned and gripped it tighter and silently demanded that his counsel intervene.

"Your Honor," Jerome sputtered. "There is no foundation for—"

"An *in camera* inspection is called for," McCall retorted. "Hand it here, Mr. Preston. I mean Doctor."

Preston hesitated, the judge gestured, Preston did as he was told. His eyes burned holes, first in D.T. and then in Jerome. The only sound in the room was the ripple of paper beneath Judge McCall's bleary eyes.

It took him only seconds. He pushed the briefcase toward the edge of the bench. "Here you are, Mr. Jones. For what they're worth." D.T. stepped forward and retrieved what he hoped would be a prize.

"No."

Nathaniel Preston surged out of the witness chair and swiped his hand at the case in D.T.'s hands. "You can't do that."

Jerome hurried to his client's side. "Yes, Your Honor. There is no basis for this. I insist on a stay so your decision can be appealed."

"Restrain yourselves, gentlemen," Judge McCall said. "As far as I can see, those papers all bear upon this case, at least conceivably. Discovery should have been completed by now, but maybe if we do it right here we can get this thing settled and off the calendar. I don't see anything of much importance, frankly, but you can look them over for a few minutes, Mr. Jones, and make whatever points you want to make. Then we can wrap it up before lunch. I'll take the matter under submission and Dr. Preston can go see some patients. I see nothing appealable about any of this, Mr. Fitzgerald."

"But . . ."

D.T. returned to his table and extracted the contents of the case. In front of him, the argument between Jerome and the judge continued. He sighed. His victory was indubitably small, proof merely that because of the break-in at his office, Preston was concerned about the loss of important bits of evidence and that Jerome had failed to give his client a basic bit of advice—that anything on Doctor Preston's person not only wasn't secure, it was liable to be ordered produced for inspection in open court. D.T. thumbed through the pile of papers.

They were what he expected—tax returns, income statements, handwritten notes, legal documents, all supporting what he now was certain was the truth—that Nathaniel Preston had not defrauded his wife seventeen years previously by concealing a portion of his holdings. Enervated, D.T. pawed his way to the bottom of the pile, going through the motions in order to justify his request to see them, certain there was nothing helpful in the lot.

The very last item was a file folder with Esther Preston's name on it. He opened it. The file contained a medical record, evidently of Esther Preston's routine checkups, administered by her husband during their marriage, maintained by him or by his nurse with an objectivity that seemed similar to the treatment of other patients. Lacking any other task, D.T. looked more closely at the scrawled notations.

Esther Preston had evidently been to see her husband professionally on two occasions in 1964, once to get a Pap smear, the other for a throat culture. The next year, the year of the divorce, there had been three visits: the first in January, the second in March, the third in April. The diagnosis was apparently inconclusive, the symptoms vague: headache, fever, nausea, weakness, fatigue. On the final sheet in the file were some handwritten notes, dated April 12, all but one in a scrawling hand. D.T. read over the page three times, then leaned toward Esther Preston.

"Is Dr. Haskell's first name Wayne?" he whispered.

She nodded, frowning.

"Then he's the one who greased your bars, moved your ramp, all the rest of it." And broke into Dr. Preston's office last night, he thought but didn't say.

"But—"

D.T. held up a hand to silence her, then stood up. "May Mr. Preston return to the stand, Your Honor?"

Judge McCall nodded. Nathaniel Preston left his lawyer's side and returned to the witness chair, looking warily at D.T. "You examined your wife from time to time in your capacity as a physician, did you not, Doctor?" D.T. asked.

Jerome objected, the judge overruled, D.T. repeated his question.

"Yes," Dr. Preston said.

"This was during your first two years of practice?"

"Yes. Until we divorced."

"So you had a professional as well as a personal relationship with her in those years?"

"I suppose so."

"Exactly when did you file for divorce, by the way? What month?"

"April, I believe. Of sixty-five."

"Yes. I see a copy of the petition right here. April 24. That's correct, is it not?"

"It sounds right."

"So of course you never examined your wife after that date. In your capacity as a physician?"

"No."

"Did she see any other doctors while you were married?"

"No. I don't believe so. Not to my knowledge."

"Did she have any major illnesses in those years?"

"No. She was in good health while we were married, other than minor colds and things." Preston looked at his wife for the first time. "Her severe problems only came later."

D.T. picked up the medical file and took it to the doctor. "This is the file you kept on your wife, isn't it?"

Preston flipped through it. "Yes."

"Is it complete?"

"I believe so."

"Has it been in your possession since you performed the examinations?"

"Yes. I guess so."

"Are the notations in the file your own?"

"Yes."

"Turn to the back page, please, Doctor."

"I have it."

"Read it. The final paragraph only."

"Objection, Your Honor," Jerome insisted. "Irrelevant and immaterial. A ridiculous waste of time."

"These are my final questions, Your Honor," D.T. responded. "I'll be finished in two minutes. The relevance of the evidence will be obvious."

"Very well," McCall said. "Go ahead, Dr. Preston."

Preston wiped his brow. "No. It's not . . . it's been changed. Something, I . . . *do* something, Fitzgerald, you stupid bastard. For God's sake *stop this!*"

"*Read it,*" D.T. thundered.

"Objection, Your Honor," Jerome called out once again, from somewhere behind D.T. "This is privileged information. And irrelevant. And—"

"The privilege is the patient's, not the doctor's, Your Honor," D.T. said. "The patient is right here. She waives it, don't you, Mrs. Preston?"

D.T. turned around. Esther Preston smiled and nodded. "Read it, Doctor," he repeated.

"No. I won't. You can't make me."

"Read it, you son of a bitch."

Preston shook his head. "Your Honor," Jerome's voice squeaked. "I insist counsel be cited for contempt. He has no right to speak to the witness in that manner."

"Yes, Mr. Jones," but Judge McCall's lips were curled into what D.T. thought might be a smile. D.T. turned back to the witness and plunged ahead.

"What was it, Doctor, when the symptoms first came on? Headache, fever, fatigue, nerves? The old housewife's syndrome, is that what you thought? Neurotic complaining, an excuse to quit the job, to hire a maid, to eat out? A lot of women get that way, don't they, Doctor? Psychosomatic basket cases, felled by their humdrum lives. Incurable by medicine, sometimes curable by divorce. Is that what you thought it was at first? I see those women all the time, too, Doctor. They're obnoxious, many of them. Nuisances."

"Yes, I—"

"But this was something different, wasn't it?" D.T. spoke while his teeth ground against each other.

"No. Esther was just—"

"Esther had MS, didn't she? *And you knew it on April 12.* You suspected that's what caused her health problems, and you referred her to your partner, Dr. Haskell, a neurologist. He confirmed your suspicions, and you divorced her a week after you learned for certain what she had. You bailed out of the marriage without telling her she had contracted MS because you knew it would cost you a bundle in the divorce settlement. You would have had to pay her medical expenses, and a huge alimony judgment because she soon would lose the ability to earn her own living. You didn't want that burden hanging over your head, so you just kept quiet and divorced her. Your partner, Haskell, insisted that you tell your wife, but you wouldn't so he pulled out of the medical partnership. And has felt guilty and frightened all these years because he didn't tell Mrs. Preston himself and he was afraid she'd find out what he'd done. Isn't that what happened, Dr. Preston? *Isn't that exactly it?*"

"No. Not at all. I had no idea."

D.T. stepped forward and pulled the file out of the doctor's rigid fingers. "It's right here, Doctor. If you'd left it home I'd never have found it. Your Honor, I request leave to read from the medical record the witness has already identified."

"I don't understand this, but go ahead."

"It's right here in black and white. At the bottom of the sheet headed 'Physician's Comments.' Quote, 'Nat. Poss. MS. See me about this soonest. Wayne.' *Look* at it, Doctor. Isn't that what Dr. Haskell wrote?"

He shoved the record under Preston's nose. Preston didn't look. "No," he said. "No, I swear. . . ." Preston grabbed for the paper and tugged it out of D.T.'s hands and ripped it down the middle.

Half the document fell to the floor. D.T. bent to retrieve it. Judge McCall's voice thundered high above him. "You do that again, Doctor, and you're in contempt of this court and subject to arrest and prosecution for the wanton destruction of evidence. I hope you understand that."

Preston started to tear the remaining portion, then stopped, as though his brain had died. D.T. removed the fragment from his hands. Then he turned to the judge. "Move to amend the complaint, Your Honor, to include fraud. Larceny by trick. Breach of a fiduciary relationship. Intentional infliction of mental distress. Prayer for two million in punitives, a million actuals."

"This is not the time for that, Mr. Jones," McCall said, standing, gathering his robe. "I take it we're finished here for now. The matter stands submitted, pending application for amendment of the pleadings. Gentlemen, I suggest you settle this matter before you leave the courtroom. It has the smell of one big mess."

Judge McCall left the bench. D.T. took the remainder of the file and put it in his briefcase and tucked the briefcase under his arm. Jerome Fitzgerald trotted to his client's side and whispered to him feverishly. D.T. looked at Esther Preston and gave her the thumbs-up sign. Her eyes would fuel him for another year.

Jerome was walking toward him, sniffling, possibly in

tears. "Two hundred thousand, D.T. Right now. So nothing leaves this room, and nothing is filed in court."

"Triple it," D.T. said.

Jerome shrugged. "Okay."

D.T. smiled and patted Jerome on the back. "I'll let you know," he said. Then he began to do some math.

■ TWENTY-FOUR

ONLY Michele could have compelled February to be so faultless. The sun was bright, the sky was cloudless, the air a balmy breath, the breeze a soothing frond. He drove through the city in a rapture, as if all its occupants were celebrating the advent of his ex-wife's second union, as if the marriage were as much a tribute to him as to the bride and groom.

Dressed in a tux that fit him like old Levi's, driving Michele's matchless cloth-top Rolls, freed from Barbara's claims upon his energies and his conscience, fresh from his triumph in the Preston case the day before, D.T. knew again the dance of youth. At a stoplight a young girl looked at him and whistled. He smiled and bowed and blew a kiss. She waved and drove away, leaving him a joyous twig. He drove on down the boulevard, captain of his ship, anchored only to his current mood. When he reached his destination the church loomed so majestically D.T. was persuaded that Michele had flown it in from Canterbury for the day.

He sailed his Silver Cloud into the parking lot and followed the directions of the security guard who protected it. After parking in the shade of the lofty spire, he marvelled that he could keep the car till Michele and George returned from Bermuda, marvelled too at the number of service vehicles that surrounded him—the large vans of florists and caterers, the tiny sports cars of hairstylists and manicurists, the huge trailer of the video outfit Michele had engaged to record it all on tape. D.T. locked the doors to the Rolls and entered the church and in the process experienced an uncommon decline in sumptuousness.

The narthex was a stage an hour before the curtain. Intense and speechless, people dashed into it and out of it like silent-screen comedians, bearing flowers, candles, bunting, finger foods, champagne. Behind a table in the corner sat Joyce Tuttle, resplendent in a viral surge of blue chiffon, an open guest book and a silver pen displayed like handicrafts before her. D.T. went over and signed in.

"How's it going, Joyce?" His eyes dwelt on the pandemonium.

"I'm fine, D.T. I hear you and that Barbara woman broke up."

"Another year without a Beltone for you, Joyce."

"I also hear you're involved with some bucolic little thing who stabbed her husband."

"If by involved you mean I'm one of her lawyers, then yes."

"There was something about a baby, too, wasn't there?"

"Yes. Something."

"It's at Michele's?"

"Till the mother's release on bail."

"Are you the father, D.T.? That's what's going around."

He looked at Joyce's meaty lips. "Yes. I am the father. Please tell everyone who signs this book that D. T. Jones is the father of a killer's child, and that if they send me a dollar and a self-addressed stamped envelope I'll send them a picture of the killer and me performing a series of unnatural acts proscribed by the laws of several southern states."

Joyce Tuttle recoiled, then started to protest his outburst, but D.T. left her and entered the sanctuary.

Various workmen swarmed over the pews and aisles, the altar and the transepts, depositing floral arrangements, fabric ornaments, and crystal containers that looked like trophies for some marvelous athletic achievement. As D.T. stood silently and tried to encompass it all, a man ran up and grabbed his arm and pointed toward the altar. "Does the white splash? Should I add jonquils as a dilutant? Or perhaps mums? But mums are so *tacky*, don't you think? Footballish, or something.''

D.T. looked down at the small man's vanishing scalp. "Jonquils are nice. Informal. This *is* her second, after all.''

The man's grip inflicted pain. "It is? Why wasn't I *told?* The entire *thrust* must be altered. My God, sir, you've saved my life. Henri! Jacques! *Tout de suite*.''

The man scurried down the aisle shouting orders to his minions. D.T. went back to the narthex and asked Joyce Tuttle where he could find Michele.

She ignored his question as she adjusted her strapless bra. "You're upset, aren't you, D.T.? I told you this didn't have to happen if you played your cards right. *You* should be the groom. Not George.''

"I've been a groom, Joyce. I'm luckier at horses.''

"I hate to see Michele end up with a wimp like George.''

"I'm sure she's comforted by your unswerving support, Joyce. And George is not a wimp. Now, where is she?''

"In the vestry.''

"Which is where?''

"That way. It's marked.''

"Is she dressed yet?''

"I think so, except for odds and ends. She's been here since five.''

D.T. walked one way and then another, found the vestry door and knocked. Mirabelle opened it and when she saw D.T. she shook her head. "We all aflutter in here, D.T. You got a pint of whiskey on you it do us *all* some good.''

"No whiskey, Mirabelle. But there's all kinds of champagne out there.''

"Champagne makes me pee, and I ain't got the time. Plus I never peed in church in all my life.''

D.T. laughed and leaned to the side to peer around Mirabelle's large body. Michele had her back to him, her hands in her hair, putting something shiny in it. "Hi there, former Mrs. Jones,'' he said. "I'm here if you need me.''

She turned toward him. "Hi.'' Her stance was shy,

awkward and girlish. "You're lovely," he said, without having to think about it, without having a doubt that it was true.

She closed her eyes and lowered her head. "Have you been in the sanctuary?"

"Yes."

"Is everything okay?"

He thought of the jonquils, of the altered thrust. "It's fine. Perfect. Don't worry about a thing."

"There'll be a brief reception here at the church, then close friends back at the house. I hope you'll come, D.T."

"Okay."

She raised her hands and watched them tremble. "Why do I feel there are certain controlled substances that would be a big help at a time like this." Her laugh was forced. He suppressed an urge to kiss her.

"Hey. Relax. It'll be great. In an hour you can get drunk and act silly and wake up in Bermuda."

Michele frowned, and started to speak, then seemed to change her mind. "Have you seen George?"

"No. You want me to find him? It's bad luck for him to see you beforehand, you know."

"I know. It's all right. I'm sure everything's fine."

"So am I. Well, I'll let you finish dressing, then I'll be back in a bit. Show time is ten o'clock. Right?"

"Right."

"Need anything?"

"Only courage."

He patted his empty pocket. "I've got a flask of it right here. I'll give you a snort just before we head down the aisle."

"Good."

"The second time's a piece of cake."

"Cake. I still have some of ours frozen, did you know that, D.T.? I guess I'll have to make room for more."

"In the freezer in the garage?"

She nodded.

"I'll just sneak in there during the reception and take it off your hands. Great cake, as I recall."

"It was." Michele's voice was low and languid. D.T. decided to depart.

"See you in a bit."

"Okay." He passed Mirabelle's still shaking head and wandered back the way he'd come and went out into the blazing winter sun.

Cars streamed past, the riders ogling the activity at the church, a few of them honking encouragement or derision, some even stopping to gape. As he watched the guests arrive, a limousine pulled to the curb and George and another man got out. When he noticed D.T., George walked quickly toward him.

D.T. extended his hand. In his morning coat and spats, George seemed about to offer a deal on a casket. "Well, today's the day," D.T. said cheerily.

George nodded and repeated the statement. "I'd like you to meet my brother Harold, D.T. My best man." They shook hands. "Harold's from Akron. He's in tires. He's also been married thirty years. I trust it runs in the family." George looked at his brother fondly. The brother only smiled and looked subservient, perhaps revealing the secret of a marathon marriage.

"Thirty years at least," D.T. agreed. "You know I wish both of you all the best."

George's face grew solemn. "I just want you to know I'll do everything I can to make her happy, D.T."

"You don't have to make any promises to me, George. I don't have any status around here."

"Oh, but you do. Michele admires you a great deal. As do I. No doubt Michele will confide in you from time to time, as is only natural, and, well, I just want you to know that I'm willing to do anything, anything at all, to make the marriage everything Michele wants it to be."

George was as earnestly nervous as a realtor with a prospect who had doubts about the deal. D.T. put a hand on his shoulder. "Relax, George. The two of you will be very happy. Michele's amazingly easy to please, believe it or not. Just be yourself, is all I can say. Be yourself, and sit back and enjoy it."

"Thank you, D.T. Your blessing means a lot."

"No problem. Well, see you at the altar, I guess."

"Yes. At the altar." George and his brother moved away toward the church. "If you're ever in Akron look us up," the brother called back. D.T. assured him he would, then decided to take a stroll.

In the small space between the church and the rectory he found a lovely shaded garden. Among the trees and vines and shrubs was a delicate wooden glider, the kind his grandmother had had on her back porch, where she and her cat had spent long portions of their summers. He sat on the glider and began to swing, back and forth, back and forth, the glider speaking to him cheerfully, as though he were a friend.

It was one of those times when life stops short and allows you to catch up to it, to prod and poke and pinch it, to edge toward its significance. As he rode the rolling glider, D.T. realized that of late his life had become sugared, had been made a tolerable bonbon instead of a bitter fruit. He tried to account for it but couldn't. It was just the cycle, the flow of fortune and forgetfulness that combined to make existence a prize to covet. The glider sang its song. He wondered how long his peace would last.

At his back, Michele and Heather were about to begin their brand new lives within the framework of a brand new family: happy, secure, and whole. That was the important thing. That was the thing for which he thanked the God to whom the little garden was dedicated, by whom the marriage would be blessed, for whom the church had been erected, from whom D.T. had hidden for years.

"Daddy, Daddy. Hi, Daddy."

"Heather. How are you? That sure is a pretty dress."

She whirled to show it off. "It cost a hundred dollars. I'm not supposed to get it dirty."

"You look beautiful, honey. So does your mother, have you seen her? It's going to be a lovely ceremony."

"I'm the flowergirl."

"Great."

"I go first."

"The best is always first."

"Are you sad today, Daddy?"

"No, honey. Why?"

"Because Michele will be living with another man. For ever and ever, if they don't get divorced."

"I'm happy for her, honey. For you, too. You still like George, don't you?"

"He's kind of old."

"But he's nice, isn't he?"

"He's okay. They're not going to sleep in the same room, Daddy."

"No?"

"George snores."

"How do you know?"

"Michele told me."

"Then I guess it's good they have separate rooms."

"Did you and Michele have different rooms?"

"No."

"Different beds?"

"No, but that's 'cause I don't snore." He patted her silken head. "You didn't tell me how I look in my tuxedo."

"You look funny. Do *real* people wear tuxedos?"

"No. Real people definitely do not wear tuxedos." He looked at his watch. "What time do you have to get ready?"

"Ten to ten."

"Well, it's about that now. You know where to go?"

"Uh huh."

"Okay. I'll see you in the church. Then afterward at the reception, okay? If you're good I'll let you have some champagne."

"I have champagne all the time."

"Oh."

"Will I have to change my name tomorrow, Daddy? Will I have to use George's name?"

"No, honey. You can keep your name. *Our* name, I mean."

"See you, Daddy."

"See you."

Heather ran off, carrying her dress above the dirt, her shoes as white as plaster hooves.

D.T. started the glider again, listened to the organ begin to play something soft and soothing, wished he wasn't a member of the wedding so he could curl up and go to sleep.

Michele and George. A mismatch, but no more so than

many. George would not resist, the way he had, would play the social games, accept the lavish gifts, see the marriage as his due or at least his obligation. D.T. thought he wished them well.

Separate bedrooms.

Good.

He smiled, then looked at his watch, then left the garden and wandered around inside the church until he found a phone.

"Dick? D.T. What's the latest on Lucinda Finders?"

"I just sprung her."

"Really? Great."

"Well, I heard social services was about to go out looking for the kid, so I thought the little mother ought to beat them to it."

"Thanks, Dick. Where'd the bail money come from?"

"My own pocket, of course. An obligation which I hereby transfer to you. Payable on demand. *My* demand."

"She'll be good for it. Or I will."

"I know you will, D.T. I don't know what went on between you two but I know it was more than the attorney-client relationship we learned about in law school."

"More than that, but less than you think."

"Sure. Anyway, last I saw she was headed for your ex-wife's place to reclaim her child."

"Good. My ex-wife is about to remarry, by the way. I'm giving her away."

"Shit, I was hoping maybe you'd be giving her to me."

"Maybe next time."

"Yeah. Hey. You know what?"

"What?"

"Your client. Lucinda. She got the curse just as I was posting her bail. I had a medico hustle down to check it out and she was right on schedule. Pre-menstrual syndrome, battered wife syndrome, a syndrome for every sin. This one will put me in the law reviews, D.T. I've already got an associate lining up the research."

"Good for you."

"It may not be good but it's gravy, as they say."

"Well, just make sure it's good for Lucinda."

"Hey. Have no fear; Dick Gardner's here."

D.T. hung up. A surge of happiness floated him toward delirium. Lucinda. She would be okay, she and her baby. Mareth Stone was okay, too, thanks to his lawlessness. And Esther Preston was as okay as money could make her. And Michele was okay, and Heather was okay, and Barbara was, well, Barbara. And Bobby E. Lee had been offered jobs by at least two law firms that were as good as law firms get. All was right with the world, or at least his share of it. D.T. sauntered down the hall and tapped on the door to the vestry.

Michele was alone in the room, from head to toe a vision, her gown as seamless as a sheet, her hair a lace of flowers and jewels, her lips enamelled and erogenous. "I shooed everyone away," she said. "Did you see Heather?"

He nodded. "She'll be the epitome of flowergirldom. She'll steal the show."

"I know." Michele's voice was reedy, haunting. "D.T.?"

"Hmmm?"

"Am I doing the right thing? Marrying George?"

He looked at her eyes and found them frightened. "You know that's not for me to say, Michele. But I'll say it anyway. Yes. You're doing the right thing. I think you'll be very happy."

"Are you sure?"

"Of course I'm not sure. But if I'm wrong, hey, at least you know a good divorce lawyer. I'll give you a rate."

She squeezed his hand. "Thanks, D.T. Time?"

"Time."

"Shall we?"

"I think we shall."

He offered his arm and she took it and they walked in grandeur from the vestry. Mirabelle stood in the hallway crying. "Bless you, Miz Conway," she said through burbling sniffles.

They reached the entry to the sanctuary. A robust woman gave the organist the high sign. Ushers hustled stragglers toward their seats. The videotape crew hit the lights and cameras, the hairstylist and cosmetician and couturier rushed to Michele and applied finishing touches while they voiced dismayed disclaimers. Joyce Tuttle clasped her friend's hand and whispered something D.T. couldn't hear. The florist handed Michele a baby's breath bouquet and pinned a boutonniere to D.T.'s lapel. With a blast from the organ, Heather gathered her basket of flowers and walked off toward the altar as if she owned it. The single bridesmaid, the mother of Heather's best friend, blew Michele a kiss and followed after. D.T. and Michele took their places in the doorway.

The organ became Wagnerian. As promised by the piece, the bride soon came, on the arm of her former groom. A hundred grinning cretins turned their faces toward them, peculiar, but rather nice. Ahead, the minister waited with a sappy smile, doubtlessly calculating the extent of Michele's next tithe.

They marched in step, soldiers of matrimony, obeying their societal mores, disciplined, reverent, each suppressing giggles. Michele squeezed his arm and he nudged her with his elbow. They glanced at each other and smiled. Up ahead, George and the man from Akron patiently gauged the progress. D.T. remembered a dance craze called the Stroll.

Up two steps, nodding at the pastor, delivering Michele to George, doing his duty, bowing, retiring to a seat on the aisle, quickly obsolescent. He glanced at Heather, caught her eye, waved surreptitiously, made her blush. George snuggled closer to his betrothed. They eyed each other gravely. The preacher cleared his throat, the organ softened, to pianissimo, then to silence.

"Dearly beloved . . ."

The words fell into place as though the air bore slots to hold them. The last time he'd seen Michele, D.T. had asked if she and George had composed their own vows, as was the vogue. Michele had allowed as how she'd give the traditional expression one more chance, to see if she could get it right this time, sort of like climbing back on the horse after you'd first been thrown. D.T. had shared her laugh. Now he shared again her vows, this time an auditor and witness, not as joint and several obligor.

"Who giveth this woman to this man?"

D.T. almost missed it, almost blew his cue. He stood up. "Her daughter and I do," he said, then sat back down, wondering why he was as nervous as he was, dismayed at his comic croak.

"If there be anyone present who . . ."

Heather was so cute. So mature. So squared away. They'd done a good job. *Michele* had done a good job. He couldn't imagine Heather taking dope or getting drunk, dropping out or turning surly. Sex, yes. He could imagine sex getting out of hand, with Heather or with anyone. But that wasn't such a problem these days. The pill. The foam. The sponge, the loop, the cap. With abortion as a convenient backup, at least for the ones with both child and money.

What the hell was going on?

The minister had stopped speaking. Michele and George faced not the altar but each other. Michele seemed to be speaking, though D.T. couldn't hear her words. George was motionless, his hands clasped behind his back. His brother was discomfited, his hands already seeking out his pockets, his weight shifting from wing-tip to wing-tip, his brow splashed suddenly with sweat.

George spoke then, a low rumble. "Are you certain?" was what D.T. thought he heard. Michele whispered an answer, George spoke back, the minister asked a question that went unanswered. George and his brother left the chancel, silently, proudly, as though ordered on a mission that they knew was suicidal.

The audience buzzed and shuffled. Michele turned toward them, started to speak, then cast her eyes for a certain face. The face she sought was his. When she found him she asked him wordlessly to join her. D.T. slid into the aisle and trotted up the steps, his mind beyond clear thought.

"I couldn't do it," she whispered when he reached her side. "I just couldn't."

"I'm sorry."

"Could you explain to everyone? We'll have the reception anyway. Tell everyone to get plastered on me."

"Okay."

"Be sure to tell them it's all my fault, that George is a wonderful man, that I just don't deserve him."

"I will. Whatever you want. Are you all right?"

"I think so."

"Do you want me to go with you?"

"No. You stay. Heather and Mirabelle can help me."

"Do you want to marry me?"

"No, I'll be all . . . what?"

"Do you want to marry me? I mean, since we're dressed for it and everything?"

"Are you serious?"

"I think so." He looked at the preacher, at the bemused bridesmaid, at his lovely daughter, then back to the preacher. "Is it all right?"

"I'm afraid not." The preacher reeked of vainglory. "The license. The blood tests. It's quite impossible."

"We've been married before, Reverend. To each other. Maybe you only have to do those things once."

The preacher looked doubtful. "It's exceedingly irregular. And of doubtful validity."

"Well, we could have the ceremony now, then check the legalities on Monday and if it didn't take we can get the license and have a civil ceremony later. What's wrong with that?"

"That may satisfy the laws of man, but I'm afraid you've left out the laws of God."

D.T. looked at Michele. "God blessed us once. I think He'd be happy if we gave Him a second chance at being right."

The preacher began to smile, despite himself, despite his calling. "There *are* a great many people here."

"Yes."

"And a great deal of champagne as well."

"Yes, indeed."

The minister looked down at his notes. "Michele Conway and . . . What is your name, sir?"

"D. T. Jones."

"And what does the D.T. stand for?"

Divorced Twice, leaped quickly to his mind.

He looked at Michele, then took her hand. He looked at Heather, and took her hand as well.

"Definitely Thrilled," he said instead.

ABOUT THE AUTHOR

Stephen Greenleaf was born in Washington, D.C., and grew up in Centerville, Iowa. He has received degrees from Carleton College, Northfield, Minnesota and from the Boalt Hall School of Law of the University of California, Berkeley. After serving two years in the Army, including a year in Vietnam, he practiced law for five years before beginning to write fiction. His four previous novels feature private detective John Marshall Tanner of San Francisco. Mr. Greenleaf lives in Oregon, with his wife, Ann, an author of children's books, and his son, Aaron. He is currently working on another Tanner novel.